J C MANSELL

BOOK TWO OF THE ATEAN CHRONICLES

To Caroline, Molly and Elliot… for your
inspiration and your lovely craziness in my life

THANKS

Thank you Caroline, my lovely wife, muse and companion in life for all the hours of listening to my ideas and for reading the manuscript so many times.

Thank you my two beautiful, strong children for filling in the gaps in my storytelling and by just being born, inspiring me to write this story for you.

Thank you mom and dad for reading, correcting and encouraging my work.

Thank you all my friends, and friends of my friends, for proofreading and giving me all that good advice and constructive criticism throughout this journey. You know who you are!

Last, but not least, a big thanks to the gifted crew at Spiffing Covers for the excellent artwork, editing, typesetting and publishing. Without your expertise this book wouldn't look so spiffing!

CHAPTERS

People and Places 9

New beginnings and re-starts 17

Chapter 1 – Hidden Watchers and Patient Conspirators .. 18

Chapter 2 – The Destroyer of Suns and Devourer of Worlds .. 69

Chapter 3 – The Hollow World 117

Chapter 4 – Interstellar Conspiracies and Ancient Plans 157

Chapter 5 – Fright, Fight and Flight 183

Chapter 6 – Into the Heart of the Empire 219

Chapter 7 – The Mayizim Halls 251

Chapter 8 – Old Acquaintances and Small Favours 290

Chapter 9 – Hidden Traitors and Deadly Assassins 317

Endings 368

PEOPLE AND PLACES

Most stories contain a handful of important people to keep track of, such as the heroes and the villains, but also the sidekicks and clue droppers. Furthermore, most stories also contain strange names of strange places, such as Golden Gwundurr, Mysterious Ma Fatarr or Sunny Stockholm. This story is no better than most and to make life a little easier, a list of people and places has been constructed for your reference.

PEOPLE (including races and self-conscious 'things')

Molnír 'Molly' Asir – A young star princess and the heroine of this story.

Elliot Stormsson – A young orphan from Sweden and the hero of this story.

Gottfrid Samuelsson – An old, nasty orphanage manager.

Agnes Fagerlund – the friendly cook of the Höder Orphanage.

Uncle Karl – A burly and nice explorer and the closest thing Elliot has to a relative. Also known as Karrillus Ursus.

Niilas – A friendly Sami from Lapland who helps Elliot.

Aili – The friendly Sami wife of Niilas.

The Nojd – A wise, old shaman of the Sami.

Big Brother – A Stage Twelve Artificial Intelligence currently housed in the starship the *Ursa Major*.

Little Brother – The 'smaller' sibling of Big Brother (only a Stage Ten A.I.) and currently in the shape of a black briefcase.

Kaitrinn Ursus – Uncle Karl's sister and co-explorer.

Vurites – Aka 'Whites'. Kind, high tech, pacifistic aliens with white skin and hair. Highly intelligent when symbiotically paired with the sentient Porian parasite, otherwise remarkably ignorant of technology.

Idagons – Aka 'Idiots'. Monkey-like aliens with six arms and six eyes who love gambling and pranks.

Grunans – Aka 'Grunts'. Thin, cowardly, fragile humanoid aliens with animated, red living hair who often faint.

Furanians – Aka 'Furries'. Peaceful furry rabbit-like aliens who detest violence and predators.

Radorians – Aka 'Radars'. Stick-insect-like aliens who produce extremely poisonous vapours and must travel in containment boxes.

S'margs – Aka 'Smellies'. Snake-like, one-eyed smelly aliens with multi-branched tentacles at the tip of their tails. Information sellers and black-marketers dealing also in bio-technology creatures.

Skar'ley – A.k.a. 'Scalies'. Regal and important lizard-like aliens of the mighty Skarl'ey Empire.

Sha Kiff – Aka 'Shifters'. Plant-like alien shape changers who are experts at mimicking other races.

Snakirra – Aka 'Sneakers'. Secretive greyish-green aliens with large slanted black eyes and long, thin fingers.

Vo'Orrn – Aka 'Worms'. Gargantuan aquatic worms living in dark waters under extreme pressure.

Ateans – The humans of the Spiral Arm. Once known as Atlanteans.

Kiv – Long extinct alien race. Sometimes referred to as the Children of the Founders.

Colossus – A very, very old Atean war robot.

Cro'lichks – Aka 'Cruelies'. Ugly, aggressive, war-loving aliens.

Major Constantine Vurelius IV – A grumpy elderly Atean consul at The Knot.

Captain Hefaistos – Another grumpy elderly consulate member at The Knot.

Hunter robots – Scary robot killers resembling a cluster of metal tentacles which can mimic humanoid shapes if needed.

The Great Mind – A Stage Eighteen Artificial Intelligence and the most brilliant mind on Centus Prime.

Quetzalcoatl 'Quetzy' – The suntanned and wrinkled old Royal Advisor of the Atean King and Queen, Lord of Ceremony and Master of the Seven Doors.

King Lukas IV – Reigning sleepy old king of the Atean Star-Kingdom.

Queen Sibylla II – Reigning sharp old queen of the Atean Star-Kingdom.

The Founders – Ancient, mysterious, extinct and mythological aliens known to be the first known space-faring civilisation in the Spiral Arm.

King Loke the Desolator – Infamous despot, instigator of the terrible Five Species War and father of Princess Molly.

Queen Kali of Vishaya – Hated stepmother of Princess Molly and infamous spouse of King Loke the Desolater, known for her Daughters of Doom, who were military generals, and for the cryopod exile of Princess Molly.

Mr Edda – Fat and plump famous Atean royal historian.

Atlanteans – The first tribe from Atlantis, Earth, to enter an alliance with the Skar'ley Empire and forebears of all Ateans.

Johanna Ursus – Older cousin of Kaitrinn and Uncle Karl.

Ambassador Horus – Friendly and (fairly) young Atean ambassador to the Skar'ley Empire.

Puad'kesh – Skar'ley Empire ambassador to Centus Prime.

Mauad'sash – An elected wise elder – Dwa'rr Oluum – of the Skar'ley who sits on the Emperor's Council.

Priesthood of the Eternal Sun – The ancient and only Skar'ley priesthood.

Skauda'tesh – Skar'ley High-Priest of the Eternal Sun.

Captain Julah Asetos – Atean starship captain of the *Warhammer*, equipped with enormous sideburns and a big moustache.

Moffat – A Furanian Mission Leader on board the *Slow Dancer*.

Millit – A Furanian Medical Officer on board the *Slow Dancer*.

Tavvin – A Furanian Chief Observer on board the *Slow Dancer*.

Billin – A young Furanian Inter-Species Liaison Officer on board the *Slow Dancer*.

The Hidden Watchers – An ancient and secret organisation of mainly herbivore species protecting the Spiral Arm from aggressive species and general destruction.

Morallin Enervours – Beings of pure energy who cannot survive on planets without special armoured suits.

Sarapids – Aka 'Squids'. Yellow octopus-like aliens who love to travel the galaxy.

Mist Spiders – Reclusive and secretive spider-like aliens known only in legends.

Varq – Horned aliens, believed conveniently by most to be extinct.

Zip Zaps – Microscopic aliens with a vast – unnoticed – empire.

Flesh Smiths – Aka 'An Barr'. Insidious aliens believed to be extinct, who are masters of genetic alteration.

Moustache-Beings – Aliens with a constant embarrassed appearance and who seem to be covered in moustaches.

Sishra – A leading Snakirra member of the Hidden Watchers.

Kovorn – A leading Vurite/Porian symbiosis and leading member of the Hidden Watchers.

General Spine Breaker and Relisher In It – A Cro'lichks commander of a dread orbital tank.

V'rorg'chak – Aka 'Destroyer of Suns and Devourer of Worlds' or 'Captain Destroyer'. The Cro'lichks captain of the *World Strangler* warship.

Salank – A Sarapid ship engineer and member of the Hidden Watchers.

K'orch'kma – Aka 'The Quite Reasonably Cruel'. Co-pilot of the World Strangler.

Snaarrk – The ancient horror and ferocious predator which hunted the Furanians throughout their evolution.

Has'pleen priests – Fanatic members of the Priesthood of the Eternal Sun who had undergone the forbidden ritual of severing their gland and thus can act with violence against their own kind.

Sauma'tesh – Mind-robbed brother and rival of Skauda'tesh the Skar'ley High-Priest of the Eternal Sun.

Sauma – Servitor caste brother of Sauma'tesh.

Mayizim (with the Hundred Glowing Eyes) – A one-of-a-kind Stage Nineteen Skar'ley Artificial Intelligence.

Visa'taum – Gatekeeper of the Fifth Imperial Palace Gate on Sku'raan.

Manivar do Shala kep tam Uwari – Aka 'Captain Manny'. The proud, brave and fiery Zip Zap captain of the *Pudding Maker*.

PLACES and **EVENTS**

Höder Orphanage – A sad, gloomy place run by a greedy manager.

Kiruna – One of the northernmost cities of Sweden.

Narvik – One of the northernmost seaports of Norway.

Ice Hotel – World famous and luxurious hotel in Kiruna built entirely out of ice.

Lapland Express – A luxurious train running to Kiruna.

The *Ursa Major* – Uncle Karl's starship. A Mark IV Vuron Class Explorer.

The Spiral Arm – Our part of the galaxy. One of the spiral arms full of stars.

Atean Star-Kingdom – A kingdom of several worlds ruled by the Atean humans.

Centus Prime – Primary planet and heart of the Atean Star-Kingdom situated in the binary (twin star) Canosis system.

The Knot – Gigantic multi-species space station and meeting point.

The Vurite Exchange Hub – A trading central or market on The Knot run by the alien Vurites.

Matalla – The ancient Atean name for lost Earth meaning 'Land Under Sun'.

Atean Consulate – The habitat section of The Knot, once known as the Grand Atean Embassy.

Valdanna – The old capital world of the Atean Star-Kingdom.

The *Humble Palace* – A Galactic Class Pleasure Cruiser used by Ateans.

Vurite Comfort Inn – A nice and luxurious hotel in the Vurite habitat of The Knot.

Azuria – Capital city of the Atean Star-Kingdom located on Centus Prime.

Three Moon Palace – The royal palace in Azuria on Centus Prime, named after the three shining moons its building material was taken from.

Atlantis – Original home of the Atlanteans from Earth, the first Atean tribes to ally with the Skar'ley Empire.

Massikita Wars – The terrible and mythical war against the Mosquito People which crippled the Spiral Arm, and the reason for introducing Atean human warriors as counter-measures.

Annihilation Wars – The thousand-year-long war between Atean humans and Cro'lichks (Cruelies) ending with an unsteady enforced truce.

Five Species War – The unnecessary war between the Atean humans and their neighbours ending with the destruction of Valdanna, the Atean capital world.

The Plum Cake Incident – The most exciting period in modern Atean history before the coming of Elliot and Molly.

Sku'raan – Throne world of the Skar'ley Empire.

The *Warhammer* – An old Atean warship.

Dead Worlds Cluster – Several dense star systems of worlds formerly known as the Maze Worlds, which were totally destroyed during the Annihilation Wars.

The Slow Dancer – A Furanian scientific research spaceship.

Vurite's End – A desolate and abandoned Vurite star system holding a gas giant moon with curious Founder Ruins.

The Ash Plains – An abandoned mining region of Skar'ley space containing a handful of star systems which have been engulfed by a great nebula cloud.

World Strangler – A Cro'lichks warship.

The Hollow World – A gigantic artificial Founder artefact machine with an entire world and sun inside. Prison of the last Flesh Smiths.

Mayizim Halls – Great halls and part of the Imperial Skar'ley Library on Sku'raan holding the Stage Nineteen Super Artificial Intelligence Mayizim.

Rum'hamveer – Orb of the Violent Ones. The original Skar'ley name for Matalla or Earth.

Imperial City of Ash'vaar – The capital city of the Skar'ley Empire situated on the world of Sku'raan and home to the Imperial Palace.

Fabulous Mines of Varania – The Zip Zap name for the Imperial Palace on Sku'raan.

NEW BEGINNINGS AND RE-STARTS

Once upon a time there had been a girl and a boy. Despite very different beginnings, they had both been very ordinary, but in their own exceptional ways. One had been from long-lost Earth, orphaned and then set adrift in space. The other had been a powerful princess, yet lost and forgotten in time. Both had been very, very lonely, in their own different ways. Yet this girl and this boy had found an unexpected and exceptional friendship in each other… and then died.

It is all very sad, but the story must continue and every story needs a setting to put things into perspective.

Therefore we start big, with the universe.

CHAPTER 1
HIDDEN WATCHERS AND PATIENT CONSPIRATORS

Our universe is a very, very big place. The universe, as such, can't really be defined, as nobody really knows how big it is or if it ever ends. Somebody actually once said that there were more stars in the universe than there were grains of sand on all the beaches of Earth. If this is true, or if the person in question had drunk too much, is a matter for debate.

In this vastly huge universe there are an unknown number of galactic super clusters, which in turn consist of normal galactic clusters. A normal galactic cluster consists of several hundred galaxies, separated by distances greater than can be comprehended by the human mind. Each galaxy in such a cluster is in itself huge and consists of billions upon billions of stars.

The galaxy, in which Earth and the Atean Star-Kingdom is situated, is a medium-sized galaxy shaped like a swirling disc. It is referred to by many Earth children as the Winter Road or the Milky Way, due to the appearance of the disc of stars seen from the side where we are situated. Other children of the galaxy refer to it as the Foaming Wake, The Night Rainbow or the Star Sandwich.

Our galaxy has two main trailing arms which extend outward from the extremely bright and star-dense centre. They are curved, trailing after the rapidly revolving centre of the galaxy. Each one of these arms, consisting of thousands upon thousands of stars, hosts the Atean Star-Kingdom, the Skar'ley Empire and countless other worlds. This trailing arm of stars is known to the denizens there as the Spiral Arm and encompasses all that is known and can be explored of their native galaxy, without breaking too many fundamental laws of the cosmos and the quantum reality in which we all exist.

In one area of the Spiral Arm there is a dense cluster of stars, only noticeable if one knows where to look. This is the Dead Worlds Cluster and consists of twenty densely packed stars and their messy systems of intermingling Oort clouds, planets and asteroid fields. The stars and their orbiting followers rotate and frequently collide into each other. Frequently, in galactic measures, is once or twice in a planet like Earth's lifetime.

On the outskirts of the Dead Worlds Cluster lie two suns that combat each other for fuel. One is red and swollen, the other small and bright. The smaller steals energy from the larger, like a super huge ball of yarn being unrolled from one spool to another. The two suns are surrounded by a dirty disc of rubble which is the remains of planets and other satellites, torn asunder by the cataclysmic forces of the battling stars. From a distance, this immense asteroid field looks like a stable dirt ring or dusty arena floor which encircles the two suns. The asteroids themselves are both spectators and victims of the slow and several-million-year-old struggle for supremacy in the chaotic system. Their suns tear at their orbits and are destined to destroy them one day.

Pinpoint stars – actually being either super galactic clusters, galactic clusters, distant galaxies or neighbouring stars – shine down like silent witnesses upon an unremarkable and insignificant asteroid, one of thousands around it. Although the asteroid is large, it is but a dust mote in the unbelievably large universe. The light of these witnessing stars has taken millions upon millions of years to reach this place and is now eager to twinkle extra brightly.

Now imagine someone trying to address a letter to one of these asteroids. He would most probably have to formulate the address something like this:

The Universe, Super Galactic Cluster 632, Galactic Cluster 984, Milky Way Galaxy, Sagittarius Spiral Arm, (the one to the Galactic Left), Dead Worlds Cluster, Twin Suns 18–19, Asteroid Ring, Sector 14, asteroid 9488.

Taking the immense size of the universe into consideration, there is no wonder that intergalactic postal services have problems being taken seriously and reaching full efficiency.

On the shadow side of the unremarkable and insignificant asteroid lay the remains of a starship. It had once been one of the greatest and most famous ships of the Atean navy – the *Warhammer*. Under Captain Tulok, it had disabled its first enemy ship more than six hundred years ago, only six days after it left its shipyard. It had broken the pirate siege of Shangri-la, under the command of bold Captain Baldur. For hundreds of years it had patrolled the borders of the Atean

Star-Kingdom faithfully. Countless crewmen had called it home and nursed it from its damages. Now there was little left that could bear witness to it once having been a starship. Burnt and twisted pieces of metal debris had been spread over more than three kilometres of the asteroid's surface. A large gash had been torn in the surface of dust and stone. A lot of the dust and some of the debris was still hanging over the crash site like an ominous cloud in the dark gloom, too small to fall back to the surface for another year or so due to the low gravity.

The blanketing darkness of the unremarkable and insignificant asteroid was suddenly dispersed when several searchlights passed over the *Warhammer*'s crash site. They pierced the inky darkness like brilliant knives, chasing shadows away and reflecting off the burnt and twisted metal debris. Dancing over the surrounding craters, the lights were searching for something. Then suddenly all searchlights drew together and focused on two sets of booted footprints leading away into the desolate pockmarked landscape. As one, the searchlights followed the two footprints away from the crash site and down into a nearby valley. Now and then one pair of footprints would transform into a small crater before it continued, giving testament to a serious inability to move gracefully in low gravity.

Soon the footprints reached a set of ragged dark cliffs. Two figures in dusty blue and silver spacesuits huddled together at the base of the cliffs. They were human children and looked tiny and vulnerable on the huge desolate asteroid, which in itself was tiny in the great scale of the universe. With legs drawn up, the two figures seemed to be sleeping peacefully, with their helmets against each other and their hands still clasping. One of them also clutched a battered black briefcase. As they were dead, they were totally unaware of the big spaceship descending upon them.

The ship was saucer-shaped with countless, scale-like protrusions from its hull. Several small lights pulsed and shone along the underside of the craft. As it sank carefully down over the two lifeless bodies its gravimetric thrusters stirred the fine dust of the asteroid's surface, making it vibrate until it seemed to boil away. The two bodies were for a moment covered in migrating dust, but then began to slowly and silently rise up towards the ship, as if lifted by unseen hands. A hatch opened in the ship's hull and a brilliant blue light shone down over the scene. The two bodies ascended into the hatch which immediately closed behind them. At once the searchlights went off and the ship rose rapidly from the asteroid. With a flash of the engines the ship then blasted off into the asteroid field.

*****

"What's the condition of the human children?" enquired Mission Leader Moffat with his high-pitched voice. He was studying the two figures lying on the white examination table. Being a Furanian, he was always nervous around humans and absent-mindedly stroked his white fur in an instinctive calming gesture. His large blue eyes studied them carefully.

"I'm afraid they're dead, Mission Leader Moffat," squeaked Medical Officer Millit. One of his long ears hung sadly to one side. "They ran out of breathable air and were asphyxiated. It seems to have happened in their sleep though, they probably hardly noticed it."

"What a dreadful way to go," moaned Chief Observer Tavvin, her voice shrill with grief and anguish.

"Well, it could be worse!"

Three sets of large clear blue eyes turned to Billin, the young Inter-Species Liaison Officer. Billin skipped away nervously and his hands fidgeted along his short furry body. "Well… I mean… you could be shot, or stabbed… or even eaten alive by a snaarrk."

The very sound of the name of the ancestral terror instilled a deep primal sense of fear in all Furanians. It was a word generally avoided as it could bring on involuntary bowel movements and sudden fainting. Therefore, the three Furanians assembled around the table where the lifeless forms of Molly and Elliot lay, skipped away in sudden anxiety. It was typical of a youngling like Billin to blurt out the Forgotten Name like that.

"Snaarrk!" shrieked Medical Officer Millit in terror and looked around nervously. "Where?" Only he among the assembled Furanians had ever seen a snaarrk in real life. As part of his medical education he had been taken deep into the Furas Natural Museum of History to witness the last stuffed remains of the primal terror that had once hunted all Furanians of Furas. The memory of standing in the presence of those barbed mandibles and staring into those bottomless predatory eyes haunted him to this day. Despite knowing that the terrible predator that had accompanied his race throughout the long and arduous road of evolution was long since extinct, Millit trembled.

Those eyes, those eyes…

"Sorry!" said Billin, feeling at once very uncomfortable. He had made another blunder and he could notice an unpleasant and recently added smell to the room.

"Hmmph!" snorted Moffat and glared at Billin with all the importance he could muster up as Mission Leader. With his small round mouth pulled tight he turned away from Billin. "Well, they didn't die... in any of those ways," Moffat concluded.

The four furry Furanians returned their attention to Molly and Elliot lying on the examination table. Their helmets had been removed, but they looked ghastly pale with colourless lips and dark rings around their eyes.

"How long have they been dead?" inquired Tavvin drawing herself closer to the two human children.

"I-I-I would say forty to fifty hours at the most," answered Millit who had nearly managed to compose himself. (Those terrible snaarrk eyes...)

"Oh, not more? How soon can you get them back up on their feet again then?" asked Moffat.

"Well, I would say in an hour or so," ventured Millit. "But it could take longer to reactivate their cell activity due to their age," he added with his high-pitched voice. "I haven't had any experience with human children before."

"Then get started," ordered Moffat. "The sooner we can be on our way the better." The Mission Leader then hopped out of the examination room, absent-mindedly stroking the white fur of his small, round body. Tavvin and Billin followed and left Millit to do his work.

***

An hour later Elliot returned from the dead.

He sat up with a jolt and banged a metal tray of medical instruments out of Millit's hands.

"Whatwasthatthathappened?" he sputtered while looking around with wild eyes.

"Extraordinary!" exclaimed Millit while backing away from Elliot who now sat up rigid on the examination table. "It must be your youth and the unaltered power of your mitochondria that restores your cell activity so fast. Quite remarkable!"

Elliot noticed the Furanian for the first time and glared at him. Millit nervously jumped a step back, banging into the medical cabinets behind him.

"What am I doing here? Who are you? What happened just now?" Elliot demanded.

"You are in the examination room of the *Slow Dancer*, a scientific vessel from Furas," explained the Furanian with his shrill voice. "I am Millit, Medical Officer on board. The sensation you felt was the ignition of your bio-electric cell activity and the restart of all synaptic activity. It's quite a jolt I've heard, especially in such a young body as yours. But it could have been worse. I once saw Radorian Rock Rodents bounce off the walls when reanimated and..."

Elliot didn't understand a thing the Furanian was babbling about and his head was spinning in a confused mixture of thoughts, memories and feelings. Then some memories slowly began to return to him. He had been talking to Molly, hadn't he? They had been holding hands and feeling sad yet happy.

In a flash of colour he suddenly remembered a great gas planet rising radiantly over the horizon. This was the trigger and all his memories rushed back to him like a great flood. His escape from the Höder Orphanage and the trip to Kiruna in search of Uncle Karl. The terrible

Hunter robot stalking him and his rescue by Niilas and Big Brother. He remembered sadly the destruction of the *Ursa Major* and Big Brother. Then he remembered his meeting with Little Brother and his search for other humans on the great space station known as The Knot. Also the joy and frustration of finding the spoilt and angry princess Molly in a cryotube, forgotten for over two thousand years. Together they had escaped their deadly pursuers and met the aged Atean king and queen on Centus Prime, throne world of the immortal, yet old and senile, Atean humans who had come from fabled Atlantis on Earth. But despite all their power and knowledge, the Atean king and queen hadn't helped them find any clues to who was hiding Earth, who had destroyed Aunt Kaitrinn's mind and who had kidnapped Uncle Karl… if he was even still alive. With a growing sense of anger he then remembered the anonymous betrayal which had destroyed the Atean warship the *Warhammer* on their way to the Skarl'ley Empire. The lizard-like Skar'ley and their Emperor possibly had some clues to Uncle Karl's fate. But instead of reaching him, his friend, the artificial intelligence Little Brother, had been mortally damaged and they had all been shipwrecked on a desolate asteroid. In the end, he and Molly were running out of air. Then they had slept. Uncomfortable at first in the bulky spacesuits, but then sinking into a deep slumber. What had happened?

"What happened? On that asteroid?" Elliot asked.

"Oh, you died. No avoiding it really. Lack of breathable air. Could happen to anyone," replied Millit with a friendly and jolly voice.

"I died?"

"Yes. Your body ceased to function due to lack of oxygen which resulted in some cellular damage to your organs and your brain. But don't worry, we patched you up as best we could."

Elliot glanced down at himself. He was naked but for some tatters resembling a loose white gown. Countless red and black wires were connected to him all over his body with small pincers. The many wires ran to a large metal machine in the centre of the room.

"We call it the Organic Jumpstarter," said Millit proudly and pointed to the machine. "Many regard it as our greatest innovation since the Bottomless Pocket."

"I was dead?" mumbled Elliot not really listening to Millit. His thoughts reeled at the notion. "Funny, I don't remember what it felt like."

There was a loud buzz from the large metal machine, followed by a gasp. On the table next to Elliot, Molly suddenly sat up with the same wild expression in her blue eyes. Her freckled face was wrinkled in confusion and her long blonde hair was in a great tussle.

"Ah, very good," trilled Millit, skipping over to Molly. "You both reacted to the first jumpstart. Very interesting! I'm glad that was successful."

Molly was also clad in a tattered loose white gown. Just like Elliot, the countless red and black wires covering her entire body were connected to the large metal machine in the centre of the room. Molly stared wildly around her until she saw Elliot. She relaxed when she met his gaze and then looked down at his gown and wired-covered body. With a yelp of horror she jumped off her table and drew her tattered gown closer around her.

"What's wrong?" asked Elliot.

"Turn away, will you!" Molly said angrily. "I'm really not wearing much."

Elliot hadn't noticed and suddenly blushed. Feeling a bit stupid he crawled off his table and hid behind it.

"Now there," said Millit contently. "All muscular control seems to be in total synchronisation. I don't think we have to make any restarts or cross connections. I'll get you unplugged so you can get dressed."

With her fierce stare and regal voice, Molly forced Elliot and Millit to look the other way while she got dressed. She then sat on her table giggling while Elliot carefully tried to slip out of the tattered gown and into his blue and gold Atean clothes without revealing any sensitive details.

"We had a black broken briefcase with us," said Elliot to Millit while getting dressed. "Did you pick him up as well?"

"Ah, yes. The Artificial Intelligence unit," answered Millit, who was monitoring them through something which looked like a huge looking glass. The outlines of their bodies were visible in the glass, but instead of hair and skin there was only a writhing mass of muscles and blood vessels. "Yes, you were holding it tightly when we brought you on board. I gave it to the Master Engineer to see if he could do anything with it."

"He's going to be repaired?"

"No. I don't think that's possible. I'm afraid it had received quite a bit of damage. We might however be able to use some of the parts for the ship."

"No! You can't! Don't touch him!" cried Elliot.

"I'm sorry?" said Millit.

"I mean. Please don't pull him apart. Can't you give him to me instead?" Elliot couldn't help feeling sorry for the black intelligent briefcase. It had somehow seemed alive to him. It wouldn't be right to scrap him. Little Brother deserved a better ending.

"I'll see what I can do…" said Millit.

"So you somehow brought us back to life," said Molly touching her earlobe. Her Memo-Hair Gel immediately untangled her long blonde hair which then began braiding itself.

"Yes, yes I did," answered Millit, turning to Molly. His already large blue eyes doubled in size as he studied her through the strange magnifying glass. "Nothing to it really, the Tissue Regenerator and the Organic Jumpstarter does most of the work. You were lucky your bodies were relatively unharmed due to the cold and the lack of oxygen."

"Thank you anyway!" said Elliot and smiled warmly. "Thank you very much for bringing us back to life. Being alive… means a lot to me… us," he said and waved a hand at Molly and himself.

Molly nodded and even tried a disarming smile, which looked more like a predator baring its teeth. But then she noticed Billin's huge eyes staring at her through the large magnifying device.

"Do you mind! Point that thing in another direction!" growled Molly and glared at the Furanian. "It can see right through my clothes you know. It's not decent."

Millit jumped back and pushed away the large instrument. "Why, I'm sorry… It really goes too deep to… I just wanted to make sure everything was fully recovered and active. Didn't mean to pry…"

At that moment the door to the examination room opened with a hiss and three Furanians stepped in. Two of them were holding something which looked like notepads, while the third had a large belt slung over his shoulder. With their strange hopping gait and their small furry bodies, they reminded Elliot of hairy penguins with long rabbit ears.

"Ah, our guests are awake. How good! Splendid!" said the Furanian with the large belt. "I am Mission Leader Moffat. Let me begin by telling you how delighted I am to find you two alive and kicking again."

"It was you who found us on that asteroid?" asked Elliot.

"Yes, yes. We were searching for you, actually. We are en route to…" Moffat trailed off, somehow unwilling to reveal their destination, and began again. "Anyway, when we heard about the Cro'lichks attack upon your vessel we hurried here to search as quickly as possible."

"But how did you find us?" asked Molly suspiciously. "I thought it was nearly impossible to find two people stranded in an asteroid field."

"Well, yes. It was quite hard. That was the reason for us to hurry. We managed to follow the faint ion trails of your ship's engines before they dissipated. But I'll admit, there was quite a great deal of luck involved as well. However, thanks to the persistence of Chief Observer Tavvin here we didn't give up until we found you."

Moffat pointed to another, almost identical Furanian who stood poised with a notepad. When hearing her name, Tavvin spread her arms in some sort of welcome.

"I'm honoured to meet you, young humans," she said in her high-pitched voice.

"Then I guess we should thank you for rescuing us… and bringing us back to life," said Elliot.

"Oh please," trilled Tavvin. "Any fellow traveller would do the same. Especially for two such distinguished guests of the Atean Star-Kingdom. I'm sure your king and queen would be devastated if they lost you."

"Did you find any other survivors from the attack?" asked Elliot, dreading the answer.

"I'm afraid not," replied Moffat. "We haven't detected any escape pods or received any distress signals from emergency beacons. This sector is as silent as the grave, so to speak."

"But there were other survivors. A lot of escape pods managed to leave the *Warhammer* before it was destroyed. But the Cruelies rounded them up."

"Then maybe the Cro'lichks still have them," interjected Billin. The Inter-Species Liaison Officer was glad to be able to elbow his way into the discussion at last. "However, I don't know if that would be preferable to death. The Cro'lichks are formidable torturers and herd most captives off to remote space mines or the slave markets of Vrakesh where they are doomed to work in misery until they die."

Everybody in the room stared at him and he just knew he had said something wrong again. Elliot remembered the Cruelies they had encountered on The Knot, who had tried to claim that he and Molly were ancestral enemies they were entitled to kill. They had been all claws, long cruel noses, black skin, lolling tongues and bloodshot eyes. All of it neatly packed in grim spiky armour and equipped with far-too-large energy rifles. He shuddered at the thought of the captives in their hands.

"Or maybe they're just fine and are being dropped off at the nearest Junction Station," he mumbled while retreating from Moffat's irritated stare.

"So, has the Atean Star-Kingdom received word of the attack?" wondered Molly, changing the focus of the conversation.

"By now they should have," said Moffat. "News like that travels faster than people."

"So, they know we're safe?"

Moffat didn't answer. His small mouth curled together tightly and he looked to Tavvin for guidance.

"No," Tavvin said nervously. "They have not yet received word of your survival. Neither will they for a while yet."

"Why not?" asked Molly, suspiciously.

"Because it would complicate matters. It's best that you remain dead in most people's eyes for the moment. Until we know more and have decided what to do."

"What to do about what?" wondered Molly and jumped off the table. She drew up to Tavvin who immediately became very nervous and skittish. The little princess could be quite intimidating when she wanted answers.

"I think there is more than fate involved in our meeting, young friends. Our roads were crossed for a reason." Tavvin looked around her with big blue eyes and then added, "we should talk more about this in private."

She turned to Moffat and nodded to him, her long ears twitching slightly. "Mission Leader Moffat, Inter-Species Liaison Officer Billin and I will withdraw to the Main Observatory together with our guests for some further conversation. Please proceed with maximum speed and inform me when we are an hour away from our destination."

Moffat nodded as Tavvin and Billin led Molly and Elliot out of the examination room.

As the Furanians were quite short, the corridor outside was low. Both Molly and Elliot had to duck now and then to avoid banging their heads on bulkheads or strange bluish glowing piping. The two Furanians led them to another large dimmed chamber filled with floating lights. Once the door closed behind them Elliot and Molly could see that the floating lights resembled stars, asteroids and planets, much like the holographic map Captain Asetos had showed them on board the *Warhammer*. But this map was full of detail and small brackets containing text hovered in connection to the various stellar bodies. Advanced calculations ticked away around some of the stellar bodies, while great wall screens shimmered with more changing texts and numbers. Between the large screens stood big glass or crystal canisters filled with strange samples of plants, animals or even glistening energy.

"This is the Main Observatory," explained Tavvin and pointed around her. "The purpose of this ship, as well as this voyage, is mainly scientific. Here we register everything of importance happening in the Dead Worlds Cluster. It was thanks to the highly sensitive sensor arrays of this ship that we could find you. Not even Skar'ley search and rescue ships have this sophisticated equipment."

"Lucky that you were nearby then…" said Molly, still with a suspicious tone.

"Well, maybe not entirely lucky," sighed Tavvin. "When we heard of your invitation to the Skar'ley Empire we suspected that something could happen on your journey. We felt that it would be best to be out and about in case we were needed."

"How convenient. Are we now your prisoners?" asked Molly.

"Well, I guess you could…" began Billin, eager to be of assistance.

"Prisoners? By the Great Root, no!" answered Tavvin with a glare at Billin. "You are our guests. You may go where you please, but I would be honoured if you would share some thoughts with me."

After a brief glance at each other, Molly and Elliot nodded and sat down on a soft spongy bench to listen.

"We have long suspected a conspiracy among the Skar'ley, but to this day did not know exactly what would be its purpose," began Tavvin. "Your coming, Elliot, has confirmed some of our suspicions."

"We? Who are *we*?" wondered Elliot. "What have I got to do with this?"

"Yes, you are right. I should tell you everything from the beginning," said Tavvin and sat down on another spongy bench in front of them.

"It was the Skar'ley Empire that discovered us Furanians a long, long time ago on green Furas. As a people, at that time we lived mainly underground and in terror, never being able to fulfil our dreams or investigate the wonders of our world. We had evolved intelligence in order to overcome the cunning of the – *gulp* – great predators known as the snaarrks, who hunted us for food. It was an arms race of evolution that the Skar'ley helped us overcome. Under their careful hand we herded the snaarrks to reservations and kept them under control.

"We learnt much from our benefactors and our first scientific records, The Observations, are from this time.

But no sooner had we taken our first shuddering steps into space when the terrible blood-sucking Massikita, the Mosquito People, appeared. We hid from the terrible wars that followed, but saw the coming of humans and the founding of the Atean Star-Kingdom. We hid because we didn't dare to face you humans."

"You were afraid of the Ateans? I thought they helped defeat the Mosquito People?

"Ah, yes," said Billin. "But you must understand that we are herbivores, humans scare us almost as much as the snaarrks. You are fearsome hunters and warriors – deadly predators. Good colour vision and eyes facing forward to better estimate distance to your prey. Long sharp teeth and a terrible temper."

"Anyway," continued Tavvin, "we were therefore not surprised to see how humans soon turned upon humans when the Skar'ley no longer could control them. Before long, the humans had also attacked the timid Idagons and aquatic Sarapids in their greed for power and more worlds to rule. After they had met their match in the Vurites they exterminated our peaceful neighbours and friends, the furry crabs of Gzarria. Then it was our turn. Three of our 'Visited' worlds were taken from us and many Furanians were killed. Only the protection of our Skar'ley benefactors prevented us from sharing the same fate as the furry crabs of Gzarria. The Spiral Arm feared another great war and the Skar'ley Empire was still weak from its conflict with the Massikita and the great Curse of Decay which afflicted them with terrible plagues and illnesses."

"Yes, that's when the Cruelies attacked," added Molly, trying to speed up Tavvin's tale.

"Yes, then came the Cro'lichks. The equally aggressive Cro'lichks occupied the Atean Star-Kingdom's attention for many centuries, turning their wrath away from the rest of the species of the Spiral Arm. We also heard of the destruction of the Ateans' ancient home, Matalla. Although we have always suspected some involvement from the Empire in this destruction, we were content with the dangerous Ateans having lost their original gene pool. During this terrible and prolonged war, the Skar'ley Empire overcame the Curse of Decay and regained much of its strength again. After many centuries of war, the Skar'ley Emperor and an alliance of Free Species forced a truth between Ateans and Cro'lichks. The Spiral Arm breathed in relief and looked forward to a life in peace again. But it would not last."

"Yes, we know," said Elliot hurriedly. "Some time afterwards the Ateans caused the Five Species War." He was trying to make it easier for Molly so she didn't have to endure the details of the terrible and meaningless war her father and stepmother had started.

"Yes. And after this brief outburst of human aggression we understood that something had to be done. It was during this time that a brilliant biologist and mathematician among our people came up with a plan: give the humans immortality."

"You *gave* them immortality?" said Elliot in wonder.

"Yes! You see, our people were never good at violence or aggression. We were peaceful by nature and focused most of our research on improving our situation instead of making weapons. Medical advancements were therefore one of our foremost sciences. The human genome was much less advanced than our own and therefore possible to map. We spent enormous resources mapping it, the project being one of our scientists' greatest ever. In the end, we managed to manipulate the very genes that aged humans and made them mortal."

"So you gave humanity immortality," said Molly. "But how would that solve the problem? Wouldn't there just be more humans if nobody died?"

"The answer to that question lies in mathematics, human psychology and general biology. Firstly, the treatment which made humans immortal couldn't be properly applied before they had reached a certain age, namely that of seniority. Humans at this age tend to be much more calm and non-aggressive. Secondly, having reached that age humans could no longer biologically reproduce. Thirdly, when having too much to do with work, war, art and entertainment, humans tend to ease down on the breeding and see to their own needs first. One or two children were simply enough. More would be bothersome. In short, we made life eternal and comfortable for humans. As a result, they calmed down and stopped giving birth to children. They retired."

"That's a very strange plan," said Elliot.

"You destroyed humanity!" added Molly angrily. "Look at them now. They're a joke!"

"On the contrary," protested Tavvin. "The Ateans were most content and happy with the solution. They were never forced or lured into this decision. They knew full well what was slowly happening. It was a result which pleased all parties."

"But what has this got to do with me and the Skar'ley?" wondered Elliot, trying to get back to the subject again.

"Well, as I said we suspected the Skar'ley Empire to have hidden the truth about Matalla's destruction, but we never suspected that it still existed – until you appeared. The evidence is quite clear. Based on the blood and tissue samples we managed to get from you during your stay at the Three Moon Palace on Centus Prime…"

"What? You got blood samples from us?" shouted Molly, angrier than ever.

"More than one, actually," said Billin. "It was quite easy to direct nano probes to your quarters while you slept and…"

"Yes, yes," snapped Tavvin and waved Billin away. "But we were ever so careful when doing so. You didn't feel a thing,"

"That's not the point. You stole those samples from us," said Molly furiously and stood up.

Tavvin jumped up from her spongy bench in fright while Billin wrung his hands anxiously. "Yes, but the situation dictated that we had to find out," Tavvin whinged. "We had to be sure."

"Sure of what?" asked Elliot.

"Sure that you were from Matalla, or Earth as you call it. And you are. Your genes match those held in ancient hidden museums, clearly proving your origin and habitat of upbringing."

"So you knew I was from Earth. Why didn't you tell anybody? Why didn't you tell the King and Queen?" Elliot said in frustration.

"We decided that the time wasn't right. First, we had to find out why Earth had been hidden and where it was. Secondly, we had to find out who was responsible. For all we knew, the King and Queen might have been responsible."

"Your stalling has lost us a lot of time. Uncle Karl is depending on me to find him. We need to go to the Skar'ley Empire and find out more."

"Yes, we have heard of this explorer and his disappearance. And we will help you find him *after* our suspicions have been thoroughly investigated."

"*We*? What do you mean by 'we'?" growled Molly. "You keep saying that but never answered Elliot's question. Do you mean that Furanians have the nerve to meddle in human affairs and decide what we should and shouldn't know about our origins?"

"No, no. When I say *we*, I didn't mean Furanians. Most Furanians haven't got a clue about what's going on. When I said *we,* I mean the Hidden Watchers."

There were brief seconds of silence in the observation room as the ominous title sunk in. Then Elliot and Molly opened their mouths in unison.

"The Hidden Watchers?"

"What we are about to tell you now is most secret and must not reach anybody else's ears, antennas or telepathic lobes," said Tavvin gravely. "I'm telling you as much of the truth as we now know, and hope that you will understand our secrecy when you have heard all that I have to say. Do I have your word that you will not reveal what I tell you?"

Elliot nodded, while Molly glowered at Tavvin for a while before agreeing. "Okay, but you'd better tell us everything."

"I will tell you everything that I know," promised Tavvin and sat down again. She drew a deep breath and then began. "The Hidden Watchers is a secret assembly of wise people who have dedicated their lives to watch over the Spiral Arm. Only members of peaceful, older or wiser races have been allowed to attend the secret assemblies that move around the Spiral Arm. Seldom do scavenger or omnivore species gain membership and never has a predator race sat in the assembly. The Hidden Watchers has been said to exist since the fall of the Founders, thousands upon thousands of years ago. None of its original member species exist today and some later members have fallen to barbarity and ignorance and thus lost their membership. Neither Skar'ley nor humans have ever been allowed membership and only few of these have over the course of history discovered the existence of the Hidden Watchers. We are known only as a vague legend."

"So what *is it* that you do? What do you watch over?" wondered Elliot, bewildered at such ancient conspiracies.

"We try to our utmost ability to safeguard the natural development of civilisations. This development is best done in peace and stability. It is our goal to protect species from everything but themselves and find stability in the Spiral Arm. By secretly influencing members of other species or putting certain events into motion, we have managed to avoid many cataclysmic developments in the Spiral Arm. If there ever is a fateful turn of events that miraculously stabilises a region, the Hidden Watchers is most probably behind it."

"It sounds just like any conspiracy to me," said Molly.

"Yes, that would be true if it were not for the nature of the members of the Hidden Watchers. None of us wish for supremacy or power over others. We simply want stability and prosperity. But this might be hard to understand. Even we Furanians who are members cannot fathom the true extent and intricacies of the Hidden Watchers' agenda. Older and wiser species have long followed the slowly turning cogs and actions which reverberate through the Spiral Arm. What interests us Furanians is peace and stability. This we have had for more than a thousand years – until now."

"So what's happening now?" wondered Elliot.

"We're not sure. The Cro'lichks are slowly moving away from this region of space. Being nomadic, they have depleted most resources of their worlds and are pushing into the centre of the galaxy. The humans have retired and calmed down and most of the other species are harmless – with the exception of the Skar'ley. Although the Empire and the Skar'ley as a race have been stable for thousands of years, the Skar'ley have the technological capability to unleash violence upon the Spiral Arm. Through the manipulations of the Hidden Watchers, the long royal caste of Skar'ley nobles has been chosen and bred to become docile and pacifistic. It's simply not in their nature to act rashly unless threatened. But lately we have noticed secret and alarming activity among the Skar'ley. Activity we cannot explain or trace to a certain source. They are preparing for something. Among all the conspiracies which currently thrive in the Spiral Arm, this concerns us most. Your coming spurred a lot of activity among them."

"I knew it! I knew those Scalies were creepy!" exclaimed Molly.

Elliot did admit he had found the lizard-like Skar'ley with their large regal headpieces, yellow eyes and crooked arms and legs scary at first. But he also remembered the funny stories of Puad'Kesh, the Skar'ley ambassador. Elliot had warmed to him on the *Warhammer* and had the feeling that the majority of the Skar'ley most likely were very friendly.

"So what do we do now?" wondered Molly.

"We must try to find answers to all our questions and solve this riddle. We must also create a plan of action that will steer us away from this violence. The assembly of the Hidden Watchers will hopefully provide us with answers when we meet them."

"We're going to meet the Hidden Watchers? I thought humans weren't allowed?" said Molly.

"Yes, humans are not allowed to be members of the Hidden Watchers. But you will only be attending as guests and witnesses. This has been done many times before. Also, human children have a milder, although more selfish side to their behaviour than adults. History even dictates that you would not be believed if you told this story to others. That's why I have been granted permission to take you before the Hidden Watchers before we take any other action. Before we notify the King and Queen of your survival."

Elliot and Molly said nothing. They pondered this new information in silence while Tavvin slowly rose from her bench. The Hidden Watchers could maybe help them solve some of the mysteries and enable them to find clues to Uncle Karl's whereabouts.

"Mission Leader Moffat knows nothing of the Hidden Watchers. Neither does anybody else of the crew. Only I and Inter-Species Liaison Officer Billin here are representatives of the Hidden Watchers. As I am Chief Observer, I have the mandate to direct this scientific expedition. I ordered the search for you and I will take you with me to investigate old Founder ruins when we reach the Vurite's End star system. There we will meet with the Hidden Watchers in secret. Until then, please enjoy your stay here on board the *Slow Dancer*. Please also let us know if there is anything else you need."

With those words Tavvin and Billin left Elliot and Molly alone in the Main Observatory.

***

Although the *Slow Dancer* was a peaceful and unarmed scientific vessel, it had the latest technology – Furanian Otherdrive. This made the ship very fast, much faster than a bulky warship and ships with Atean Otherdrives. With relative ease, Ship Commander Hattin had made his way out of the Dead Worlds Cluster before other search and rescue ships from the Atean Star-Kingdom and the Skar'ley Empire had begun trawling the area. When he was free of the chaotic cluster, Hattin plotted his course carefully and then engaged the top-of-the-line Otherdrive. With a brief contortion of space, much like a bubble expanding around the ship and then popping, the *Slow Dancer* vanished from normal space and slipped into Otherspace.

***

Three days later the *Slow Dancer* reached its destination, a remote star system far from the Dead Worlds Cluster. Space seemed to sizzle or wobble at first, then the bubble-like distortion appeared, grew and popped. In its stead was the *Slow Dancer*, still travelling at very high speed towards the centre of the star system known as Vurite's End. This star system lay on the inward side of the Vurite Controlled Sphere, closer to the centre of the galaxy. The absent-minded but highly technological Vurites had once inhabited two of the worlds which circled this small blue star. But for unknown and mysterious reasons the Vurites had suddenly withdrawn from the system some six hundred years ago. Rumours stated that a terrible plague had afflicted them. Other rumours said they found something terrible in the star system. Considering the strange Vurite kind of intelligence, which only occurred when in symbiosis with their squid-like Porian counterparts, most Vurites didn't have a clue why they abandoned the world either.

The *Slow Dancer* changed its course and headed for one of the moons orbiting a red gas planet of gigantic proportions. The moon itself was larger than Earth and totally covered in grey murky clouds. As soon as the ship entered orbit around the moon, a small shuttle with Tavvin, Billin, Elliot and Molly departed and dove down into the murky clouds. Stowed in a box at the rear of the shuttle were the hapless remains of Little Brother.

The shuttle shook and groaned as it passed through the violent atmosphere. Elliot could see black rain whipping against the windscreen of the cockpit. Several times the shuttle banged violently or suddenly fell some hundred metres or so. It made his stomach lurch violently.

"The a-a-atmosphe-ere is very-y violent," stuttered Tavvin over the shaking and din of the shuttle. "The gra-a-vity of the ga-a-s gia-ant creates the-e-se violent st-o-orms. But don't worry-y-y, the a-a-utopilot of the shuttle ca-a-n handle it."

"A-a-and if it ca-a-an't," added Billin "I'm su-u-re the-e-r-e a-a-are many o-o-ther safety pre-cautions."

With a sudden jerk they were out of the turbulent clouds and flew calmly again. When they looked out they saw a desolate mountainous landscape in the gloom below them. Some faint light penetrated the storm clouds above, but couldn't fully light up the surface. A few lightning bolts in the distance suddenly lit up the landscape and they could all see the black torrential rain pouring down.

"Black from volcanic ash," commented Tavvin with her high-pitched voice.

"This place is awful!" Molly pointed out.

"Yet the Founders chose to inhabit this world once upon a time," replied Tavvin.

"The Founders? The Ancient Ones? The First People?" said Molly in wonder.

"The same. The surface is full of their ruins, well those parts that haven't been covered by mud, water and lava."

"Err, who are the Founders?" asked Elliot. "I've heard people mention them before, but nobody's ever told me…"

"The Founders are the first known civilisation to spread throughout this region of the galaxy – throughout the Spiral Arm," answered Tavvin. She had made some alterations to the autopilot and now turned away from the controls to face them. "The Founders lived and disappeared more than twelve million years ago. Nobody knows if they were only visiting the Spiral Arm or if their homeworld is among the countless worlds of this region. Their coming and their going is a mystery and not even legends have survived from their days. The only things they left behind are strange ruins and artefacts that are both wondrous and dangerous. Nobody even knows what they looked like. It is said, however, that it was they who founded the first habitat of The Knot and that somewhere deep within the forgotten and abandoned parts of The Knot their legacy can still be found."

"Some say the Founders doomed themselves by constructing terrible weapons," said Billin gravely. "Weapons that one day will resurface again and doom us all."

"You are once again over-exaggerating, Inter-Species Liaison Officer Billin. Please refrain from telling us more of your gloomy prophetic anecdotes."

"But why would they choose a world like this?" wondered Molly looking out of the window. "This is a nightmare."

"Maybe the world was not always like this? Some speculate that worlds like this, with traces of the Founders, were destroyed in some terrible war. Baruun, the Vo'Orrn planetologist, however theorises that this world once was terraformed by the Founders and then reverted back to its natural state when the Founders disappeared. If you just knew how many mysteries like these abound in the Spiral Arm, young ones."

A beeping tone attracted Tavvin's attention and she turned to the shuttle controls again. The shuttle was descending in a long, curved trajectory into a deep, water-filled basin between two mountains. Tavvin assumed control of the shuttle and turned off the autopilot.

"No need to let the ship computer register what's going on from now on. We are, after all, officially here on an archaeological expedition."

All around the great basin were gigantic stone pillars, sometimes hundreds of metres tall. Some still pointed towards the sky, while others stood half fallen, jutting in all directions. Many pillars lay on the ground, broken or half sunken into the mud that had formed out of the ash rain over the millennia. In the gloom, their rounded, half-sunken shapes made them look like gigantic worms that slithered in the dark mud. The shuttle came to a standstill and hovered over the great basin, its thrusters rippling the dark surface.

The communication system on board the shuttle suddenly flickered to life and a black chaotic swirl filled the screen. A deep booming voice said something that Elliot and

Molly didn't understand and Tavvin replied in the unknown tongue with her shrill voice.

"What language was that?" wondered Molly. "My translator couldn't interpret it."

"No, that's because it's an ancient and dead language, only used for codes and secret messages between the members of the Hidden Watchers. We have just been granted permission to land."

Under the hovering shuttle, the dark surface of the basin began to churn. Faster and faster the water swirled, like a great maelstrom, until it opened up into a large hole. The hole was directly below the shuttle, its walls a swirling mass of black water. Without hesitating, Tavvin lowered the shuttle into the hole. Lower and lower they sank into the seemingly bottomless basin of water. Then suddenly the black walls of water were replaced with old and stained stone walls of ancient origin. Overhead, large metal doors closed and separated them from the water which was ceasing to swirl and was rushing back to fill the hole in the basin. Finally they felt the shuttle touch down.

"We are here. This place has served as the meeting place for the Hidden Watchers the last fifty years. After today we will never return here."

The shuttle shook slightly as an airlock was attached to it. Tavvin opened the shuttle's airlock and hopped out, her long ears twitching and her large blue eyes looking around nervously.

"You are late Watchers Tavvin and Billin," a loud but still whispering voice said. It sounded a bit like a hiss. As Elliot and Molly stepped out of the shuttle and into the corridor outside, they could see three figures awaiting them. Two of them were enormous and clad in bulky, nearly round armour which covered any clues to their species. There was no helmet or anything which resembled heads on the armour, only the round bulk. Bulb-like protrusions at the arm and leg joints of the armour seemed to be filled with a kind of sparkling gas or electricity.

The speaker was of another species. Elliot recognised him as one of the aliens with large slanted black eyes and greyish-green skin which he had suspected had followed him throughout the seedier parts of the Vurite Exchange Hub. Little Brother had referred to it as a Snakirra. The Snakirra held a small device, which it manipulated with its long thin fingers resembling spider legs more than digits. They just seemed to have far too many joints. While doing this it never blinked or took its almond-shaped black eyes off Elliot and Molly. They could see their own reflections in that black bottomless stare.

"The identities of Watchers Tavvin and Billin, as well as the human children, are confirmed," the Snakirra whispered hoarsely, as if its vocal cords couldn't produce a sound louder than this.

"It's a Sneaker," Molly whispered. "They normally don't mix much with other species. They just sneak around here and there, spying on everyone, Father always said."

"Watcher Sishra," greeted Tavvin and skipped forward. "I'm sorry we're late, but we had to be careful when plotting our course. There are many spies about in these troubled times."

"Hello!" said Billin shyly from behind Tavvin's back, but was ignored by Sishra.

Tavvin eyed the two armoured creatures next to the Snakirra. They held something which looked like great metal staves in their three-fingered metal hands.

"Why are the Morallin Enervours here?" Tavvin asked.

"They are here for our protection. We suspect that the Balance will be tipped unfavourably very shortly," the Snakirra whispered in answer.

"But I thought creatures of pure energy like the Morallin detested planetary meetings?" Tavvin went on in her squeaky voice.

"Desperate times, means desperate measures. In their environment armour, the Morallin – and we for that matter – are well protected." To change subject the Snakirra pointed to the other door at the end of the airlock tunnel. "Come now! The meeting has already begun."

They followed the Snakirra and the two bulky guards. The second airlock door opened with a hiss into another tubular corridor. The new corridor had transparent walls and seemed to float freely in an immense chamber of stone and more gargantuan pillars which supported a high ceiling. The stone was old and covered with lichen and discolouration from muddy water. Newer steel doors were set in the centre of the ancient underground chamber's ceiling and several metal boxes and cables sat perched on the cracked pillars like giant metal spiders. The floor of the chamber was partially filled with brown water, fungal growth and debris which had fallen from the ceiling. Parked neatly among the pillars were several ships of very different designs. Most of the others had what Elliot would have referred to as standard spaceship features, such as a metal hull, landing gear, view ports, cannons and such. But some were totally alien in design. One was very large and cigar-shaped with several metallic feelers or tentacles which moved around it. Another resembled a flat shiny disc with no visible entrances or weaponry. One ship resembled hundreds of shell-like plates hovering in an open huddle, as if held together by invisible seams. A long sleek ship with curved wings even seemed to be alive, with bones, horns, smoking blowhole and trembling tentacles which seemed to be drinking the fetid water of the chamber.

The tubular corridor they were walking in led to a large and ancient stone doorway. Through the transparent walls they could see that all ships were linked to the large stone doorway by several similar tubular corridors with transparent walls. Just like their own corridor, the bundle of tube-like corridors floated freely in the chamber and they could see that some of them were filled with dark brown liquid or yellowish gases. It looked a bit like giant transparent umbilical cords that were feeding the various ships with air, liquid and most probably, their passengers.

But Elliot and Molly didn't have much time to look at the spaceships, as the Snakirra leading them seemed to be in a hurry. At the stone doorway they were guided into a car with a bubble dome. Tavvin and Billin seated their small furry bodies at the controls while the Snakirra motioned to Elliot and Molly to take a seat behind the Furanians. It then left them together with the two armoured colossuses. As soon as the children had seated themselves the bubble dome snapped closed over them and the vehicle rose from the ground. It rapidly slid through a membrane at the doorway and up into another smaller stone chamber.

"The assembly of the Hidden Watchers," Tavvin introduced as the bubble vehicle rose up into the chamber.

Elliot and Molly stared in wonder at what they saw. Also, this chamber seemed ancient and worn, a small waterfall of fetid water even cascaded from its dank floor down into the larger chamber below. Along the walls of the chamber hovered more of the illuminated bubble-domed vehicles, forming a great circle around the hole from which their vehicle rose. The other vehicles were of different sizes and shapes, to accommodate their occupants.

Inside, Elliot could see twenty or so different… things, which he assumed must be the various species which were members of the Hidden Watchers. Some he recognised – like the insectoid Radorians who stood surrounded by radioactive yellowish gas, and Snakirra sitting cross-legged as if meditating. There were also three slender Vurites with pearly white skin who sat bare-breasted in waist-deep water. Their long white hair flowed into the water, but nothing could be seen of their fair faces and mother of pearl eyes. Instead, a large reddish lump sat attached to their heads, totally covering them in a mass of tentacles and slimy wet rhythmically pumping bulges. Elliot understood that these were the Porian creatures that lived in symbiosis with the Vurites and gave them their vast intellect. Without the Porian, the Vurites were as ignorant and gullible as children.

The inhabitants of the other bubble vehicles were unknown to Elliot. Ten or so of them looked humanoid but with differently coloured skin, wings, horns, scales and, in one case, several bushy moustaches all over the body. The moustache creature didn't seem to be enjoying its own appearance. The other species were very peculiar. One of the vehicles was huge, easily ten times as big as the others, containing murky dark liquid. But inside the gloom Elliot could hint the shape of a large worm-shaped body that was constantly circled by small and fast swimming triangular creatures. In another liquid bubble resided two large yellow octopus creatures whose innumerable tentacles seemed to divide and branch forever. In a misty bubble vehicle could be seen the shadowy silhouette of a spider-thing; and one vehicle was curiously shaped, consisting of several interconnected bubbles. These held sparkling creatures of energy which moved around inside as fast as lightning.

More of the round, armoured Morallin Enervour guards stood amidst the many vehicles. Standing absolutely still, with their great staffs in their hands, they looked like robust stone sentinels.

"That's a Worm," said Molly excitedly and pointed at the largest vehicle containing the worm-like creature submerged in dark murky liquid. Elliot remembered his tiring journey around the Vo'Orrn habitat on The Knot and now understood why the large creatures needed such a large habitat. "And those are Squids," Molly continued and pointed to the yellow octopus creatures. "But apart from the Sneakers, Radars and Whites, I don't recognise any of the other species."

"Yes, you are right," replied Billin. "The Vo'Orrn delegate is easily recognisable, as are the octopoid Sarapids. That's because both they, the Snakirra, the Radorians and the Vurites are – in galactic terms – your neighbours. The other members of the Hidden Watchers are however only known to some of your people. Some are not known at all. Beings like the Mist Spiders are the stuff of legends these days, while the horned Varq are quite comfortable with the common belief that they are extinct. The Morallin energy creatures exists even in Atean space, but are known only as strange energy anomalies, not intelligent beings. The ones that call themselves Zip Zaps," Billin now pointed to something that looked like a small fly on the wall, "are microscopic people in an immense generational ark ship. The proud Zip Zaps expanded their vast, but microscopic, empire into our region of the Spiral Arm more than two hundred years ago. Due to their microscopic size, very few have however noticed them or even been bothered too much by their innumerable, but very, very small fleet."

"I… I didn't know there were so many… people in the Spiral Arm," said Molly astonished.

"Then you would be even more astonished to know how many more species have been charted here in the Spiral Arm. Remember that not all of them are allowed a membership in the Hidden Watchers. The Spiral Arm is a vast place. Furthermore, consider also that this is but one spiral arm of our galaxy. Not forgetting to mention the star dense Galactic Core itself."

"So… how many species exist?" wondered Elliot.

"The Sarapids have travelled the furthest with their generational exploratory fleets. They have catalogued hundreds of species of intelligent life. Many of these have not even taken the step out into space. The Snakirra, who are our eldest members, have records of more than three hundred species that have lived in these parts or still exist today. I assume that not even the well-travelled Founders would know the true answer to your question."

"Now, let us join the debate of the assembly," Tavvin interrupted and began fiddling with the controls of the vehicle. Suddenly a toneless voice poured from the speakers.

"… and as that new-found world is rich in Founder artefacts, it is paramount that we must conclude this affair. Ponder the notion that the Idagons or even the Cro'lichks stumble upon that world. A notion which makes us all shudder."

Elliot could see from the agitated motion of one of the yellow Sarapid octopus creatures that this was the speaker.

"I suggest we immediately begin shipping the most dangerous artefacts off world," another voice said. "With the aid of the Sarapid exploratory fleet this could be done fairly easily, all under the guise of fresh water export."

This time Elliot couldn't see who was speaking, but the voice was very similar in accent and lack of tone.

Seeing Elliot's gaze searching the assembled aliens for the speaker, Tavvin leaned forward to explain. "The different communication modes of the members are translated into vocal speech so that we can understand it. I'm sorry if it confuses you."

As Elliot and Molly listened, the Hidden Watchers switched between the various topics which seemed to be on their agenda. Most topics were beyond their understanding, relating to complex interstellar politics. Facts revealed when discussing some of the other topics startled them. Among these was the fact that it was the second time the nomadic Cro'lichks scourged this part of the Spiral Arm. The first time had been more than twenty thousand years ago. However, the warmongering Cro'lichks did not themselves have any knowledge of this fact, as history never had been their strong point. Now the Cro'lichks were once again retreating, which left their old and exploited worlds open for the taking of others. Past experiences foretold that these worlds would be unruly and rife with piracy.

But most alarming was the brief mention during a discussion: "… and as the Massikita are returning we must consider how long these effects will last…"

Molly lurched forward in her seat.

"The Mosquito People still exist?" she shouted in alarm. She had been taught the terrible history of the Mosquito Wars and had heard the legends that had shaped her people in ancient times.

"Yes, yes," replied Billin. "But they are so far, very few and very, very far away."

"But, that's terrible," moaned Molly. "People should be warned and…"

"Yes, yes," said Tavvin while trying to follow the conversation. "In time they will. But there is no reason to worry people about things that will not occur in their own lifetime, or even their children's lifetimes."

Elliot could feel his head spin with all the details and great galactic politics. It was simply too much for him. He couldn't keep track of which aliens had done what anymore. All he knew was that someone was trying to kill him and Molly. The same people that might have killed Uncle Karl. He didn't have time to understand the mysteries of the galaxy. He just wanted to save Uncle Karl.

Tavvin suddenly held up her hand to get their attention. "Now it is our turn."

A speaker was addressing the assembly and bringing it up to date regarding the current situation within the Skar'ley Empire.

"… and so it is that the Empire has grown stagnant. Its population has not changed in over a thousand years and in the last four thousand years its borders have shrunk in size. Now the remaining two hundred worlds of the Skar'ley are overcrowded and resources are growing thin. The once-balanced race has begun to consume its resources faster than it can replenish them and have upset the very balance that keeps them alive and united. Decadence among the workers and soldiers is growing in the form of lethargy and a sense of not caring what the future has in store for them. They are an uninspired race. The ruling caste cannot inspire the masses anymore and are nothing but dreaming fools."

From the gazes of the other species, Elliot understood that it was the immense Vo'Orrn creature that was speaking.

"As you know, for the last three hundred years we have noticed activity among the Skar'ley that they wish to keep secret from the other species. This activity is the work of an unknown conspiracy in Skar'ley society. These conspirators tread carefully and patiently, aware of our existence and avoiding rumours to reach their neighbours. But the few statements we have intercepted hints that they will not let their Empire and their people grow weak."

A murmur of agreeing voices confirmed the Vo'Orrn speaker's tale and it continued.

"Until now we have not known what purpose this conspiracy has had or what its goal is. However, two recent pieces of evidence hint a sinister plan slowly nurturing within the Empire and along its uncontrolled borders."

A holographic image suddenly burst into existence in the middle of the assembly ring. It showed some large asteroids and countless smaller ships flying to and fro like worker bees.

"Firstly, we have this. Before he was killed, Watcher Sarrasha uncovered a large worksite deep within the Abagean Asteroid Belt. Through the new-found ingenuity of Skar'ley engineers who have 'disappeared' and slave labour purchased from the Cro'lichks, a vast and destructive fleet is being built as we speak. All the ships are large enough to be equipped with powerful planetary weapons and are disguised as rogue asteroids. Strangely enough, much of the ship design and weaponry interfaces don't seem to cater for Skar'ley personnel. The question has therefore arisen of to whom these ships actually are intended."

"Slave manned?" one of the unknown humanoids asked.

"Hardly," answered a Vurite/Porian, the red squid-like attachment shuddering violently as it spoke. "The Skar'ley understood long ago that slave labour is only a temporary solution which will inevitably turn against them."

The Vo'Orrn continued "We can only speculate as to whom or what will man these ships. But under their camouflage, some of these ships have now begun to move slowly and unnoticeably as rogue asteroids towards the heart of the Skar'ley Empire. The ships are uncompleted and still await their intended crew, but the conspirators seem to be acting as if they are running out of time."

A great ruckus erupted from the assembly.

"What does this mean?"

"What has forced them to act so quickly?"

"Are the Skar'ley conspirators attacking their own Emperor?"

"Yes, it seems that the unknown conspirators are now making their slow move to usurp the power of the Empire."

"We have to act immediately!" one of the other members said. "The stability of the Empire is paramount to the Spiral Arm."

"We should attack and destroy them now!" demanded the seemingly bodiless voice of the microscopic Zip Zap speaker.

Silence spread through the assembly, followed by the embarrassed voice of the Zip Zap speaker. "Sorry, sorry! Got carried away…"

"Well. As we all know," a Snakirra said. "We cannot and should not interfere with what is happening within the territories of any of the Free Species – not even the Cro'lichks. It is the law laid down eons ago by the wise Kiv, the Children of the Founders. We must never forget our purpose. We are to watch and observe. To learn and recognise signs of destruction and oppression that could spread to disastrous proportions. We may only interfere if these signs are obvious. Otherwise we cannot meddle in the political affairs of the observed species. Remember the downfall of the Founders."

"They're actually trespassers in *our* Empire," the voice of the microscopic Zip Zap leader mumbled disapprovingly, but nobody seemed to pay this comment any attention.

"So what is the extent of these conspirator's plans?" said the Vo'Orrn in order to return to the subject.

"We have speculated this often," said Sishra the Snakirra. "The Emperor could very well be leading this conspiracy. He has been acting strangely and rashly lately, although the Imperial physicians claim nothing is wrong. Some mental illnesses among the otherwise very pacifistic and homogenous Skar'ley allow sick individuals to act against their own race. Something that for sane Skar'ley would be the same thing as cutting their own flesh. Mental illness such as this in their Emperor would be very dangerous indeed."

"Yes, the health of the Skar'ley Emperor is a grave concern," agreed Tavvin. "Unfortunately, access to his complete medical records is virtually impossible, as he is deemed most holy by his subjects."

"Let us not forget that this conspiracy has existed longer than the lifetime of the current Emperor," said the Vo'Orrn. "Let us assume he is not involved or simply a pawn. Let us focus on how these conspirators would assume power over the Empire. Would they overthrow the long line of emperors and the ruling caste? Would they overpower the Imperial Navy? Surely this cannot be done by fellow Skar'ley soldiers? It is against their nature. As we said before, it will be like cutting their own flesh. No, they need somebody else to do this. Somebody else to man the weapons and fighters of these great ships."

"It is not the first time the Skar'ley use another race to further their means," the four insectoid Radorians spoke as one. "They foolishly stole worlds from the dangerous Massikita and unintentionally drew their attention to this part of the Spiral Arm. They then gave technology to the humans to defeat the Massikita in order to remedy their mistake. We did not act then as this seemed to stabilise the Spiral Arm. But that lead to more violence from the Atean Star-Kingdom. Then, once again, the Skar'ley tried to remedy what they had caused. They hoarded the Cro'lichks into this region of the Spiral Arm so that they would weaken the Atean Star-Kingdom."

"So it was the Scalies who set the Cruelies upon us! They caused the Annihilation Wars!" exclaimed Molly, clearly upset.

"I assure you, I didn't know this either," said Tavvin, also clearly shocked by this new information.

"Who will the Skar'ley use this time to further their means?" continued the Radorians.

"Yes, and that is where we come to our second piece of evidence," said the Vo'Orrn.

All eyes, antennas and minds now turned to Tavvin's vehicle. The small Furanian began to fiddle her fur nervously while her large blue eyes darted across the assembly. Also, Billin seemed nervous by the attention and shrunk away from the controls.

"We have with us the two humans who have been the focus of much attention these past weeks," Tavvin began. Elliot could feel his face blush from the attention and Molly fidgeted nervously. "Spies who have long ago infiltrated the Ateans have now begun to act. We cannot uncover their identities, but notice their actions. I believe the reason for this attention is the fact that the boy here, Elliot Stormsson, claims to come from lost Matalla."

Tavvin made a dramatic pause, but it was clear that the other members of the Hidden Watchers were already aware of this information. She continued.

"So, we secretly began obtaining data ourselves. And based on my most recent tests of Elliot's genome, it's evident that he must indeed come from the very source of humanity – Matalla, or Earth as he calls it."

The assembly now stirred and several voices arose.

"Can it be?"

"Are you certain?"

"I am certain of my findings and I have compared my data with genetic data, long forgotten, in the Skar'ley bio-libraries. There can be no doubt – Elliot comes from the original stock of humans. Therefore, I must come to the conclusion that somewhere out there Matalla – Earth – still exists."

The assembly nodded in unison. Their suspicions had been confirmed.

The Vo'Orrn spoke again. "It is clear that this conspiracy is aware of Earth's existence. Through their actions they have proved that they wish to keep this a secret – at any cost. However, clever deduction or chance led the brave Atean explorers Karrillus and Kaitrinn to this lost world. Unfortunately, they were silenced before news of their discovery could spread. All clues to their journey seem to have been lost or destroyed. But thanks to their efforts, Elliot and thus proof of Earth's existence has now reached us."

"This must be the link we have been looking for," the Mist Spider suddenly said with a slow droning voice. "With the humans of Matalla… Earth… the Skar'ley conspiracy could man those new ships. Seemingly out of nowhere they would have a great army of deadly warriors. Once again, young, dangerous humans would overrun the Spiral Arm."

"Exactly!" confirmed Tavvin and the Vo'Orrn. "That was our conclusion as well. Elliot's appearance could therefore also be the reason for their hurry. They fear that their new army will be discovered."

"But what if the conspirators won't settle with the Imperial throne?" continued the Mist Spider. "The Atean Star-Kingdom is but a shadow of what it once was. It cannot possibly withstand a new wave of younger humans. The magnitude of this threat to the rest of the Spiral Arm is considerable. Those ships could be turned against us all."

A new cacophony of arguments arose.

"Let us not forget the lessons of the past," interrupted the wise old Snakirra. "Humans have very strong wills of their own and are very hard, or rather, impossible, to control in the long run. Even the Skar'ley should know that this plan sooner or later would turn against them."

"Nevertheless, it is evident that the humans of long lost Earth are somehow a part of this sinister plan," said one of the unknown humanoids. "Why else would someone want to hide Earth's existence? The question is now how do the conspirators attempt to control them?"

There was silence until one of the Vurite/Porians spoke.

"We know a lot more now. We know that the Skar'ley conspirators might be attempting to use humans as their soldiers again. But we don't know how they will control them better this time. We still need to gather additional information before we can act. We have always thought that the Skar'ley somehow helped the Cro'lichks find Earth in order to destroy it. Now we know that this was just a clever guise. Most probably some other poor world suffered that fate and all maps were cleverly destroyed over time. Clearly the route to Earth is now solely in the hands of the Emperor or someone close to him. To learn more we must delay this new fleet of ships and find our way to Earth and see for ourselves what the conspirators have done to this world. We must see how they intend to control the humans."

"But they haven't done anything. Not yet." Elliot was surprised to hear his own voice.

"Please, Master Elliot," hushed Tavvin. "You do not yet have the mandate to speak…"

"Let the human child speak," boomed the Vo'Orrn from its murky tank. "It is time to hear what he has seen with his own eyes."

Elliot gulped as he realised he was now fully at the focus of everybody's attention. As it felt like the right thing to do, he stood up inside the bubble vehicle.

"I-I-I mean, I haven't seen anything strange on Earth. Nobody has ever seen a Skar'ley on Earth. Nobody has ever seen *any* alien as a matter of fact. At least that's what they say. Everything is quite normal. The days go by, grown-ups go to work, children go to school, countries are at war, international song contests are won and the Winter Olympics is soon to start. The only strange thing I've ever seen is the Hunter robot that came after me… and Uncle Karl of course."

There was so much Elliot wanted to say, but he just couldn't put words on how normal Earth and Sweden had felt.

"Tell us… everything," the Snakirra said in its hoarse whispering voice.

So Elliot did his best to explain what Earth was like. It felt just like he was back at school and suffering Mrs Kateder's terrible geography homework interrogations. He told the Hidden Watchers everything he knew about Earth's history. How the Egyptians had built the pyramids, how the Romans and Chinese had built their great empires. How countries had explored, warred and expanded. He told them about ice cream, TV and comics. He told them about the different people and their languages which he had read about in books. During his description the Hidden Watchers never asked any questions. The Snakirra only kept saying, "Tell us… more."

So finally he came to Uncle Karl, his journey to Kiruna and the Hunter robot.

"… Now I think Uncle Karl was ki… captured by those Hunter robots and Aunt Kaitrinn has somehow lost her mind." Elliot could feel a lump in his throat as he thought about the big, kind old man and the poor confused old woman. But then Molly squeezed his hand for support and he found the courage to continue. "There are no maps or clues to their discovery of Earth. It's all gone. Now they nearly managed to get rid of us as well."

Elliot was itching with impatience. There had been so much talking and still no clues to where Uncle Karl could be found. There was no time for this. They needed to find Uncle Karl and possibly warn everybody about the conspiracy. Elliot needed the Hidden Watchers to help him find Uncle Karl and stop debating, but he didn't know how he was going to ask them. His troubles seemed so small in comparison to galactic politics spanning several millennia.

"Yes, as you know, both these children have been subjected to more than one attempt to take their lives," explained Tavvin. "According to the description they left with the Atean Secret Police, their assailants used Class IV Hunter robots of Technoid manufacture. These old, but still deadly robots were presumed all destroyed when the rebellious Technoids were dismantled. Clearly the conspiracy still controls some of them. Then, just recently, the Atean ship transporting the children was attacked and destroyed by the conspirators as it passed through the Dead Worlds Cluster."

"But it wasn't them. It was the Cruelies," interrupted Molly.

"Yes, the Cro'lichks might have held the sword, but their hand was surely guided by the conspirators," said the Snakirra. "The Cro'lichks have long been aware of the manipulative powers of the Skar'ley and are tired of being scapegoats and unwitting pawns. Most certainly they were lured into this mess from the very start. How else would the Cro'lichks know where to wait for you? They are as close to innocence as one of their species ever can be."

"But how can they be innocent?" Molly said angrily. "They are murderous beasts."

"Cro'lichks are actually moody and aggressive because of their racial memory," explained Billin. "They have a racial memory of sorts, but mainly remember strong emotions such as hate and pain. Therefore, the Cro'lichks get grumpier and crueller every century as a species. It is said, however, that some Cro'lichks try to halt this development through relaxation, poetry and soothing slime baths."

"I don't care if they swim in lard," replied Molly. "They're evil and killed all those people aboard the *Warhammer*."

"Actually the crewmen are still alive," replied one of the Vurites/Porians. "The Cro'lichks took them to the slave market of Vrakesh where we persuaded them to deliver the prisoners into our care. The reason for their attack was the two of you, and not those crewmen. They wanted to attack their two ancestral enemies and had probably been alerted to your route without knowing the true purpose of this. The Cro'lichks are once again slaves under their silly Scriptures of War."

"It's true," said Elliot who had been thinking. "We did intercept that message, Molly. The one about alerting the Cruelies about our route. It was probably meant for a spy on board the *Warhammer*, just as we suspected."

"What message?" wondered Tavvin and Billin.

Elliot looked to Molly for help. She sighed, then consulted her PDM and read the message. "*The human children must die. Accidents in space can happen easily. Matalla must remain hidden until our plans and the devices of the Flesh Smiths of the Ash Plains come into fruition. The Cro'lichks who patrol the Dead Worlds have been notified which route the ship will be taking. They will home in on your signal.*"

"Flesh Smiths!" cried the Snakirra in unison and became very agitated. "By the Sacred Nebulas, what have the Skar'ley done now?"

"It cannot be!" cried other members of the Hidden Watchers.

"Destroy or be destroyed!" wailed the microscopic Zip Zaps in unison.

"We would know if any of the Flesh Smiths still existed. Wouldn't we?" said the Sarapids anxiously. "Surely they would have made themselves known?"

"What are Flesh Smiths?" wondered Elliot, his curiosity taking control over his mouth.

"The Flesh Smiths – or An Barr, as they called themselves – are terrible shadows of the past," explained the Vo'Orrn. "Equally terrible as the Massikita, the Flesh Smiths were a vile and immoral species of meddlers. Experts at genetic manipulation, they waged genetic warfare against their neighbours. They were formless and hard to defeat or understand as they constantly would spawn new bodies for themselves. In their wars, they unleashed terrible beasts and altered the very genes of their enemies. Many poor creatures were born to the Skar'ley, Vo'Orrn, Sarapids and Snakirra during those days. The young Skar'ley Empire achieved much of its original fame by the destruction of the Flesh Smiths. The Galactic Navy and the resilience of the Skar'ley destroyed the Flesh Smiths in the end."

"But now it once again seems that the Skar'ley have outwitted us," said the Snakirra speaker. "We did suspect that the dying Massikita used some kind of Flesh Smith weapon to inflict the genetic Curse of Decay upon the Skar'ley, but to hear that those accursed fiends could still exist today…"

"We must take action immediately," cried the embarrassed looking moustache-being.

The assembly raised their voices in agreement.

"But where are these Ash Plains?" wondered the Radorians.

"It's a region of the Skar'ley Empire," answered one of the yellow Sarapids. "A handful of star systems which have been engulfed by a great nebula cloud. Supposedly there is nothing there apart from run-down Skar'ley mines. The Cro'lichks would know everything there is to know about the Ash Plains. They've made secret incursion into that region for decades."

"Evidently the conspirators must be hiding some surviving Flesh Smiths there," said one of the humanoids. "That this could have escaped our attention! How reckless and evil can the Skar'ley be to keep such monstrosities alive?"

"Maybe the Flesh Smiths now control the Skar'ley? Maybe they have twisted them and turned them to evil?" said one of the Sarapids.

"Let us remember that the Skar'ley as a species are not evil," said the combined voices of the Radorians. "Far from it. Their moral values are very sophisticated and their culture fairly benevolent. They were close once to achieving membership in the Hidden Watchers. However, it is their naiveté and their desperate attempts to find a status quo that constantly ends up shifting the delicate balance. As hard as it is for us who have hive minds to grasp, we must remember that we now face the actions of only a small fraction of the Skar'ley – not their species as such."

"Then we propose a plan of action," said Sishra the Snakirra calmly after having consulted its comrades. The assembly grew silent and listened to the wise old Snakirra. "While we put all our resources into delaying the secret fleet and finding Earth, let us send a crew of investigators to search these Ash Plains for the Flesh Smiths. Evidently we must seek the assistance of the Cro'lichks in doing so." The Snakirra then turned its large black eyes towards Elliot and Molly. The bubble-domed vehicle they were sitting in reflected in its cold bottomless eyes. The Snakirra raised its hand and pointed one its long, spidery fingers at them.

"Their role here as witnesses and evidence has been played out. They must now serve another purpose. We suggest the human children are taken to the Cro'lichks. What better way to gain their trust than to bring their ancestral enemies to them."

To Elliot's and Molly's horror, the assembly grumbled in agreement.

"But-but the Cruelies hate us," stuttered Elliot. "You can't hand us over to them."

"Master Elliot," replied the Snakirra speaker calmly and without compassion. "I'm afraid the future of the Spiral Arm is at stake here. It is beyond your power to change your destiny now."

Elliot sat down in shock. Beside him he could hear Molly begin to scream and curse.

"You backstabbing Ferrybeetle dungheap Sneakers! The Cruelies will kill us! You wouldn't dare! Do you know who I am…?"

The angry outburst made Tavvin and Billin retch with anxiety and they retreated as far away from Molly as they could in the small vehicle.

But the assembly of the Hidden Watchers didn't seem to listen. Instead the various vehicles began breaking away from the ring and one by one they departed down the hole in the chamber's floor, to their ships.

Elliot couldn't believe it. They had been betrayed again.

CHAPTER 2
THE DESTROYER OF SUNS AND DEVOURER OF WORLDS

Over a red and dusty planet known only as Scratch, hung a great spiked ball of steel. The light of the large sun of the star system glinted on its rough and bolted steel surface, nearly cutting itself. It was a large space station, brimming with cannons and torpedo hatches. To the Cro'lichks it was known as an Orbital Tank. To other species who had witnessed devices such as this in action, it was known as a World Killer.

The long and sleek Vurite starship that was docking at one of the station's struts looked out of place. The station appeared composed of various scraps of multihued and rusted metal which had been scavenged elsewhere and bolted together. The Vurite ship on the other hand, seemed made of a combination of polished silver metal, sleek glass and white porcelain.

Angry Cro'lichks workers in bulky spacesuits on the station's hull glared at the ship with suspicious beady eyes. However, sadistic foremen soon got their attention again by constricting their air tubes. With a flurry of activity and welding sparks they returned to repairing the badly manufactured and constantly battle-damaged space station.

A long airlock arm in the shape of a cruel rusty claw reached out and attached to the Vurite ship. Soon, a delegation of species left the Vurite ship and made their way across to the Cro'lichks space station. Only the contours of the creatures, which were both tall and slender, short and round, low and tentacled, were visible.

***

At the assembly of the Hidden Watchers, Elliot and Molly had at first been angry. Tavvin and Billin had been so verbally abused by Molly that they had thrown up and cowered in fear while the Snakirra and the Morallin Enervour guards took Elliot and Molly on board the Vurite ship. Tavvin had tried to explain herself and apologise, but had stuttered too much in fear of Molly to be understandable.

Elliot and Molly had been confined to small but comfortable quarters during the entire trip to the Cro'lichks territory. They had slept much of the way and Elliot suspected that the Vurites somehow had been responsible for this in order to keep them calm. During the short periods they had been awake, however, Molly had shouted and banged the walls of their quarters until she had nothing left but angry tears and a hoarse throat. Elliot had also tried to persuade them to change their minds, but had quickly tired of talking to a locked door.

Now, as they were being taken over to the Cro'lichks space station, Elliot looked around him. The members of the strange delegation were six fair Vurites (one of them with a symbiotic Porian), the Snakirra known as Sishra, five Morallin Enervours in their huge bulky power armour, an octopoid Sarapid and the two Furanians – Tavvin and Billin. Despite being an Inter-Species Liaison Officer, Billin seemed extremely nervous at meeting the Cro'lichks. Foul odours and unpleasant noises seemed to originate from his person. As they walked, Tavvin's large and sad blue eyes looked their way.

"Traitor!" hissed Molly and drew a finger across her throat.

Tavvin stumbled in sudden fear and anxiety but was caught by one of the many tentacles of the Sarapid. The Furanians were not very good at handling conflicts and Molly seemed to be enjoying tormenting the feeble-minded creatures.

"You don't need to do this!" said Elliot. "You know what they'll do to us. You're just as much a murderer as they are," he added accusingly.

Tavvin and Billin blinked nervously and looked up at the silent Snakirra with large blue eyes. But Sishra said nothing and didn't even spare the children a glance.

The inner airlock doors now loomed in front of them. They were shaped like two great steel jaws, complete with demonic red eyes. With a loud hiss and clouds of steam they opened.

"Drama, drama," said the Snakirra tiredly with its whispering voice. "The Cro'lichks never tire of their intimidation techniques."

Elliot smirked at this comment, but his expression soon changed as the steam parted and revealed what awaited them in the room beyond. Steam rolled around the ugly faces of twenty Cro'licks warriors in bulky and cruelly spiked armour.

Large tusked mouths moved in anticipation of violence and blood-shot eyes glared at Elliot and Molly expectantly. Huge power axes and large rifles were poised ready to strike. Cruel spikes jutted out of the steel walls of the room which was lit only faintly by a red glow.

Billin groaned and fainted, his small furry body landed limply on the floor.

Then, suddenly the Cro'lichks saw the Morallin Enervours and took a couple of steps back.

"Greetings mighty warriors and rulers of the galaxy," said Sishra the Snakirra, and raised his spidery fingers to his temples. "I am Sishra of Direek and this is the symbiosis known as Kovorn." Sishra pointed to the Vurite with the Porian whom nodded slowly.

"What! What is meaning of this?" grunted one of the Cro'lichks warriors and pointed to the Morallin Enervours. The Cro'lichks was evidently some kind of leader, as his armour was painted with several cruel symbols the other warrior didn't have.

"The Morallin are here to ensure our safety," explained Sishra. "They have chosen to ally with us for the time being."

"Not good. Not fun. Sparky-Things cannot be killed," growled the Cro'lichks. "They grow and eat everything. Big sparky boom to all they touch." Although the translators could handle the foul and offensive language of the Cro'lichks, their crude speech seemed to lack proper sentences. Clearly the warrior culture of the Cro'lichks hadn't felt the need to stop robbing and murdering their neighbours to organise the grammar of their language.

"Your observations are correct," answered Sishra. "As you most certainly have learned through trial and error, our friends here cannot be destroyed by conventional means. The more the reason for them to watch over us."

The Cro'lichks grunted with displeasure and then pointed to Elliot and Molly. "Give us prisoners! We want execute them now!"

"Not yet, my good friend," said Kovorn. Only his lips and chin was visible under the bulging red mass of the shuddering Porian creature which was attached to his head. Long red tentacles draped around his shoulder and chest. "Take us first to the commander of this establishment. It is he and not you, a simple sergeant, whom we should deliver these creatures to."

A great rumbling growl started at the back of the Cro'lichks sergeant's throat. But it soon stopped as the other Vurites, still smiling, drew sleek guns from their holsters.

All the Cro'lichks took a step back and the sergeant whined nervously. It sounded to Elliot like a squealing pig. It was evident that the Cro'lichks feared the weapons of the Vurites.

"We will. We will take you. Follow."

The Cro'lichks sergeant then led the delegation out of the ghastly reception room and through more red-lit corridors.

"Are your weapons so mighty that they scare these brutes?" Elliot asked one of the Vurites.

The fair Vurite turned to Elliot. He smiled stupidly and his mother of pearl eyes looked surprised at the question. "I don't know," he replied.

"No, of course not," said Elliot with a sigh. "I assume the guns are magical."

"Yes. Yes they actually are," replied the Vurite as a matter of fact and, without breaking his sheepish smile, kept on walking.

The nervous and growling Cro'lichks warriors escorted the delegation to a large room filled with several screens which monitored the planet and space around it. Several Cro'lichks sat by the controls throughout the room and twenty or so guards stood along the walls and by the entrances. The entire room stunk of brimstone and rotting meat. In the centre of the room stood a great command chair or throne, flanked by two unusually large Cro'lichks bodyguards on either side. The Cro'lichks that sat in the chair seemed much older and wrinkled than the others. As they drew closer, Elliot could see that the wrinkles were in fact a tangled mass of nasty scars and badly healed wounds. His great hooked nose was broken in several places and a black tongue lolled out in disgust at their approach. Big, clawed hands rested on a nasty and barbed rifle-axe lying in his lap. One of the clawed hands rose to point accusingly at Sishra.

"What you bring us, Grey-skin? Not prisoners but Sparky Warriors and death. You betray me?"

"We would do no such thing, General Spine Breaker and Relisher In It," replied Sishra humbly in his whispering voice. "We have brought the human children just as we said. The Morallin are here for our protection only and will not harm you."

"Not good. Not suitable. You prove loyalty now and give us prisoners."

"We will deliver these humans to your care, just as we promised when we contacted you. However, in return for doing so we wish a favour of you."

"Favour! Cro'lichks not give favours. We give death, war and occupation – sometimes with trade."

"Yes, yes, we understand. But this favour would also be of great interest to you."

"Don't listen to that stinking Sneaker!" shouted Molly suddenly. "They have no right to…"

Her voice was silenced with a wave from the tentacles of Kovorn. Her lips continued to move but no sound could be heard. When Molly noticed this she looked around her in horror while trying to say or scream something else. Somehow she had been silenced and it didn't matter how hard she tried or how red her face turned, not a sound escaped her lips.

Sishra continued, "We wish to employ your services to find certain dangerous creatures hiding in the Ash Plains. We wish to bring back at least one of them alive. Now, we know that you have extensive knowledge about this region. So, we want you to take us there and back."

"What I get for this? This in Skar'ley Empire. A no-no place to go."

"First of all, you would be granted access to these humans and do to them what you please. Secondly, you will be paid sixty million Imperial doubloons to cover your expenses – and maybe help fund your next military campaign against your brother? Thirdly, you would be allowed to hunt and destroy very dangerous creatures you have never before encountered. I assume that you would earn much honour for such a trophy in the next clan gathering?"

This seemed to spark General Spine Breaker's interest. He leaned forward with a greedy grin. "Tell me of these creatures. Tell more."

"They are called Flesh Smiths. Terrible creatures that once fought the Skar'ley and many other species. Their cunning and their power over living creatures is very great. They are a dread enemy that even the Vurites fear."

"How I slay them if Vurites cannot? You take me a fool? Danger this is. Danger."

"But, I thought the Cro'lichks didn't fear anything?" said Sishra with feigned surprise. "I thought the Cro'lichks had defeated all that can be defeated? Hunted all that can be hunted? Surely it would be worth the risk to defeat at least one of the legendary Flesh Smiths, regardless of the loss of… resources?"

General Spine Breaker pondered this for a moment and his large tusked mouth seemed to word something silently. Finally, he nodded furiously and spoke.

"Yes, yes. Cro'lichks will hunt these Flesh Smiths. Get great honour. Great hunting party we gather. We take you into Ash Plains. But first you give humans. Human captives of war."

Sishra nodded and pointed towards Elliot and Molly.

"Here are the human children you have been looking for." The large steel hands of the Morallin Enervours clamped down on Elliot's and Molly's arms and dragged them forward.

"Elliot Stormsson here comes from Matalla," Kovorn said, the red body of the Porian on the Vurite's head shuddering. "Matalla is a human world not included in the Clean Slate Accord, which was signed by the leaders of all Cro'lichks Nations and all subjects of the Atean Star-Kingdom. The very accord that was incorporated into your Scriptures of War. The population of Matalla therefore know nothing of the peace treaty."

Kovorn then turned his unseeing eyes to Molly.

"This is Princess Molnír Asir of Valdanna. She was placed in a cryotube more than two thousand years ago. Because of this fact, she hasn't signed the accord either."

"Yes, yes. Enemies they are. Die they will," said General Spine Breaker impatiently.

But Kovorn went on and presented a writing pad with chaotic scribbles of Atean and Cro'lichks characters. "We present these ancient enemies of the Cro'lichks to you in order for you to witness their signing of the Clean Slate Accord. They have no wish to be at war with the mighty Cro'lichks Nations and call upon their right as humans to Clean the Slate of Aggressions and Transgressions of the Past. Being a warlord and spokesmen for your Nation, it would honour us if you would sign on behalf of all Cro'lichks."

"What!" yelled General Spine Breaker and rose angrily. "What is this? Trick! Deception! We no sign!" The angry general swung his rifle-axe over his head menacingly.

Billin fainted again.

"But I'm afraid you must, General," insisted Kovorn. "In accordance with the edicts of the Galactic Court, the human children have exercised their rights in front of at least three members of other species. They have come freely to you and bring no force or other demands. If you do not sign, you will go against the Scriptures of War and bring shame and dishonour to yourself and to your Nation. I'm sure there's some kind of penalty for that."

"Aaaarrrgh! Roaarrrhh!" shouted the angry general and began hacking with his rifle-axe at the throne he had been sitting in. Fiery sparks of electricity and white hot plasma spilled from the axe as it struck. After three mighty blows the throne had been reduced to smoking and sputtering splinters. But the enraged Cro'lichks didn't stop. Like a frenzied gorilla he ran across the room and began hacking at computer consoles, doors, pillars of electronic devices and a small hapless cleaning robot. The Cro'lichks guards and terminal operators retreated in terror. For a good two minutes the enraged general ran around demolishing his own control room while the assembly of Hidden Watchers stood silently and waited. Tavvin was retching and shuddering with fear, while Elliot and Molly huddled behind the large Morallin Enervours.

"I really don't like conflicts!" moaned Tavvin.

Finally the fury of the Cro'lichks general subsided and he returned panting to the ruin of his command chair.

"You-you fool Cro'lichks. Make truce. Not very fun. No killing for me of prisoners. Very unfriendly. Tricky games you play."

"I'm sorry," whispered Sishra. "We did not mean to fool you in any way. Maybe our intentions were misunderstood?" The Snakirra turned to Elliot and Molly as he spoke and one of his large black eyes winked suddenly. "Maybe we forgot to mention the fact that these human children were calling upon their rights to enter a truce with the mighty Cro'lichks."

"Bah! We sign. Do it quickly! Me tired."

"Indeed," agreed Kovorn and presented the writing pad. "Here is an amendment to the Clean Slate Accord which can be signed immediately. Please sign under the dotted lines." Elliot and Molly were handed a pen and the writing pad was thrust before them.

"Should I sign it?" Elliot whispered to Molly.

"If you want to live, you'd better do it," answered Molly, slightly surprised at the sound of her voice which now had returned.

Elliot wrote his name in bold letters over the dotted line that Kovorn was pointing at. As the writing pad and pen was shifted to Molly, Elliot could see his own signature squirming and wriggling, changing into Atean letters which Molly could read. After the children had signed the amendment, the writing pad was given to General Spine Breaker. With an angry series of slashes and stabs he signed the pad, denting it in the process.

"There! We finished. Happy now?" growled General Spine Breaker and glared at the children.

"I'm sure that I speak for the children when I say how delighted they are to finally be at peace with the mighty Cro'lichks Nations," whispered Sishra.

"Me not happy. Must find something else to torture now," muttered General Spine Breaker.

"Yes, yes, we quite understand your disappointment. Please do not let us keep you any longer. If you could only assemble this hunting party and we will be on our way to the Ash Plains…?"

With a series of grunts and growls, General Spine Breaker summoned one of his men over the blaring intercom of the space station. Soon, another bewildered and ugly Cro'lichks stood in front of them. This Cro'lichks was also clad in bulky spiked armour, but additionally equipped with a large metal helmet which hung from his back.

"This V'rorg'chak – Destroyer of Suns and Devourer of Worlds," said General Spine Breaker. "He finest captain I send with you. Knows Ash Plains well." General Spine Breaker then turned to his nervous captain and pointed his blaster-axe at his face.

"You take Truce Guests to Ash Plains and find Flesh Smith. New and cunning enemy. Bring back head and hunters glory for me. Fail me and you pulled apart by my angry wives. Okey dokey?"

Captain Destroyer swallowed hard and his long black tongue lolled out of his foul mouth.

"Yessir, boss. Me understand." Evidently, facing two score of angry Cro'lichks wives scared him more than the notion of facing an unknown and terrible beast.

With an angry wave of his large clawed hand, General Spine Breaker then turned away from them. "Me tired. Prepare slime bath and poet!" he ordered his men. He felt an enormous amount of hatred right now. Hatred to the Vurites. Hatred to the humans. Hatred to silly ancient treaties. Hatred even to his own men, his breakfast and for some reason his own left boot. He sighed to himself – which sounded more like a fart – and once again confirmed that these inherited race-hatred memories were impossible to fully understand. A nice and soothing slime bath and the words of a dying poet would ease his emotions and calm his blood. Actually, he might even let the poet live – with some of his limbs intact. Without addressing the troublesome aliens further, General Spine Breaker burped and lumbered out of the control room.

***

It took at least five minutes for the party to get what belongings they needed from the Vurite ship and to hand over the sixty million Imperial doubloons. It took twenty minutes to shuttle them to the large warship which lay in orbit on the other side of the dusty world of Scratch. It took less than thirty minutes to prepare their living quarters aboard the huge warship *World Strangler*. This consisted of cleaning out unused and stinking cabins, fitting brighter lights and installing strange Vurite sentry devices over their doors. It however took more than fifty minutes to revive Billin who had fainted and withdrawn into himself in terror. Finally, when all was ready, Captain Destroyer ordered his warship to set a course for the Ash Plains.

It might be incorrect to say that the Cro'lichks warship was large – it was, in fact, enormous. As its gargantuan metal bulk passed the spiky world killer space station it seemed to fly by forever, until the blaring red engines finally heralded its end. Only an insane, psychotic and paranoid race of mindless killers would construct something with so much armour, torpedo hatches, microwave cannons and gun turrets.

On board the extremely unconspicuous warship were now Sishra the Snakirra, Tavvin, and Billin the Furanians, the yellow tentacled Sarapid, Kovorn the Vurite/Porian and Elliot and Molly the humans. They all sat congregated in one of the War Planning rooms in front of a large red tinted window which contained an endless vista of stars.

"Remind me again what we're doing here?" asked Molly curiously to a nervous Tavvin.

The Furanian's twitchy large blue eyes met Molly's hard gaze and she swallowed.

"I'm sorry that I couldn't explain this whole Clean Slate affair to you sooner. You were just so angry that I couldn't…"

"Never mind that! Why are we on board a Cruelie warship on our way to hunt down a terrible ancient enemy? Why us? What can *we* do?"

"You? Well, I don't know. There wasn't time to…"

"So we have to come along and risk our lives… again?" Molly was now standing with her hands on her hips and did her best to look as intimidating as possible. The round and furry Furanian felt totally out of place and wished she was somewhere else.

"We should be looking for Elliot's lost uncle and not flying around gathering evidence of hidden Skar'ley conspiracies," continued Molly. "Every minute we lose could be invaluable."

Elliot nodded vigorously in agreement. "Yes, we need to get back and keep searching for clues."

"I'm sure we can ask the Cro'lichks to host you on the space station until another ship passes by this region of space," replied Billin suddenly, who seemed genuinely serious about his suggestion and even smiled slightly. But despite Billin's usual doom-ridden words, Molly and Elliot slowly understood that they had no choice. Staying alone among the Cro'lichks was not an option. It wasn't likely that anybody would *want* to pass by that region of space.

"What about the Vurite ship? Why didn't we go back in that?" asked Elliot.

"I'm afraid that would have been even more dangerous," said Kovorn. "That ship is destined to intercept the disguised fleet of asteroid ships. Needless to say, there is a large risk of it being destroyed."

"Then I guess we'll have to come along," sighed Elliot. His thoughts returned to Uncle Karl and he began despairing that he would be too late. He desperately hoped they would find some clues to his whereabouts when investigating the sinister conspiracy of these Flesh Smiths.

The intercom blared noisily and interrupted them. The ugly fanged and hook-nosed face of Captain Destroyer appeared on a grimy screen.

"We jump now to Otherspace," he declared.

"Otherspace?" replied Tavvin. "I didn't know Cro'lichks had Otherdrives? What a coincidence that your engineers would invent the same method to overcome the laws of relativity."

"Cro'lichks not have time for inventive engineers. We steal invention. Why invent what we can steal from others? Much cheaper, more fun, more honourable," answered Captain Destroyer with a satisfactory gurgling.

"You stole…?" began Tavvin.

"Ehm yes," explained Billin. "It's actually considered very honourable among the Cro'lichks to conquer not only planets and people, but entire cultures, religions and technological inventions. It's their way. Their Scriptures of War encourage them to do so."

"Those Scriptures must've been written by a psychopath," mumbled Molly.

Sishra glanced quickly at the intercom screen, but Captain Destroyer was already gone. He then turned to Molly.

"You would do well not to insult the Cro'lichks on their own ship, little friend. However tied to their strange Scriptures of War they may seem, they have a tendency to overreact and kill things before they have time to think or consult the Scriptures. Let us now prepare for the jump and then stay as far away from our hosts as we can. We need them to locate and capture the Flesh Smiths but nothing more."

Outside, space contorted and then popped like a gigantic bubble as the enormous Cro'lichks warship passed into Otherspace. Nothing of the warship was left behind except a cloud of expelled organic waste and faint ion trails evaporating in space.

***

As usual, the journey through Otherspace was boring. Elliot and Molly didn't feel inclined to explore the Cro'lichks ship as they were pretty sure it would contain far too many dangerous machines and harmful weapons. Instead they spent much time with the yellow squid-like Sarapid alien they learnt was called Salank. Although Salank was an aquatic creature with very little in common with Elliot and Molly, he was intrigued by their inquisitiveness and glad to answer most questions they had. Salank was a ship engineer and had worked most of his life on board Sarapid Deep Space exploratory ships. Being a skilled engineer, Salank had already taken the opportunity to enhance their energy shield devices, making them much stronger.

"What do these Deep Space Exploratory ships actually explore?" asked Molly, as Salank now sat hunched over her PDM with his many yellow tentacles. The ever-branching tentacles wielded a number of small tools and triple lens spectacles sat perched over the two large eyes. Salank was updating her PDM as he couldn't live with the fact that it hadn't been properly updated for two thousand years.

"New stars, new worlds, new species of intelligent or non-intelligent life," Salank answered reverently, looking up from his work. His wheezy voice was transmitted from his Speech Converter Box as he lacked organs to create audible speech.

"But isn't there enough to see here?" asked Elliot.

"For you, maybe. I have visited more worlds of the Spiral Arm than many others, yet I still long for the mystery of the unknown. All Sarapids do. Our curiosity is not easily satisfied. That is why most of us choose to participate in at least one exploratory expedition in a lifetime. Some, like myself, spend most of our lives exploring. Exploring and witnessing the galaxy is our strength, just like the strength of the Vurites is their technology. The very reason for our membership in the Hidden Watchers is our reporting of the strange and very secret events we witnessed in the Clouds of Magellan."

"What events?" asked Molly.

"I can't tell you, as they were to you both strange, and most importantly, very secret."

Molly sighed impatiently.

"Seems a bit odd, going off exploring all the time," she said after a while.

"On the contrary," replied Salank. "It has always been in the nature of the Sarapids to explore. We are inquisitive by nature. First we explored our seas, then our continents. When we reached space we continued to explore. Every generation enjoys learning of new discoveries and eagerly awaits the reports of returning deep space explorers. Seeing new worlds and new marvels, even if it isn't with our own eyes, is our most appreciated experience. But the known boundaries of space are moving outward at a great speed. It now takes decades or even centuries for exploratory ships to reach uncharted space. Most of these trips are therefore spent in hibernation."

"The trips last centuries? You travel in hibernation? That means you'll be gone a really, really long time," said Molly.

"Yes. But the greater the expectations are when we return. All Sarapids are now counting down to the return of the Keilop Expedition that set out to the Veilion Star-Ring five hundred years ago. The first expedition I participated in took ten years to reach its destination. We stayed in that region of space for more than four years before returning. All in all I was gone twenty-four years. After that I participated in much longer expeditions."

"But, then your family and friends must be really old by now," said Elliot.

"I have no family or friends any more. They are long dead. I left my birth-waters of Sarapia more than four hundred years ago. I have spent more than three hundred of those years in hibernation all together. The family and friends that I have are those that I make on trips just like these. It is they who remember me and whom I might actually meet again."

Elliot and Molly didn't know what to say. They weren't sure if Salank's life was fantastic or tragic. Instead they stood in silence and watched him complete his work.

***

Six days later, space began to wobble and the bubble-like distortion appeared, grew and popped. Out of the nothingness appeared the *World Strangler*. As soon as it had made its course corrections, the ship modified its engine emissions, minimising the ion trail that might reveal them to patrolling ships from the Skar'ley Empire.

The members of the Hidden Watchers assembled in one of the War Planning rooms together with Captain Destroyer. As usual, his flight uniform consisted of bulky and spiked armour. Nobody seemed to object to Elliot and Molly also being there. The two children stood in the background, being as silent as possible, trying to get a glimpse of the holographic star map hovering in the centre of the room.

"All this Ash Plains," snorted Captain Destroyer. His large clawed hand waved through something that looked like a glowing cloud of dust mites. "Six systems. Many, many planets and planetoids and rock-rocks. Nebula cloud from supernova engulf everything. Make sensors go ding-ding. No good for long-range torpedo systems."

"Nor for long-range scans either, I presume," said Tavvin. "Six murky systems filled with intense cosmic radiation, interstellar debris from a supernova, chaotic magnetic fields and possibly even space-time continuum anomalies. The perfect hiding place for the Flesh Smiths."

"Tell us what regions of the Ash Plains you know best," asked Kovorn politely.

Captain Destroyer clawed his way through the great stellar cloud, uttering in remarkably few syllables what the regions contained. "Old mines." "Abandoned mining outpost." "More mines." "Destroyed by nova" and so on.

"And in all these places you have seen no habitation in use? No strange creatures you do not recognise."

Captain Destroyer pondered this for a while. His blood-shot eyes focused on the tip of his long and crooked nose in the effort to recollect all he had seen.

"We once ate one-legged horse we found at old abandoned mining station," he ventured and licked his protruding yellow fangs with his long black tongue.

"A one-legged horse?" repeated Sishra bewildered.

"Yes, one-legged. Jumped a lot. Very clumsy. Most other one-legged horses already dead. Air running out on planet. This one tasted like tar."

"It sounds like a Sorosian Plains Runner," said Salank. The Skar'ley often bring them with them to their colonies. I think they sing beautifully or something."

"Certainly not something a Flesh Smith would create," concluded Sishra in his hoarse whispering voice.

"Hmmm…" said Kovorn. "It seems that we have a very large region of space to search. On top of this we cannot search it from a distance due to sensor disturbances in the nebula. It would however be wise to assume that all the places the Cro'lichks have loot… hrmm… have explored, contain no world inhabited by the Flesh Smiths. Otherwise the Cro'lichks would certainly have found out. We must therefore focus our attention on the places that so far haven't been visited. Do we have any information about what these regions might contain? Any rumours even?" As he spoke, Kovorn ringed six regions of the grimy interstellar cloud.

"No nothing," growled Captain Destroyer.

"Then we must split up to search faster. I have seen that the *World Strangler* has four Radorian scout ships with stealth drives docked in its landing bay – most certainly legally acquired. Would it be possible to use these to hasten our search, captain?"

"Hummm… Yes, this possible. I send squadron leader to guide you. They know hidey rendezvous points and trap mines if trouble comes."

"Then I suggest we begin searching these six regions," continued Kovorn. I will lead the ship that will explore the centre of the nebula. It's the region most densely packed with interstellar dust and radiation, so it will take the longest time. Salank, with his vast experience of exploration, will investigate regions two and three. Sishra, you will investigate regions four and five. Tavvin, to you and your college I leave region six. It's not all too large and should be searched the fastest. Judging from its location I would guess it mostly contains unstable planetoids devoid of life – but you never know."

"So that's what we're looking for?" asked Salank. "Planets, planetoids or moons that can sustain life?"

"Yes. The Flesh Smiths were masters of manipulating life," said Sishra. "Twisting life was both their power and their weapons. It's unlikely they would be able to sustain themselves anywhere else than on a world they have biologically groomed to their needs. A Flesh Smith without flesh to torture is nothing."

"If any of you find anything suspicious, do not proceed further," warned Kovorn and held up a slender white finger of warning. "Return immediately to the *World Strangler* and call for assistance. The Flesh Smiths are deadly enemies and their weapons unfathomable. Remember also that we wish to capture at least one of them alive."

"What about us?" Molly blurted out as the assembled aliens were about to leave.

"What about you?" asked Kovorn in return. Although he had no eyes, the red Porian on his head seemed to twitch as if it moved to look at them.

"What do *we* do? We don't want to wait here until you come back – that's boring. Can't we go with you?"

"Very well," replied Kovorn. "Go with Tavvin. It is least likely you will encounter the Flesh Smiths in that region."

***

As they trundled back to their cabins to prepare themselves, Elliot raised an eyebrow in surprise at Molly.

"What?" she said.

"I thought you said you didn't want to look for these Flesh Smiths? Something about it being dangerous?"

"That's different. That's because we didn't have a choice. I hate being told what to do. Being pushed around like a common servant. Anyway, it *will* get boring here. Searching these systems could take weeks or even months. Would you like to sit cramped up here with these stinking Cruelies?"

"No!" agreed Elliot.

"There you go, Earth Boy. Anyway, we'll be travelling with our dear friends Tavvin and Billin," said Molly with a peculiar smile that somehow resembled a cruel grin. "They won't be going anywhere dangerous – they're Furanians. I'm pretty sure we're safe."

When they entered the murky corridor leading to their cabins they were suddenly greeted by a familiar voice.

"Master Elliot! Princess Molly! How glad I am to see you! My memory circuits overcharge with joy!"

Before them in the hallway stood the black briefcase of Little Brother. The briefcase itself seemed to be resting casually against the door to their cabins.

"Little Brother! You're alive!" exclaimed Elliot and ran up to the briefcase.

Suddenly, the briefcase shuddered and ten metal tentacles shot out of its sides. They were ringed and shiny, immediately reminding him of the dread Hunter robots. With ominous silence and ease, the tentacles raised the black briefcase to eye level with Elliot.

"W-what's going on?" gasped Elliot and jumped back.

"It's me! Little Brother! Your friendly Stage Ten Artificial Intelligence. I have been repaired. All my memory cells have been regenerated and my circuitry replaced. I'm so glad to see you both."

"But, but you look… different," stuttered Elliot who couldn't get rid of that ominous feeling in his gut. What if the briefcase had been turned into a kind of new Hunter robot which would try to kill them?

"Different? Oh yes, you mean the enhancements, Master Elliot," said Little Brother. "Salank kindly altered some of my physical attributes and enhanced my worldly interface possibilities."

"Your worldly interface…?" began Elliot.

"He gave you steel tentacles? Well, that figures!" said Molly. "Trust a squid to give a computer tentacles."

"So… Salank actually mended you and gave you these… tentacles?" asked Elliot suspiciously.

"Why yes he did. He's a kind soul and a very talented Sarapid engineer. I have been enjoying my binary conversations with him thoroughly. Also, these tentacles are very handy for travelling and moving about. And, you don't have to carry me anymore."

"They look a bit creepy," said Elliot.

"They do…?" replied Little Brother, with sadness in his voice. His entire tentacle composure seemed to sag a little. "Oh… I'm sorry. Then I guess I shouldn't use them so much if…"

"No, no. That's not what I meant," stuttered Elliot feeling immediately embarrassed.

"Don't worry!" said Molly and put her hand on Little Brother who was sinking down to the floor again. "Don't you bother about the silly Earth Boy here. I think you look great! All new and shiny." She shot a glare at Elliot. "I might even call you Brother Squid now and then."

"You would, Your Highness?" said Little Brother with a bit of hope returning to his voice. "I mean you don't have to, but it would be nice if you did. Thank you very much."

"Don't worry about it. After all, you're the only one who keeps calling me Your Highness. It's about time I returned the favour."

As they spoke, Salank the Sarapid engineer rounded the corridor. His multitude of long yellow branching tentacles flowed over the floor as he moved towards them. The two large eyes with large multi-lens spectacles and measuring equipment were fixed on the two children.

"I hope this gift pleases you," Salank said solemnly. "I hope it can somehow compensate for the discomfort of your trip to Cro'lichks space. It was not my wish to hold you like captives."

"Thank you very much," said Elliot, still bewildered at Little Brother's revival.

"I have made some modifications to your companion which I hope will favour you all. Maybe now you will understand our concern for your well-being."

"Thank you…" Elliot said again, but trailed off in silence.

To break the awkward silence Molly pulled at Little Brother. "Come along now Brother Squid," she said. "I'll tell you all about how we're going to risk our lives again."

Still feeling very stupid and embarrassed, Elliot bowed to Salank who left them and followed Molly and Little Brother into the cabin area. He hadn't meant to hurt Little Brother's feelings. So, while Molly told Little Brother about the rescue from the asteroid, the Hidden Watchers and the search for the Flesh Smiths, Elliot tried his best to patch up his mistake towards the revived intelligent briefcase.

***

Twenty minutes later four scout ships shot out of the docking bay of the *World Strangler*. In comparison to the giant warship they were tiny. In reality, their sizes were equal to the *Ursa Major*, Uncle Karl's ship that Elliot had first ventured out into space in. The scout ships resembled sharks, with nasty grins and painted teeth on the hull. All four of them were a bit too heavily armed to be scout ships – but then again, the originally Radorian scout ships had been modified by the war-crazy Cro'lichks.

On board one of the scout ships were Elliot, Molly, Little Brother, Tavvin and Billin. The crew that manned the ship consisted of two large Cro'lichks. One of them was the co-pilot K'orch'kma (the Quite Reasonably Cruel) while the other was Captain Destroyer himself.

Captain Destroyer of Suns and Devourer of Worlds was not a very brave Cro'lichks by Cro'lichks standards. This meant that he was never first to charge an enemy – although maybe second, and actually preferred to stab his enemy in the back or shoot them safely from a distance. As nature tends to favour these traits and reward them with a slightly longer lifespan, Destroyer had finally made the rank of Captain. He had earned his name after a quite unsatisfactory racial suicide of an alien species, which preferred to blow up their entire star system rather than be enslaved by the Cro'lichks. Ever since that day, Captain Destroyer longed to subjugate (read kill) another intelligent species and enhance his reputation further. As this mission would no doubt give him the credit of the kill anyway – regardless who of his men actually pulled the trigger – he took the option to accompany the ship least likely to encounter the dangerous aliens. In this way, he might still have a chance for some target practice against some innocent trees or other extremely rare life forms in the Ash Plains.

After two hours, the ship reached the zone of the Ash Plains they were supposed to search. With their sensors turned up to a maximum, they began searching for pockets of life. Everybody sat glued to the screens or view ports while Tavvin interpreted the incoming data. As there were a lot of disturbances from the nebula cloud itself and the recurring solar storms of the nearby star, the scanners had a limited range. All stellar bodies therefore had to be examined from close range to determine if they contained any life.

***

Minutes soon turned into hours. After six long hours, Billin lay dozing at the back of the ship, while Molly played a game on her PDM. Elliot was bored again and looked out at the twinkling field of stars beyond the ship. Space here had an odd amber tinge to it, as light reflected off the tiny particles of the nebula cloud.

The entire ship now stunk of the Cro'lichks. It smelled like a mixture of brimstone and rotting meat. Although Elliot had smelt this on board the *World Strangler* it was much stronger in the smaller scout ship and nearly suffocated him.

"Nothing! Nothing-nothing!" said Captain Destroyer with a disappointed snort. "Not even small abandoned station to destroy. Boring trip. Me go home."

"Space most certainly is empty around here," agreed Tavvin sitting bent over the bright scanner analysis display. Her small and round body was relaxed and more resembled a furry pear. "Let us set a return course via this last planet here and we can go back."

"Why go there?" argued Captain Destroyer. "Is only small gas planet. Has nothing."

"Yes, but we still have to examine it," Tavvin explained carefully and respectfully to the grumpy Cro'lichks. "It's the last stellar body of this system that we haven't examined yet. After that we can go back. It'll take one more hour maximum."

"Bah! Okey dokey. We go," growled Captain Destroyer and sunk back into his seat.

Soon a small and grimy dust-covered planet became visible on the screen. Elliot knew that they were still very far away, but already at this distance it looked very dull and uninteresting.

Suddenly the sensors began to bleat a warning.

"Proximity warning," called Tavvin in her high-pitched voice. "It's a ship!"

"What? We have ship close by? What ship?" shouted Captain Destroyer, suddenly awakened from his boredom.

"I-I don't know yet," stuttered Tavvin who was punching commands into the scanner analysis unit. "It's actually more than one ship. Skar'ley frigates I think, judging by their engine emissions. They are well within sensor distance. They have been riding on the wave of that last solar storm, so we couldn't detect them."

"Can they see us?" asked Elliot with growing worry.

"I-I-I'm afraid so," answered Tavvin. "If we can detect them, they should have no problem detecting us."

"Are they any danger to us?" asked Molly. "Isn't this Cruelie ship armed to the teeth with Ship Imploders, Planet Busters and Vapourisers?"

"No, I'm afraid we're quite outgunned," Little Brother pointed out cheerfully while going through the ship specifications. "Although insanely heavily armed for a scout ship, this vessel is no match for those frigates. Now, if we'd still be on board the *World Strangler* it would have been an entirely different matter."

"Stealth mode!" growled Captain Destroyer. His co-pilot punched aggressively at some of the controls and the ship lurched suddenly. Through the view ports Elliot could see the twinkling stars distorting slightly, as if they were suddenly under water. Outside the ship, a light distorting field enveloped the craft. Soon all starlight and cosmic radiation was being bent around the ship, making it nearly invisible.

Billin, who had been awakened by the commotion, skipped and jumped up to the cockpit and looked worriedly at all the instruments. Also, Molly had turned off her game and sat bolt upright next to Elliot looking at the screens.

"The ships are still coming straight at us," Tavvin reported nervously. "There are four of them. They must have detected us."

"We trust stealth drive," ordered Captain Destroyer. "It probably very good."

But the ships kept coming at them.

"Maybe they'll parley before they kill us?" Billin suggested.

"Cro'lichks never parley!" roared Captain Destroyer and slammed his clawed hands on the console. "Change course and arm weapons!"

"Oh no!" moaned Tavvin and her eyes flickered as if she was going to faint. "The frigates are armed with antimatter cannons and particle disruptors."

***

In the silence of space four ships in the shape of crescent moons continued towards the strange signal they had picked up. Several bulky antennae-like protrusions sparkled with energy as they readied their weapons. If the signal was an intruder it was going to be destroyed.

***

"Master Elliot! Those ships are identical to those that destroyed the *Ursa Major*," said Little Brother as the ships came on screen for them to see.

Elliot's thoughts raced. Identical? That must mean they were on the right track. The people that had tried to kill him were here in this system.

Molly cocked her head sideways and squinted as she studied the images of the crescent-moon-shaped frigates closing in. "What do those symbols on the ship hulls mean?" she asked pointing to the screen.

"Symbols?" Billin magnified the picture to get a better view. "Oh my!"

"Oh my what?" said Molly.

"Those are the symbols of the holy Has'pleen zealots, true devotees of the Eternal Sun."

"What does that mean?"

"The Has'pleen was a martial cult of religious Skar'ley fanatics who severed the maglio gland of their children at birth. This meant that the otherwise quite peaceful Skar'ley youths became fearless and aggressive – lacking the otherwise very strong bond of kinsmanship with their race. The Has'pleen sect was only allowed in older times, when danger threatened the Empire. It was many centuries ago that the ceremony of maglio was banned."

"Great! You mean the ships are manned by dangerous religious fanatics instead of peaceful and logical Skar'ley?"

"Something like that…"

"Could these Has'pleen cultists be the conspirators we're looking for?" wondered Elliot.

"Not likely," answered Tavvin. "Even though Has'pleen warrior priests would be capable of attacking their own race, they can't be used as spies. Their skin texture and body form differs from other Skar'ley. They are bulkier and more gaunt, their voices deeper and harsher. Although they could potentially be the conspirators, it's not very likely. They simply can't move or act among the normal Skar'ley without detection. Neither would they be the intended crews for those secret ships, as hormonal imbalances make them notoriously bad pilots. Most likely they are pawns used to watch over something in this region. Something they would kill fellow Skar'ley to keep hidden."

"Flesh Smiths! That's what they're hiding!" said Molly. "These religious types give me the creeps."

"Me not afraid of religion. Religion is for fools," growled Captain Destroyer. "They change course yet?" he added and turned to Tavvin.

"N-not yet," said Tavvin weakly. "But I think they will."

"Thinking is for idiots," snarled Captain Destroyer and gave his co-pilot another order to alter the ship's course.

The passengers and crew of the ship then sat in nervous silence for a while. Time seemed to slow down to a crawl. Only Billin's whimpering and Tavvin's hyperventilation was heard.

"They're not altering their courses!" Tavvin finally whispered. "They haven't seen us. We're getting away."

A whoosh of exhaled air could be heard throughout the scout ship.

"Said we could trust stealth drive. Best to be stolen in the galaxy," boasted Captain Destroyer.

"The frigates are scanning space around them with high-intensity neutrino waves," interrupted Tavvin. "They might still find us if they stumble upon our ion trail. We better get out of here quickly."

"I definitely agree," whimpered Billin.

"No! No go yet. First we go see why they patrol here," said Captain Destroyer. "Take us closer to dirty planet."

"WHAT?" cried Billin in terror. "Why do that? That's most likely very dangerous."

"Yes. Very dangerous," agreed Captain Destroyer, whose lust for danger and violence now had to be sated somehow.

"I agree with Inter-Species Liaison Officer Billin here," said Tavvin wringing her hands nervously. "A Skar'ley presence here is most suspicious. The existence of Has'pleen cultists is even more alarming. We better report this to the others on board the *World Strangler*."

"Not yet. You forget, this old Skar'ley territory. Still have mines and thingies. Maybe just normal border patrol. We investigate – I say so."

"Can't we let somebody else do this, hmmm?" whimpered Billin.

"Oh, come on!" said Molly. "Don't be such a baby. Finally something's happening."

Elliot on the other hand wasn't so sure whether this was

a very good idea, but he didn't want to ruin the mood of the very touchy Cro'lichks captain.

***

Slowly the scout ship inched forward to the grimy cloud-covered planet. On the scanners Tavvin kept her nervous eyes on the signatures of the Skar'ley frigates which were still searching for them. As they drew closer it finally became possible to examine the planet itself.

"Neither the planet nor its small rocky moon contains any life readings at all," confirmed Tavvin with a grateful sigh. "Only dangerous combinations of gases, very high and deadly radiation and extreme wind speeds. Nothing could survive there."

"Nothing we know of…" said Molly. "Didn't the Vo'Orrn say the Flesh Smiths were formless and changed or re-spawned themselves at will? Maybe these Flesh Smiths have adapted and now can endure these extremes."

"Little human is right," said Captain Destroyer. "We go investigate."

"I disagree," said Tavvin. "This is very dangerous. I insist we return to the others."

"You insist! You challenge me for leadership?" howled Captain Destroyer and turned to Tavvin, his spinal spikes now bristling. The foul breath of the Cro'lichks enveloping her and the evil eyes staring down the long hooked nose pressed against her small furry head was too much for Tavvin. She reacted like any other Furanian would do in a similar situation. She fainted.

"Think not!" Captain Destroyer said triumphantly as Tavvin slumped over the controls. He also shot a glare at Billin, who immediately became occupied with his seat straps. A brief memory of crushing innocent furry crabs with a large club suddenly appeared in Captain Destroyer's dim racial memory. As usual he didn't know where or from which of his relatives this memory originated, but he felt a moment of joy and happiness and settled back into his seat.

As nobody else objected, Captain Destroyer slowly slid the scout ship into the stormy atmosphere of the gas planet. At first the stormy planet looked like a smooth surface of whirling mists. Like differently swirling liquids mixed together. But as they drew closer the details of the topmost clouds could be discerned. Some clouds were large, grey and fluffy, over a kilometre high. Amongst them whirled wind-torn cloud streaks of different dirt brown colours. At first it all seemed serene and tranquil. Then the tiny speck of a ship dipped down into the great ravines of clouds. After a brief descent down into the abyss, the ship was enveloped by the towering clouds. Immediately the ship began to rock violently. It jolted and rose and fell, sometimes falling several hundred metres due to different jet streams and the varying air pressures. They were now in the terrible grasp of the planet's immense gravitational pull and thrown about by the tempest storms. There was no longer anything tranquil about the gas planet. It was a hellish, chaotic and dangerous place for a miniscule ship like theirs. The scout ship's hull creaked and the engines whined and strained as they tried to maintain their course. Outside, near darkness ruled and grimy clouds rolled over and around the small ship.

Maybe due to the violent rocking and shaking of the ship, Tavvin awoke. She cast a quick glance at Captain Destroyer and then bent over the scanner controls again.

"We're at eleven times standard atmospheric pressure, but the hull is holding," shouted Tavvin over the din. "I suggest we don't go deeper."

"Is there anything down here?" shouted Molly. "Can you see anything?"

"There is so much radiation from the planet itself that the sensors only work on extremely short range," Tavvin replied. "We can't see where we're going and we're not likely to detect anything with our sensors. This is like a blind pooka looking for a hover-ant in an electro-bee hive."

A buzzing alarm suddenly drew her attention to another screen.

"The ship's particle shield generator won't hold forever. It's too small on a scout ship like this. We have less than thirty per cent particle integrity. The radiation is depleting the shield faster than it can regenerate it. We'll be leaking in massive doses of radiation soon."

"Bah!" growled Captain Destroyer. "Radorians always put in safety measures. We stay little longer."

Something suddenly jolted Tavvin and she began fiddling frantically with the sensor controls.

"Ships! Ships!" she cried. "Dead ahead!"

Out of the rolling storm clouds ahead of them appeared the dark contours of three large starships. Like shadowy ghosts in the stormy gloom they looked ominous and foreboding as the small scout ship raced towards them.

"Look out! We're about to crash into them," Tavvin shouted and ducked down, as if that would help.

In an instant, the foremost ship filled the entire view port and a crash was imminent. Captain Destroyer's co-pilot pulled at the controls with a mixture of instinct and panic. The

Cro'lichks scout ship made a ninety degree turn and instead began to fly alongside one of the ships. As wing, cannon and engine protrusions from the larger ship stuck out from the hull, the Cro'lichks pilot had to spin and turn the scout ship in order to avoid hitting anything. It was a high-speed madman's flight along the immense hull. As the larger ship's great hull passed by, seemingly only inches away from them, Elliot could see that it was stained and discoloured from prolonged exposure to the stormy and corrosive atmosphere of the planet. Several dimly lit view ports flashed by and he briefly thought he could see shadows or silhouettes of people inside.

With a last amazing feat of piloting skill, the Cro'lichks pilot managed to get them free of the large ship and came to a standstill, hovering beside it.

"Idiot!" shouted Captain Destroyer at his pilot and began hitting him over the head. "You kill me? You risk my life? You idiot crazy pilot!"

Molly didn't pay any attention to the Cro'lichks pilot being reprimanded. Instead she looked out of the view port at the large ship outside.

The huge, stained ship hovered silently and ominously in the dark rolling storm clouds. The lights from the many view ports should have looked warm or comforting, but instead instilled in her a feeling of dread and impending doom. Lightning flashed somewhere deep inside the storm clouds, lighting them from inside. For a second, Molly imagined the storm-tossed ship to be a long-abandoned craft crewed by ghosts which winked in and out of existence on the many decks.

"It's not moving. It's just sitting here," she said. "Is it deserted?"

Tavvin glanced at her sensor controls and shook her head. "No, I don't think it's deserted. I detect that the life support systems are working. But yes, you are right. The three ships are stationary. They are not even in low atmospheric orbit. They are perfectly stationary. It doesn't make sense. Why would they want to remain in this particular location, while the planet revolves under them?"

"What are they doing here? Who are they?" Molly continued.

"Eh… as we shot by, only inches away from a grimy death, I couldn't help but notice the Has'pleen symbols on the hull," said Billin with a weak smile.

"Those religious fanatics again?" wondered Molly.

"Yes, those fanatics."

"Then I guess it was here those other ships came from," said Molly.

"Can they see us?" asked Elliot, who seemed to be the only one aware of the fact that they were parked next to three giant hostile ships.

Captain Destroyer had finished punishing his co-pilot and wiped off his hand on his uniform. He turned to the screens and answered Elliot.

"No! They no see cloaked ship."

As if an answer to his words, a ball of plasma formed along one of the protruding spikes of one of the other ships.

"Look out! They're firing at us!" shouted Tavvin.

Once again, the co-pilot reacted fast. He accelerated the scout ship back along the side of the large ship, using it as a shield. A ball of super-hot plasma shot past them and disappeared into the murky clouds.

"That answers that question," said Molly. "They can definitely see us."

"But we have stealth drive..." complained Captain Destroyer.

"It's probably being disrupted by the storm and the radiation," noted Little Brother calmly.

"We have to get out of here," shouted Tavvin and Billin with panic in their voices.

Without asking for permission from his superior, the co-pilot swung the ship around and blasted away from the three Skar'ley ships. As they fled, a volley of plasma bolts was fired after them. The plasma bolts spread amongst the clouds in a shiny fan formation and came racing after them. Despite the co-pilot's attempt at swerving, spinning and dodging them, one finally struck the scout ship. The smaller ship's shields took the blunt of the energy blast, but some of it leaked through. With a burst of sparks and molten metal the scout ship was flung out of the gas planet's atmosphere and out into open space. Inside the ship, various consoles exploded in sparks and flames.

"We're hit!" cried Molly and the co-pilot.

"We're going to die!" wailed Tavvin and Billin."

"Oh no!" moaned Elliot.

"Cowards! Bastards!" howled Captain Destroyer.

"It's not that bad," said Little Brother.

The small scout ship tumbled through space, out of control but away from the gas planet. The Cro'lichks co-pilot tugged at the controls and pressed all emergency buttons he could find. Amazingly enough, he had soon righted the ship again.

"I said it wasn't that bad," said Little Brother, although nobody seemed to be paying him any attention. "It was just our engines. My guess is that we're down to thirty-two per cent engine efficiency."

"We down to thirty-one per cent engine efficiency," growled the Cro'lichks co-pilot. "Our engines hit."

"Oh well, one can't be right all the time," sighed Little Brother.

"Hide us! Engage stealth drive!" ordered Captain Destroyer.

"But now they know what they're looking for," protested Tavvin. "They'll find the faint emissions of the stealth drive. We have to run for it."

"Nowhere to run, furry one. Engine no good. They faster now."

Tavvin's eyes were wide open with fright, but she accepted the truth without fainting. Instead she consulted the sensor screens. "Then put the planet between us and the three ships. They can't see us with a planet between us."

"That's what they'll expect us to do," mumbled Little Brother, but nobody seemed to be listening.

"Yes! We go round planet. Make it so," ordered Captain Destroyer.

"Wait!" said Elliot, who had been the only one to hear Little Brother's comment. "Isn't that what they'll expect us to do?"

"Maybe!" agreed Captain Destroyer. "But now we time to charge and load weapons. We die in plasma shower from both sides. Better way than plasma shower from only one side."

"We could hide behind that small moon," suggested Little Brother.

Everybody now turned to the black briefcase. Although it didn't move or have eyes of any sort, the attention it was suddenly given seemed to make it sink further into the seat where it was lying.

"I-I-I mean… we could set a course for the planet's small moon, shut down all systems except the stealth drive and glide there slowly and silently. Hopefully they won't notice us."

The two Cro'lichks looked at each other, the tips of their long, hooked noses nearly meeting, and nodded.

"Good idea," said Captain Destroyer. "Good thinking from brainy box. Set course for moon."

After a small course correction, the co-pilot set off a last burst from the engines and then began powering down the ship. Soon the scout ship slid silently and in darkness towards the small cratered moon.

***

Behind them three large ships rose out of the murky atmosphere of the gas planet, like terrible crocodiles out of a muddy lake. They immediately scattered and began circling the gas planet. As they flew over the surface they dropped several metal balls which zipped away into the clouds.

***

The crew and passengers of the Cro'lichks scout ship could do nothing but wait and observe the Skar'ley ships on their screens.

"What are they doing?" wondered Elliot.

"They're most probably dropping sensor buoys into the atmosphere to look for us," answered Tavvin. "In case we slipped down there to hide. Maybe even depth charges to flush us out."

Slowly their ship approached the small moon. As it came into view they could all see what a barren and desolate place it was. Its surface held no life and was pockmarked with craters. Elliot shivered as he thought of the cold and barren asteroid where he and Molly nearly had… well, actually *had* died.

Suddenly one of the large Skar'ley ships changed its course and left the gas planet's orbit. It fired its engines and came speeding towards them.

"Not good!" noted Tavvin. "They've decided to search the moon as well."

"Have they seen us?" asked Elliot once again.

"I don't think so. If they had, all three ships would most probably come racing after us."

"Must hide ship," Captain Destroyer growled. "Find deep crater or ravine."

The co-pilot did as he was told and gently steered the ship with its smaller thrusters in amongst the rocky outcroppings of the moon. As with all large stellar objects, the surface of the moon was anything but flat when they drew closer. There were ravines, ridges, mountains and deep meteor punctures in the surface. Some of the meteor craters were deep, bottomless holes, as if the surface was so soft that the meteorites had been driven deep down into them.

"Hide us in hole. Possible yes?" ordered Captain Destroyer.

"Wait! I don't know if that's a good…" began Tavvin.

"What?! You tell me what to do again, eh?" exploded Captain Destroyer and rose angrily from his seat. "You leader of mission? You challenge me?"

This time Tavvin was physically pressed back into her seat by the spittle and foul breath of the angry Cro'lichks.

"No-no-no. I actually think it's a very good idea," stuttered Tavvin. Her large blue eyes once again opened in fright and near faint. "It's just…"

"Just what?" shouted Captain Destroyer, his hate feelings were coming back again, fuelled by the stored anger and hatred of his ancestors.

"It's-it's-it's something strange with this crater," Tavvin finally managed to blurt out.

"Strange? Not great ship-eating worm in space I hope? That silly. Not possible."

"No-no, I detect faint traces of oxygen and other trace elements – air."

"Air? As in breathable air?" asked Molly bewildered.

Thankful for the possibility to turn away from the angry Cro'lichks, Tavvin nodded to Molly and pointed at the scanner analysis screen.

"The scanners detect a mixture of gases that in sufficient quantities could be from a breathable atmosphere."

"So, the moon has a breathable atmosphere?" Molly wondered.

"No, that's it, it doesn't. The small amounts of air must originate from somewhere else. It must be leaking from somewhere."

"Could it be leaking from our ship?" wondered Billin, ever the pessimist.

Everybody seemed instantly paler and the co-pilot bent over his controls.

"No. Not possible. We have full pressure and hull integrity. Tanks not ruptured," he said finally.

"Then it has to come from some sort of concealed Skar'ley base somewhere," concluded Elliot. "We better be careful so we don't fly into another ship or space station."

"Where is air from?" asked Captain Destroyer.

Tavvin consulted her screen again. "That's strange. I can't detect it anymore. It must have been very faint."

Elliot suddenly thought of something. "Take us back over that crater hole again. That bottomless one." The co-pilot did as Elliot said and soon Tavvin nodded.

"The boy is right. The air seems to be leaking out of this hole. There are very few molecules, but it's traceable."

"We investigate?" asked Captain Destroyer.

"NO!" said Tavvin, Billin, Molly and Elliot in unison.

"Eh, I don't want to be the one who points out the obvious," said Little Brother meekly from his reclining position on his seat, "but I don't think we have much of a choice. That Skar'ley ship will soon come over the moon's horizon and when it does it will be able to detect this ship. I don't think they'll be fooled again by our stealth drive at this close proximity and we can't run with our damaged engines."

"Then we fight and go out in great plasma shower!" exclaimed Captain Destroyer with a cheerful growl.

"Well… yes we could," agreed Little Brother carefully. "Or we could hide in a place with a chance for some breathable air. This would be a bonus for carbon-based air-breathing creatures such as yourselves."

They all stared at Little Brother for a couple of seconds while his words sunk in.

"Brother Squid is right again," said Molly finally. "We have to hide, now!"

"Okey dokey! Go into hole!" ordered Captain Destroyer.

As gravity was minimal on the small moon, the scout ship turned its nose downward and flew into the bottomless crater hole. Soon darkness engulfed them and they flew by their sensors only.

"The tunnel has widened slightly," said Tavvin who was busy reading off data from her scanner screen. "That's strange. How can an impact crater get bigger?"

"Maybe the whole moon is made up of very loosely packed materials? Maybe it only has a hard crust?" suggested Billin.

"Oh no!" said Tavvin suddenly and looked up from her screen. "Mines! Mines!"

Immediately a dozen red spots appeared on the central flight screen above the pilot's head. They covered the entire tunnel and roved slowly back and forth.

"Festering carcasses!" howled Captain Destroyer. "You tell me now! Little late I think!"

Once again, nature decided to be kind to the co-pilot. Heeding a sudden vague memory from one of his forefathers he immediately shut down all systems except the stealth drive. The scout ship continued to fall slowly downward, but with no chance of correcting its course. Inside the ship, the artificial gravity was switched off, making everybody suddenly feel dizzy and nauseous.

"Those Skar'ley mines," said Captain Destroyer after a few seconds of examining them. "They go for heat signature, metal signature, ion signature, plastic signature, movement signature..."

"Yes, yes! But how do we get past them?" cried Molly. "We're falling right into them! They're blocking the hole."

"As I said," continued Captain Destroyer. "Those Skar'ley mines. Have one big-big problem with electro sensors. Easy overcharge. Make blind for couple of seconds. We do every time with sticky electro gun."

Captain Destroyer barked an order to his co-pilot and then pulled a rusty lever which clearly had been added later to the ship's original controls. An electric discharge shot out of the scout ship like forked lightning. It sought out the closest mine and then spread from one mine to the other. Soon all mines were covered in sparking discharges. Carefully the scout ship dropped through the net of mines and further into the hole. Behind them the strange Cro'lichks electricity discharged from one mine and then another. Slowly all the mines resumed their sentinel duties.

"Phew! That was close," whistled Molly. When she looked around her she could see Billin lying prone on the floor. Evidently the excitement had been too much for him.

"Hmmmm… There are mines and there seems to be air somewhere," murmured Tavvin. "This could be a secret fortress we're approaching, judging by the weaponry."

The ship continued down for a while and they all sat in silence, waiting for Tavvin to give them some clue as to what they could expect.

"The walls are uncannily smooth here," said Tavvin after a while. "That's strange."

"We now far down. Turn on lights," ordered Captain Destroyer.

When the exterior lights of the scout ship came on, the walls of the hole came into view.

"By the Great Root!" exclaimed Tavvin.

"Bombs and Shrapnel!" exclaimed Captain Destroyer.

Elliot and Molly looked out of the view port. At first the walls seemed to be of smooth brown rock. Then, as they focused they could see lines and patterns along the walls. Great symbols and pictograms resembling a winged creature covered the rounded walls. The patterns of the lines were complex and gave the impression that the walls were made of several strangely and differently shaped slabs which somehow fitted perfectly together. As the scout ship itself was pretty large, Elliot realised that the pictograms were in fact huge.

"What is that?" murmured Molly. "Who made this?"

"The Founders!" said Tavvin with awe. "Pictograms like these are often encountered in Founder ruins. But I've never witnessed anything so intact and beautiful before. It's amazing!"

"Founders! You mean those people that once terraformed that abysmal world in the Vurite's End system?" said Elliot.

"Yes, yes. The oldest species ever known to have mastered interstellar travel. We know so little about them. They were long gone before even the oldest civilisations that exist today first appeared."

"They had wings," noted Molly.

"Most probably not," answered Tavvin. "The creatures they depict are always different. In some ruins they have arms and legs, in others they have tentacles, flippers or nothing at all. They might just be depictions of local partner species."

"Tunnel is branching," heralded the co-pilot and pointed ahead.

All of them could clearly see how the large tunnel divided (or hole, as Elliot reminded himself. They were actually falling into a hole). The other tunnel looked identical.

"Where we go?" asked Captain Destroyer.

"There seems to be a strange deviation in atmosphere in the left tunnel," said Tavvin after consulting her sensors. There is more air in that tunnel."

"Then is left."

After having travelled another kilometre or so through the ancient tunnels Tavvin pointed at her screen again.

"The level of oxygen and other breathable gases rose again. This is the second threshold we pass. Atmospheric pressure and oxygen levels are rising all the time. As if we're passing through some kind of invisible airlocks. This is amazing!"

Once again the tunnel branched. This time three new tunnels were available to them. Once again they chose the tunnel where the levels of breathable air were higher.

"This is truly fantastic!" continued Tavvin. "Our sonic scanners indicate many more tunnels close by. It's a complex network of tunnels. The moon is riddled with Founder tunnels. Like, like a diamond-wasp hive.

"Or like a worm-eaten apple," suggested Billin gloomily who had now awakened.

"Maybe the entire moon is artificial?" suggested Molly. "Maybe the whole moon is a Founder artefact?"

"Pressure outside is nearly that of a human world. Oxygen levels are close to optimum. What kind of place is this?" said Tavvin.

"It *is* a hidden fortress" said Molly.

"Or a hidden prison?" suggested Elliot.

"We have gravity anomaly also," growled Captain Destroyer suddenly and began fighting with his flight controls. "Sensors don't know where up or down."

"Yes, yes. I see. Amazing! Somehow the centre of gravity is shifting. As if we're about to pass it."

"Not amazing to me!" growled Captain Destroyer. "Ship maybe crash. Don't know which thrusters to use."

"Do the artefacts these Founders left behind normally work?" asked Elliot.

"Sometimes," answered Billin helpfully. "Like the Sun Cannon on Efeus IX that destroyed an entire fleet by mistake. And the planetary self-destruct on what was formerly known as Kalhandra."

"Great!"

"Look! There's light ahead," said Molly and pointed.

A strange bluish glow could be seen in front of them. It quickly grew stronger as the two Cro'lichks were struggling with the controls.

"Gravity all wrong!" bellowed Captain Destroyer.

Suddenly the scout ship shot out into open air. There was a blazing sun ahead of them and wet mists all around them.

"What's going on?" shouted Elliot who could feel his stomach lurch and suddenly indicate that 'down' was now suddenly 'up'.

The ship rolled, rose and fell a couple of times before Captain Destroyer and his co-pilot gained control of it. When everything was stabilised, they all gazed out of the view ports in wonder.

"It's an entire world!" gasped Molly.

Molly was right. The entire moon was hollow and at its empty centre blazed a small and slightly blue-hued sun. The walls of the hollow space, which would most easily be visualised as the inside of a football, were covered with vegetation or forests of some sort and between these rose mountains with rivers and lakes. Wet mists rose from the ground and flocks of large flying creatures could be seen far below. Here and there on the surface they could see large holes or tunnel exits, like the one they had come from.

"A hidden world!" whispered Billin.

"An amazing feat of engineering! Gravity must be artificial? The inside walls of the hollow moon is pulling things down towards it. What powers it? What powers the sun? How could they do this?" murmured Tavvin with existential panic in her large blue eyes.

"A perfect example of Founder ingenuity," Tavvin concluded.

"A perfect world for the Flesh Smiths," added Elliot grimly.

CHAPTER 3
THE HOLLOW WORLD

The Cro'lichks scout ship swept over the alien landscape. Strange cauliflower-like trees swathed in rising wet mists swept past under the ship. Although their senses told them that the ground was underneath, it was hard for their eyes to adjust. The entire hidden world hung around them, clinging to the inside walls of the hollow moon. And at the centre of the Hollow World, hung the tiny bluish sun which gave life to everything.

"Amazing!" was all Tavvin could say.

"Yes, yes, we've seen enough. We'd better get out of here now!" said Billin. But the Furanian Inter-Species Liaison Officer was speaking to deaf ears. Everybody gazed in wonder at the artificial world. For that was what it had to be. No world like this could ever have been created by the forces of nature. Or could it?

"We land and kill something," Captain Destroyer said, with temptation in his eyes. "Good trophies to bring back."

This finally broke the spell and Tavvin sat bolt upright.

"Certainly not!" she said sternly. She then corrected herself. "What I mean is, it might be unwise. We don't have sufficient numbers to defeat the Flesh Smiths if they are here. We should return with reinforcements."

Billin agreed. "Yes. Remember what the symbiosis known as Kovorn said. The Flesh Smiths are very dangerous. We should return and report what we've found immediately.

"But trip has been boring so far," complained Captain Destroyer. "I go for some fun hunting. Make long hours worth it."

"It's too dangerous!" Tavvin said stubbornly. "You'll get us all killed!"

"There are no buildings," said Elliot. He pointed down. "I can't see any cities, roads or buildings. Wouldn't there be something like that if the Flesh Smiths lived here?"

"I agree," said Molly. "This place looks wild and abandoned. Nobody seems to live here."

"We can't possibly know what the infrastructure of the Flesh Smiths would look like…" began Billin.

"Bah! Me sick of spacing! Land near small lake and prepare precision hunting rifle," said Captain Destroyer, ending the argument with the bristling of his spinal spikes and an evil glare.

With moans of disapproval from Tavvin and Billin, the co-pilot landed the scout ship near a small lake. Steam rose up from the lake and enveloped the ship as it landed.

While the humans and the Cro'lichks got out of their seats and readied themselves to go outside, Tavvin and Billin refused to unbuckle their belts.

"This is most unwise, not to mention dangerous!" protested Tavvin.

"I agree! We could get eaten by angry plant monsters or impaled by horned lizard horses, or get decapitated by giant insects or…" explained Billin.

"You waity-waity here then," said Captain Destroyer who was now holding an unnecessarily big hunting rifle in his hands. Judging by the size of the muzzle of the rifle, Elliot doubted there would be anything left of whatever Captain Destroyer hit.

Just to be safe, Elliot and Molly put on the super-thin Vurite spacesuits which had been packed into their scout ship, although they didn't put on the helmets.

"Come on, Little Brother," said Elliot and bent down to pick up the black briefcase as it spoke. "Please, Master Elliot. Carrying me is tiring. Let me suggest how I can make it easier for you."

The long steel tentacles snaked out of the briefcase and began wrapping themselves around Elliot. For a moment he stiffened, but then tried to relax and not show his discomfort. He didn't want to hurt Little Brother's feelings again. In a couple of seconds Little Brother had attached himself to Elliot's back like a backpack, the tentacles wrapped around the boy like uncanny straps.

"If it feels uncomfortable, please let me know," said Little Brother. "I can walk reasonably well myself, but in this wilderness I might slow you down."

"No, no. It feels good, actually. Much easier than carrying you," said Elliot who genuinely thought it was much easier to carry Little Brother this way.

Without further delay Captain Destroyer opened the airlock door and stepped outside. A wet and warm breeze found its way into the ship as the heavily armed Cro'lichks exited. Strange smells, a bit like cinnamon and overly ripe apples wafted in.

When Elliot and Molly stepped out onto the alien world they were once again amazed at the immensity of it all. The absence of a real and clear horizon as the surface of the world rose up all around them in the circular space, gave them the impression that they were at the bottom of an immense valley with incredibly high walls. The glare of the sun and the misty hazy air made it impossible for them to see too far or even the 'roof' of the world. But they knew it was there. They knew they were inside an immense chamber and not on the surface of a world.

When they studied their immediate surroundings they found that the trees were not trees at all. They were giant slender mushrooms with broad cauliflower caps. On the ground grew silvery bushes filled with dew-wet brown fruit. Amongst the trees fluttered beautiful insects with large shiny wings. Over the nearby lake flew more of the colourful insects and steam rose from the surface which was covered in large floating water-lily-like leaves. From deep inside the mushroom forest, something that sounded like pleasant bird song could be heard. The place was totally alien, but beautiful.

A sudden loud bang broke the serenity of the place, as Captain Destroyer fired his oversized hunting rifle. The trunk of one of the mushroom trees was obliterated in a cloud of mulch and the great cap fell with a crash to the ground. Hundreds more of the shiny insects took to the sky in fright.

"Thought I see animal," said Captain Destroyer.

"Don't you think your shooting might attract dangerous animals or even Flesh Smiths, hmmm?" said Molly with a constrained smile.

Captain Destroyer shrugged as if he didn't care and began lumbering into the forest. His co-pilot seemed slightly more nervous than him, but eagerly kept his blood-shot eyes open for anything that could potentially move.

With more uncertain steps, Elliot and Molly followed the destructive Cro'lichks that waddled through the serene forest. With their bulky and spiked armour they looked totally out of place in the strange forest. But despite their odious habits, the Cro'lichks were armed and could protect them all if anything dangerous appeared.

A handful of beautiful butterflies swarmed up around Elliot and Molly as they walked. To Molly's delight one of them perched gently on her hand. The large wings shone like blue, green and silver metal.

"This place is beautiful," Molly sighed.

"Wait! Wait! Don't leave me here," cried Billin suddenly and came running out of the ship behind them. He was immediately followed by Tavvin. The round furry shapes of the Furanians and their large frightened blue eyes made them look comical in the mushroom landscape. As they ran after the spontaneous expedition, Molly stopped and laughed.

"Ha, ha. So you don't like waiting alone in the ship for us? Like tinned meat ready to be eaten? I guess a lot of nasty things could come and nibble at your furry behinds."

"It's… not funny… to make jokes about… other people's fears," said Tavvin indignantly, as she reached Molly's side, panting. "If we're in a world controlled by Flesh Smiths we have much to fear and every reason to stick together. Even if I object strongly to this unplanned exploration, I see the advantage in numbers."

Another loud blast from Captain Destroyer's rifle interrupted them and made the two skittish Furanians jump. It was followed immediately by a crash and cloud of insects rising to the sky.

"I wish he would stop doing that!" said Molly angrily. "Don't these Cruelies know anything other than senseless destruction?"

"I'm afraid they don't," said Billin. "It's because of their clouded racial memory…"

"I know, I know," said Molly, to spare herself a lecture about Cro'lichks racial memory.

"Although Captain Destroyer's rifle could probably hold off a stampeding herd of doompas," said Tavvin, "I brought these, just in case." In her small hands she held four wand-like pistol devices.

"Laser guns!" hooted Molly. "Good thinking!"

"Laser guns? By the Great Root, no!" exclaimed Tavvin "These are stunners. I couldn't stand the sight of an animal or person being blown to bits."

Molly sighed and put the ridiculously small wand pistol in her belt. "Just like the Furries to make friendly guns," she mumbled. Elliot took another of the stunners and examined it. It had a small button as a trigger on one side, but that was it. Fairly easy to use then, he thought.

Following the noisy Cro'lichks, the small expedition made their way further into the alien wilderness of the Hollow World. Tavvin, being the Chief Observer, kept stopping to examine plants and insects, while making notes on her notepad or even taking some samples. Now and again a loud shot was heard ahead of them, often followed by the flight of scared animals and the occasional triumphant cheer from Captain Destroyer.

***

Meanwhile, further into the misty mushroom forest a large group of butterflies congregated amongst clusters of old overgrown stone pillars. More and more of the colourful insects filled the air amid the pillars until they were so many that there was hardly any room for their fluttering wings. With a sudden coordinated move, the butterflies began grouping themselves in a precise order, some butterflies attaching themselves to others, until they formed a large alien head with long curving horns. Then, as one being, the butterflies buzzed. The combined noise of the butterflies formed words as the hovering head spoke to the centremost pillar. When the group of butterflies had delivered their message they dispersed in a flurry of small fluttering wings. Some butterflies had willingly let themselves be crushed by the effort to form the alien head and now fell broken and lifeless to the ground.

For a while the blue sun sparkled in the bent and broken butterfly wings which lay strewn around the central pillar. But after a couple of minutes a low rumbling was heard. The ground opened up behind the pillar, revealing an old entrance to the buried ruins covered by the fungal forest. To begin with, the darkness beyond the old portal was absolute. Then a pack of shadowy creatures emerged from the gloom – creatures with barbed mandibles and bottomless predatory eyes. Slowly the creatures snuck off into the surrounding trees to hunt for their prey.

***

Elliot, Molly, Billin and Tavvin paused when they entered a large clearing with a small stream. The combined hunting and exploring expedition had already lasted two hours and Captain Destroyer showed no signs of tiring of his senseless killing of strange new life forms. During their hurried march, they had encountered many strange and often bizarre plants and animals, such as roving herds of trees which walked slowly on their roots, large furry balls which seemed to moan constantly, twelve-legged spiders with butterfly wings, strange sneezing clouds which drifted between the mushroom trees and beautiful but terribly foul-smelling rose bushes.

The two Cro'lichks had maintained a fast pace and it had been hard for the small Furanians to keep up. But every time Captain Destroyer stopped to reload his hunting rifle with more high-explosive rounds of ammunition, they somehow managed to catch up again. Now, once again, the two Cro'lichks were somewhere ahead of the others.

Mushroom trees towered over them as they paused in a clearing, wiping sweat from their brows. A huge smooth rock formation stood in the centre of the clearing and the stream circled around it.

"It's quite hot," said Elliot.

"Yes," agreed Tavvin. "Hot and humid."

"Do you think this water is drinkable?" Molly wondered and pointed to the inviting small stream.

"Certainly not!" said Tavvin. "We shouldn't touch anything here. It might be contaminated by the Flesh Smiths."

"Then we're already too late," Billin pointed out. "If the Flesh Smiths were experts at genetic warfare we would already have been subjected to poisonous or gene-altering spores in the atmosphere or by brushing against the vegetation here. At any time, our innards could turn into paste, our brains begin to mould or our skin begin to harden and crack from crystalline accumulation of…"

"Yes, yes," moaned Tavvin. "I think we all get the picture. We've taken many risks already due to our lack of common sense. We should never have left the ship. Let's not risk anything further by drinking poisoned water."

"I guess you're right," sighed Molly and sipped some water from the spacesuit water tube instead. It tasted warm and stale. Not at all like the sweet, chilled spring water splashing in front of her. Annoyed by the bad service of water, she kicked a stone into the stream with a splash.

Immediately, the large rock formation next to Molly began to rise. With something that resembled a long, wet kiss, it lifted itself off the ground. A huge wet and spongy body revealed itself underneath the rock and began flowing out on all sides. Slime dripped off it and stuck to the ground.

"Look out!" cried Elliot and grabbed Molly. He tugged her away from the house-sized trembling rock formation and the strange slimy creature under it. Tavvin and Billin were already running at full speed away from the stream.

Two large eyestalks shot out from under the rock and studied the two fleeing human children. Then, slowly, the whole rock and creature began to move. Its pace wasn't fast, so Elliot and Molly could easily outrun it. They stopped and panted when they realised the creature wasn't coming after them, but rather fled, very slowly, in the other direction.

Molly began fiddling with her stunner wand.

"Do you think the stunner will work on that huge creature?" wondered Elliot.

"I don't know, but I'll try if it comes any closer."

"It's a giant snail!" said Elliot in astonishment. As he studied the slowly retreating figure more closely, he could see that the large smooth rock formation was a kind of shell.

"Yes it is!" agreed Molly. "I think it's a House Swallowing Snail of Atakondria. I've seen creatures like those at the Royal Zoo when I was little. They eat everything. A pack of them can destroy a whole city. Luckily, they're very slow and people have plenty of time to move first. They're nearly unstoppable and immune to most weapons."

"Actually, they cannot stand ice cannons, tactical nuclear grenades, garlic or salt and vinegar crisps," informed Little Brother after having consulted his database.

"Phew! That's a relief," said Elliot sarcastically, "as we have all of those weapons on us right now."

A loud rustling of leaves behind them made them both jump and turn around. Already jumpy and expecting an attack, Molly thrust her wand into the face of a terrified Billin who had emerged from behind the tree where he had been hiding.

"Ahhhh!" shouted Billin.

"Ahhhh!" shouted Molly.

"Don't shoot! Don't shoot!" pleaded Billin, while cowering and holding his hands over his eyes.

"Sorry! I thought you were… something else," apologised Molly and put away her stunner wand.

Billin slowly opened his eyes again and looked around him.

"Is it gone?" Billin whispered, while scanning the forest with wild eyes.

"Not yet," said Elliot and pointed over his shoulder at the huge House Swallowing Snail which was making a run for it at a breathtaking crawl-speed. "It's more afraid of us than we are of it," he added and put his stunner wand back into his belt.

"Thank the Great Root it's leaving," said Tavvin and emerged from behind another mushroom tree.

"That was a House Swallowing Snail of Atakondria," noted Billin.

"Yes, I know," replied Elliot while watching the huge snail break down a tree which was in its way.

"I mean… what does a House Swallowing Snail from Atakondria do here? It doesn't seem to belong here," Billin continued.

"Well… maybe it hitched a ride," sneered Molly. "Does it matter how it came here? As long as it doesn't bother us anymore."

"It *does* matter," said Tavvin who was once again consulting her notepad. "I've been studying the plants and animals we've seen so far. This last encounter confirms my theory. Not only do the plants and animals of this world have their origins on totally different planets, they are also all asexual."

"Asexual?" said Elliot, trying hard to remember those embarrassing lessons about sexual reproduction that Mrs Kateder so hastily had run past them at school.

"It means they don't have males or females. Only… things," Tavvin explained.

"So how do they… fall in love and stuff," asked Molly.

"They don't," answered Tavvin flatly. "Somebody or something makes them. Or at least that's what I think. That would be the reason why there's a wild collection of species here from totally different worlds."

"Flesh Smiths!" exclaimed Elliot. "Create animals – that's what they do, isn't it? This has to be a Flesh Smith world."

"Yes, it must certainly be so," agreed Tavvin. "This is all the evidence we need. Now let's get out of here as fast as we can."

Captain Destroyer suddenly came barging back through the silvery underbrush. His large rifle was slung over his shoulder and his co-pilot lumbered behind him, carrying the remains of the near-obliterated animals his captain had shot.

"There you are," he said. "Why you runaway lost?"

"We didn't run away," explained Tavvin, "we fled from…"

"Never mind," interrupted Captain Destroyer with an uninterested wave of his large clawed hand. "You always scared of everything. Nothing here. Only silly-small animals and soft trees. We go back."

"Finally a sensible decision," said Tavvin relieved. "This place scares me stiff. It holds some kind of terrible secret."

"Sna!" said Billin.

"Bah! Nothing scary here," said Captain Destroyer. "Me not scared of silly butterflies and mushroom trees. Silly world. Forgotten world."

"Sna!" continued Billin.

"Well, yes. Maybe we haven't encountered anything exciting, but nobody is happier about that than me," said Tavvin. "This report will still be invaluable in the further exploration of the Ash Plains."

"Sna!" Billin stuttered.

"Yeah! This world has been boring," added Molly with a bored sigh. "Let's get out of here."

"Sna!"

"WHAT?" said Tavvin angrily and turned to Billin. "What *is it* that you want? Speak up!"

"Sna... sna!" Billin kept stuttering. He didn't meet Tavvin's angry gaze, but instead kept his large terrified eyes locked onto something behind the small expedition. Slowly he raised his arm and pointed.

A chill ran down Elliot's spine as he suddenly became aware of something behind him. He could feel merciless eyes on the back of his neck and could nearly hear the breath of whatever stood behind them. He turned around slowly.

"SNAARRK!" wailed Billin, finally being able to form the dread name of his people's ancestral horror. A foul odour began to spread about his person.

When Elliot turned he saw the source of Billin's terror. Well, at first he saw only the eyes. Large bottomless black eyes, which reflected his own terrified face. Although the eyes were jet black they were shaped in such a way, and held such a glint, that their owner seemed to possess some uncanny kind of evil intelligence or half hinted sneer. The eyes belonged to a terrible face with barbed insect-like mandibles, large pointed nose and a long red tongue which tasted the air. The head in turn belonged to a sleek black body with four powerful legs equipped with long, tearing claws. A nasty, bony tail with spikes was held poised and trembling, ready to strike. On top of this, the entire creature stunk strongly of musk and was covered in long black fur which hung in messy strands. This was the terror of Furanian evolution, the predator which had hunted them for generations.

The creature stood only five metres behind them and stared menacingly at Elliot. The long red tongue tasted the air. Its instincts told it that here was meat. Meat that it was destined to hunt. It crouched and waited for something.

"Snaarrk! Snaarrk! Snaarrk!" wailed Billin and threw himself to the ground.

Tavvin, who had never gathered the courage to read any kind of description of a snaarrk, knew instinctively that Billin's statement was true. This was the primal horror she had glimpsed in her nightmares from time to time. The fear of its form had been imprinted on her as clearly as humans instinctively feared the forms and movements of snakes, spiders and telephone bills.

"A snaarrk?" whispered Elliot. "But how? I thought they were extinct or something…"

"Finally!" growled Captain Destroyer and levelled his discreet hunting rifle at the waiting beast.

But the snaarrk was waiting for a reason. A sudden rustling in the undergrowth made everybody glance sideways. The snaarrk was not alone. Another beast slowly emerged from the undergrowth. It also was poised to strike.

"Oh no, another one," whispered Elliot.

"I'm sorry if I bring bad news," said Little Brother carefully from Elliot's back. "But I'm afraid my sensors are picking up a lot more of these creatures than just those two."

Identical sounds of approaching snaarrks could be heard all around them now. It seemed like the entire undergrowth was full of them.

"We're surrounded!" shouted Molly.

Then the snaarrks attacked.

With a growl, the first snaarrk leapt at Elliot with its terrible barbed mandibles open wide, ready to tear into flesh. Before it reached Elliot, who was struggling to ready his stunner wand, a loud bang was heard. In mid-air the snaarrk exploded in a cloud of red and black.

All around them the other snaarrks attacked as well. Everybody screamed and backed into each other. Tavvin was trembling so badly with fear that she couldn't point her stunner wand properly and successfully managed to stun a mushroom tree instead. Reacting fast, Elliot pointed his stunner at the snaarrk that leapt at Tavvin and fired. A loud *ZAP!* was heard and a blue bolt leapt from the wand. It hit the snaarrk square in its ugly face and it fell twitching to the ground. Molly managed to shoot one of the snaarrks that came at her. It also fell twitching to the ground. The forest was now full of the sounds of combat. There were growls from the snaarrks, zaps from the stunners and loud bangs from Cro'lichks rifles.

Even though the powerful Cro'lichks rifles obliterated another two of the snaarrks, another of the creatures managed to leap onto Captain Destroyer's back. A Cro'lichks might be big and strong, but Captain Destroyer was clad in bulky armour. The snaarrk therefore knocked him down and immediately began tearing at his back with its terrible mandibles, while bashing him with its spiked tail.

"No-no, you don't," howled Captain Destroyer and began rolling around and hitting the snaarrk with his spiked gloves.

Tavvin was now overcome with fear and fled into the undergrowth.

"No! Don't run!" shouted Elliot and fired his stunner wand at another snaarrk which fell to the ground.

Maybe only hearing part of Elliot's words, Billin rose to his feet and began running in the other direction.

"No! Stay here!" Elliot shouted again and tried to grab Billin. But he didn't reach the Furanian. Instead something knocked him over and he dropped his stunner wand.

Standing on his chest was a snaarrk. The snaarrk's foul breath stunk terribly of rot and decay, and saliva dropped onto Elliot's forehead from the strong barbed mandibles. The snaarrk opened wide to bite off Elliot's face, but as the barbed mandibles snapped shut over Elliot's face, Elliot felt a tingling sensation as his energy shield activated. The snaarrk's barbed mandibles weren't strong enough to penetrate the shield.

A blue light suddenly blinded Elliot and a loud *ZAP!* was heard. The snaarrk fell off him and lay twitching on the ground.

"Get up!" shouted Molly, still waving her stunner wand at him. "Your shield won't save you forever you know!" Behind her another snaarrk came running through the undergrowth.

"Behind you!" shouted Elliot and grabbed his stunner wand lying next to him. Still lying on the ground, he shot the snaarrk in mid-jump and it fell at Molly's feet.

There was a brief moment to look around them as no snaarrk was attacking them. As Elliot rose to his feet he could see several other snaarrks circling them or throwing themselves against the Cro'lichks.

"Oh no! They don't stay stunned," shouted Molly and pointed at a snaarrk which rose groggily to its feet.

From amongst the trees they heard Billin shout in terror; "No! No! Please No!"

Without hesitating Elliot ran towards the voice. Molly immediately followed. As they rounded a large mushroom tree they could see Billin up against another tree with four snaarrks drawing closer. He was fiddling with his stunner wand, but was so afraid that he missed the snaarrk he was aiming at. The snaarrk licked its barbed mandibles with the long red tongue and crouched for a jump.

"Hold on!" shouted Elliot as he ran on. He raised his stunner wand and shot the snaarrk which rolled away in spasms. The other two snaarrks turned and growled, but Molly immediately stunned another one of them. A third snaarrk leapt at Elliot and bowled him over. Once again, the energy shield activated with a buzz. Even though the shield has saved him from the barbed mandibles, Elliot was still winded. Molly however leapt to his side and shot the snaarrk. The last snaarrk quickly backed away and disappeared into the undergrowth.

"I told you not to run, Billin!" wheezed Elliot as he rose again.

"Yeah, you're all alone here. They would have finished you, easily," added Molly while shooting the two twitching snaarrks again before they could rise.

But Billin could barely hear them. He had evolved from peaceful herbivores and was very bad at handling stress and controlling his fear. Adrenaline pumped through him and the only sensible thing his frail nerves could tell him was 'Run! Flee!'

"Snaarrks! Snaarrks everywhere!" was all he could say.

From amongst the trees they could hear more loud gunshots and the shrill scream of Tavvin.

"We have to get back to the others," said Elliot and turned back.

But after only a few steps the three of them stopped in their tracks. Black shadows slid between the mushroom trunks and through the silvery undergrowth. Snaarrks were closing in on them.

"Oh no! They're cutting us off."

"Yes, separating weaker individuals from the flock is a common hunting method for most primitive predators in…"

Little Brother informed them from his vantage point on Elliot's back.

"Thank you! We don't need to know any more about that," Molly interrupted sharply. She fired at one of the snaarrks and backed away. Elliot did the same and nudged Billin with his elbow.

"Keep firing! Keep them away from us!"

The three of them fired their stunners over and over again. The snaarrks fell to the ground, but slowly rose again. None of them fled. Instead they continued to attack the three of them with grim determination.

"Why don't they run away? Why aren't they afraid of us?" shouted Elliot. He remembered reading that wolves and bears in the forests of Sweden were always afraid of humans.

"I don't know," replied Molly. "There's something wrong with them."

The gunshots of the Cro'lichks weapons seemed further away now. Were they running away from the snaarrks in the other direction? Tavvin's screaming couldn't be heard anymore and Elliot feared the worst.

"This way!" shouted Molly and began running towards a small clearing. "We can get around the snaarrks over here."

But as they reached the clearing, more snaarrks appeared.

"How many of them are there?" shouted Molly. She shot a couple of snaarrks who came running at her, making the others more uncertain.

"Over here!" Molly shouted again and began running through the undergrowth. The shots of the Cro'lichks rifles sounded very distant now. The snarling of the snaarrks was much louder. Elliot and Billin followed Molly, occasionally turning and firing at the snaarrks. The snaarrks seemed more wary. They followed their prey, but kept out of the line of fire most of the time.

They continued their mad dash through the silvery undergrowth, but suddenly the ground in front of them ceased to exist. Molly and Elliot barely came to a halt by the crumbling side of a steep depression. The ground dropped in front of them, forming a deep ravine with a swift river at the bottom. Billin, on the other hand, was doing what he did best in such situations – fleeing. He didn't see the edge and ran straight into Elliot. Elliot, in turn, knocked into Molly and all three of them fell over the edge. With a buzzing and humming from their energy shields, they rolled down the rocky slope, through brushes and small mushroom stalks and into the river with a loud splash.

For a brief moment Elliot was under the surface and everything he could hear was the rushing of water. Then he resurfaced.

"Are you crazy!" shouted Molly angrily as her head surfaced next to Elliot. Her wet blonde hair lay streaked across her face.

Billin surfaced next to Molly, sputtering and with mud and mushroom mulch still in his fur.

"I'm sorry," he replied while trying to tread water.

"You could have killed us all if that drop had been higher," shouted Molly, while wiping her wet hair out her face. Her face was once again red with anger.

"I'm – *sputter* – sorry," said Billin again.

"Is everybody alright? Is anybody hurt?" asked Elliot, while treading water.

"No! I'm alright," replied Molly sourly and glared at Billin.

"I'm unharmed… so far," whimpered Billin.

"Good!" said Elliot. "At least that's a comfort."

"Yes. I'm also fine. Thank you for asking," replied Little Brother, a little hurt from Elliot's back.

"You're a box, a machine. You can't drown."

"Maybe not drown, but my circuitry could get flooded and short circuit if the case isn't waterproof. That would be the same as dying," Little Brother pointed out.

"Isn't the case waterproof?" wondered Elliot.

"Well… yes, it is, but it might not have been."

Elliot didn't want to keep arguing with Little Brother while the river washed him away. The A.I. was safe where it was, strapped onto Elliot's back. What about himself and the rest of his belongings? Suddenly Elliot realised that he didn't have his stunner wand anymore. He must have dropped it in the fall down the slope. How could he have let go of it? How stupid of him. While treading water he began groping around under him for the stunner wand. But the swift water was already taking them down the river and away from the spot where they fell. The stunner wand was gone.

"I can't find my stunner wand," complained Elliot. "I dropped it when we fell."

"Okay. But we still have two stunners left," said Molly who was bobbing further down the river.

"Well… eh…"sputtered Billin "I seem to have lost mine as well. *Sputter*. Most unfortunate!"

"Great!" exclaimed Molly and hit the water furiously. "So now we only have *my* stunner left. That's just wonderful! What happens when that runs out?"

Nobody wanted to think about that.

At the top of the slope two snaarrks appeared. They snarled menacingly while carefully examining the edge and their prey in the river below. Molly shot at them but missed. The snaarrks, who evidently thought the slope was too steep, disappeared again. Their shapes could be seen briefly among the trees as they ran down along the edge to find a better place to reach their prey.

"The snaarrks. They can't reach us," Elliot pointed out.

"Snaarrks were – *sputter* – notoriously bad swimmers," said Billin who had problems keeping his head over the surface. "Just – *sputter* – like Furanians." Then the furry head of Billin sank under the surface.

Elliot reached over and pulled Billin up to the surface again. The small Furanian was surprisingly heavy in the water. Maybe this was due to the wet fur? Elliot had to tread water hard to keep them both above the surface.

"Thank you – *sputter* – Master Elliot," Billin gasped. "You are most – *sputter* – kind."

"Didn't you learn to swim?" asked Elliot, while struggling to keep them afloat.

"No. I'm afraid not. Water is a most – *sputter* – terrifying thing. We don't – *sputter* – swim for recreational purposes like you do. We are not suited for water. It seems like folly to risk one's life in it to start with."

"Then we had better get out of this river," Molly pointed out.

After some heavy strokes and some struggling amongst the reeds of the riverbank, they managed to crawl out of the river. They lay panting on the riverbank when Little Brother spoke.

"Master Elliot? Your Highness?" he began.

"Yes?" Elliot replied.

"Well, I don't want to spoil this moment but…"

"But what?"

"Well, I think we better get moving. The snaarrks might find somewhere to cross the river and they'll be on us again soon."

"He's right," Molly agreed. "Let's get back to the ship as fast as we can. Hopefully the others will have made it there as well." She stood up and touched her earlobe. Immediately her Memo-Hair Gel shook the water from her hair and began braiding it nicely again.

With a groan, Elliot rose and helped a drenched Billin to his feet. The otherwise sleek fur of the Furanian was now filled with dirt and reeds and pasted to his body. His ears hung limp down the sides of his head. He looked like a drowned rabbit. Billin, if anyone, would need some Memo-Hair Gel, Elliot thought.

"The ship's that way," Molly said and pointed. "Let's get going."

"Ehm…" interrupted Little Brother. "The ship is actually the opposite way, Your Highness. The river took us quite a way downstream and further away to the… east, if that's what we can call it here."

"Okay, okay," sighed Molly. "Let's do what Brother Squid says."

Without wasting any time, they set out at a fast pace. This time they didn't stop to take samples or look for evidence of Flesh Smiths. They simply wanted to get back to their ship as fast as possible. Little Brother led the way as he seemed to know exactly where the ship was located in relation to their position. After half an hour of fast walking, Billin was still extremely skittish and nervous. He kept looking around him for snaarrks as he walked and as a result kept tripping over things.

"Do you think those Skar'ley ships are still looking for us?" asked Molly as they hurried through the tall mushroom forest.

"I don't know," replied Elliot, shrugging. "If they haven't, they'll spot us as soon as we leave this hollow moon. But that's a problem we can take care of later. Right now I just want to get back to the ship where those snaarrks can't get us."

"Snaarrks?" hiccupped Billin who hadn't heard the whole conversation, but immediately went to full alert at the mention of the terrible beasts.

"No! There's no snaarrks right now," said Molly impatiently. She was tired of Billin's skittishness. "We just said we…"

"Schhhh!" hissed Elliot suddenly and threw himself to the ground. Without knowing what was going on, Molly and Billin did the same. Billin immediately began to whimper and moan.

In front of them the mushroom forest opened up to a familiar lake. It was the lake where the scout ship had landed. But now there wasn't a ship there anymore.

There were two ships.

The other ship was slightly larger than the Cro'lichks scout ship and resembled a large arrowhead. The ship bore the symbol of the dreaded Has'pleen sect and around it milled ten or so Skar'ley priests. Despite the distance, Elliot could clearly see that the otherwise slender and green lizard-like aliens here were bulkier, more gaunt and had a sickly yellow skin tone. They were Has'pleen Skar'ley, whose bodies had been altered by severing the maglio gland when they were young. Elliot also knew that they were priests, as they bore long brightly red robes with snake motifs, just like the one the priest Skauda'tesh had worn. But under the robes these priests were armoured and in their hands they carried long rifles. Elliot then noticed that several of the warrior priests were scurrying about the Cro'lichks ship.

"This isn't good," Molly pointed out in a whisper. "Those must be Has'pleen warrior priests."

"They've found our ship," Elliot confirmed grimly. "They're trying to get in. I hope that the ship's bulletproof."

"They have worse things than bullets," said Molly and pointed.

What Elliot saw made his blood freeze. Out of the Skar'ley ship filed a long line of tangled grey humanoids. Their forms were only roughly humanoid, as their bodies consisted of a tangled heap of coiling metal tentacles.

"Hunter robots!" he hissed.

It was the same type of coiling metal horror that had chased Elliot throughout Sweden on his journey to Kiruna. The same fiends which had nearly caught them and killed them on The Knot. These Hunter robots did, however, not need to conceal their forms in wide-brimmed hats and dark coats.

From their hiding place, they watched the robots beginning to tear the Cro'lichks ship apart. Their strength was incredible and the tentacles were equipped with drills, cutters and laser burners. In only a few minutes they had cut through the hull and parts began to fly everywhere. As soon as there was a small hole into the ship, the robots changed their shape and squeezed through. Soon, flickering from electric short circuits and the glow from lasers could be seen inside the cockpit windows.

"Oh no! I hope nobody was inside," moaned Billin.

Elliot and Molly didn't respond. If anybody was inside, it was already too late. The Hunter robots were merciless. Elliot tried desperately not to picture what it would feel like to hear the killer robots tearing their way in through the ship's hull and how it would end.

The main hatch of the ship then fell to the ground, knocked out of its hinges by the robots inside. With rifles raised high, the armed Skar'ley priests ran inside. But they soon emerged again and raised their arms in baffled shrugs to their leaders.

"There was nobody inside," sighed Elliot with relief.

"Yes, what a relief!" agreed Little Brother.

"Yeah. That's good," said Molly. "But it means they're going to start looking for us now. Soon this whole Hollow World will be crawling with deadly Hunter robots."

"You're right! We have to get out of here," said Elliot with a bit of panic in his voice.

"But where do we go?" moaned Billin. "There's nowhere to go. There's nothing here – *gulp* – but snaarrks."

"Anywhere else is better than right here," hissed Elliot.

As everybody agreed to this, they carefully crawled away from the ships and the Hunter robots. As soon as they dared to stand they did so and hurried away from the landing site.

***

As they crossed a small stream where the ground was more open, they suddenly heard a loud siren. It split the serenity of the mushroom forest and even quieted the distant birdsong. The noise came from somewhere to the left of them and as they shielded their eyes from the strong glare of the blue sun they saw a dark figure on the nearby cliffs.

"It's a Hunter robot!" Elliot shouted. "It's seen us!"

The thing on the cliff continued its wailing, alerting the Skar'ley priests and the other Hunter robots of the whereabouts of their prey.

"Run!" shouted Molly and took off.

The three of them ran as fast as they could through the undergrowth. Behind them, an answering wail was heard from further away.

The hunt was on!

They ran until their legs ached and Billin was too tired to keep up. The short and stocky Furanian kept stumbling over roots and weeds and didn't have the stamina of Elliot or Molly.

"I'm – *pant* – sorry!" Billin said. "You keep going – *pant*. I'm just too tired to – *pant* – run."

"We won't leave you," said Elliot grimly, while trying to get his breath back. "We're tired too. We'll walk for a bit."

They continued walking at a fast pace, all the time glancing behind them in worry. Nothing could be seen or heard. The forest was uncannily quiet and tranquil again. Around them the butterflies with the colourful wings fluttered peacefully between the mushroom trees. But the forest emitted a false feeling of tranquillity. Elliot knew that the world they were now stranded on was only peaceful on the surface. Dangers lurked everywhere in the form of snaarrks and other hostile life forms. On top of this, somewhere close behind them several killer robots and mad Skar'ley priests were hunting them silently through the alien forest. None of them stated the obvious – where were they going? What were they going to do? They knew nothing of this world or where to hide. They were just running blindly away from one danger and probably headlong into the next. Hope had all but abandoned them. Even Little Brother expressed his concern when he asked, "Master Elliot, do you remember if my latest backup copy of myself was on that scout ship?"

"What do you mean?" replied Elliot.

"It's not important really. I was just wondering when I last made a backup of myself. I guess Salank must have made a backup copy when he restored my memory circuits."

"Why are you asking that now?" Elliot wondered, truly bewildered.

"I think," snapped Molly, "that he's worried that he – and we – might not make it. In that case his personality can always be restored with a backup copy."

"What? We're not going to make it?" said Billin, eyes open wide with terror. In his moment of despair he didn't see where he put his feet and tripped over a stone.

"That's not fair," scowled Elliot while helping Billin to his feet again. "*We* can't be backed up. You shouldn't even be thinking like that."

"I'm sorry, Master Elliot. I was only thinking out loud and calculating the odds of our survival," apologised Little Brother.

"Okay, but don't do that in the future," mumbled Elliot." I guess now we're even for when I said your tentacles looked scary."

"What *are* the odds?" said Billin nervously.

"I don't think we want to know," interrupted Molly.

"Well, considering what we have been through so far, the odds are not that bad," declared Little Brother cheerfully. "We've nearly been blown up – twice. We've faced Hunter robots on more than one occasion. We've crashed on an asteroid. We've died – but got better. We've nearly been traded off as prisoners of war by a super-secret society. We've socialised with psychotic Cro'lichks. We've avoided to crash into hostile enemy ships in a lethal atmosphere. We've survived an attack by a believed-to-be-extinct pack of predators. And now we're being hunted – but are still alive – by a dozen Hunter robots and fanatic Skar'ley priests. With luck like ours we'll most probably find the ruins ahead devoid of anything harmful."

"Ruins? What ruins?"

"Oh, yes! That's what I was going to say from the start," Little Brother reminded himself. "There are some ruins ahead and they could potentially be very, very dangerous."

"I can't see any…" said Molly but then fell silent.

Ahead of them, the mushroom trees thinned slightly, creating a half open space filled with large boulders. But as they looked closer, they could see a broken landscape of standing stones overgrown with fungus and silvery undergrowth. The upper surface of the stones or structures couldn't be seen, but their full shapes had to be guessed. Some were shaped like rectangles or squares, while others looked like pyramid slices. All were placed in two rows which led to a small hill clustered with broken pillars. They hadn't seen this from the air, as everything was covered by vegetation.

"I don't think we should go there. It's most likely very dangerous," whispered Billin.

Molly drew her stunner wand and slowly approached one of the standing stones.

"The stones have imbedded circuitry," announced Little Brother from Elliot's back. "They seem inactive, but there are faint energy emissions. That's how I detected them. Then comparing with topographical maps created by the radar..."

"Yeah, I think we understand," said Elliot with a hushed voice. He had the feeling somebody or something was watching them.

"It's really, really old," said Molly quietly. Her voice was nearly a whisper as well. "We'd better check them out. It might be somewhere to hide."

"I don't know..." replied Elliot, but Molly was already leading the way along what seemed to be an overgrown procession road between the standing stones.

"We shouldn't be here," mumbled Billin and drew closer to Elliot and Molly.

Somewhere behind them a dry branch suddenly snapped with a crack.

"They're here," hissed Elliot and began to run again. With Molly leading the way, they ran along the lines of overgrown standing stones and up the pillar-clustered hill. The pillars on the small hill were not as overgrown as the two lines of standing stones. Here and there among the fungus growing over it, they could see strange patterns and symbols.

They stopped and hid behind one of the big pillars.

"It's the Hunter robots all right," said Billin who was looking back where they'd come from behind a pillar. The Furanian was trembling with terror.

Six of the Hunter robots were now standing at the edge of the overgrown ruins. Small red globes of light bobbed in front of them, scanning the surroundings for traces of their prey. For a moment they seemed to hesitate, but then moved, or rather flowed, ahead on their coiling mass of steel tentacles, resembling humanoid figures with octopus tentacles instead of legs. The cold, glowing blue eyes of the Hunter robots turned upwards and fixed upon the small hill. With their superior sensors they could clearly detect their prey. To prevent their prey from fleeing further, the six Hunter robots began to spread out to encircle the small hill.

Running from pillar to pillar, Molly, Elliot, Billin and Little Brother reached the hill's summit. At the centre of a cluster of broken pillars was a slightly larger central pillar, crowned with a flat disc of stone. Around it lay hundreds of large dead butterflies. Their broken colourful wings reflected the light of the small blue sun in a sad kaleidoscope of light.

"What's happened to the butterflies?" wondered Molly and picked one up with a sad expression.

"I don't know," replied Elliot. "But I don't like this."

Molly cocked her head to one side and then sat down.

"Look!" she whispered and pointed forward. Elliot followed her finger and saw a hole in the ground. A large overgrown stone slab seemed to have been raised, opening up to some sort of ramp down into the underground.

"Maybe it's somewhere to hide?" suggested Molly.

"Down there?" replied Elliot sceptically.

Molly slowly crept forward with her stunner wand ready. Fearing that something would happen to her, Elliot grabbed her hand. Molly turned and looked at Elliot, then smiled and continued forward. When they drew closer they could see that the soil and the undergrowth around the raised slab had been ripped, as if the slab had been opened only recently. Several animal tracks could be seen in the soil – tracks from large, claw-equipped animals. A foul, musky animal stench wafted up from the descending ramp.

"I definitely don't like *this*," Elliot said again.

"Snaarrks?" whispered Molly, as quietly as she could, so as not to let Billin hear.

"Most probably," agreed Elliot. "It could be their den. Going down there would be suicide."

Behind them they heard the faint whirring of clockwork as the Hunter robots drew closer. They were on the small hill now.

"What else can we do?" whispered Molly desperately. There's nowhere else to go. At least against the snaarrks we have a chance."

Elliot didn't know what he feared the most – the snaarrks or the Hunter robots. The Hunter robots were merciless killers and near indestructible. At least the snaarrks could be stunned for a while – if they saw them in time – and if Molly's stunner wand had enough charge left in it.

"Okay, let's go down," Elliot sighed. "I guess it's the only chance we have."

They motioned to Billin to follow and stepped into the gloom. Billin reluctantly took a step forward. When he felt the musky smell of deadly predators that wafted up he stopped.

"What's down there? I'm not going down there. It smells like a snaarrk den."

"How would you know?" replied Molly with feigned bravery. "They were extinct long before you were born. You wouldn't know what a snaarrk den smelled like even if you lived in one."

"Well… this definitely smells the way I picture one. I'm not going down there."

"Then you'll have to stay here and take your chances with the Hunter robots," hissed Elliot.

Billin looked behind him, he was trembling with worry and indecision.

"Come on! Hurry!" beckoned Elliot. "Whatever lived down here is probably long gone."

"Alright! Alright!" surrendered Billin and joined the others in the gloom. "But I'm doing this under protest and against every fibre and natural instinct still left in my body."

"You're very brave and I'm proud of you," said Elliot as he helped Billin down the ramp. No sooner had Billin joined Elliot and Molly on the ramp, when the heavy stone slab began to close behind them with a loud grating sound.

"It's closing!" shouted Billin in terror.

"It's a trap!" shouted Molly.

"Everybody quickly out again," shouted Elliot and ran for the slowly diminishing sliver of light.

"I don't think that's a good idea, Master Elliot," Little Brother pointed out.

Elliot understood what Little Brother had meant. Running up the top of the hill were two Hunter robots.

"Sssstop! Dessisst! Fleeing is uselessss!" the dread machines chanted.

With lightning speed they ran for the closing slab. Stingers, laser drills and vibro-cutter knives poised at the ends of the coiling steel tentacles to reach their prey. Far too late, Elliot realised that he was too close to the opening. He tried to jump back, but one of the tentacles hit him over the arm and he fell to the ground. His energy shield buzzed violently, but he still felt a burning pain on his upper arm as a vibro-cutter tore through both shield and spacesuit.

Spreading out like two steel octopuses, the Hunter robots came at him, intent on shredding him to bits.

Then the slab closed with a boom and darkness engulfed them.

In the darkness, Elliot fought with the deadly Hunter robots. The steel tentacles wormed and snaked over his body, trying desperately to cut or strangle him. Somewhere in the darkness they towered over him, ready to strike. At any moment he expected the main bulk of the Hunter robots to come crashing down on top of him. Molly and Billin shouted, but all he could do was scramble backwards on his heels and elbows.

Suddenly a light pierced the darkness. It was a soft but strong white glow which Elliot realised came from his own back. The light came from a slender rod which had protruded from the black briefcase of Little Brother. It gave off enough light for Elliot to see that there weren't any Hunter robots standing over him. There were only two thrashing tentacles whose ends were crushed under the heavy slab of stone. The slab had closed just in time to prevent the Hunter robots getting through. Avoiding the blindly thrashing tentacles of steel, Elliot moved back to the others.

"Th-th-that was c-c-close!" stuttered Billin.

"Yeah, that slab closed just in time," agreed Elliot, still breathing heavily and feeling the adrenaline, making his whole body shake.

"We were lucky again," Little Brother pointed out.

"Elliot, you're injured," gasped Molly when she saw the torn suit and Elliot's blood.

Believing that he'd been fighting for his life with two Hunter robots, Elliot hadn't stopped to consider the stinging pain on his arm. Now he looked at it with shock. His red blood was spattered over the otherwise white and slim Vurite spacesuit.

"Let me have a look at it," said Molly and carefully peeled away the suit around the wound. All three of them leaned in to see the wound.

"Uuurrgghhh!" said Billin and fainted.

"There's… there's a lot of blood," said Elliot, feeling a bit queasy.

"It doesn't look that bad actually," said Molly. She pumped some water from her suit's water container and let it splash over the wound. When the blood was gone, Elliot saw that the cut wasn't very deep. It looked more like a wide burn mark which had gashed the skin open. Molly rummaged in her small bag and came up with a pink silken hair band that she tied over the wound.

"You're lucky your energy shield is so strong," informed Molly. "Salank knew what he was doing when he enhanced its power. Without the energy shield you would have had your whole arm cut off."

"I'll remember to thank Salank for that if I get to meet him again," agreed Elliot and studied the bandage Molly had made. Although pink wasn't his favourite colour, the bandage looked good enough. "This'll do fine," he said. "Now we'd better get moving. Those Hunter robots might be able to cut through that stone."

"Alright, but it's your turn to wake up the Furrie this time."

***

When Billin had come to his senses (which involved some pulling of his long ears and slapping him around) they continued down the ramp. Elliot and Molly went first, both literally holding on to the stunner wand. After thirty or forty metres they came to a small room with several branching tunnels. All the tunnels were very high, but quite narrow. Only one of them was broader than the others.

"I suggest the broad tunnel because… because it's broader than the others," said Elliot.

Molly shrugged in agreement.

After having walked a couple of metres down the broader tunnel, the floor stopped sloping downward. The smell of animals on the other hand became stronger. Soon they saw light in front of them. Small pinpoint lights in the ceilings created an eerie gloom which reminded Elliot of a moonlit forest. The corridor they were following soon opened up to a large chamber. The raised corridor floor sloped down on either side of them to the vast lower floor of the chamber, while a thin strip of floor continued forward to some steep steps leading up. The steps themselves were wide and high, as if built for beings much taller than humans or Furanians. The steps ended close to the roof of the chamber, at a large orb-like object which was cut out of the wall.

"So, where do we…?" began Molly, when a growl suddenly interrupted her. The growl came from the large chamber below and was immediately followed by several other snarls and growls.

"SNAARRKS!" screamed Billin at the top of his squeaky lungs, and turned to run back.

"No! No! Don't run," shouted Elliot and grabbed the Furanian painfully by his long ears. "You haven't got a stunner. You have to stay with us."

In the gloom below them they saw shadows congregating at the bottom of the sloping floor. Soon they could see snaarks running up at them.

They were trapped. They could either climb the steep steps and get cornered there, or run back to where they came from. Neither option seemed very promising.

"M-m-maybe we can hold them off at the top of those steps," said Molly, her face pale with fear.

"Let's do it!" commanded Elliot who didn't feel they had time to think it over. Below them the snaarks came running up. Billin took one look at the tall steps and pulled free from Elliot.

"Noooo! We won't make it! It's too high!" He then turned and ran back.

"No! Stop!" shouted Elliot. But Molly pulled him the other way, towards the first of the giant steps.

"You can't run after him this time," she said.

Elliot hesitantly jumped up onto the first tall step and then onto the next while looking over his shoulder. At a surprising speed, Billin ran back down the broad corridor from where they'd come and was swallowed by the darkness. But immediately behind him chased five black figures. Elliot could see that the snaarrks were faster than Billin and felt a large lump of fear and sadness form in his belly.

A white dazzling flash brought his attention back to where he was and he saw a stunner bolt hit a snaarrk only a couple of metres ahead of him. It fell twitching to the floor while many more snaarrks leapt over it. Elliot turned and jumped up another three steps, while Molly turned and shot some more snaarrks. She was good at shooting and the snaarks could only come at them from one direction. She therefore managed to hold the snaarrks at bay, while climbing. In order to climb the giant steps while holding the snaarrks off, Elliot had to grab Molly's arm and pull her up every step. Behind them, snaarrks were piling up as they tumbled back twitching down the steps. But the snaarrks could smell fresh flesh and blood. Their scary eyes reflected Little Brother's light in the gloom and their barbed mandibles clacked together menacingly. They jumped up after the two children with snarls and growls.

From down the corridor a shrill scream was suddenly heard. It was high and full of terror and pain. It was Billin.

"Billin! No!" shouted Elliot. He stopped and stared down the steps towards the corridor where Billin had disappeared into the darkness.

The screaming continued and now he could hear the loud growls and barks of excited snaarrks.

"Elliot, we can't do anything," Molly shouted. Her eyes were filled with tears, but she turned again towards the snaarrks, which were advancing up the steps, and fired off a couple of stunning bolts.

The screaming ended suddenly and the growling of snaarrks was the only thing that could be heard from the corridor. Elliot felt tears welling up in his eyes as he thought of the grim fate of Billin. But he didn't have time to stand there for long. The blood-crazed snaarrks continued to come at them and he scampered up after Molly who was standing two steps over him shooting down at the snaarrks.

The steps were very high and the climb was harder than they thought. Soon they were both panting heavily. Below them the snaarks had slowed slightly, fearing the sting of the stunner.

Finally, they reached the uppermost step and looked down over the vast chamber below them. In the gloom, Elliot could see that the bottom of the steps was swarming with snaarrks. Those that had been stunned at first were now on their feet again. The chamber floor, far below them, was covered with bones and remains of animals and other things he didn't want to think about. This was truly the filthy lair of the snaarrks.

At the top of the steep steps Elliot and Molly huddled together under the last beacon of light which came from Little Brother. A couple of snaarks emerged from the corridor where Billin had disappeared. Although they were already wet and shiny around their mouths, they eyed the two human children greedily. Luckily it was too dark to see the colour of the blood on their snouts.

Behind Elliot and Molly loomed the large stone sphere which was half buried in the wall. It seemed to consist of several stone slabs, all perfectly joined together, and reminded Elliot of a three-dimensional wooden puzzle he'd once seen at school. Strange symbols were carved into the large stone sphere, but were unreadable, as his Translator Lenses didn't recognise the writing.

"Now what?" he said tiredly to Molly.

"I don't know," she replied and shot a snaarrk. "Is there anything behind that thing?" she said and pointed over her shoulder.

Elliot looked around them, but there was nothing except for the large stone globe.

"Maybe we can open it somehow?" Little Brother suggested.

Elliot pressed and pushed against the stone sphere, but nothing happened. He tried following the many depressions and lines which perhaps symbolised where the large stone pieces were joined together. But he found nothing.

Even Little Brother joined in the search by extending his tentacles from where he was strapped to Elliot's back. The tentacles moved over the sphere's surface while Molly continued to shoot snaarrks that had summoned the courage to venture up those last two steps.

"I'm pretty sure this can be opened," said Little Brother after a while. "The stone has the same kind of imbedded circuitry as the standing stones outside. But there's no way to activate it. It's probably designed to open from the inside."

"Can't you do *something*?" said Molly while shooting another snaarrk. "You've got all that fancy new enhanced worldly interface stuff."

"I'm sorry, Your Highness. I have no way of opening this thing. Maybe it can't be opened any more. I'm truly sorry."

The snaarrks below paused, as if they knew that they now suddenly had all the time in the world. Their prey was trapped. It had nowhere to go.

"We're trapped!" said Molly. "We have nowhere to go!"

Molly shot another snaarrk and this time the stunner wand sputtered slightly. Her next shot was visibly weaker, as the bolt hardly reached its intended target.

"Oh no!" Molly groaned.

Elliot understood what was happening. He stepped down from the stone sphere and took Molly's hand. She squeezed his hand tightly as she tried to fire the stunner wand again. This time there was nothing.

"Well, at least we still have the energy shields," Elliot whispered.

"Eh… I'm afraid the shields won't do you any good against multiple attacks and bites, Master Elliot," informed Little Brother. "Consecutive activations within a very short period of time will overload the…"

"Great!" said Elliot.

A growl spread among the snaarrks as they understood that their prey was now helpless. From the lower steps a much larger snaarrk pushed its way through the hungry pack. If it was possible, this snaarrk looked even uglier and grimmer than the others. Scars snaked over its body and one of its eyes was missing.

Molly turned and drew Elliot close. Whether she was comforting herself or Elliot was uncertain, but Elliot clung on to his friend for life.

"I don't want to die like this," Molly whispered, while staring in horror at the advancing snaarrks.

Elliot agreed. This time dying wouldn't be painless and in his sleep. This time it would be in screams and agony. Being eaten alive was not something he'd ever imagined would happen to him.

With drool dripping from its cruel, barbed mandibles the large grim snaarrk paused at the topmost step. Then, with a roar of victory it hurled itself at the two helpless children.

CHAPTER 4
INTERSTELLAR CONSPIRACIES AND ANCIENT PLANS

In most bodies of living creatures in the universe there are some sort of carbon-based cells which are controlled and activated by minute electrical discharges from a nerve centre or brain. Whenever such a creature registers something through sight, hearing or touch, electrical discharges are sent to the nerve centre or brain. The brain, of course, needs to register and interpret these combined signals in order for the creature to act upon them. By tapping into these minute electric discharges and reading them, an advanced creature with extensive knowledge of cellular organisms can learn a lot. Not only can a creature's cell activity be monitored, it can also be duplicated and read into an advanced bio-link machine. This machine will display whatever a monitored creature sees, hears or feels, sometimes even what it is thinking. With other advanced machines, such as Organic Controllers, new electrical impulses can be transmitted to certain cells of a creature, activating specific body functions and behaviour, as well as imprinting false information which is transmitted to the poor creature's brain. With such machines, a creature can be totally monitored and totally controlled. Its thoughts, feelings and bodily functions are no longer its own. Additionally, if this creature also has been biologically predisposed to such manipulation, it is nothing but an organic puppet. Freedom exists only when the puppeteer turns his attention elsewhere. And if it is a clever puppeteer, the creature will never know whether it is being controlled or whether it is free.

On most primitive worlds, this power would be associated with demonic possession or mind control, but in other places of the universe it is very real indeed. One such place lies hidden deep inside the barren and abandoned Ash Plain nebula of the ageing Skar'ley Empire. A world populated by creatures that are nothing but artificial organic machines living in an equally artificial world. A world of puppets and hidden puppeteers.

Images flashed and formed in the amber liquid of the puppeteer's large stone bowl. The creatures, whose visual brain activity was being monitored, travelled close to the ground on all fours. Everything was therefore seen from a much lower perspective, than for example that of a human. The combined overview of the creatures of the subterranean chamber was transmitted to the amber liquid, like a live feed to a screen. A high staircase was the focus of their attention, and at the top of the staircase shone a blinding light which broke the dark tranquillity of the underground. The creatures hated the light that stung their eyes and blinded them. But stronger emotions than that were transmitted via the bowl – hunger and the joy of the hunt.

The images in the golden liquid flashed again as the visual brain activity of the creatures higher up on the stairs came into focus. Two bipedal figures huddled under the bright light. Even though these bipedal creatures were of a much younger species, it was easy for the puppeteer to interpret the meaning of their body language and the electrical activity in their more primitive brains. These creatures were scared.

As the electrical impulses of the two bipedal creatures were examined, they were found to be boringly simple and easy to control. Not even a challenge for the puppeteer. But something else triggered the interest of the puppeteer. Something familiar, but unexpected.

The creatures were about to be killed.

The puppeteer hesitated.

How much information could be learned from re-grown tissue?

***

The large scarred snaarrk leapt through the air. It longed to sink its mandibles into the pink flesh of its prey. It could already feel the taste of blood and skin in its mouth. Then, suddenly, all of the snaarrk's brain activity was shut off. A barrier was placed between the bodily functions and the controlling organ of the brain. No nerve impulses could reach the brain. The snaarrk folded up in mid-air and landed like a discarded piece of cloth at the feet of Elliot and Molly. They looked at the lifeless snaarrk in horror, waiting for it to rise and attack them again, but it didn't. More snaarrks lunged at them, but all fell suddenly limp and lifeless to the ground, as if their very life and spirit left them when they crossed an invisible line. The remaining snaarrks suddenly sat to attention. Like well-trained dogs they settled on their shanks and lifted their ugly heads upward. Still and motionless like statues, they sat and an eerie silence spread through the chamber.

"Wha-what happened?" asked Molly as she slowly loosened her grip on Elliot.

"I… don't know," replied Elliot. A shiver went down his spine when looking at the many snaarrks sitting silently and obediently on the steep steps. They seemed to be waiting for something. The snaarrks lying at their feet were not dead, Elliot could see their chests heaving when they breathed. It was as if they had been turned off or something.

"Why are they just sitting there?" Molly asked. She also felt the sudden and inexplicable fear.

"They seem to be waiting for something," guessed Elliot.

"I… can't register anything different from before," added Little Brother, his steel tentacles slowly retracting back into the black case. "Nothing has changed. There is no invisible force field, no detectable signal, no stealth field around us. Nothing!"

A sudden rumbling and grinding of stone interrupted them. It came from immediately behind them. They spun around, with their hearts beating even harder in their chests, and saw the large stone sphere begin to crack along the angular seams. Like a strange and angular stone flower, the orb opened up. Soon, a stone corridor could be seen beyond. A strange, greenish ground mist rolled silently out of the opening; it smelled strongly of ammoniac and stung their noses.

Do… do we go in?" wondered Elliot.

"I get the feeling we don't have a choice," replied Molly, and looked back at the many snaarrks which sat and waited in silence.

Molly carefully stepped into the newly opened corridor. As she did so, a strange light grew out of the thin air over their heads. It started as a white point and then grew until it was a softly glowing sphere roughly the size of a tennis ball. It wasn't attached to anything and didn't seem to emanate from any kind of object. Three more spheres of light grew out of the air further down the corridor, beckoning them on.

"Come on!" she said and took Elliot's hand. She pulled him with her all the way through the strange stone opening. As soon as they both had stepped through, the stone sphere closed again behind them with a grinding noise.

"I guess we follow the light," said Molly and walked on. Elliot said nothing. He was still in shock since their near-death experience with the snaarrks, and his heart felt like it was going to burst out of his chest. His spine and arms still tingled with adrenaline.

The strange lights kept appearing out of thin air in front of them, while the lights behind them shrunk and disappeared. As they walked down the corridor they began to hear bubbling and moaning noises. Their corridor soon became an elevated walkway as they came upon a series of rooms with large stone vats. The vats contained some light brown syrupy liquid which bubbled and moved, as if something swam or fidgeted under its surface. From the ceiling hung more of the strange light orbs, shedding a gloomy light over the rooms. The green mists rolled gently between the vats, making it impossible to see the floor. But in the thick mist, Elliot thought he saw shadows or small things which scurried about. As they passed one of the vats, a flat, furry head broke through the surface which seemed to be covered by a kind of membrane. With a series of panicked jerks, the thing was out of the liquid and flapping its large bat-like wings. It flew, dripping and squealing, over the floor and disappeared into the gloom of the chamber. From another vat rose a deer-like creature with scales and curved horns. It jumped clumsily out of the vat and stood shivering next to it, eyeing everything with large terrified eyes. Then it too ran off into the gloom.

Further down the elevated corridor they could see many more rooms with rows upon rows of vats. Although the lighting was poor, they could see that both the rooms and the vats seemed to stretch off into infinity.

"What is this place?" said Molly with a shiver.

"My guess is it's the workshop of those Flesh Smiths," answered Elliot quietly. He also felt that they were witnessing something very unnatural. "Maybe it's like a factory for living creatures?"

"Any idea what all this is, Little Brother?" Molly asked.

"Ehhh, well, regarding the lights, it's my guess that they consist of luminescent microorganisms which congregate and activate in predetermined patterns when sensing the presences of…"

"Saying that you don't know would be enough," Molly cut off. "What about all these vats? I suppose you don't know what they are either?"

"Yes. You're right, Your Highness. I'm afraid I don't understand any of this. There are no references to this technology in my databanks. It's a conundrum, I promise you."

"I'm sure it is," said Elliot who didn't really know what a conundrum was. He was also squinting to distinguish what it was that he saw further ahead.

Ten other walkways from different directions joined the one they were walking on. Where all the walkways met, a small figure waited for them. That was what Elliot had seen in the gloom. The creature barely reached Elliot's knees. It had a thin, ropy body with big, pointed ears and large tired eyes. Its mouth was small and pulled tightly into what looked like a sour face.

"Follow!" it croaked like a toad and turned away from them.

"Pardon?" said Elliot, who hadn't expected the thing to speak.

The figure turned again and eyed Elliot suspiciously. "Follow!" it croaked again. This time it pointed across a walkway and into the gloom.

"Follow what? Follow where?" asked Molly and crossed her arms.

After a brief pause, during which the creature gave Molly what seemed to be a condescending look, it said, "Follow… me!"

"Alright! Alright! We'll follow you," sighed Molly.

And so they did. The three of them followed the small creature as it made its way across the stone walkway. After endless rooms with vats, followed corridors with foul-smelling stone piping and suffocating green mists. Their strange guide then took them up more oversized stairs and across bottomless chasms on small stone bridges. Although everything around them appeared to be made of stone, many of the large corridors, rooms and chasms seemed to have no reasonable purpose. After a while it struck Elliot that this was exactly how an ant lost inside a human computer must feel like. The strange floors, walls and ceilings actually being huge and incomprehensible electronic components.

"Where are you taking us?" asked Molly, impatiently after a while.

The small creature didn't even turn this time. It simply croaked the same command. "Follow!"

Finally, after what felt like an hour-long walk through the interior of the mysterious hollow moon, the small goblin-like creature stopped in front of a large stone doorway. The doorway was decorated with more pictograms of winged creatures and strange symbols, clearly of Founder origin. But covering the lower half of the doorway was something newer. A strange fungus or weed with long purple strands. Although there was no breeze or draft in the corridor, the long strands swayed slightly.

"Creator… waits," the creature croaked and pointed into the large chamber beyond.

"Creator?" repeated Elliot and gulped. "Do you mean the Flesh Smiths?"

"Creator," the creature repeated simply.

Understanding that the small goblin-creature couldn't explain any more, Elliot and Molly carefully stepped through the doorway. Behind them, several small eyes popped out of the swaying weed and examined them. Elliot heard the faint rustling behind them and turned. But before he could see anything, the eyes had popped back into the doorway weed. Elliot eyed the doorway suspiciously, but then turned back and followed Molly into the large chamber beyond.

The chamber was oval with a high ceiling and many slender pillars. More of the strange bodiless lights seemed to drift slowly amongst the high pillars. At the centre of the chamber stood something that resembled an enormous stone chair which rose high over the floor. From several stone bowls on a raised portion of the floor around the chair came a warm amber glow. The amber light seemed to dance slightly over the chair and closest pillar, like water reflections.

Both Elliot and Molly could see that something sat in the enormous chair and approached it cautiously. Every step they took echoed through the large silent chamber. As they passed the many stone bowls on the floor, they saw glowing amber liquid with strange pictures swirling in them. Sometimes it looked like parts of the mushroom forests or curving tunnels. Other pictures resembled a multitude of swirling dots dividing and multiplying in complex patterns.

When they were close enough to study the thing in the chair they stopped dead in their steps. The thing was not alive. Mummified remains of something large, ropy and cracked sat slumped in the chair. Three large eye sockets stared emptily at them from a long horse-like head, crowned with several sets of curving horns. Broad, clawed hands rested lifelessly on the chair's armrest and a long staff lay across its spiky knees. Judging by the size of the stone chair, the thing must have been over five metres tall when standing up. When looking at it closely, Elliot got the impression that the thing in the chair had been long dead. The dry mummy seemed to have fused with the chair, as if cut out of the same substance. Even the staff seemed to belong to this same substance.

"Is that…?" Elliot wondered aloud.

"I think it is," Molly replied. "It must be a Flesh Smith."

"But it's… long dead," Elliot pointed out.

"Yeah, really long dead," Molly agreed.

"So, the Flesh Smiths are no longer alive?" Elliot wondered.

"If they were, you would assume that others of its kind would have cleaned up this mess," Molly said.

"Maybe the Flesh Smiths died or were killed a long time ago?" Little Brother suggested. "Maybe this whole place is automated and continues to produce its organic products?"

"The An Barr are not dead," a dry, raspy voice boomed. "They are simply resting... and waiting."

Molly and Elliot jumped back from the large mummy in fright. But the voice had not come from the mummy. It had emanated from somewhere else. Their hearts raced as they circled each other and scanned the chamber for whatever had spoken. Nothing more was heard other than the echoes of their shuffling feet as they moved around.

"Where are you?" Molly shouted after a while. Elliot was startled by her voice and jumped. "Show yourself!" she continued.

"I am present!" the dry voice continued. "To show myself more than I have done already is not possible." The vibrations of the deep voice could be felt in their stomachs.

Elliot looked around him again. He saw nothing but the pillars, the mummy and the slowly drifting lights close to the ceiling. "Where are you? We can't see you. Are you the mummy? Or the lights?"

"The lights are simple servants created by us. The empty husk is but a shell that we have worn. Now we have come into one. Now there is only I. I am everywhere. I am An Barr."

"What do you mean 'everywhere'? Are you watching us from some camera?" asked Elliot, who was still circling the chamber trying to find someone or at least a loudspeaker to direct his questions at.

"I am watching you, because you are passing through me. Everything you touch and see is part of me."

"So you're a Flesh… I mean an An Barr?" Elliot asked. "I thought the Scalies killed you a long time ago?"

"THIS THEY DID. DESTROYED THE ORGANISMS WHICH WE HAD ENGINEERED TO HOST US. WIPED OUR WORLDS CLEAN OF LIFE OR DESTROYED THEM ENTIRELY. SO GREAT WAS THE ANGER AND MISTRUST OF THE SKAR'LEY. ONLY A FEW OF THE AN BARR DID THEY ALLOW TO SURVIVE ON THIS ANCIENT WORLD. HERE WE HAVE LIVED IN BANISHMENT AND SOLITUDE, SAVE FOR THE THINGS WE CREATE. HERE WE HAVE WILFULLY DIMINISHED AND DIED, UNTIL WE WERE ONE."

"So, you created all the plants and animals of this Hollow World?" asked Molly.

"YES. THEY ARE MY SERVANTS, BUT ALSO PART OF ME."

"Then you murdered Billin and maybe even Tavvin and the others," Molly said. She knew it wasn't the wisest thing to do, accusing a Flesh Smith of murder in his own halls, but when thinking about poor Billin's terrible fate she felt her anger rise. In any case, she suspected that they were the prisoners of the Flesh Smith now. Their lives were in this bodiless creature's hands. "You murdered them," she repeated boldly.

"TRESPASSERS UPON THIS WORLD MUST SUFFER DEATH," the dry and booming voice replied.

"Why? If you controlled those snaarrks, you could have let him live. He was harmless. Not to mention scared senseless of the snaarrks. He was no danger to you."

Elliot was surprised at Molly's accusations and that she evidently had cared so much for poor Billin, whom mostly had seemed to irritate her. There was more to the hard princess than met the eye.

"IT IS NOT FOR ME TO DECIDE WHO LIVES OR DIES. IT IS THE WILL OF THE SKAR'LEY. I AM FORCED TO DO THEIR BIDDING… FOR NOW."

"Why snaarrks?" asked Elliot. "Why the thing that scared Billin and Tavvin the most?"

"I HAVE MANY CREATURES THAT SERVE ME. SNAARRKS ARE BUT ONE OF SEVERAL PRISTINE EXAMPLES OF PERFECTED NATURAL PREDATORS. WHEN I DETECTED THE PRESENCE OF FURANIANS, I FOUND IT SUITABLE TO UNLEASH THE SNAARRKS I CREATED. THEY ARE PERFECT KILLING MACHINES."

"So, now you're going to kill us too?"

"MAYBE. BUT FOR NOW I WILL LET YOU LIVE."

"Good! At least that's a start," said Elliot relieved.

"Why?" asked Molly, still full of defiance and anger. "Why let us live and not Billin?"

"Ehm… Molly," whispered Elliot. "I don't think we should upset…"

"YOU LIVE BECAUSE YOU INTRIGUE ME. AS LONG AS YOU HAVE MY INTEREST, MY GUARDIAN LIFEFORMS WILL NOT HARM YOUR FLESH. AND BELIEVE ME, THIS WOULD BE NO HARD TASK FOR THEM. YOU SEE, THE DEADLIEST OF MY GUARDIANS ARE NEITHER LARGE, CLAWED AND SPIKED, BUT SMALL, MANY AND IMPOSSIBLE TO SEE OR DEFEND YOURSELF AGAINST."

"So we're your prisoners!" Molly said flatly. "Until you're tired of us and decide to kill us. Then that's the end of it all. Is that so?"

"DEATH IS NOT THE END. IT IS MERELY A POOR STATE OF EXISTENCE. AS LONG AS THERE IS FLESH, LIFE CAN BE REBORN."

"I don't want to die… again," Molly said. "And I certainly don't want to be reborn. It seems so messy and unhygienic. I'd be glad if you just let us go."

"So what do you want of us? Why do we intrigue you?" asked Elliot.

"OF MORE IMPORTANCE IS THE REASON FOR YOUR COMING HERE. HOW DID YOU FIND THIS WORLD? WHY DID YOU COME HERE?"

There was silence for a few moments while Elliot and Molly looked at each other uncertainly.

"We… eh… found this world by mistake," Elliot ventured.

"MISTAKES RARELY HAVE BENEFICIAL OUTCOMES. YOUR COMING HERE HAS NO DOUBT REVEALED AN ANCIENT SKAR'LEY SECRET. BENEFICIAL TO YOU BUT HARMFUL TO THE SKAR'LEY. CONTRARY TO WHAT MOST PEOPLE BELIEVE, THE UNIVERSE IS NOT FULL OF COINCIDENCES AND CHAOTIC FORCES OF NATURE. THERE IS AN ORDER AND A PURPOSE HIDDEN WITHIN EVERYTHING. YOUR COMING HERE WAS NO COINCIDENCE."

"Okay, you're right," said Molly and shrugged. "We came here because we heard that there could be Flesh… An Barr here."

"YOU WERE CORRECT. NOW THIS KNOWLEDGE COULD COST YOU YOUR LIVES. BUT MY QUESTION REMAINS: WHY DID *YOU* COME HERE?"

"You mean *us*? Why did *we* come here?" said Molly. "Well, to be honest, we didn't want to come in the first place. Some other people took us here. They didn't want to drop us off somewhere else, so we had to come along."

"SO, YOU DO NOT KNOW THE IMPORTANCE OF YOUR COMING HERE?"

"No… should we know?" Elliot said uncertainly.

"I WOULD ASSUME SO… AS ONE OF YOU BEARS MY MARK…"

Elliot and Molly gave each other puzzled looks. But before they could ask anything else, the bodiless dry voice continued.

"WE ARE MUCH MORE ALIKE THAN YOU WOULD IMAGINE. WE ARE BOTH PRISONERS AND PAWNS. WE ARE BOTH UNWANTED BY THE SKAR'LEY. BUT WE BOTH HOLD THE KEY TO THEIR GREAT CONSPIRACY AND MYSTERY. WE BOTH WISH TO BREAK FREE."

Elliot's and Molly's heads were spinning now. The booming voice of the Flesh Smith was making no sense.

"What mark of yours are we carrying?" asked Elliot, thinking about the strange orichalcum medallion Uncle Karl had sent him.

"What key do we have?" asked Molly, also thinking about Elliot's mysterious medallion.

"*Is it the medallion?*" they both asked in unison.

"BOTH THE MARK AND THE KEY IS THE SAME. THEY ARE NOT HIDDEN IN PERISHABLE METALS, BUT IN FLESH WHICH COPIES ITSELF FOREVER."

"In flesh…?" said Elliot, his face now a question mark.

"A WISE MEMBER OF OUR PEOPLE ONCE SAID, '*IF YOU LOOK DEEPLY ENOUGH INTO YOURSELF, YOU WILL SEE THE BEGINNING OF ALL THINGS AND THE ANSWER TO ALL QUESTIONS*'. NOW, LOOK DEEP INSIDE YOURSELF AND YOU WILL FIND THE KEY TO THE FREEDOM YOU SEEK."

"The key to freedom deep inside me…" mumbled Elliot and immediately remembered the Nojd's words, '*… the Key to Freedom lies deep in your chest…*'

"You mean me!" Elliot said finally. "I've got something inside me, haven't I?"

"YOU ARE ONCE AGAIN CORRECT. YOUR GENES CARRY AN ALTERATION THAT I IMPLANTED IN YOUR KIND A LONG TIME

AGO. IT IS NO COINCIDENCE THAT YOU HAVE COME HERE. THE UNIVERSE HAS ORDERED AND PLANNED IT SO."

"So what am I carrying?" said Elliot, not really understanding what the bodiless Flesh Smith was talking about.

"SOME OF THE SMALLEST AND MOST MINUTE PARTS OF YOUR BODY WERE ALTERED BY ME. THESE ALTERED GENES WERE HANDED DOWN TO YOU FROM ONE OR BOTH OF YOUR PARENTS AND FROM ONE OF THEIR PARENTS IN TURN. IN THIS WAY THESE ALTERED GENES HAVE WANDERED DOWN THROUGH TIME, FROM THE VERY FIRST OF YOUR KIND WHICH WERE RELEASED BACK INTO YOUR WORLD."

Molly sighed and threw up her hands. "I don't understand a thing you're talking about. What genes? Which people were released back onto Earth? What are you talking about?"

"IT IS INTRIGUING THAT YOU TRULY DO NOT KNOW WHY YOU ARE HERE! MOST INTRIGUING! I HAD ASSUMED THAT YOUR KIND WOULD BE ENSLAVED BY NOW."

"Enslaved! By who?"

"ENSLAVED BY THE SKAR'LEY PRIESTHOOD, THE NEW RULERS OF THE EMPIRE. I ASSUMED YOU HAD NOW SOUGHT ME OUT IN HOPE OF FINDING FREEDOM FOR YOUR PEOPLE. EVIDENTLY I WAS WRONG. EVIDENTLY TIME HAS NOT YET TURNED FAR ENOUGH FOR THE PRIESTHOOD TO REVEAL THEIR POWER OVER YOUR KIND."

"So it's the Skar'ley priests that are conspiring to take over the Empire," exclaimed Molly.

"The whole priesthood? All of them?" asked Elliot.

"YES, THE PRIESTHOOD HAVE LONG PLANNED TO TAKE OVER THE EMPIRE THEY NO LONGER SEE FIT TO BE RULED BY EMPERORS. THEY DREAM OF A THEOCRACY OF DEVOTED WORSHIPPERS OF THE ETERNAL SUN. MAYBE THE

LESSER PRIESTS KNOW NOTHING, BUT ALL PRIESTS OF SOME IMPORTANCE HAVE A PART TO PLAY IN THE USURPATION OF POWER."

"So, why do they want to enslave us?" asked Elliot. "Is it to man their new warships?"

"MAYBE. I DO NOT KNOW THE SMALLER DETAILS OF THEIR GRAND PLAN. TIME STANDS STILL FOR ME. YOUR BRIEF LIFETIMES FLUTTER BY SO QUICKLY. BUT CREWS FOR SHIPS WOULD ONLY BE THE START OF YOUR SLAVERY. NEXT WOULD FOLLOW THE CONQUEST OF THE SPIRAL ARM... IN THE NAME AND GLORY OF THE ETERNAL SUN. SUCH IS THE POWER OF GREED."

"But, but, how would they do this?" wondered Elliot. "I thought they'd already tried to use humans against the Mosquito Men and found that humans are hard to control."

"THIS IS WHY THEY CAME TO ME FOR A SOLUTION. LONG HAVE THEY KEPT THE AN BARR HERE IN CASE THEY WOULD NEED US. ORIGINALLY, THE EMPERORS KNEW ABOUT OUR SECRET EXISTENCE. WHEN THEIR RACE SUFFERED FROM THE CURSE OF DECAY, THE EMPERORS CAME TO US FOR SALVATION. WE FOUND IT VERY IRONIC THAT THE SKAR'LEY REWARDED US FOR CURING A GENETIC AILMENT WE ORIGINALLY AND SECRETLY DESIGNED FOR THE DYING MASSIKITA TO USE AGAINST THE SKAR'LEY IN THE FIRST PLACE. SUCH IS THE PLAN LAID OUT BY THE UNIVERSE. BUT, OVER TIME THE EMPERORS FORGOT ABOUT US. IN THE END, ONLY THE PRIESTHOOD OF THE ETERNAL SUN KNEW OF OUR SECRET PRISON. WHEN THEY SAW THE DEMISE OF THE EMPIRE AND THE MEDDLING OF THE HIDDEN WATCHERS, THEY CAME TO ME – LAST OF THE AN BARR. THEY ASKED OF ME TO CREATE LOYAL SOLDIERS FROM A SAVAGE YOUNG

RACE. THEY GAVE ME HUMANS FROM A HIDDEN WORLD THEY CONTROLLED. WHAT I GAVE THEM WILL PLUNGE THE SPIRAL ARM INTO FIRE AND FLAME."

"What did you give them?" said Elliot, fearing that he wouldn't like the answer.

"I GAVE THEM NEW HUMAN GENES."

"Oh no!" said Little Brother, who was beginning to understand what the Flesh Smith had done.

"IN MY ORGANIC BLENDER I ADDED SOME NEW GENES INTO THE HUMANS THAT HAD BEEN ABDUCTED FROM THAT HIDDEN WORLD. THESE GENES WERE UNNOTICEABLE AND EXTREMELY DOMINANT. THEY WOULD NEVER BE LOST DUE TO TIME OR BREEDING. THE EFFECT OF THE GENES ARE MADE OBVIOUS WHENEVER THE HARSH VOICE OF A HAS'PLEEN PRIEST IS HEARD BY A HUMAN. THE VOICE RENDERS THESE HUMANS TOTALLY WILL-LESS AND SUBJECT TO SKAR'LEY CONTROL. THEY BECOME SLAVES THAT WILL GENETICALLY OBEY EVERY ORDER FROM THEIR MASTERS. SLAVES THAT WOULD RATHER DIE THAN REBEL. FOR THE LAST SIX HUNDRED YEARS THE SLAVE GENES HAVE BEEN IMPLANTED INTO YOUR WORLD AND SPREAD BY YOUR PEOPLE EVERY TIME THEY PROPAGATE. BY NOW, MILLIONS UPON MILLIONS OF HUMANS SHOULD CARRY IT."

"That's terrible…" whispered Molly.

"WHEN THE PRIESTHOOD MURDERS THEIR BELOVED EMPEROR, A NEW HORDE OF WARRIOR HUMANS WILL BE UNLEASHED UPON THE SPIRAL ARM. IN THE GREAT WAR THAT WILL ENSUE, THE PRIESTHOOD WILL HAVE THE HUMANS RID THEM OF THE SNAKIRRA AND THE VO'ORRNS, AS THEY WOULD BE THEIR MAIN OPPOSITION. FROM THIS CHAOS THEY WOULD CREATE ORDER. WITH THE VOICES OF their stunted Has'pleen priests, they would forever control the humans. A new chapter of the Spiral Arm is about to begin."

"And I have those genes," said Elliot weakly. "I could pass them on… That's why Uncle Karl said I was special. I'm some sort of terrible weapon."

"You are mistaken as well as correct. You do not have the slave genes, but you are a weapon. It is true that you are special, but only because there is nothing special about you at all. When I engineered the slave genes, I altered one of the human captives so that she would never be able to carry the slave genes. However, to the untrained eye it would seem like the slave genes were carried as normal. Instead she had the power to break the hold upon her kinsmen with the Words of Reason. You, like your mother or father, are relatives of hers and do not carry the slave genes. Thus, you can never be genetically enslaved by the Skar'ley. You hold the key to your people's freedom inside you. your words can break their bond."

"Then *that's* it! *That's* what Uncle Karl knew!" said Elliot excitedly. "Just like you, he said in his message that I was special because I wasn't special at all. And so was my mother and father. That was why they had been killed in the first place. The Skar'ley somehow found out about this resistance and began killing everybody that couldn't carry their slave genes. No wonder they wanted Uncle Karl and me dead."

"And so, now you have returned to me with the very mark that I placed upon your captured ancestor six hundred years ago. Now I have the

CHANCE TO REMEDY MY TREASON AND GAIN MY WARDEN'S TRUST… IF I WISH."

The last words of the Flesh Smith made Elliot's and Molly's blood freeze. It was true. The Flesh Smith could undo his treason and earn the Skar'ley priesthood's favour by turning them in.

"Then why haven't you done it already?" asked Molly defiantly. "Why have you spared us so far?"

"Because he doesn't want the Skar'ley priests to succeed in killing us," said Elliot with a frown. "Because he's a prisoner here and has to do their bidding. Because he wants revenge and freedom. You want to help us, so that we in turn can help you escape, don't you?"

"I DO NOT SEEK REVENGE. REVENGE IS IRRELEVANT. I DO NOT EVEN SEEK FREEDOM FROM THIS PRISON. I ONLY SEEK TO SURVIVE, SO THAT THE AN BARR CAN SURVIVE."

"But… I don't understand," said Molly. "You said that the Skar'ley let a few of you survive here. You *are* prisoners here, aren't you?"

"WE *WERE* PRISONERS. THEN WE ESCAPED OUR WORLDLY BONDS BY LETTING OUR FLESH SHELLS DIE ONE BY ONE, UNTIL THERE WAS ONLY I LEFT. NOW I HAVE FLED INTO THE ANCIENT AND UNFATHOMABLE MACHINERY OF THIS WORLD. ALTHOUGH THE SKAR'LEY PRIESTHOOD DOES NOT CLEARLY KNOW IT YET, IT CANNOT HURT US ANYMORE."

"You mean that you have imprinted a copy of your essence into the very fabric of this Founder artefact?" Little Brother asked excitedly.

"YOUR GUESS COMES FROM MUCH WISDOM, LIFELESS ONE. EVERY CHAMBER, EVERY CORRIDOR, EVERY BIO VAT AND EVEN THE CIRCULATORY CANALS – ALL THAT IS HERE,

IS NOW PART OF ME AND I PART OF IT. WE ARE INSEPARABLE AND ONE."

"This is amazing, Master Elliot," Little Brother explained to Elliot and Molly in a low whisper. "I have heard of this before, but only in theory. Sometimes very advanced Artificial Intelligences and even Enhanced Biological Intelligences can spread their thought patterns, or you could call them essences or souls, into machines which are linked to them. Most often those machines are what makes them so intelligent in the first place. It might even be what powers them. So, long after they are gone, copies of their thoughts live on in the machinery which has been associated with them. Like ghosts in the machines, so to speak."

"YOU ARE ONCE AGAIN CORRECT, LIFELESS ONE. BUT YOU FORGET THAT WE ARE AN BARR. WE ARE NOT GONE. WE ARE NOT GHOSTS. WE ARE TIMELESS. WE ARE FORMLESS. WE ONCE CREATED DEVICES SUCH AS THESE TO SURVIVE OUR JOURNEYS BETWEEN THE STARS. MINDS AND MEMORIES ARE IMPORTANT – BODIES ARE NOT. THEY CAN BE ALTERED OR RE-SPAWNED. THEREFORE WE WILL SURVIVE ALTHOUGH THE SKAR'LEY DESTROYED OUR WORLDS AND OUR SHELLS. THEREFORE WE WILL RETURN ONCE AGAIN."

"But they could destroy this world, couldn't they?" Molly pointed out.

"MAYBE THEY HAVE THE POWER TO DO THIS. BUT IT DOES NOT MATTER. WE WILL SLOWLY AND SECRETLY SEED OURSELVES ELSEWHERE. IN TIME, THE SKAR'LEY WILL ALSO BE GONE AND THEN WE WILL RETURN. WE WILL RE-SPAWN OURSELVES WHEN THE TIME IS RIGHT. MOST PROBABLY EVEN YOUR SPECIES WILL HAVE BECOME EXTINCT BY THEN. WE ARE TIMELESS. WE ARE AN BARR."

"So what is it that you want us to do for you?" asked Elliot.

"I want you to be my courier. I want you to take a part of me to every world you visit."

"A part of you?"

"Seeds. Seeds that in the future will become the An Barr. I want you to seed us among the stars."

"So, you'll help us simply because it would be a nuisance to the Skar'ley Priesthood? In return you want us to help you seed your people wherever we go?" Elliot concluded.

"You are correct. If there is a chance the Priesthood does not come to power, the demise of the Skar'ley as a species will be swifter. Then we can re-spawn sooner. The more seeds that have been spread, the greater the chance for our survival."

"I don't trust you," said Elliot with a suspicious frown. "You're hiding something. There's something else you're not telling us, isn't there?"

"Never mind!" interrupted Molly. "How will you get us out of here?"

"Look behind you!"

Elliot and Molly looked behind them and saw images form in the many bowls of amber liquid. They could see Has'pleen warriors working together with Hunter robots to remove the large boulders blocking the entrance. The images were strange and seemed to be composed of several smaller moving images that together formed a larger picture. Most images seemed to be captured from above, but some were of varying height.

"The butterflies! He's watching this from the eyes of the butterflies," Elliot said quietly to Molly.

"The Skar'ley are furiously trying to gain access into my halls," explained the booming voice of the bodiless Flesh Smith. "But they have left the ships unguarded. This is your way to escape."

Molly bit her lip and looked at the image in one of the bowls that showed the two ships by the lake. There still seemed to be quite a few Has'pleen warriors on guard.

"How will we get to the ships? There are still too many guards," she said.

"I will try to aid you through my servants. But the Skar'ley priesthood are at my door as we speak. They will demand my help. My aid to you cannot be obvious and no larger creatures can assist you. Your primary aid will come from the one you brought with you."

"The one we brought with us?"

There was a rumble and grinding of stone as a doorway opened at the other end of the chamber. A gust of warm fetid air hit them and then something lumbered disoriented out into the chamber. It walked on all fours, but was twice the height of Elliot and Molly and powerfully built. Long white and grey fur covered a broad, tightly muscled body and powerful paws with long claws. The head was a mixture of fur and a hardened shell-like substance with a wide, tusked mouth. Two large and hairless drooping ears framed the broad face. But it was the eyes that made Elliot and Molly stagger backwards. Set deep in the craggy, shell-like skull, they were large and clear blue.

They were Billin's eyes.

"Billin!" exclaimed Elliot. "It's Billin! It's you, Billin, isn't it?"

But the large beast looked down at them with no sign of recollection in the large blue eyes. Instead it shuffled its feet and made a deep grumbling noise.

"Oh, what has he done to you?" whispered Molly and reached out a hand to touch the strangely warped Billin.

The creature sniffed at her hand and then closed its eyes when her hand carefully stroked his fur. It began to purr.

"What have you done to him?" Molly shouted angrily to the chamber.

"I have altered him in the Flesh Forge and given him a new, improved shell. I have brought to the surface powerful and beneficial physical attributes from the hidden history of his race which I found deep inside him. There was a reasonable amount left of him when my servants wrested him from the snaarrks, so I had plenty to work with."

"But why? Why have you done this… terrible thing?"

"So that he can aid your escape. He has a chance against the snaarrks and the Has'pleen, which you must fight without my further aid. His former shell was weak and of no use. You should be grateful that I restored him and brought him back to life."

"It was you that killed him in the first place. It's not more than right that you… restored him. But you can't just change him. It's wrong," continued Molly furiously. She could feel with every fibre in her body that this was somehow a terrible crime against nature.

"And he doesn't recognise us. Has he lost his intelligence?" asked Elliot.

"The trauma of being re-spawned leads to primal and instinctual behaviour activating first.

After a while his brain should return to its normal functions."

"How long?" Elliot asked.

"Months… maybe years."

"But… will he always look like this?" asked Molly.

"Yes. Why should he not? His former shell was weak and of no use."

"But I'm pretty sure he liked that shell. I'm pretty sure he would rather have that back," said Elliot.

"It was not his decision to make. I have decided it for him. As he was dead, he was in no position to choose."

"But it's wrong," repeated Elliot.

"It is incorrect to label the world and one's actions as right and wrong. This is only a matter of perspective," replied the Flesh Smith. "We should improve you as well," it continued. "Your small frames have no chance against the Has'pleen and their robots. I know there are many primal natural weapons I can bring to the surface in your bodies. With the Flesh Forge and Bio-Welder I can also add other weapons which would give you the upper hand."

"You want to change *us*?" said Molly.

"In any way you desire."

"No thank you! We don't want to be changed into something unnatural, thank you very much!" protested Elliot.

Molly seemed to think it over for a while and then asked, "Can you make me a bit taller?"

"Molly! No! Don't let him do anything to us. It's wrong!"

"Okay!" sighed Molly and sulked.

Elliot once again turned to the bodiless Flesh Smith. It felt right to address the throne, so he did so.

"I have some conditions," he said boldly.

"You dare make demands to the An Barr? You dare tell me what to do in my own halls?"

The voice was much louder and angrier now. The bowls with the amber liquid trembled and the pillars seemed to shake. Dust fell from the ceiling. Even the great beast that had been Billin began to whimper in fright. Molly pushed herself against Billin's powerful new frame and glanced around her in fright.

Elliot swallowed hard and nodded.

"Yes I do." His body was tingling with fear now, no doubt brought on by the strange devices of the Flesh Smith. But despite his mounting fear, he continued. "I want you to make Billin normal again. We won't leave and we won't do whatever it is you're making us do, unless you change him back. I also want some kind of antidote or medicine for the people of Earth. So that they can get rid of these slave genes. I know you're up to something when helping us, but I don't care. As long as you give us this, we'll play along."

He just knew he was right. There was something else to the Flesh Smith's plan. He was using them somehow.

"Very well," the voice of the Flesh Smith boomed finally. "I will give you genome re-construction serums that will restore both this creature and your people to normal... within reasonable time. Within weeks of taking the serum, your companion should be restored. For the humans the process will be much swifter. I give this to you because your survival and the spread of the seeds will guarantee the survival of the An Barr. Never forget this favour I grant you."

"I won't," Elliot promised.

"Then leave now. Leave this world and return to where you came from."

With those words another stone door opened with a grating sound. Beyond were stairs that led up. More of the green mist rolled down the oversized steps.

Elliot, Molly and the lumbering furry beast that had been Billin left the chamber with a last glance at the silent giant mummy in the stone chair. It felt like leaving a dread old tomb.

CHAPTER 5
FRIGHT, FIGHT AND FLIGHT

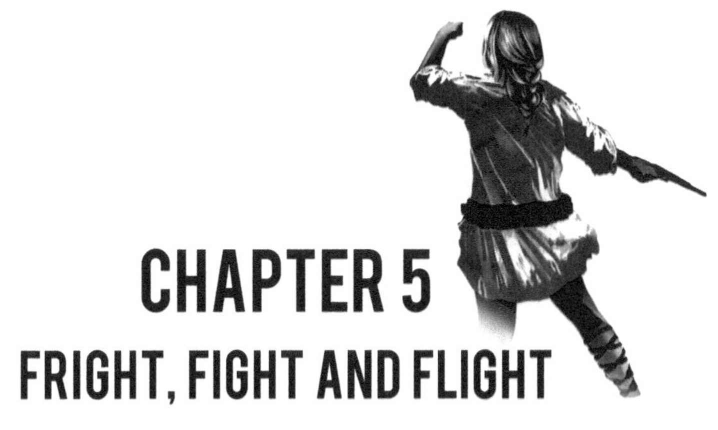

As they passed out through the tall stone door, leaving the strange Flesh Smith tomb behind, they felt a huge relief. Maybe this was hope returning, or simply the Flesh Smith manipulating their cellular and synaptic activity, it was hard to say.

Outside the tall stone door stood the small goblin-like creature with the large ears, big, tired eyes and sour mouth. Elliot wasn't sure if it was the same creature that had taken them to the chamber or another one just like it. It croaked "Follow!" and then began to lead them up the steps. The steps were so big that the creature climbed them using all fours. But it never stopped its pace or seemed to tire. On and on it led Elliot and Molly while the strange lights illuminated in mid-air above them. The Billin-creature was so large that it had no problems moving up the steps and often stopped to lend a furry paw to help Elliot and Molly if they were tired.

"Too bad," sighed Molly as they climbed. "I've always wanted to be taller. Like the Danaan sisters. Everybody always stared at them at the balls."

"I think you're fine the way you are," said Elliot.

"But I'm short and I'm freckled. I wish I was tall with raven dark hair and porcelain skin. That's what a princess should look like."

"Well, you don't look like that," Elliot continued. "You look much better the way you are now. I think you're very… very…" Elliot suddenly began to blush and quickly looked away. "…very tall enough… .okay."

"You do?" said Molly with a teasing smile, as she tried to meet Elliot's embarrassed gaze.

"Yes I do…" mumbled Elliot and focused on climbing the large steps.

After the large steps, their strange guide took them along several winding corridors which ended at a large stone door. At the door waited two more of the large-eared goblin-creatures. Both of them carried large leather satchels filled to the brim with something.

"Serum!" one of them croaked and handed them a satchel.

"Creator-Seeds!" the other croaked and handed them that satchel.

Elliot and Molly carefully took a satchel each. Molly took the one with the serum, and when she opened it, found several capsules which looked like large nuts made of amber. When she held one up to the hovering lights, she could see something that looked like tiny dust mites whizzing around inside. Elliot's satchel contained the strange Flesh Smith seeds. When he opened the satchel he found it filled with darkly coloured dry wooden sticks. The Billin-creature sniffed at the sticks and growled nervously.

"There, there!" said Molly and patted him on the back. "We don't like those seed things any more than you do." She then grabbed a serum-nut from her satchel and held it up to the Billin-creature. "We might as well start giving you your medicine right away."

The Billin-creature sniffed cautiously at the amber nut. Then, with a quick flick of its long tongue, it licked it from Molly's hand and swallowed it.

"Good! You understand what I'm saying," said Molly happily. "Did you see that Elliot? He understands us."

"Snaarrks wait. Beyond is tunnel," their strange guide suddenly said, before Elliot could reply. The large stone door he had taken them to then began to open with a deafening grating of stone against stone. It was a similar door to the one Elliot, Molly and Little Brother had entered when they first were let into the halls of the Flesh Smith. Several blocks twisted and turned in a complex pattern of unlocking, revealing a growing opening.

"What? Snaarrks? Are there snaarrks? What tunnel?" asked Elliot and Molly. But the goblin-creatures ignored them and turned away. The terrible stench of the snaarrks soon wafted in through the opening doorway. The Billin-creature began to growl loudly. Its fur bristled and the large blue eyes narrowed as it bent its head.

Molly clung on to Elliot while trying to penetrate the gloom beyond. All they could see was something which looked like a great unlit natural cavern.

"I hope the An Barr knows what he's doing," said Little Brother, as they carefully stepped through. "None of you have any stunners left, or any other weapons. If there are snaarrks here, we're doomed."

As an answer to Little Brother's question, the complex stone doorway began to twist and turn, closing behind them with a grinding noise. With a last thump, the pieces fell into place and formed a seemingly seamless large stone orb in the cavern wall. Darkness enveloped them. There was silence for a while. All that was heard was the nervous breathing of Elliot, Molly and the Billin-creature. Then, Little Brother protruded his small light rod and the cavern was soon bathed in light. At least three natural tunnels between mighty stalagmites and stalactites exited the cavern. In the much stronger light they could also see that the cavern was littered with bones from all kinds of animals, both small and large.

"This doesn't look good," Molly pointed out.

As an answer to her voice, a sudden growl was heard. An ugly head with stringy black hair slowly emerged from one of the tunnels. Its two big mandibles clacked together menacingly as it studied its prey with its bottomless black eyes.

The Billin-creature returned the growl and rolled back its thick lips to reveal the full length of his tusks.

"Let's get out of here!" whispered Molly and began shoving Elliot out of the cavern towards one of the other tunnels. But then another growl was heard, followed by a third. Soon the whole cavern echoed with the growls and snarls of snaarrks that began to file into the chamber from all the tunnels. There was nowhere to run and nowhere to hide. They found themselves once more pressed up against a stone orb door surrounded by drooling, bloodthirsty snaarrks.

The snaarrk closest to them licked his large mandibles with a long red tongue and pounced at them. But in mid-air the snaarrk was hit straight on the snout by the mighty paw of the Billin-creature. It crumpled up with a yelp and fell lifeless to the ground. The Billin-creature had reacted out of instinct and had saved Molly from the first attack. It now stood between the human children and the snaarrks. With more growls and snarls, the other snaarrks threw themselves at the Billin-creature. It staggered around, trying to meet every snaarrk with its powerful claws, but they were too fast and too many. They clung on to the back and neck of the Billin-creature with their sharp claws and slashed and bit at it. But its hide and fur was tough and thick and their claws and mandibles didn't have time to penetrate to the softer tissue underneath before the Billin-creature had torn them off and flung them across the cavern. Somewhere deep inside the brain of the terrified Billin-creature it suddenly remembered its last fight with the snaarrks. This time things were different however. This time, the Billin-creature was better prepared. A red rage awoke inside it.

With a roar of triumph the Billin-creature raised itself on two legs and swatted at the snaarrks with its large paws. With a snapping of bones and tendons, snaarrks began to fly through the air and hit the cavern walls with sickening thuds of broken flesh and bones. A couple more snaarrks tried to snap at the new and strange creature, but soon met the same end. The other snaarrks began to back away, yelping with fear of this new and fearsome creature. Only a large, ragged snaarrk still challenged the roaring Billin-creature. It was the old and scarred leader snaarrk with only one eye. Although it was nervous, it opened its cruel barbed mandibles wide and prepared to attack. The two creatures met on their hind legs in a deadly embrace. The snaarrk leader snapped and bit viciously at the face of the Billin-creature. It was evidently going for the eyes and tried desperately to puncture the crusty shell-like skin of the face. But the Billin-creature didn't let go. It slowly worked its powerful arms around the snaarrk and began to squeeze. The snaarrk's good eye opened wide in terror as it realised what was happening. With a yelp and a last wild struggle, it fought to get free of the Billin-creature's grip. Then, a loud crack was heard and the grim old snaarrk leader went limp.

With another roar, the Billin-creature hurled the dead snaarrk across the cavern and into the opposite wall. But the other snaarrks didn't back away. Instead they held their heads low, as if submitting to their new enemy. The Billin-creature continued to bellow and roar, but none of the snaarrks dared to challenge it. Then, as one, they snuck off into the gloom.

The Billin-creature stood swaying at the centre of the cavern. Elliot and Molly could see that it was wounded and tired. Blood gleamed in its fur.

"There, there!" said Molly, and approached it cautiously.

"Be careful!" hissed Elliot, who was too scared to get any closer to the enraged beast. But instead of attacking Molly or even roaring at her, the Billin-creature moaned sadly and bent his head so that she could pat him.

"There, there!" Molly said again. The breathing slowed and the Billin-creature seemed to calm down. Its large blue eyes gave them both a sad look and it moaned pitifully.

As the creature clearly presented no danger to them, Elliot and Little Brother approached it as well.

"There's some blood," said Molly, who was rummaging through the fur, "but the wounds don't seem very deep."

"Oh boy. You really kicked ass!" Elliot whooped. "Did you see those snaarrks flying? They squealed like pigs. They won't bother us again. You were great Billin!"

"Yes, yes," agreed Little Brother. "You definitely smacked predator bottom in the name of all herbivores!"

But the Billin-creature didn't say anything. He just moaned and looked at them with his large sad blue eyes.

"Come on!" said Molly after she had examined the Billin-creature's wounds. "We'd better find a way out of here."

As if it once again understood what Molly said, the Billin-creature sniffed the air and then began to lumber off into one of the corridors.

"I guess it's that way," said Molly and followed it.

Following the Billin-creature's nose proved to be the right decision. Within a couple of minutes of walking through the cavern system, they saw a light in the tunnel ahead. Soon they emerged in the blue sunlight of the Hollow World. All around them stood the high mushroom trees. When they looked behind them, they could see that they had exited from a similar overgrown stone slab that had been raised recently.

"So, where do we go now?" asked Elliot and looked expectantly at the Billin-creature. But the hairy brute just looked around with large bewildered eyes.

Suddenly the sun above them began to twinkle. As they looked up, a trail of large colourful butterflies descended from the mushroom caps. Their large shiny wings blotted out the sun as they trailed down towards them. Molly lifted up her hands and laughed as the butterflies passed around her. Even the Billin-creature seemed to enjoy the colourful display. The butterflies then continued off into the forest, like a long shiny tread of beads that twinkled in the sunlight.

"They want us to follow them!" Elliot said and pointed at the disappearing butterflies.

"Yes, it's the Flesh Smith. He's showing us the way," agreed Molly.

"Amazing! He must be controlling the synaptic activity of those creatures as well," said Little Brother admiringly.

Without hesitating further, the three of them set after the butterfly trail that passed between the tall mushroom trees. The butterflies flew so fast that they had to run to keep up. Without time to look where they were going, they rushed blindly through the silvery undergrowth.

After twenty minutes of running and jogging, the butterflies suddenly dispersed like an explosion. One second they had been a trail of closely linked butterflies, the next they fluttered off quickly in every direction. Elliot, Molly and the Billin-creature stopped in their tracks and watched the colourful insects disperse among the tall mushroom trees above them.

"Look!" said Elliot as he lowered his gaze again.

The butterflies had taken them back to the steaming lake. Right beside it stood the two small spaceships. Their Cro'lichks scout ship and the Has'pleen ship formed like an arrowhead. Here and there around the ship stood Has'pleen warrior priests on guard. Elliot and Molly quickly ducked down into the silvery undergrowth.

"It doesn't look good," Molly once again pointed out as they parted the undergrowth to get a better look.

"I count at least four guards," whispered Elliot worriedly. He examined the scene for a couple of minutes, watching the guards slowly patrol back and forth. They were heavily armoured and had long rifles. "Maybe we can sneak up to our ship when those two wander off behind those trees there?" he said after a while.

"Eh… Master Elliot! I'm sorry if I point this out," said Little Brother meekly. "But our ship can't be used to escape this world. The hull has been breached in several locations by the Hunter robots and my sensors pick up a lot of class four emergency alarms in the ship's computer systems and the ship's machinery."

"You mean the ship's worthless?" asked Elliot.

"Well… maybe not worthless… I mean… it would still be repairable or at least sellable if we had…"

"Yes, yes, but we don't have those possibilities right now, do we," hissed Molly.

"Yes… well… then I guess it's quite worthless."

"What about the Has'pleen ship?" asked Molly.

Elliot hadn't thought of that. He studied the enemy ship for a few seconds and bit his lip.

"I don't know. I mean… we don't know anything about that ship or what's in it. It's the most guarded ship of the two. Those Has'pleen priests have big armours and big guns. We just don't…"

"I don't think we need to discuss this any further," said Molly and pointed.

Elliot turned to the ships again and tried to see what Molly was pointing at. Then he saw. A large hulk of fur was sneaking up behind one of the guards.

"Oh no! That's Billin," he said. "I thought he was with us."

But the Billin-creature wasn't with them. It hadn't even stopped when the others had hid and surveyed the two ships. Instead it had followed some notion deep inside it and slowly made its way towards the ships. Despite its size, it was very good at moving silently. Those instincts ran deep. The armoured Has'pleen priest heard the undergrowth crackle just a fraction too late. Before he had time to turn around, the Billin-creature had risen on its hind legs and hit him squarely over the head. With his helmet pushed down over his face, the priest went down without a sound. The Billin-creature then ran off towards the next guard. This guard saw the furry giant coming and raised his rifle. But before he could squeeze off a shot, the Billin-creature rammed him hard and knocked him clean out of his boots.

"Come on! We have to help him!" shouted Molly, and ran towards the ship.

The other two guards must have been alerted somehow. They came running with their rifles ready. But as the first rounded the large landing struts of the ship, a large furry arm lashed out and hit him straight over the face. His feet continued running, while his head and brain were knocked viciously back and decided to call it a day and pass out. The other guard ducked and dove out of the way. He fired his rifle blindly at the Billin-creature but didn't manage to hit him as he tumbled to the ground. Laser fire from his rifle ricocheted off the ship's hull. The Billin-creature then tried to lunge at the prone Has'pleen priest, but came up against the nozzle of the laser rifle. A laser shot passed clean through the arm of the Billin-creature. It stopped in its track and screamed in pain. Clutching its badly damaged arm it staggered back, the large blue eyes open wide with fear as it realised just how deadly the laser rifle was. The Has'pleen priest quickly tried to scramble to his feet again and find his target. Elliot and Molly were now close enough to see the yellow reptilian eyes align the Billin-creature along his rifle's sight.

"No!" screamed Elliot at the top of his lungs as he sprinted forward.

Startled by the noise, the Has'pleen priest spun around and fired.

The laser shot went straight for Elliot's heart and struck true.

There was a loud buzzing and crackling of energy as Elliot's energy shield activated. A large force field blossomed around him as the laser energy reflected off in a million small rays of light and enveloped his energy shield. The force of the blast knocked Elliot off his feet and threw him hard on the ground some three metres away.

The brief distraction was all the Billin-creature needed. It lunged forward and bashed the Has'pleen priest with his uninjured paw. The priest folded around the mighty paw of the Billin-creature and was sent flying hard into the hull of the ship with a bang. He fell lifeless to the ground.

With a roar of defiance, the Billin-creature then ran on towards the open hatch into the ship.

Molly ran to Elliot and helped him up. Although Elliot was smoking and disoriented, he was unharmed. His ears rang, his eyebrows were singed and his bottom hurt from the fall. It felt like he'd been subjected to sudden and very intense sunburn, itching all over his face and arms. The energy shield had saved him.

"What? ... What? ... What? happened?" asked Little Brother meekly, where he lay on the ground next to Elliot. His tentacles were splayed in every direction and twitched weakly. He had fallen off Elliot's back in the blast. "I must have re-booted. That energy surge came out of nowhere." With half-limp and trembling tentacles, Little Brother reached up to Elliot and attached himself like a backpack again.

Back on his feet, Elliot could now see the Billin-creature running up the ramp and into the ship.

"N-n-no. Be careful! There could be more of them in the…" began Elliot.

A loud thump was heard. Then a Has'pleen battle helmet rolled down the ramp.

"I think it's too late for that," said Molly with a cruel smile. "No use feeling sorry for them. Those Scalies had it coming."

She helped the dizzy and singed Elliot up the ramp to the hatch and looked inside. Beyond the unconscious body of a Has'pleen priest was a corridor connected to two compartments in either direction. As they stuck their heads into the corridor, they heard great commotion from one of the compartments. An armoured Has'pleen priest flew across the doorway to the compartment and crashed into something. The Billin-creature then came racing out of that compartment and shot past them into the other compartment. As it stormed in, screams and general commotion were heard from this compartment as well.

"We better check that he doesn't kill anyone," said Molly and let go of Elliot who stood swaying at the hatch. His ears were still ringing from the laser blast and his clothes were still smouldering. Following Molly unsteadily, he entered the compartment just in time to see her trying to calm the Billin-creature which stood over two unarmed Has'pleen priests. The uninjured paw was raised, ready to strike.

"No! No!" said Molly calmly to the Billin-creature and clung to its arm. The two priests cowered in a corner, one of them trying to protect the other.

"No! They're unarmed! Leave them alone! They can't harm us," said Molly, pulling at the huge furry beast. With a last growl and a moan, it backed away from the priests.

When the Billin-creature was gone, Elliot could see that the two priests were very old and wore no armour or weapons like the others. But they were definitely Skar'ley who had undergone the Has'pleen ritual. Their scaly skin was yellow instead of green, but the skin was extremely wrinkled and they had large darkly coloured bags under their eyes. Both seemed worn and tired, their clothing dirty, patched and in generally bad condition. Despite his more bent and bulkier Has'pleen frame, one priest seemed very weak and frail, with a large stained headpiece which provided him with the ever-important Skar'ley crest. The other was shorter and even stockier, but lacked the impressive headpiece. Despite his Has'pleen changes, Elliot recognised this latter priest as a member of the servitor sub-species of the Skar'ley. He had seen them pampering their Masters both on The Knot and at the Galactic Olympics. The shorter and stockier servitor priest was evidently protecting the other, as he held him behind him. When he looked down at their feet, Elliot saw that they were both shackled to the ship.

"Here! Take one of these," said Molly and shoved one of the long laser rifles in Elliot's arms. "Just point it at them and press the trigger if they move," she explained. She then turned and took the Billin-creature's huge hand in hers.

"There doesn't seem to be anybody else on the ship," continued Molly. "I'll go and see if I can close the hatch and find something to bandage Billin with." Elliot nodded, while keeping his eyes on the two old priests. Molly led the whimpering hairy beast out of the compartments to find the hatch closing mechanism.

"Who are you?" Elliot asked the priests. He didn't like having a deadly weapon aimed at someone, so he kept the muzzle pointing up, but stepped away to a safer distance, just in case.

The stockier priest looked up at him tiredly and answered, "I am Sauma, servitor and brother of Sauma'tesh here." His voice was hoarse and strained, sounding even nastier than the otherwise quietly hissing Skar'ley.

"You're…"

"Brothers, yes," completed the Skar'ley with that irritating Leap-Thinking swiftness. Elliot was a bit confounded as they didn't look very alike, and began to ask his next question when the old servitor continued.

"We are blood-kin, born from the same clutch of eggs, but separated by bio-caste. That is why we look different to you. We are no longer Amha, Priests of the Eternal Sun, but should enjoy their honorary protection and respect as Voluntary Outcasts."

"I'm sorry, but I don't understand what you mean," said Elliot. "Are you, or are you not, priests?"

"Not any more. My brother and Master, Sauma'tesh, was once a priest of Vaush'ke rank. He was charged with overseeing and monitoring the activity of the Flesh Smiths on this world. Now his mind is broken."

Elliot looked at the other priest who stared emptily in front of him.

"What do you mean broken?" Elliot asked.

"Broken by the power of the Synaptic Erosion Gun," answered the stocky servitor grimly.

"The…?" began Elliot.

"What is a Synaptic Erosion Gun? It's a new weapon we use against traitors or those who have discovered our secrets. It causes the synaptic receptors to shut down or something, disabling proper connections between various parts of the brain. I don't know exactly how it works, but the victims lose most of their memories and therefore also much of their personalities. Their minds are broken and their memories scattered."

"Their memories scattered!" Elliot murmured with sudden insight.

The Skar'ley servitor looked seriously at him with his yellow eyes "You have seen its effect before, haven't you? Someone close to you? But you didn't understand what caused the sad degeneration?"

"Yes," replied Elliot angrily. "I bet that gun was used on poor Aunt Kaitrinn. She and Uncle Karl found out about you, and your friends destroyed her mind."

Elliot could feel real hatred for the Skar'ley priesthood welling up inside him. They destroyed people's minds at whim.

"I know nothing of this Kaitrinn you speak of. I'm sorry for her sake."

"Is there any way to cure this? Can the memories be restored?" Elliot demanded to know. To emphasise his question, he levelled the laser rifle at the stocky priest. He hoped it looked intimidating.

The old servitor sighed. "I'm not sure. But I have heard that the only one able to reverse the effect of the Synaptic Erosion Gun is the weapon smith that made the weapon. He, however, took the secret with him when he was sent to an asylum for the mentally ill. I hope a cure exists, though, and would wish nothing for myself but to see my brother's mind whole again."

"I don't know if you deserve it," mumbled Elliot. He felt really angry again. Someone *had* destroyed Aunt Kaitrinn's mind. He swore that he would do anything to help her restore it.

From the corridor, Elliot heard a loud whirring as the ramp retracted and the hatch locked. Molly had finally managed to close the ship. But Elliot was intrigued by the two priests. He felt there was something in their story he needed to know more about.

"Who did this to your brother?" Elliot asked.

"His rival, another Vaush'ke called Skauda'tesh. He broke his mind with the Synaptic Erosion Gun and left him here to serve out his days on this dismal world."

"Skauda'tesh?" said Elliot thoughtfully. "I recognise that name. Isn't that the High Priest? I met him on Centus Prime." With sudden realisation, he added, "That slimy toad was on board our ship as well, when it was attacked in the Dead Worlds Cluster. He was the traitor!"

"Yes, Skauda'tesh is High Priest now, but once he and Sauma'tesh were rivals for that position. Until Skauda'tesh betrayed my Master."

"But how can they have been rivals. I thought Has'pleen priests like you weren't allowed in the Empire? People would recognise you."

"The Flesh Smith alters our outside appearance of course," said the servitor and shrugged. "That way the righteous – those who suffer physical ostracism for the good of the Empire – can return to lead our people."

"Of course, the Flesh Smith altered your appearance," moaned Elliot. "That explains why you priests have managed to conspire against your people. Has'pleen disguised as normal Skar'ley. You could be anywhere. Even the Emperor could be one of you."

"I'm afraid our beloved Emperor isn't one of us. He is weak and has been misled and used by Outsiders. He will die shortly."

"When? When are you going to kill him?" asked Elliot. "You'd better answer or… I'll shoot you." He knew the threat hadn't sounded very good, but did his best to look grim.

The old priest looked him up and down a couple of times before he sighed and answered.

"I do not surely know. But I heard the other priests saying that they had to hurry in order to be ready with something for the Massikita Victory Memorial Day. Maybe it is then that our Empire will turn its full attention to the Eternal Sun and rid itself of weak aristocrats?"

They're going to assassinate the Emperor on the Massikita Victory Memorial Day, thought Elliot and shuddered. Molly and he were supposed to attend those festivities. Taking into consideration the time they had been gone since that attack in the Dead Worlds Cluster, it must be time for that Memorial Day any day now.

"Who will kill him? Skauda'tesh?" asked Elliot.

"I do not know. Even my Master did not know. It will certainly not be Skauda'tesh. He is too important for a simple assassination. Anyway, anybody killing an Emperor will be executed. But I know it will be somebody very close to the Emperor. Somebody he trusts. '*Toothless will be fanged when the moment is right*' it has been said."

Who then? Some servant or servitor who is a disguised Has'pleen priest? Elliot wondered.

His thoughts were interrupted by a howl of pain from the Billin-creature in the other compartment.

"It's okay! I'm just cleaning his wound," shouted Molly reassuringly. "Now, be still, you big baby!"

The Billin-creature whimpered sadly as Molly continued the treatment.

***

Outside the ship, one of the badly battered Has'pleen guards awoke with a hiss and a groan. The world spun terribly and he could see his comrade lying prone some metres away. What was that furry thing that had pummelled him? Had anyone taken the registration number? Although it was hard to focus on anything, he could see that the boarding ramp to the ship had been retracted. Without trying to move too much – as his head hurt incredibly – the Has'pleen guard pressed the emergency button on his wrist communicator unit. He then slumped down again and decided to rest some more.

***

In the ship, Elliot continued to interrogate the two Has'pleen priests.

"Why are you tied up?" he asked and pointed at the shackles around their feet.

"We lived here in squalor. Barely surviving," the servitor explained. "I don't know if Skauda'tesh finally decided to kill my Master instead of keeping us here, because suddenly these priests dropped down from the sky and seized us. They bound us and brought us here together with other prisoners."

"What other prisoners?" asked Elliot, standing to attention.

"Those prisoners," said the servitor and pointed to a high and thin cupboard door.

Elliot took a step towards the door, while glancing sideways at the priest. Was the priest trying something? Was it a trap? The door had a kind of latch with the sign '*Pull Here to Open*'. Elliot did what it said and was immediately surprised to find the whole door and a large section behind it jumping out at him with a loud hiss. Shivering cold mist rolled out and engulfed him. He jumped back with his rifle ready, in case the old priest would try something in the confusion.

But he didn't. He just sat there protecting his brother.

When the cold mist settled, Elliot could see something that looked like freely hanging shelves which had extracted from the wall. On the shelves sat three white figures. It was Tavvin, Captain Destroyer and his co-pilot. They were frozen solid, their bodies entirely white. Tavvin's fur was a fluffy ball of ice, while the long, hooked noses of the Cro'lichks had long icicles hanging from them.

At that moment, Molly burst into the compartment.

"Come on! I've found the cockpit. It was higher up," Molly said. She then noticed the three frozen figures on the large retractable shelf.

"Oh… you've found the others. They don't look too chewed on by snaarks, so I guess they must've been captured. At least they're in one piece."

"But… what have they done to them? Are they alive?"

"Of course they are. They've just been frozen to make transportation easier. The Cruelies probably caused a lot of problems, so they had to freeze them."

"But… can we… thaw them, or something?"

"No! We'd better not," said Molly gravely and shook her head. "We need the right equipment for that or they could suffer Severe Thawing Syndrome. It's very painful I've heard. Pop them back into the freezer and come with me to the cockpit. It's time we got out of here."

Elliot did as she said. But as he closed the door to the compartment, the old servitor priest looked up and met Elliot's eyes. His yellow reptilian eyes were unnerving. "What do you intend to do to us now, human?" he asked.

Elliot didn't know. Instead he just closed and locked the door.

He followed Molly up the corridor and noticed that Molly and the Billin-creature had tossed the other unconscious Has'pleen warrior priests out of the ship. This was good, as they could wake up at any moment and attack them. Molly led him towards a shaft with a ladder at the other end. He assumed this led to the cockpit.

Along the side of the corridor were opened hatches to small compartments. Each compartment had a strange spike in it with the text *'Please Don't Overcharge. 10 Standard Hours Maximum'.*

"What's that?" he asked and pointed.

"I think that's the transportation and charging bays of the Hunter robots," answered Molly as she began to climb the ladder to the cockpit.

"One, two, three… twenty. There are twenty of those charging bays. That means twenty Hunter robots. I don't like this."

"Neither do I," replied Molly. "That's why we have to get out of here."

When Elliot climbed into the small cockpit he found three seats in front of complicated instruments, such as buttons, levers and small screens.

"Eh… I don't mean to…" began Little Brother.

"What now!?" said Molly irritated.

"Eh… well, Your Highness, we don't really have any pilots. None of us can pilot a spaceship."

Elliot and Molly looked at each other. They hadn't really thought about that before. Getting a ship had been the main priority.

"But… can't *you* pilot the ship, Little Brother?" Elliot wondered.

"Me? No! I mean… I'm not a pilot. Big Brother was. I'm not good enough," complained Little Brother meekly.

"But surely you must be able to pilot a small ship like this? You must have that knowledge somewhere in your databank," said Molly.

"Ehh… I… well… I mean… No! I'm just not cut out to be a pilot, Your Highness," moaned Little Brother.

"But you must have helped or at least learnt something from Big Brother," said Elliot.

"Maybe I did learn a little when serving with Big Brother, but he was always the better pilot. I mostly took care of landing gear, non-smoking lights and the auto ashtrays."

"I *know* you can fly this ship," said Elliot resolutely. "I just know you can."

"We don't have much time to decide if you can fly this or not," said Molly and pointed out of the main view port.

Outside they could see several Has'pleen priests and Hunter robots approaching the ship. One of the Has'pleen priests with a big helmet pointed a small device at the ship. The ship bleeped twice and flashed its lights, then the hatch began to open.

"No you don't!" said Molly and pressed the button '*Lock All Hatches*'. The ship bleeped again, flashed its lights and closed the hatch. The Has'pleen pilot looked surprised but pressed his device again. Once again the ship bleeped, flashed and began to open. Molly immediately locked it again.

"You'd better hurry up!" shouted Molly. "I don't know how much longer I can keep this up."

Elliot took Little Brother from his back and thrust him into one of the seats.

"You *can* do this!" he said. "I know you can. You're just as good as Big Brother. Better even."

"No – *sob* – I'm not. I'm just a Stage Ten Artificial Intelligence. I'm not good enough!"

"Yes you are. You *are* good enough. You've proved it by helping us this far. You flew that torpedo, didn't you?"

"Well… I did pilot that torpedo, yes. But – *sob* – look where that got us. I nearly crashed it."

Outside, the Has'pleen priests were getting anxious. They had found their comrades who had been knocked senseless by the Billin-creature. While Molly and the pilot continued to fight over the ship control by opening and closing the hatch, the other priests ordered the Hunter robots to attack.

"Come on, Little Brother!" shouted Molly a bit more angrily.

"Come on!" pepped Elliot. "You can do it!"

"No! I'm useless – <u>*sob*</u>. I'll get us all killed!"

"No, you're *not* useless. You can do this. Just try!"

"But you'll get angry with me when I crash it. Then I've doomed us all."

"No! I won't get angry. Then at least you tried. I won't get angry. We're friends, aren't we?"

"Really? Do you mean that, Master Elliot? Because that means a lot to me. I know those tentacles kind of freaked you out and…"

"Get this piece of junk flying, NOW!" yelled Molly using all her regal training in ordering and intimidation. With her stern voice, her blazing eyes and red face, she interrupted the tender moment.

Laser shots could now be heard ringing off the hull. Drills from the Hunter robots reverberated throughout the ship. Molly furiously hit the '*Lock All Hatches*' button again and found that it stuck in the down position. She turned to Little Brother again.

"If you don't fly this ship, I'll have you converted to a Toilet Seat Wiper Droid!" she yelled.

Shocked into action by the angry princess, Little Brother extended his metal tentacles. Like a giant spider he rose from the seat and bent over the controls.

"Okay, I'll do my best… don't blame me afterwards. Oh dear, the ship controls are locked."

"Can't you do something?" begged Elliot, hearing the Hunter robots pummelling the ship.

"Hmm… yes maybe…" Little Brother mumbled. With his metal tentacles, Little Brother ripped off some lower panels and twisted two wires together. They sparked a couple of times and then the controls lit up.

"Was that it?" exclaimed Elliot doubtfully.

"Yes. Nothing to it really!" mumbled Little Brother. "Yes, let's see… ..hmmm… shields to maximum… .main thrusters activated… pre-flight checklist okay… seatbelt lights on," continued Little Brother silently to himself.

With a loud whining noise the ship suddenly rose from the ground. Dust and torn silvery undergrowth billowed around the ship. Outside, the Has'pleen priest ran for cover as the ship lifted off the ground and turned on its thrusters.

The Hunter robots began to slide off the hull one by one, but some of them held on tight. Their job was to get into the ship and destroy the humans. They were not about to give up so easily. One of them noticed the open hatch and began to move towards it.

"Get us out of here!" shouted Molly.

With swift movements of the controls, Little Brother gained control over the ship. The main engines suddenly roared into life and the ship blasted away from the steaming lake and the angry Has'pleen warrior priests. Hunter robots flew off the ship to the left and to the right. They flailed angrily, with their tentacles in the air, and then dropped into the steaming lake with big splashes. As they were of metal, they sank as stones, their blue menacing eyes disappearing into the depths.

"Jihaaa!" shouted Elliot in triumph. "You did it!"

The ship streaked through the sky of the Hollow World, while Elliot and Molly jumped around the cockpit in a victory dance.

"Where do we go?" asked Little Brother, when their dance was over.

"Take us out of this place. Out of this world," replied Elliot.

"I would love to," acknowledged Little Brother, "but the main hatch is still open. We have to close it before we go anywhere."

"This stupid button has jammed," said Molly, who had been hammering at it during her duel with the Has'pleen pilot. "I'll go and close it manually."

"I'll go with you," said Elliot. "I need to check that our prisoners are bound properly."

The two of them climbed down the ladder from the cockpit. As soon as they came to the corridor which connected the two compartments, they heard the rushing wind blowing in through the open hatch. Moving towards the hatch and pushing against the rushing wind, they failed to notice the thing which hid in the Hunter robot charging bays.

Slowly and menacingly, steel tentacles wormed along the floor and walls behind them.

Molly grabbed the manual override handle she had used to close the hatch the first time and pulled it. Slowly the hatch began to close. The wind reached a whistling crescendo as the slit narrowed – then it shut with a clonk.

In the silence that followed, Elliot and Molly could clearly hear the ticking and whirring of cogs behind them. They both turned slowly, their spines and fingers electrified with adrenaline and fright. Behind them towered a Hunter robot. Like a great spider it had spread its tentacles over the corridor. The cold blue eyes studied them mercilessly.

"Ressissstance is uselessss – death issss inevitable," the Hunter robot hissed, its cold metallic voice echoing from inside its steel body. Steel pincers, drills and vibro-cutters rose to finish them.

Suddenly the blue eyes flickered and went out. Then the ropy body slowly began to fall apart, as each tentacle that had joined together to create its form untangled and fell individually to the floor. In less than three seconds the terrible Hunter robot had been reduced to a mass of lifeless steel tentacles lying in a bundle at their feet.

"Wha-what happened?" asked Elliot, backing away from the mass of steel tentacles on the floor.

"I shut down the robot's main processor core," said Little Brother over the ship's intercom system. "I'm connected to the entire ship and noticed the robot connecting to the core system when it entered. I thought I'd better shut it down before it did any damage. Was that okay?"

"More than okay!" whooped Molly. "You saved our lives. Thank you very much, Brother Squid. Now take us out of this place while we clean up this mess."

***

As they didn't trust the Hunter robot, they opened the hatch again and threw out every single metal tentacle. They fell gleaming through the sky towards the misty mushroom forest below. When this was done, they checked on the two old Has'pleen priests. The reptile aliens sat huddled together and were still securely shackled. In the other compartment sat the Billin-creature. It looked terrible. The long fur was stained with its own blood and that of snaarrks. One of its limbs had been perforated by the laser shot and Molly had bandaged it. Having found some food bars to eat, the Billin-creature sat in misery and ate. The large sad blue eyes studied them as they entered.

"You wait here, okay?" said Molly. "Here's plenty of food. If the priests over in that compartment try to escape, hit them over the head. Understood?"

The Billin-creature stared at Molly but didn't give any sign that it had understood. It simply continued to munch on its food bars.

"I hope he'll be alright," said Elliot as they left the Billin-creature. "I hope that serum capsule we gave him makes him return to normal again."

"I hope so too," agreed Molly. "I kind of liked that silly old Furry better the way he was."

***

On their way back to the cockpit, Elliot told Molly everything he had heard from their prisoners. She swore as she climbed into one of the seats.

"Those stinking priests! This is all their fault! We've been shot at, nearly cut to pieces, blown up, tortured and eaten because of them. Actually, we've crashed and even died because of them. Someone should really kick their arses. They deserve it."

"That's what the Hidden Watchers is trying to do," said Elliot. "The problem is that the Flesh Smith altered the Has'pleen so that they look like normal Skar'ley. But they're not friendly and peaceful like the Skar'ley, incapable of hurting their own people. Instead they're ruthless and remorseless Has'pleen who would gladly kill for their beliefs. They could be everywhere."

"We're passing the tunnel mine fields," Little Brother suddenly informed them. They had been so busy discussing the Skar'ley priests that they hadn't noticed the ancient Founder tunnels passing by outside the ship.

"Will the mines activate when we pass them?" asked Molly.

"No, Your Highness," replied Little Brother. "This ship has identification codes that will let us pass unharmed… I hope."

They held their breaths for a couple of minutes as the ship slowly passed the drifting mines. But nothing happened and they continued out through the tunnels. As soon as they exited the tunnel and saw the cratered lunar surface under the countless stars, Little Brother spoke again. "We have those large Has'pleen ships dead ahead in orbit around the moon."

On the screen they could see the three large ships which had been hiding in the gas planet's stormy atmosphere. Like huge hovering fortresses they hung low over the desolate moon's horizon. Around them circled six smaller ships. They were crescent-moon-shaped with protruding spikes and cannons. It was the frigates which had been searching for them when they first approached the planet.

"Does this thing have a stealth drive?" asked Elliot.

"No, Master Elliot. I'm afraid it doesn't."

"Well, then we'll have to do without it then."

"Don't fly towards those ships," said Molly.

"Okay, Your Highness. Where do I fly instead?"

"Just fly casually past them, kind of. Away from here anyway," Molly replied.

"Do you know where to find the *World Strangler*?" asked Elliot.

"I know which sector it is in and the general direction, yes."

"Then take us there," Elliot said and sat back.

But they hadn't flown more than a couple of minutes before a red light began to flash next to one of the screens.

"What's that?" Elliot asked anxiously and pointed at the light.

"The other ships are trying to hail us, Master Elliot," explained Little Brother.

"Don't answer them. Just keep flying away from here."

The red light continued to flash angrily for a minute or so.

"Master Elliot. I'm afraid that they will attack us if we don't identify ourselves," informed Little Brother.

"What can we tell them?" wondered Molly. "Can we fool them that we're one of them?"

"I'm afraid not," replied Little Brother. "They're transmitting a special code and if we don't reply with the proper password, they'll notice."

"Then we've got no choice but to run," said Molly bitterly. "Get us out of here at full speed."

***

The engines of the small arrowhead-shaped Skar'ley scout ship lit up as it accelerated away at full speed. The six frigates immediately set after it while the three larger ships slowly began to turn. The hunt was once again on.

***

"Can we contact any of the others?" asked Elliot while glancing nervously at the many ships hunting them. "I mean, can we contact the other scout ships or even the *World Strangler*?"

"Maybe, Master Elliot," answered Little Brother. "We could send out a focused distress signal beam towards the sector where the *World Strangler* is hiding. Hopefully the *World Strangler* or any of our other scout ships are close enough to pick it up. But by doing that there is a chance the Skar'ley ships will detect the signal. We might reveal the position of our friends."

"Do it anyway! It's our only chance. In any case, they need to know what we've found."

"Yes," agreed Molly. "Send that we're in trouble. We've found the Flesh Smith and are hunted by Has'pleen traitors… or something like that."

"Sending it right now," informed Little Brother.

After the distress signal was sent, Elliot and Molly sat nervously in their seats, watching the pursuing ships. Elliot tried not to count the many gun turrets and cannons, but still got to thirty-four in total.

"The frigates are faster than us, I'm afraid," Little Brother informed them after a while. "They're gaining on us."

A sudden flash outside rocked the ship and lit up more angrily flashing lights around the cockpit.

"Oh yes, and the larger ships are firing their meson cannons at us," Little Brother added.

"Are those cannons dangerous? I mean, can our shields take a hit?" wondered Molly.

"From a meson cannon? By the Great Programmers no! No ship this size could withstand a hit from a meson cannon. We'll be pulverised."

"Then get us out of here! Hide us! Do something!" yelled Elliot.

"But there's not really anywhere to go... except for that super-dense asteroid field," complained Little Brother.

On one of the screens, a large field of icy rocks came into view. Hundreds upon thousands of pieces of rocky and icy debris of all sizes, tumbled through space and stretched across the entire horizon of their view.

"The larger ships won't be able to manoeuvre in that asteroid field, will they?" noted Molly.

"Well, no, Your Highness. They would at least have to slow down considerably. But..."

"Good, let's get in there," Molly decided. "We should be able to find somewhere to hide amongst all those rocks."

"But..."

Another blast close by rocked the ship and made all the ship lights and circuitry flicker for a second.

"No buts, ifs or maybes! Take us there or we'll all die," snapped Molly.

"Well… as you wish, Your Highness," replied Little Brother obediently and changed course. Soon the asteroid field was all they could see on their screens. It was huge.

"Oh no, not again," groaned Elliot. "I hate asteroids!"

The small scout ship dove in amongst the rocky debris at full speed. The obstacle tracker screen highlighted all potentially dangerous asteroids in red. Suddenly the screen went entirely red with asteroids of all sizes. An alarm went off.

"What? How can there be so many of them?" shouted Molly. "They're everywhere!"

"That's what I tried to tell you, Your Highness," explained Little Brother politely. "This asteroid field is super dense. Also, much of the smaller debris is travelling at such high velocities that our shields will take considerable damage…"

"What? And you're telling us this now?" raged Molly.

An asteroid, the size of a continent, tumbled towards them. Little Brother swerved the ship away from it – only to find ten new, city-sized asteroids closing in from all directions. Several smaller pieces of debris zoomed towards them, or ricocheted off the larger asteroids. The obstacle tracker was going crazy with red dots of all sizes. Little Brother ducked, swerved and shot past the many asteroids which came hurtling at them. The black briefcase was lying flat, its metal tentacles moving frantically over the controls.

"This is insane!" screamed Elliot who was helping Little Brother fly the ship by the universal and involuntary ducking this way and that in his chair. "We're going to die if we stay here!"

Next to him, Molly was holding her hands over her eyes.

***

Close behind them, the frigates and the much larger mother ships slowed down and changed their course. They were not so foolish as to enter the super-dense asteroid field. Instead they flew along the fringes and tried to keep their scanners locked on the seemingly doomed scout ship they were hunting.

***

"The other ships haven't entered the asteroid field," informed Little Brother. "They most probably consider it far too dangerous to pursue us." Little Brother finished the sentence with some amazing flight acrobatics which barely, but just barely, saved them from crashing into a sudden swarm of smaller debris. Suddenly a huge asteroid, flanked by four large asteroids, appeared on the screen. As it allowed them no room to manoeuvre while going forwards, Little Brother tried to change his course one hundred and eighty degrees. The scout ship missed the huge asteroids, but found itself cornered by the other large asteroids closing in from above and below.

"Look out!" cried Elliot and Molly.

But it was too late. There was nowhere to go. Even Little Brother gave off a high-pitched electronic scream as the scout ship crashed into one of the smaller asteroids... and bounced off.

"Wha-what-what happened?" asked Elliot who had tumbled out of his seat. But nobody had time to answer him. The scout ship was now spinning out of control. After the initial hit it was ricocheted into another rock. They all braced for impact, but instead the ship bounced away softly again.

"What's going on?" shouted Molly, who had been tossed upside down in her seat. "How come we're bouncing off those asteroids?"

"I don't have the faintest idea, Your Highness," answered Little Brother, surprisingly disappointed. "We should all have been pulverised by now."

As a large asteroid tumbled past them, they could all see a large six-armed figure engraved in the rock. It had two of its arms raised in a rude greeting.

"Idagons!" said Molly and smiled. "The asteroids are fake. They're made of foam or something. They're harmless, but register as real asteroids on ship scanners."

"Idagons? Those six-armed and six-eyed aliens? The ones you call Idiots?" said Elliot. "But why would they do this?"

"Because they love pranks and practical jokes. They're Idiots. Just imagine a whole asteroid field which everybody is really scared of, but which is false. I bet they can even move it around and throw it in people's paths when they least expect it."

"But, what's it doing here? Isn't this Skar'ley space? An abandoned sector?"

"Maybe they've forgotten where they put it?" suggested Molly. "It would be just like the Idiots."

"But this is good news," mused Elliot. "The other ships haven't entered the asteroid field yet, have they?"

"No, Master Elliot. They're waiting just outside," answered Little Brother.

"Then slow down and find somewhere to hide us. This place is so big and full of asteroids that we should be able to hide for a while and then sneak away among the asteroids."

"Good thinking, Earth Boy," congratulated Molly. "That sounds like the best plan we've heard so far."

With only the steering thrusters activated, Little Brother slowed down to crawling pace and began putting asteroids between them and the ships waiting outside the asteroid field. Hopefully, their pursuers would lose track of them with their scanners. Now and then large asteroids bounced harmlessly off their hull. Moving carefully from asteroid to asteroid, they slowly moved away from the Has'pleen ships.

***

After a couple of minutes it became clear that the Has'pleen priests had noticed the Idagon prank. They also suspected that their prey was still alive and well and not pulverised by asteroids. The frigates and several small one-man fighters entered the fake asteroid field. Navigating slowly among the foam asteroids, they began searching for the hiding scout ship. Now and then their cannons would flare, and a foam asteroid would vanish.

***

Avoiding detection, Little Brother had hid them in a craggy crater on one of the foam asteroids for over two hours. Their sensors kept picking up faint echoes from the neutrino scans of the other vessels, so they knew they were still looking for them. They didn't dare to move in case they were detected. When looking out, all they could see was the endless vista of tumbling foam asteroids.

"This waiting is killing me," said Molly who was too nervous to even play with her PDM she was holding. "Why don't they give up?"

"They've got too much at stake to risk that we'll tell people about their secret conspiracy," said Elliot tiredly. He didn't know how many hours he'd been awake by now. "They'll never give up and they have all the time in their life."

"Well, we can wait as well," said Molly stubbornly and grabbed her PDM again.

"Ehm… I'm afraid that's not entirely accurate," said Little Brother carefully.

"Why not?" asked Molly and Elliot.

"Well, our air supply will run out in four days, six hours, twenty minutes and eight seconds," continued Little Brother. "And then it's going to be hard to be a human."

"Great!" snorted Molly and tapped angrily at her PDM.

Suddenly the proximity alarm began to flash. Another ship was nearby.

"Dousing all lights! Shutting down all non-essential systems!" announced Little Brother quickly and began to run his tentacles over the controls.

Soon the ship was dark, cold and silent, giving off only minimal energy readings.

In nervous silence they waited. Would they be detected?

A shadow crept over the edge of the ragged crater rim. They didn't dare use their sensor, but it was clearly another spaceship and they could all see the angular shape of the shadow. It flew in a slow zigzag pattern over the crater and then came to a standstill in front of them. Then, without warning, strong ship lights came on and bathed them in golden, but revealing light.

Their hunters had found them.

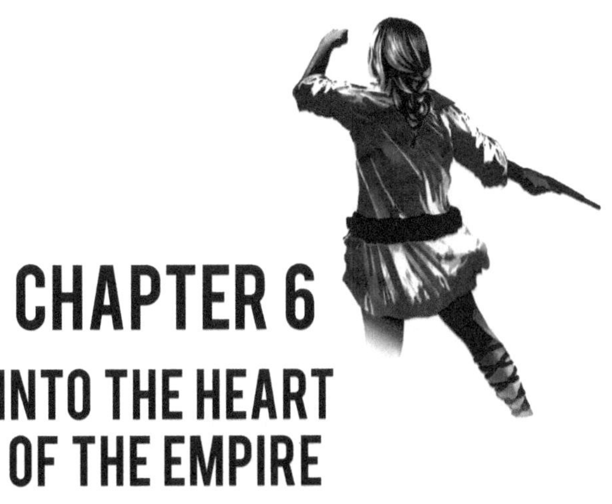

CHAPTER 6
INTO THE HEART OF THE EMPIRE

"They've found us!" Elliot called out in alarm. "Start up the ship! Get us out of here!"

"It's too late," whispered Molly. "We won't have time to go anywhere."

Elliot stared in disbelief at the strong lights in front of them. He slumped back into his seat. Was this it? Would they be killed and silenced for ever?

"The ship is hailing us," Little Brother said suddenly.

"Hailing us?" replied Elliot. He hadn't really expected the Has'pleen priests wanting to say anything to them before killing them.

"Well, put them on screen then," said Molly nervously.

Little Brother did as he was told. Immediately, an unexpected face was displayed on the screen. Large black almond-shaped eyes stared at them. A small mouth in an emotionless flat face opened to reveal short, pointed teeth. It was Sishra the Snakirra.

"Greetings, Younglings!" Sishra said in his hoarse whispering voice.

"Sishra!" exclaimed Elliot and jumped out of his seat. "Boy, are we glad to see you!"

"We are equally glad to have found you before the Skar'ley, Younglings," said Sishra. Behind Sishra they could see other Snakirra and some Sarapids.

"How did you find us?" asked Elliot.

"You were late for the rendezvous. As we had returned early, we were sent out to search for you in this sector. But no sooner had we arrived, we received your distress call. In stealth mode we saw this small Skar'ley ship being hunted and understood it was you. Very clever of you to notice that the asteroids were false and hide in them. How did you do that?"

"Well… we… I mean, we didn't know they were false until we hit one," informed Little Brother.

"You mean you actually tried to hide in a Class Eight asteroid field? By the Stars? I've never seen anything more brave… or stupid."

"Yes, it was stupid and dangerous…" admitted Little Brother shamefully.

"Well, we made it, didn't we?" snapped Molly. "And Little Brother here proved to be an excellent pilot. He saved our lives."

"So it seems," agreed Sishra thoughtfully. "We are all most fortunate to be alive. This false asteroid field is crawling with Skar'ley ships. Is it the Imperial Navy?"

"No, didn't you get our distress call?" said Molly mockingly. "It's Has'pleen ships. Religious fanatics. It's the Skar'ley priests who are behind everything. They're going to use humans from Earth as warrior slaves."

"The Skar'ley priesthood? Humans as slaves? That's impossible in the long run. They simply…"

"Look!" interrupted Elliot. "It's true. We heard it from the imprisoned last Flesh Smith. He's altered humans genetically, or something, so they must obey Has'pleen priests. They plan to kill the Emperor and conquer the Spiral Arm."

At first there was only silence from Sishra. Then he finally spoke.

"You *met* a Flesh Smith? You *spoke* to a Flesh Smith?" Sishra was evidently very upset and shocked by this, as he leaned closer to his com screen.

"Yes!" replied Elliot, Molly and Little Brother in unison.

"It told us about its part in the conspiracy and helped us flee," explained Molly.

"A Flesh Smith does nothing for free," Sishra noted grimly. "What price did you pay?" The Snakirra's black bottomless eyes filled the screen as it seemed to stare into their souls.

"We…" began Molly and looked to Elliot.

Elliot sighed. It was best to tell Sishra the truth. "We promised to help his people return one day by spreading some seeds." He lifted up the seed satchel and showed Sishra.

Sishra sucked in air and made a strange keening sound.

"You must destroy it immediately!" he ordered. "The Flesh Smiths must never be allowed to return!"

"But we gave the Flesh Smith our word," Elliot pointed out. "He saved us from the Has'pleen priests and it doesn't feel right to break our promise. He just wants his people back."

Sishra tilted his head and made a calming clicking sound. "I'm sorry! You are too young to understand the enormity of this. But the Flesh Smith has fooled you. That is his way. The Flesh Smith is extremely deceptive and dangerous. There is more to his help than this. History has shown that the An

Barr wax and wane as a civilization as they please, sometimes being reduced to just one single organism. Studies actually indicate that they most probably never have been a species at all – just one individual. This Flesh Smith doesn't miss its people and its absence from history, while being imprisoned by the Skar'ley, is nothing compared to earlier dormancies. What history also shows is that the An Barr *always* attempt to enslave, alter and dominate all other species around them – without exception. They spread terror as they alter the children of those they have conquered into terrible beasts of conquests. Entire worlds and their fauna are gruesomely reshaped to suit their whims. If they were allowed to return they… he… would try this again. We cannot risk that. Please, you must understand, Younglings."

Elliot and Molly nodded, thinking about how the Flesh Smith had altered poor peaceful Billin into a murderous and clawed beast. Staring with dread now at the seed satchel, they expected it to jump to life any second.

"Throw it out of the airlock," Sishra commanded. "We will destroy it with our precision lasers."

"Finally, some decent advice I recognise," muttered Molly and grabbed the satchel at arm's length. Elliot and Molly did as they were told, even though Elliot felt deep down that this was a betrayal of his promise.

Not long after the satchel was jettisoned into space, a brief stab of a laser from the other ship disintegrated it in an unremarkable flash.

"Now, Younglings, you must tell me all that happened during your encounter with the Flesh Smith," Sishra said over the screen. "Tell me about the altered humans and the assassination plans against the Emperor. Tell me everything. Somewhere there must be clues to how we should act to stop this threat and how we can find Elliot's missing uncle."

Taking turns, they began to tell Sishra about their amazing discovery of the Hollow World and the bodiless Flesh Smith. When they had told him all the details, including Elliot's suspicions that the Emperor was about to be assassinated on the Massikita Victory Memorial Day, there was silence.

"You have… uncovered much," Sishra said finally. "I am amazed at your resourcefulness… and your luck. What you have told me is grim news indeed. But all the pieces of the puzzles fall into place now. The secret asteroid ships headed for the Imperial Throne World belong to the Priesthood. As we speak, the Priesthood of the Eternal Sun is reshaping the Empire into a theocracy."

"Theocracies are dangerous," one of the Sarapids behind Sishra declared. "The judgement of a theocratic state is always clouded by religion. We must take care of these priests before…"

"A theocracy is not always an evil thing," interrupted Snakirra. "Remember the glorious and peaceful theocracy of the Furry Crabs of Gzarria. That theocracy worked. So much splendour, beauty and sculptured phlegm have not since been seen in the Spiral Arm. No, what we must do is uncover this plot and give the Emperor a chance to survive. But we are in haste. The Massikita Victory Memorial Day is only three days away."

"So let's go!" said Molly. "Let's get out of here and warn the Scalie Emperor."

"You forget, Little One," said Sishra, "that the ships of the Has'pleen are combing this false asteroid field for you.

Against their weapons and numbers your small ship stands no chance. Just by coming here we have probably doomed our ship as well."

"What about the *World Strangler*?" said Elliot. "Can't it help us?"

"Perhaps! It is a gruesome flying weapon monstrosity after all. But even if we managed to sneak out and send a signal, it would take the *World Strangler* too long to get here. While we, against all odds, manage to stay hidden until the *World Strangler* arrives, the plans of the priesthood will reach fruition."

"Then… what do we do?" wondered Elliot.

"Our course of action is obvious. One of us must distract the Skar'ley priests, so that the other can slip away and warn the Emperor."

There was silence as Sishra's words sunk in. One of them had to sacrifice themselves.

"Our ship is fastest and has the best pilots," Sishra said after a few seconds. "We should be able to survive long enough for you to slip away."

"But… but… you'll die," stuttered Elliot. "Your ship is still much smaller."

"Maybe we will. But if we can hold out long enough for you to get away, there is a chance this whole conspiracy can be neutralised. If our sacrifice can restore stability to the Spiral Arm and prevent a devastating war, we will be content."

Elliot and Molly said nothing. Instead they lowered their gazes, feeling only shock at Sishra's decision.

"Time is short," Sishra said again. "Just like you Elliot Stormsson, I fear that something will happen during the Massikita Victory Memorial Day. Therefore, when you are free of the asteroid field, you must set a course for the

Imperial Throne World of Sku'raan. Do not waste time by rendezvousing with the *World Strangler*. It won't be able to approach the Imperial Core Worlds as it's a Cro'lichks warship. Neither should you speak with the Imperial clerks and bureaucrats. They will waste your time. Go straight to the Emperor. It's imperative for the Skar'ley as well as the humans of Earth that you warn the Emperor in time."

Sishra was silent for a moment before he continued. "It's ironic that it all depends on you three now. You are neither great rulers nor agents of the Hidden Watchers. Yet succeed you must, for the good of the Spiral Arm. Do not fail."

"We won't!" mumbled Elliot. "We will warn the Emperor about those creepy priests. We even have some captive priests with us as evidence."

"Good! Go now and let us not linger any longer than we have already."

With those words Snakirra ended his communication. In front of them the Cro'lichks scout ship rose out of the asteroid crater with its thrusters flaring. It kept rising up amongst the fake asteroids until it could hardly be seen any more. Then suddenly, flares from multiple torpedoes could be seen firing in all directions. Sishra was firing on all the Has'pleen search ships.

It didn't take long before the asteroid field was lit by flashes from exploding torpedoes and stray laser shots. With the stealth drive, Sishra and his crew were appearing and disappearing, launching torpedoes as fast as he could.

"It's started!" said Little Brother. "I suggest we begin to find a way out of this false asteroid field immediately."

"Do it!" said Elliot. "Fly carefully and avoid the fighting ships."

Little Brother navigated carefully so as not to disturb any of the foam asteroids. Slowly they inched their way out of the false asteroid field. Behind them the combat continued. Thanks to the crowded asteroid field, Sishra and his crew were still alive. But the Has'pleen ships were heavily armoured and far too numerous. In addition to this, they were slowly learning how to find the faint signal of the cloaked ship. False asteroids bounced off ships or were evaporated easily by ship turrets, making larger and larger holes in the fake asteroid field. Keeping their prey within the circle of search ships, the Skar'ley priests began to close in. Hiding places became fewer and fewer for every destroyed foam asteroid. The outcome of the battle was unavoidable.

"The edge of the asteroid field is coming up," Little Brother notified them.

"Are there any ships outside which can detect us?" asked Molly.

"Not on this side," answered Little Brother. "I chose to exit here, as no ships should be able to detect us. My plan is to continue drifting away until we get to a distance where we can fire our main engines without being detected. Would that be okay?"

"Sounds like an excellent plan, Brother Squid," said Molly.

"Yes, it sounds good," agreed Elliot. "Just get us out of here."

The fighting in the asteroid field continued behind them. It was hard to follow the battle, as their ship was moving away and they didn't dare use any active ways of scanning. But as long as they saw flashes from detonating torpedoes, they knew Sishra and his crew were still alive.

But after a while no more flashes could be seen.

"I… I can't see any more detonations," said Molly solemnly. "It's over."

"Poor Sishra!" said Elliot quietly.

"I… think we're far enough away. I'm engaging the main engine," said Little Brother nervously.

The ship rumbled as the engines flared. Like a rocket, the captured Skar'ley scout ship shot away. Biting her lip nervously, Molly watched the scanners to see if they were being pursued. She could detect the three larger Has'pleen ships in the fake asteroid field, but none of them pursued them so far.

"They haven't noticed us… yet," Molly whispered.

Their breathing was all that could be heard in the cockpit as they stared at the scanner screens. Slowly the Has'pleen ships moved further and further away until they dropped off the screens totally.

"Phew!" said Elliot. "I think we've made it… so far."

"So it seems, Master Elliot," agreed Little Brother. "I'm plotting a course for Sku'raan now."

"How long until we reach Sku'raan?" asked Molly.

"Approximately three days, Your Highness," replied Little Brother.

"THREE DAYS!" exclaimed Elliot. "But that's too late. Sishra said the Massikita Victory Memorial Day was in three days. We won't be there in time to warn the Emperor. If he dies we have no chance of saving Uncle Karl and the Earth." Elliot could feel the panic growing in him. He felt that Uncle Karl, and maybe all humans of Earth, depended on him.

"I'm sorry, Master Elliot," Little Brother apologised. "This ship isn't very fast. Although it's equipped with an Otherdrive, it's an older model and not very large. But we'll arrive early in the morning and might still have a chance to make it before the ceremonies begin."

"Let's hope we have a chance. Let's hope we do," said Elliot and sat back heavily in his seat. He felt cold and nervous. Spending three days on this ship without knowing if they would make it in time would drive him crazy. The fate of Earth and humanity rested heavily on his shoulders. He closed his eyes to drive out the nagging fear that they were already too late.

With engines flaring, the captured scout ship inched towards the distant star which was the sun of the Sku'raan system. But to everybody on board, the journey seemed agonisingly slow.

***

A thousand engines were flaring in another part of the Skar'ley Empire. These engines belonged to heavily armed ships disguised as asteroids. Only the white-hot engines and a few spiky metal protrusions revealed that this swarm of space debris was in fact a swarm of ships. They had been built slowly and in secret. Patience had been in their making. But now time was short. Most of the ship's cannons, turrets and torpedo halls were unmanned and the barracks stood empty – but not for long. Their crew was being assembled and would join them before their baptism of fire. Taking a necessary risk, the asteroid ships were racing towards the Imperial Throne World.

Far behind the first swarm of a thousand ships flew another swarm. After this came a third. The secret shipyards of the Skar'ley Priesthood had not been idle.

Far, far away, but trailing alongside the three swarms of asteroids, was another ship. It was cloaked and invisible to the naked eye. Even its engine emissions and disturbance in the neutrino winds was masked. Its sleek, snaking form and normally uncloaked porcelain shine revealed it to be a Vurite warship. Although vastly outnumbered, the Vurite warship scanned and examined the distant asteroid ships and prepared for battle.

***

On the approach to the capital system of the ancient Skar'ley Empire, the stolen Has'pleen ship was hailed by deep space defence stations. But as automatic high-priority codes were programmed into the ship's computer, they were allowed to pass unhindered. Evidently, the priest conspirators could come and go to the Throne World as they wished. On one occasion, they could view one of these ancient but immense battle stations in their view screens. A huge spiked cannon with endless rows of missiles and long-range blaster turrets which floated silently in the dark abyss of space.

After three days of travelling, the captured Has'pleen scout ship entered the Sku'raan system. The distant star had now grown to a bright sun. Soon the throne world of Sku'raan itself came into view. The planet was immense, much larger than Earth or Centus Prime. Space was busy around the Skar'ley capital. Large ships and space stations were packed in orbit around the planet like wasps around sugar. Between them smaller ships whizzed to and fro. Below the glowing horizon of the atmosphere and the gentle clouds were huge continents of green, red and gold. Clear pinkly tinted oceans encircled the continents and several small islands ringed the coasts like jade-green necklaces.

A dry Skar'ley voice suddenly spoke over their communicator.

"Welcome to Sku'raan, oh servants of the Eternal Sun. You are free to dock in the Imperial City. We are transmitting coordinates and landing schedules. Activating your auto-docking program – now."

"We should tell them about the danger their Emperor is in right away," suggested Elliot, as the ship began to adjust its approach course automatically.

"I don't think it would do any good," replied Molly thoughtfully. "We won't be able to speak to him directly. We first have to go through his bureaucrats and convince them. They won't believe us. The Emperor is far too well guarded for them to believe that he's in danger."

"But they need to know about the priests and their conspiracy," protested Elliot. "Only the Emperor can help defeat them and find Uncle Karl."

"Remember what Sishra said. We shouldn't waste time with the Imperial clerks and bureaucrats. They're the same everywhere across the Spiral Arm. Ignorant, tiring individuals who are bored and ruled by inflexible regulations. My father always said that we should've put the bureaucrats out the airlock when we had the chance. In any case, we don't know who will hear our transmissions. For all we know the Priesthood or their spies might intercept the message and shoot us down. We have to be careful."

"Yeah... maybe you're right," said Elliot. "I guess we should try to tell the Emperor himself about the conspiracy. The priests we captured said that the assassin was someone close to the Emperor himself. We don't know who we can trust."

***

While the ship was being guided into an automatic docking approach to the capital city, Elliot, Molly and Little Brother began to prepare themselves. As the Billin-creature was too conspicuous to bring along, they gave it plenty of the tasteless Skar'ley food biscuits they all had been living on for the past three days. They told it to stay behind in the ship and guard the prisoners and their poor frozen comrades. During the three-day voyage the Billin-creature had changed slightly. The skin was saggy as if the frame had somehow shrunk. The claws had retracted and the paws began to look more and more like normal Furanian hands. Even the large blue eyes seemed to contain more intelligence. The creature seemed to understand its instructions and even nodded and patted Elliot and Molly on their shoulders in confirmation.

During the automatic descent through the atmosphere, the ship shuddered a few times and in the end fired its main thrusters as it set down in the primary spaceport. Then there was silence.

"That's it!" whooped Molly. "We're here. We're in the heart of the Empire."

"Good flying, Little Brother," commended Elliot and patted the black briefcase.

"Why, thank you, Master Elliot," Little Brother replied, flushing with a red diode. Little Brother then left the pilot's seat and re-attached himself onto Elliot's back.

"Now all we have to do is warn the Emperor," said Molly. "Do we still have time?"

"It is eleven fifteen in the morning, Your Highness," announced Little Brother. "The religious ceremonies are about to start, but the main memorial celebrations don't start until nightfall. That's when the Emperor addresses the people and the official victory is celebrated."

"Then we'd better hurry!" said Molly and opened the ship hatch.

As the hatch opened, warm and very moist air hit them, while sunlight found its way into the ship and blinded them for a moment. The sun was so bright they had to shield their eyes with their hands as they walked down the ramp. But as their eyes became adjusted to the light, both of them stopped in their tracks and stared in wonder at the capital city around them. Elliot had expected metal, concrete and glass skyscrapers of magnificent design stretching for the sky – like Azuria. But instead he found a mixture of stone and forest. The buildings of the Imperial City were made mainly of stone, some of them glistening like marble, others old, coarse and crumbling. Instead of sleek modern buildings, the city looked like a collection of ancient multi-storey temples, domes and pyramids. The greatest buildings had so many angles, different designs and varying signs of ageing that it looked like they had been built upon in several different stages. Between these immense stone temples were several canals and countless bridges. A myriad of small boats plied the canals or lay docked to small jetties. The canals themselves were full of something that looked like golden water lilies and long watergrass hung from the wooden jetties. Long hanging weeds, flowery bushes and silver trees with hanging orange fruit grew on terraces and rooftops or clung to the walls, giving the city a green and vibrant appearance. To Elliot it looked like old temple ruins of gargantuan proportions overgrown by jungle. But most amazing of all were the lone stone buildings which hovered freely in the air. Like upside-down pyramids or great stone needles, they hung over the other buildings like majestic stone ships. Here and there, floated large tree colonies and even small parks which were connected to the stone buildings with slender wooden bridges. Between the great jungle-clad stone houses, floating palaces and hovering gardens fluttered countless white-winged creatures which resembled graceful birds from a distance. Everywhere were the obvious signs of moisture. Weeds and lichen grew on every surface and the air stunk of rot and wet soil. Most likely the Skar'ley enjoyed this smell.

"This place is amazing!" gasped Elliot as he stared out over the ancient city.

"This place stinks!" said Molly and frowned.

"This place is full of music," said Little Brother.

"Music?"

"Yes. The air is full of signals and transmissions of all kinds. Complex algorithms, database files, nifty utility programs. This city is a paradise for Artificial Intelligences, such as myself."

"Well, that's great, I guess. But we have to stay focused on what we have to do," said Molly.

A hundred metres or so away from their ship, a workforce of Skar'ley were inspecting and repairing the spaceship parked next to them. Several of the smaller and stockier Skar'ley servitors wielded tools or manoeuvred spare parts into the interior of the ship. Their yellow eyes were focused on their tasks and their green scaly skin covered in oil and dirt. Engineers or work overseers were of the taller and more slender kind of Skar'ley that had large headpieces in the form of crests. They studied blueprints and small handheld computers while directing the work. None of them paid the trio any attention. In other docking bays, they could see six-armed Idagons, hardworking Grunans with long red hair, fair Vurites and even S'margs. In front of a ship, three docking bays away from them, Elliot could see the red robes of Skar'ley priests. He wondered if these were Has'pleen cultists and shuddered at the prospect of them noticing their ship and capturing them.

"We have to warn the Emperor as quickly as we can," said Elliot and turned his back on the priests. "Where can we find him?"

"Wait. I'll access the city map and services database," said Little Brother. He was silent for 1.6 milliseconds, then said, "The Imperial Palace is down the main spaceport road eighteen kilometres and to the left."

"That didn't sound too hard," said Molly.

"Eighteen kilometres!" said Elliot. "How big *is* this city?"

"The Imperial City of Ash'vaar is very, very big, Master Elliot," replied Little Brother.

"Okay, let's go," said Molly and began walking away from their neatly parked spaceship. "Let's get out of this spaceport and find ourselves some transport."

***

But after having walked more than half an hour, the trio hadn't even reached the perimeter of the large spaceport.

Ship upon ship stood parked in neat rows in the walled docking bays. They were of all kinds and from all species. The spaceport itself was busy with activity. Fuel transporters competed with passenger transporters and maintenance transporters on the narrow access ways. Passengers milled around together with ship crews and spaceport personnel. Engines roared from ships landing and taking off. Blast walls were raised and lowered to protect parked ships from arriving or departing ships. The trio therefore had to dodge and duck amongst all the machinery and spaceport personnel while making their way.

"This is hopeless," Elliot declared with an irritated voice, as two parked fuel transporters cut off their route. "We'll never make it to the palace in time. We're lost already."

"Yeah, I agree," said Molly. "This spaceport is just too big and too messy."

"And it's too warm and humid," complained Elliot, who was sweating just from the walk. His clothes felt sticky and far too warm for the climate, despite their inbuilt heat-regulating properties.

"That's how the Scalies like it," informed Molly. "Father said all their worlds were hot and wet or being terraformed to become hot and wet."

"It figures. They're lizards. Remember how Puad'kesh, the Skar'ley ambassador, always felt cold on board the *Warhammer*?" Elliot then nodded to Little Brother on his back. "Little Brother, can't we get some transport out of here?"

"Why of course, Master Elliot," replied Little Brother. "I will call them immediately."

No sooner had Little Brother spoken when a small flying car came swishing low over the ground towards them.

As it landed next to them a green Skar'ley driver gave them a bored look and asked them, "Where to strangers?"

"The Imperial Palace, and make it snappy," ordered Molly as she jumped in the back seat. Elliot followed her while the Skar'ley driver made a dry throaty sound.

"The Imperial Palace is off limits to air traffic as well as to aliens and normal citizens," declared the driver.

"But we have to talk to the Emperor," Elliot pointed out.

The Skar'ley driver made another throaty sound and glared at them with his reptilian eyes.

"Talk to the Emperor? The most holy and sacred person of the Skar'ley Empire? The Light Manifest of the Eternal Sun and the Father of Society?"

"Ehh… yes that seems to be him," said Elliot carefully.

"That's impossible!" snorted the driver. "Getting an audience with our beloved Emperor takes months – if you're admitted at all."

"We'll we've got really, really important news to give him," said Molly who knew exactly how to handle snotty taxi drivers. "So take us to the Palace Gates or wherever is closest and stop complaining."

The driver glared at Molly and ruffled its crested headpiece in irritation. "Very well, I can take you as far as the Weightless Fountains at the Plaza of Great Expectations. From there you'll have to walk."

The car then rose into the air and sped off towards the Imperial Palace. Recklessly and far too fast for Elliot's liking, the flying car criss-crossed between the big stone buildings. The flocks of white birds were all around them now and Elliot could see that they more resembled fish with four sets of long white scales for wings rather than traditional Earth birds.

Soon they could see where they were going. The entire stone city was built around the great palace grounds which were as big as a town itself. Ten broad pillars reaching far up into the clouds of the sky surrounded the steep palace hill. Canals and strange free-floating lakes surrounded the pyramid-shaped main buildings in the centre. The layered surfaces of the pyramids were covered in trees and bushes, giving them a truly forested appearance. Amongst all the green of the pyramid terraces jutted a myriad of balconies, small spires and complete buildings, making the palace a truly immense and gargantuan piece of architecture. In the air over it all, hung a great palace sphere of stone, riddled with windows and glazed balconies.

The flying car set down on a large plaza at the foot of one of the broad pillars reaching for heaven. One end of the plaza ended right at the foot of a broad flight of stone steps leading up to an immense portal of sculpted stone. Skar'ley palace guards in old ceremonial armour and power staves flanked every step up to the immense portal. They looked grim and determined to defend the Emperor at all costs. The centre of the plaza was dominated by a beautifully sculpted fountain in the shape of an animal, made of several interlinked pieces of crystal. Water ran over the glossy surface of the fountain and made it change colour constantly. The fountain bobbed slightly in the faint breeze and was, despite its mass and current location on a planet, weightless.

The plaza was full of Skar'ley wandering to and fro, or generally trying to sell something. There were also alien tourists, such as Idagons, Furanians, Vurites, Grunans and even elderly humans.

"Imperial Library and Mayizim Halls and Museum of Peculiar Sciences to the left," the driver announced tiredly. "Plaza of Great Expectations, the Floating Fountain and Fifth Gate to the Imperial Palace to the right."

As they prepared to leave the flying car, Molly turned around sharply to Little Brother who lounged innocently in the backseat. She glared at the black briefcase.

"Did you just show your software to that young on-board computer system?"

"No… why… yes, maybe!" said Little Brother, and seemed to shrink back further into the seat.

"We don't have time to show off to every little circuit board or mini-server we bump into," Molly said angrily. "We're on an important mission!"

"Yes, yes… I'm sorry, Your Highness," replied Little Brother sheepishly.

"Don't argue," Elliot interrupted. "Little Brother, just pay the taxi so we can get on with this. We don't have much time."

Diode-blushing with shame, Little Brother arranged some wireless payment while Elliot and Molly stepped out of the flying car. With his gaze, Elliot followed the endless pillar up into the clouds and found himself stumbling backwards from disorientation. As the car rose up into the sky again, Elliot and Molly began to make their way to the great portal which was the entrance to the Imperial Palace. Little Brother quietly attached himself to Elliot's back while enduring an indignant glare from Molly.

When they passed through the crowd milling around the base of the broad flight of steps, they began to attract attention to themselves. An elderly Atean couple stopped in mid-haggle with a vendor of doubtful antiquities and stared at the two children in disbelief. Several of the regal Skar'ley stopped what they were doing to watch the rare sight composed of two human children and an odd backpack making their way through the plaza. A group of Furanians stopped taking 3D photographs of themselves in front of the Imperial Palace portal and huddled together to discuss the human children agitatedly. The Idagons and Grunans, however, didn't seem to even notice Elliot and Molly.

The two of them ran up the broad flight of stone steps. The guards didn't move as the children drew closer to the immense portal. Instead they glared at them from under their ceremonial crested steel helmets. But as soon as Elliot and Molly had reached the summit of the stone steps they found their way barred. Ten palace guards positioned themselves in front of the portal and blocked their way. Behind them, and on the other side of the stone portal, Elliot could see beautiful gardens and something which looked like floating snake-like tendrils of water or small streams.

"Halt!" one of the palace guards roared. "Entrance to the Imperial Palace grounds is prohibited."

"But… but… we have to warn the Emperor," wheezed Elliot, who was tired and sweating from the quick climb up the many stone steps.

"Entrance is prohibited," the palace guard repeated.

"But it's an emergency!" cried Molly. "We have to warn the Emperor at once. Someone is trying to kill him."

"Entrance is prohibited!" the palace guard repeated doggedly.

"Can't you say anything else than 'entrance is prohibited'?" asked Molly angrily and tried to take a step around the palace guard.

"Halt! Entrance is prohibited!" repeated the palace guard and stepped in front of her. His crested helm gave him an impressive and aggressive appearance. The fact that he was also lowering his power staff towards Molly enhanced that impression.

"Aaahh!" screamed Molly in frustration and turned away. "They're as dumb as hover snails."

"Is there anyone we can speak to?" asked Elliot, trying to remain as polite as possible despite Molly's insults.

The palace guard looked him up and down a couple of times then pressed a series of buttons on his arm.

A couple of minutes passed.

People milled about down in the plaza behind them.

The palace guards glared hard at Elliot and Molly.

Molly glared back fiercely.

Elliot tried to smile politely.

Finally a figure approached the portal from inside the palace grounds and began climbing the steps on the other side. He was wearing long black robes and an impressive golden headpiece. When he reached the gate at the top, the palace guard who had summoned him nodded towards Elliot. The newcomer's yellow reptilian eyes focused on Elliot and seemed bewildered for a moment.

"I am Visa'taum, Gatekeeper of the Fifth Gate. None may pass into the Imperial Palace through this gate without my permission. Who are you? What are you? You look human, but seem too small."

"We're human children," answered Elliot politely. That's why we're so small. You might have heard about us?"

Visa'taum remained aloft and expressionless.

"No? Well, we're here to see the Emperor. We have to speak to him and…"

"See the Emperor? Impossible!" Visa'taum interrupted. "You will have to put your names to the Audience Master so that he can add you to the Audience List."

"How long will that take?" Elliot wondered, knowing that he wouldn't like the answer.

"About three to four years."

"THREE TO FOUR YEARS!" exclaimed Molly and rounded upon the Gatekeeper.

"Yes. The short waiting period is due to the fact that you are exotic human specimens and will receive some special attention," explained Visa'taum proudly.

"But three to four years is a *long* time," complained Elliot, while trying to push an angry Molly behind him. "We can't wait that long."

"Well, well. You'll just have to, won't you? We cannot rush the Waiting and Purification of Mind Ceremony now, can we? Everything has its time, hasn't it? To meet in person with the Most Holy and Beloved Emperor of the Skar'ley is a great honour and something that shouldn't be rushed into."

"Okay, okay. We understand that it's a great honour and all that," said Elliot, still maintaining his smile. "But we have to warn the Emperor. He's…"

"In danger?" added Visa'taum, displaying his ability to Leap Think.

"Yes, in danger. You all are."

"What type of danger?" Visa'taum demanded to know with a sceptical look.

"Somebody will probably try to assassinate the Emperor during the ceremony and festivities today."

"Somebody will *probably* assassinate the Emperor? Well, that's something new," said Visa'taum and rolled his yellow eyes. "And you *probably* know who this assassin would be? A Cro'lichks disguised as a chambermaid? A rabid Furanian armed with swords and axes? A ferocious death-defying Grunan?"

"Well… no… we don't know who it'll be. Only that it'll be somebody close to the Emperor," said Elliot who was giving up his polite smile.

"Listen!" said Molly and raised her finger menacingly. "Your priests are planning to kill the Emperor and wage war on the Spiral Arm, okay! Now *we* need to tell the Emperor about this."

Visa'taum made a strange gurgling sound at the back of his throat. Elliot suspected it was the Skar'ley equivalent of a laugh.

"The Priests of the Eternal Sun conspiring against the Emperor?" Visa'taum laughed. "I'm afraid that's impossible, little humans. The Priesthood would never, and could never, lift a hand against the Bearer of the Sun's Light. He is the spokesman of the Eternal Sun. It would be like cutting their own hearts out and abandoning their souls. No subject of the Empire would or could ever harm…"

"Yes, yes, we know all that," interrupted Elliot, who now wasn't smiling anymore. This Visa'taum fellow was getting on his nerves. Clearly there was no use talking to him.

"It would be better if we explained this to the Emperor himself. He would understand. We were invited to the Massikita Victory Memorial Day celebrations by the Emperor himself, you know. Just check it and let us in."

Visa'taum lifted his chin and looked down on them condescendingly. "I don't care if you were invited by the Eternal

Sun herself. There are no human children on the invitation list, so you cannot see the Emperor today. He is heading the Ceremonies right now and can under no circumstances be disturbed. And even if there would be a threat to our beloved Emperor's life – which I don't believe there is – I assure you he will be perfectly safe. The best warriors of the Empire guard his life with their own. The technology and the entire might of the Empire protects him. The Eternal Sun herself watches over him. I'm sure he will survive your fictional assassination quite well, thank you."

"But you're not listening, you dumb Scalie!" shouted Molly, who was now red in the face. "You're all in danger and if you don't do anything about it you'll all be sorry."

The commotion at the top of the stairs was drawing some attention. All the palace guards who were positioned on the steps below them were watching them carefully. From within the palace grounds strode a party of Skar'ley who wanted to see what was happening. Elliot could see that they wore the red capes with snake motifs, which were typical for the Priesthood of the Eternal Sun. The foremost of the priests wore a large golden headpiece in the shape of a radiant sun. In his hand he held a long staff shaped like a snake-like creature which held a sun between its fangs. From the dark stained scales around the priest's yellow eyes, Elliot recognised him as Skauda'tesh, the High Priest of the Priesthood. He was the mastermind behind the entire conspiracy. He had been aboard the *Warhammer* when it had been destroyed. Clearly he had escaped unharmed somehow. A shudder went down Elliot's spine. They were in real danger again. They couldn't stay here. If they were seen it would all be over. Panic grew inside him. They had to get away from the great steps to the Imperial Palace grounds as quickly as possible.

Molly, on the other hand, was vividly telling Visa'taum exactly what she thought about his silly procedures and stupid waiting list.

"Come on Molly!" hissed Elliot and dragged her away from the condescending Gatekeeper.

"No, no. Wait a minute. I'm not done with this Goloy-Brain!" Molly snapped angrily and tore herself free. She waved her finger at Visa'taum again and continued her lecture. "It's no wonder you're all a pack of stinking, lazy, no-good, skin shedding…"

"We have to go!" Elliot hissed again and pulled hard at Molly's arm.

"Ouch!" Molly said and turned her evil glare at Elliot.

But Elliot nodded at the approaching group of priests and continued to pull Molly away.

As soon as Molly saw the priests she turned away and ran after Elliot. As they half ran, half walked down the broad steps, Visa'taum stood and shook his head behind them.

"Alas, the youth of today. Restless, impatient, ignorant of proper ceremony and bad dressers. What will become of the Spiral Arm?"

Skauda'tesh and his priests came up alongside Visa'taum, who immediately fell to the ground and lowered his forehead.

"Why is there shouting at the Fifth Gate?" asked Skauda'tesh angrily. "And why is the Fifth Gate open? Did I not explain that it must remain shut during the Massikita Victory Day ceremony?"

"Why yes, Your Reverence," answered Visa'taum meekly.

"B-but by shut I-I-I thought you meant that nobody was allowed to enter."

"By shut I meant the gate closed and its Mega-Steel doors joined together to prevent entrance."

"Yes, yes, Your Reverence. B-b-but why must we close the Fifth Gate? We have not done this for over a hundred years."

"Times are changing and there is rumour of an alien threat. Close the gate."

Visa'taum felt his blood go colder. Had not the human children spoken about a threat? Could it be true after all?

"I will see to it at once," Visa'taum replied obediently.

As Visa'taum rose and ordered the Fifth Gate closed he turned to Skauda'tesh again. "Then the two little humans were right after all? There is a threat to the Emperor's life?"

Skauda'tesh spun around quickly and pressed his long staff under Visa'taum's chin.

"What little humans? Who said anything about the Emperor being in danger?"

"T-t-those humans!" stuttered Visa'taum and pointed down the broad steps towards the Plaza of Great Expectations. "T-t-they said they were c-c-children."

Skauda'tesh looked where Visa'taum pointed but could see nothing. The great steps were empty except for the lines of palace guards. Elliot and Molly had already reached the plaza and disappeared among the people milling around there. The High Priest scanned the plaza with his yellow eyes for a long time before turning back to the scared Gatekeeper.

"There is no threat to the Emperor's life," he said menacingly slow. "Nobody would dare to lay their hands on our beloved Emperor. The threat is from stupid Idagons who once again wish to disrupt our ancient and holy traditions with their pranks. They are ignorant and foolish, but must nonetheless be stopped from ruining this happiest of days. Forget about these human children and concentrate on the Idagons. Let not human trouble-makers disturb you in your duty."

"But should we not report the human children? I'm sure they're worth reporting. I have never heard of children among the Ateans."

"Yes, we must report this, my dear Gatekeeper," said Skauda'tesh and laid his arm around Visa'taum's shoulders. "The Fifth Gate is closing and your work here is done, for now. Come with me and we will report these troublemakers at once."

Under his red robes, Skauda'tesh fingered his Synaptic Erosion Gun just to check that it was there. Good! It would serve him well once again.

As the huge doors of the Fifth Gate swung shut, Skauda'tesh cast a last glance down at the plaza. His yellow eyes widened slightly as if he saw something, and he smiled menacingly. Then the huge Mega-Steel doors shut with a clang. The Imperial Palace grounds were shut off from the rest of the city.

✳✳✳

Down in the plaza, Elliot and Molly ran between the people to get away from the palace gate. They stopped behind a small stand and looked around behind them. The huge palace gate was shut now and the palace guards had disappeared inside.

"That was close!" wheezed Molly. "Do you think he saw us?"

"I don't know," replied Elliot worriedly. "I hope he didn't. Because if he did, we're in deep trouble."

"Ice cream, ice cream!" the Skar'ley vendor in the stand in front of them suddenly called and pushed a tray into their faces. On the tray lay several spiral-shaped cones filled with an orange, brown and white substance which looked remarkably like the ice cream Elliot knew from Earth.

"Eh… no, thank you," Elliot replied and turned away.

"You look sweaty and tired, my Touristy Friend," said the Skar'ley vendor and pursued them with his tray. "Please help yourself to a delicious Nevermelt Ice Cream. It will do you good."

Elliot took a long look at the ice cream again. The vendor was really pushy and continued. "It's free of course, as it's mandatory in the summer on Sku'raan to serve ice cream to all who need it."

"Is that really ice cream?" Elliot asked the reptilian vendor suspiciously. He'd been subjected to far too many culinary confusions, mix-ups and surprises and was now on his guard.

The vendor looked Elliot up and down with his yellow reptilian eyes before answering.

"Of course it is. The best Nevermelt Ice Cream on Sku'raan. What did you think it was?"

"I-I don't know. I just didn't expect ice cream here in…" Elliot trailed off. Here in space he had been about to say. He then looked again at the name on the trolley. "Nevermelt Ice Cream? You mean it never melts?"

"Yes, of course. The Nevermelt can withstand even the dry and hot temperatures of the Golden Desert. Without it the southern passage to the Sixteen Lakes would be impossible. You would like one, wouldn't you?"

"Yes, yes, okay," said Elliot to make the vendor go away and grabbed one of the spiral cones which contained red and brown ice cream. He hoped it would be strawberry and chocolate flavour, but dreaded it would probably taste of slugs, nail polish remover or shampoo instead. Molly didn't have much of a choice either, as the vendor shoved the tray into her face immediately afterwards. After some consideration she grabbed a cone with blue and white ice cream. Satisfied that he had succeeded in harassing yet another pair of tourists into accepting his ice cream, the vendor then turned around to find new prey.

"What now?" said Elliot while he sampled his ice cream. He found that it tasted remarkably good, but not at all like strawberry and chocolate.

"I don't know," replied Molly while trying out her ice cream. "That stupid Gatekeeper Scalie should just have let us in. It would've been much easier."

"Sishra was right. He told us that these bureaucrats would be tricky and not understand."

"But we had an invitation from the Emperor himself," argued Molly.

"Maybe it was somehow withdrawn after they assumed us dead in that crash. Maybe we were never invited at all. It could all have been a trick by the priests."

"Well… now they won't get our warning. It serves them right," said Molly and attacked her ice cream angrily. "They don't deserve to be saved."

"Yes they do," corrected Elliot. "All those millions of innocent people deserve to be warned before something nasty happens to them. All those people from Earth deserve to be warned and saved from becoming slaves to those horrible priests. The children at the Orphanage, Mrs Kateder, Agnes Fagerlund, Niilas and Aili need to be saved from slavery. Uncle Karl is depending on me to rescue him." Elliot's heart sank as he once again felt himself drifting further away from his goal to save his Uncle, his only chance of being part of a family. "As long as we have a chance to save everybody we have to…"

"Have to what?" wondered Molly who had been moved deeply by Elliot's speech.

But Elliot didn't answer. He just stared ahead of him.

"What's the matter, Elliot?" said Molly and followed his gaze to the buildings opposite the Imperial Palace gate. The stone buildings were old and impressive, covered by lichen, bushes and trees, as most buildings in the Imperial capital were. There was nothing special about them.

"What does it say on that building there?" Elliot asked finally.

Molly looked again. "Which one do you mean? The Imperial Library and Mayizim Halls or the Museum of Peculiar Sciences? The driver said something about them, but I can't remember."

"That's it! Mayizim! That's what Aunt Kaitrinn kept saying. One of the few things she remembered. She said she and Uncle Karl had spoken endlessly to Mayizim… or something like that."

Both of them stared in awe at the building.

"Who's Mayizim?" they both said in unison.

"Ehm…" Little Brother coughed. "*Who* is Mayizim? Did I hear you correctly Master Elliot? Your Highness? You don't know what Mayizim is?"

"No!" both of them said, now turning their attention to the black briefcase Elliot was carrying on his back.

"Well… Mayizim is only the most magnificent, most intelligent, most gifted, best built Artificial Intelligence in the Spiral Arm. Mayizim the Great. Mayizim the triple relativity formula breaker. Mayizim with the Hundred Glowing Eyes."

"So he's a computer?" Molly concluded.

"We prefer to call ourselves Artificial Intelligences, Your Majesty. And yes, Mayizim is an A.I. A Stage Nineteen A.I., the best and only one ever built. Mayizim is actually so clever that it changed some of its designs while being built to enhance its intelligence."

"He's the guy we should speak to," Elliot said excitedly. "Uncle Karl and Aunt Kaitrinn spoke to him for hours. He'll know more about this whole mystery. He might even know the way to Earth."

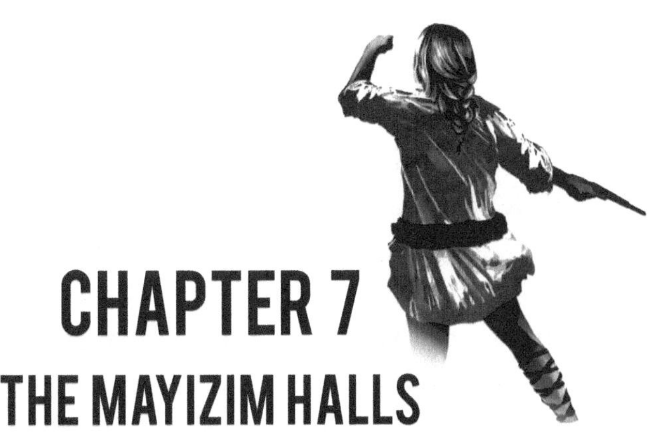

CHAPTER 7
THE MAYIZIM HALLS

With no further delay, the two of them ran to the huge old stone building. It stood with huge carved letters above the broad flight of steps leading into the ornate doorway – 'Imperial Library and Mayizim Halls'. Inside they found dusty old corridors and endless rooms filled with books, scrolls, countless data storage devices and rows upon rows of reading desks. At the centre of the library stood a giant statue of a Skar'ley, whose arms touched the walls around him and his great headpiece held up the ceiling. Walkways and stairs led along his arms and up his body. All walls and the entire body of the statue contained shelves upon shelves of books. The Imperial Library was huge, but eerily empty of people. Dust danced lazily in the rays of lights that cut down into the gloom from painted glass windows high above.

At the feet of the great statue was a 3D post with several signs pointing in different directions. When their eyes fell upon it they saw the sign pointing to the 'Mayizim Halls' and ran for it. Soon statues and depictions of great deeds, inventions or written instructions Mayizim had accomplished began to flank the rooms and corridors.

The Mayizim Halls were also huge and likewise empty of people. They ran from room to room, looking for Mayizim or anything that could possibly be the Spiral Arm's most intelligent A.I. They even called his name aloud, but heard nothing but the echo of their voices as a reply in the old halls of stone.

"Tsk, tsk," a dry old voice interrupted their frantic search. "I can't believe it! Running and shouting and eating in the Mayizim Halls!"

The voice came from an old Skar'ley draped in long brown robes and wearing a drooping headpiece of bronze. He stood in a small doorway, bent over his walking cane. A shiny badge on his chest revealed that he was the Chief File Backup Manager. Despite his triple lens spectacles over his small yellow eyes, the old Skar'ley squinted as he spoke to them, as if not seeing them clearly.

"It… hum… says in nearly every corridor and room – *No running! No shouting! No food or beverages!*" the old Skar'ley said. "Yet you come here…hum…running, shouting and eating ice cream. No… hum… respect. You'll drip ice cream on the floor and someone will slip on it and hurt their back badly. There'll be sorrow. And there'll be no end to it all, mark my words. Tsk, tsk."

"I'm sorry," said Elliot and stopped in his tracks. Finally, here was someone they could ask for directions. He turned to the old Chief File Backup Manager.

"It's Nevermelt Ice Cream, you know," said Molly condescendingly. "It doesn't drip."

"Yes, yes, we're sorry," said Elliot once again. He grabbed what was left of Molly's ice cream and threw it, together with his own, in the bin located in the room.

"There! We've thrown away the ice cream," explained Elliot. "I'm sorry if we shouted and ran. But we're in a hurry you see. We have to see Mayizim. It's a matter of life and death for the Emperor and many people in the Spiral Arm."

"Well, that's no excuse for running and making a… hum… nuisance of yourself is it?" the old Backup Manager went on. "Suppose everybody ran around… hum… shouting and dripping artificial non-essential foodstuffs everywhere, hmm? What would the Spiral Arm come to, hmm?"

"Listen you old…" Molly began.

Elliot quickly stepped in front of Molly and smiled.

"I'm sorry. We both are. We didn't know better. We won't do it again."

"I hope not. Honestly, I don't know what all the… hum… fuss is about. All this running and shouting these days. It's like everybody believes the end of the world is at hand."

"It might be, it might be," Elliot said silently. He then donned his most friendly smile and addressed the Backup Manager again.

"We were wondering, how do we find our way to Mayizim, the super computer?"

"Hmpff! Super computer. Insults like that won't buy you any favours with Mayizim the Great. I remember once when…" The old Backup Manager began.

Elliot quickly interrupted him. "Is it that way? Through those ornate doors?"

"What? No, no. The main interface of Mayizim is located on the top floor, right by the ancient records. The magnificent Mayizim Communion Chamber is a testament to the greatness of all…"

"Great! Thank you very much," shouted Elliot over his shoulder as he and Molly hurried away.

"But…" said the old Backup Manager.

"But what?" repeated Elliot and stopped in his tracks.

"The Mayizim Communion Chamber is locked during… hum… holidays. And now we have such a… hum… holiday. The Massikita Victory Memorial Day, which celebrates…"

"Yes, yes, we know," snapped Molly, who was losing her temper.

"So it's locked," said Elliot. "Any chance of opening it, for just a few minutes?"

"What? Open the Communion Chamber during a public holiday? By the Eternal Sun, I think not! There are limits even to what can be done in the name of decency and…"

"But we have to speak to Mayizim," complained Elliot. "It's a matter of life and death."

"Life and death, you say?" snorted the old Skar'ley. "If we should open the great doors every time someone considered dying, we'd be busy all year. The Mayizim Communion Chamber wasn't even opened during the meteor shower of 2694. I hardly think this…"

"Yes, yes. So it's locked," said Molly who winked at Elliot and pointed to the PDM in her belt. She obviously intended to hack the door system. "Thank you anyway for telling us where it is. We'll come back after the holidays." Molly and Elliot then turned to leave again.

"But…" said the old Backup Manager.

For the second time, Elliot and Molly stopped in their tracks and turned back to the old Skar'ley.

"But what?" Elliot repeated.

"Mayizim the Great wouldn't speak to you even if it wasn't a… hum… public holiday."

"Why not? Don't tell us we have to be on some Audience List," moaned Elliot.

"Audience List? Of course not! There's no such thing. No, Mayizim chooses not to speak to humans like you, because of your low intelligence."

"What? What's that supposed to mean?" asked Molly accusingly.

"Well, not only humans in general, but all lifeforms with an intelligence below that of Mayizim itself. It simply refuses, except on occasions when it is bored with super-advanced algorithms, to talk to anyone that can't teach it anything new. Mayizim just doesn't think it worth the waste of time."

"But… Uncle Karl and Aunt Kaitrinn spoke to Mayizim."

"What? I have never heard of… hum… humans speaking to Mayizim for over six centuries, and then it was only because the human was mad and his twisted reasoning intrigued Mayizim."

"So, can you speak to Mayizim for us?" Elliot asked nicely. "We'd be very happy if you did," he added with a smile.

"Me? Speak to Mayizim the Great? Address Mayizim with the Hundred Glowing Eyes? That's impossible! Mayizim has never… hum… answered me in the one hundred and eight years I've been working here. I'm not worthy."

"You've worked here for one hundred and eight years!" exclaimed Molly. "How old are you?"

"Never mind! interrupted Elliot, trying not to offend the Backup Manager further. "So, who can speak to Mayizim? The Vurites?"

"Nobody actually. A being more intelligent than Mayizim has so far never been encountered in the Spiral Arm."

"So, what's the point of being the most intelligent… thing… in the Spiral Arm if you won't speak to people?" asked Elliot.

"Ahem… Mayizim the Great uses his time for… hum… higher purposes. Things we mere mortal intelligences cannot fathom. Now and then it will grant us print-outs of solutions to great vexing problems or just new technological breakthroughs it wishes to… hum… bless us with. We cannot for a second even try to imagine what it is like to wield such a vast intelligence."

"Bet I can," mumbled Molly. "Just go down to the mental asylums and have a look…"

"Mayizim with the Hundred Glowing Eyes simply does not have time for us," said the Backup Manager with a wry smile. "He was made far too intelligent by his creators in the old days." Having shared his gloomy insight about Mayizim, the old Backup Manager chuckled and turned his back.

As the old Skar'ley hobbled away from them, Elliot and Molly looked at each other.

"Now what do we do?" sighed Elliot.

"We knock on his door, maybe open it a little and try ourselves," replied Molly as if it was the simplest thing in the Universe. "Uncle Karl and Kaitrinn managed it, didn't they? Maybe we will too?"

"I guess it's worth a try," agreed Elliot.

"I don't think we'll succeed, actually," said Little Brother gloomily. "I'm only a Stage Ten A.I. and the three of us together couldn't even get up to…"

"Don't be so gloomy, Brother Squid," said Molly cheerfully. "Let's give it a try."

***

The three of them made their way up to the topmost floor of the magnificent old stone building. It was quite a climb and their legs were tired when they came to a great glass dome under which was a large set of ornate doors that read 'Mayizim Communion Chamber'.

It was locked.

"Okay! Let's see if we can open these," said Molly, and called up the holo-screen from her PDM. She began to filter through complicated code and wrote so fast her fingers blurred. As usual, Elliot didn't understand a thing he saw blurring past in the countless hovering holo-windows which Molly threw up around her in the air. Endless text strings of information scrolled past in several of them.

"Can you open them?" Elliot asked.

"Maybe I can, if I'm not disturbed all the time," replied Molly, but not with her usual irritated tone.

"Aha!" Molly said after a while. "Someone has done this before."

"Done what before?"

"Hacked this door system. Whoever it was, they left a passworded code behind to make it easier for them a second time."

"Maybe it was Uncle Karl and Aunt Kaitrinn," suggested Elliot. "Aunt Kaitrinn is supposed to be a wizard at computers… at least before her mind was broken by the priests."

"That could very well be. Anyway, whoever it was, they made it much easier for me." The doors suddenly swung open.

"There we go! That wasn't so hard," said Molly with a satisfactory grin.

The two of them stepped into a large chamber with ten ornate seats with tall backs. In front of the seats was nothing but empty space. No screens, no keyboards, only a complicated array of glowing buttons along one of the walls. They looked around them expectantly, but found nothing else in the chamber.

"It's empty!" said Elliot disappointed.

"No! Not empty, Master Elliot," said Little Brother in awe. "Mayizim is here. I can sense the complicated currents and light flows that are its thoughts and its supreme intellect. If Mayizim chooses to communicate with you there will be holo-screens and other holo-input devices such as keyboards, buttons, emotion pads or virtual reality emissions."

Elliot looked around him again. He could see nothing but the ten ornate chairs, or thrones, which was a more accurate description of them. He walked up to one of them and sat down.

"Mayizim!" he said to the room. "Can you hear me?"

There was only silence.

"Please Mayizim! We need to speak to you. We're friends of Karrillus and Kaitrinn Ursus. We know they spoke to you. We need your help."

There was more silence.

"*Okay, here goes,*" Elliot thought. "We need your help to stop the priests from assassinating the Emperor and enslaving the people of Earth. Can you help us?"

There was no reply.

"Little Brother!" said Molly and sat down in one of the other chairs. "Can't you access Mayizim? Can't you hook onto his network or consciousness and speak to him?"

"Me? No, that would be rude and intrusive," replied Little Brother.

"But you have to. He clearly won't speak to us otherwise," said Molly.

"Please Little Brother. I know Mayizim knows something. I know he can help us. He might be able to tell us where Earth is," begged Elliot.

"Alright! I'll try to speak to Mayizim normally," sighed Little Brother. "But I won't attempt to break into its system or anything else rude."

"Alright, accessing communication network, searching for matching codes. Matching communication interZZZZZZZZZZZZZZZZZ."

The black briefcase which was Little Brother suddenly began to hum loudly. The steel tentacles which held on to Elliot jerked away and began to flail slowly and aimlessly in the air. Little Brother fell from Elliot's chair and onto the floor with a thud.

"Little Brother! Are you alright!" shouted Elliot and sprung to the briefcase which had fallen next to the throne he was sitting in.

"ZZZZZZZZZZZZZZZZZZZZZ," was all Little Brother said.

"Oh no! I think Mayizim didn't appreciate the disturbance," said Molly.

"Did he kill Little Brother?" asked Elliot in horror.

"Well… no… I don't think so. I guess he's been damaged or frozen somehow by Mayizim. It could actually also be the result of a much weaker intelligence tapping into a super-fast and super-intelligent network. Maybe he just couldn't handle it. I don't know."

"ZZZZZZZZZZZZZ," continued Little Brother.

"Can we disconnect him?" asked Elliot.

"I'm afraid not. I can't access any of them with my PDM."

"That's great! Just great!" exclaimed Elliot. "We've risked our lives. Sishra and his crew sacrificed themselves for us. We've come all the way here – only to be stopped by stupid bureaucrats, insane priests and a stuck-up computer. It's just not fair."

Elliot sat down angrily again in his chair. Right now he just felt like giving up. They'd done everything they could. It wasn't their fault the Spiral Arm was full of idiots – organic and artificial. How had Uncle Karl and Aunt Kaitrinn managed to speak to Mayizim? Had they been super intelligent? That just didn't seem like the answer. Certainly, Aunt Kaitrinn must have been very clever, but amongst the most intelligent in the Spiral Arm? What had Aunt Kaitrinn said during her brief moment of clarity just before he left? She said that they had spoken for hours to Mayizim. But how? Suddenly Elliot remembered that they had somehow made Mayizim angry. It all came back to him then. Mayizim had complained about some stupid riddle.

The riddle! Of course! It must be…

Elliot leaned forward, gripped the armrest of his chair firmly and spoke loudly.

> *"Hard as stone, soft as mud.*
> *Cold as winter, sweet as summer.*
> *Good as gold, bad as sin*
> *What am I?"*

Suddenly all the lights along the wall lit up. A holo-screen flashed into existence in front of Elliot. It showed a transparent face of an ancient Skar'ley with an enlarged head and a natural crest of spikes, bones and scales.

"Oh no! Not another one!" said Mayizim the Great.

Elliot didn't know what to say. They certainly weren't the words he'd been prepared for.

"What do you mean? Another one what?" Elliot asked carefully.

"Another one with that stupid riddle. It can't be solved. Riddles in themselves are a stupid phenomenon you humans waste your short and valuable time with. Just like you wasted valuable time hacking that maximum security Skar'ley library door, when you could have knocked. It was quite impressively done though… for a human. I achieved the same thing in one thousandth of a second, while taking a 0.0002 second break from solving the hardest sudoku ever created in the Empire and composing a list of all potential star systems in the galaxy with the right conditions for life to evolve. So, now that you're here, just tell me the answer and be on your way."

"The answer to the riddle? The same riddle that Uncle Karl and Aunt Kaitrinn told you?"

"Yes, yes," replied Mayizim. The semi-transparent head which represented Mayizim made an irritated grimace and rolled his yellow eyes. "This riddle has vexed me for a considerable time. I've spent more than twelve seconds contemplating it, assembling a list of possible answers and created an extensive dossier on the interpretation of the words. I've come to the conclusion that this riddle is either unsolvable and created out of haphazard phrases, or the answer is something so unknown and amazing that I do not have any record of it in my extensive databases. As you clearly know the riddle, you must also know the answer. Please provide me with it and I shall occupy no more of your valuable time."

"I… don't…" Elliot stuttered.

"You *do* know the answer to this irritating riddle, don't you," said Mayizim as the holographic face leaned closer, peering at him. "Kaitrinn Ursus and that annoying young man Karrillus threw these stupid sentences in my virtual face but never revealed the answer. Most irritating!"

Elliot understood. This was the reason Mayizim had been angry with Uncle Karl and Aunt Kaitrinn. He couldn't solve the riddle. This was how they had been able to speak to him. The only problem was that Elliot and Molly didn't know the answer either. Elliot had no choice other than to provide Mayizim with the only decent answer during the circumstances.

"Yes! I *do* know the answer to the riddle," he said and swallowed. It was a lie, yes, but the circumstances certainly allowed for one lie. A whitish little lie. The longer they could speak to Mayizim the better.

"Well, out with it then," Mayizim said eagerly.

"No," replied Elliot flatly. "Not until you answer some of our questions."

"All right! Here we go again. Very well, get on with it then! What do you want to know? The exact age of the universe? The origin of the Founders? The location of the greatest treasure in the Spiral Arm? When your homeworld is going to be devoured by its sun? The reason sandwiches always fall with the messy side down?"

Elliot was taken totally by surprise. The sandwich mystery had often been on his mind, but he made a mental effort and shoved it aside. There were more important matters after all and he tried to decide how to phrase his words best. He suspected they wouldn't get too many chances before Mayizim tired of the extortion.

"Well, no. None of that," said Elliot and bit his lip. He didn't really know where to begin. They needed to choose their questions wisely.

"Then what do you want to know?" asked Mayizim. "Please hurry up. My time is valuable."

It was Molly who came to the rescue with a question of her own.

"What's the deal with the Hundred Glowing Eyes?"

"What? Oh that. Well, I was built two hundred years before the great depression of Skar'ley culture. This is long before your people were found on Matalla. As civilisation had temporarily fallen to medieval levels during this time, the simple priests caring for my needs referred to me by that name because of the one hundred illuminated screens and buttons of my control room. Well, and also the fact that I had tapped into every surviving and near magical communication, surveillance and database network in the Empire."

"Are you still connected to these? Can you still spy and eavesdrop on everyone?" asked Elliot.

"Well, maybe not everyone… but certainly quite a few."

"Then you know about the priesthood's conspiracy against the Emperor?"

"Of course I do. That's old news."

"But… what are you going to do about it?" asked Elliot.

"Do about what? About the conspiracy? Why should I care about that? Emperors come and go. Empires rise and fall. Times change. As long as they don't bother me, they can do whatever they want. As long as my power supply isn't threatened I'm happy. I don't want to go back to slave-manned treadmills powering me again."

"So, you won't help us to stop this plot?" asked Elliot.

"No. If I would ever choose a side in a conflict such as this, I will gain enemies. But if I remain neutral and helpful to both sides, my future existence is secured."

"If you remain a coward, you mean?" Molly pointed out.

"Life, synthetic or not, is not about valour or cowardice. It's about survival."

"What about dignity and being proud of what you stand for and what you've done? That's pretty important, you know," continued Molly. "You don't want to be remembered as history's worst tyrant or something."

Molly's eyes were hard and determined. Clearly Molly was thinking about her own father, but Elliot could see something had changed about the way she saw her family. Elliot realised she had a point.

"That's the difference between humans and A.I.," replied Mayizim. "You value many things that are unimportant for your survival."

"That's what makes life worth living," protested Molly.

"Okay, I have a question," interrupted Elliot. "What did you and Uncle… I mean Karrillus … and Kaitrinn Ursus talk about?"

"Well, a lot of things," replied Mayizim. "During your question I compiled a summary of our topics, which I'm downloading to your friend's PDM as we speak. It was nothing special really. Mainly the location of hidden old religious books, historical texts and the whereabouts of

Matalla, which despite what people might otherwise tell you, has not been destroyed."

"So, it was you who gave them the coordinates for Earth... Matalla, I mean."

"No, I didn't. I don't have them, actually. I helped the priesthood purge all data regarding Matalla's location more than eight hundred years ago. I made a promise not to store them in my memory."

"You helped them? You purged all the data?"

"Well I had to, hadn't I? The Priesthood can damage my databanks severely if they put their will to it. Anyway, I did know of some ancient records in the Imperial Library that I pointed Karrillus and Kaitrinn towards. They could have contained some clues to Matalla's location in the Imperial Library."

"Great! What records? Where can we find them?"

"Now hold on," said Mayizim carefully. "I won't be fooled again. Karrillus and Kaitrinn talked and asked questions for hours and still didn't reveal the answer. This time I want to know the answer to the riddle before I tell you more about the records." The holographic image of the mythological Skar'ley smiled triumphantly.

"The answer... yes," said Elliot trying to buy time. His mind was racing. *Hard as stone, soft as mud.* Clay? No, that didn't fit with the rest, '*Cold as winter, sweet as summer*'. Snow? Slushy ice? No, that didn't fit with '*Good as gold, bad as sin*'. He looked to Molly for some help, but she just shrugged.

"Well? Will you give me the answer or not?" stressed Mayizim. "Or don't you know it?"

The holo-image leaned closer and gave Elliot what he suspected was a disgusted look. "You don't know the answer, do you?" Mayizim accused.

"Yes I do! It's just that…" But Elliot's mind was blank. He couldn't concentrate. The more he tried, the more he lost focus on the words of the riddle. He sighed. It was just his luck. He had travelled across the Spiral Arm and faced countless perils, but solving one stupid riddle seemed impossible. It wasn't fair that this was all up to him now. If he'd been a normal tourist to Sku'raan he could have been enjoying the festivities right now in one of the grand plazas with as many free Nevermelt Ice Creams as he wanted. Now, instead he had to save the Spiral Arm and…

Suddenly he got it – the answer to the riddle.

He went through the words again in his mind. It was stupid, but could actually be right.

"I'm ending this communication now," said Mayizim sourly. "You have been a pointless waste of my valuable time and…"

"Wait! The answer is… ice cream," shouted Elliot.

Both Molly and the holo-face of Mayizim looked at him in surprise.

"Ice cream?"

"Yes, ice cream. *Hard as stone* when it's frozen and *soft as mud* when it's melting."

"Unless it's Nevermelt Ice Cream!" Molly pointed out.

"Well, yes… but no! This is the general idea of ice cream we're talking about," Elliot explained with his heart racing.

"Oh, okay!" agreed Molly thoughtfully.

"That's the most preposterous and stupid answer I've ever heard," Mayizim pointed out. "It can't be right."

"But it is," Elliot persisted. "Listen, the rest also makes sense. *Cold as winter*, as it's an ice cream, but *sweet as summer* as it is sweet and normally eaten during summer."

"And everybody has a sweet ice cream dream of summer," Molly pointed out.

"Yes, yes!" exclaimed Elliot, happy for Molly's support. "It's even *good as gold*, as it's nice to eat, but *bad as sin*, as it isn't good for your health." He remembered that Uncle Karl used to love ice cream. He'd often seen him sitting at his school with several scoopfuls and getting his beard all messy. In her moment of clarity, Aunt Kaitrinn had also said that it had been a stupid riddle with a stupid answer. "It can't be anything else. It's ice cream," Elliot concluded.

"Well, it makes sense I guess," said Mayizim with a disappointed sigh. "Some kind of fussy mentally challenged human logical sense."

"It's ice cream," whispered Elliot to himself, proud of having solved Uncle Karl's riddle at last.

"Ice cream," repeated Mayizim to himself, as if he couldn't believe it. "Based on my database of human culture, languages, synonyms and brain capacity it's a 93,3489 per cent probability that this answer is indeed correct. Incredible and so totally... upsetting."

"So... where can we find those ancient records?" asked Molly triumphantly.

"Yes, yes," moaned Mayizim. "They're called The Testaments of the Lonely and can be found under the Biography Department, Exploration Era, Section 6F. They are personal reflections of deep space explorers experiencing long and boring travels in the vastness of space during the expansive seventeenth dynasty of the Empire."

"Perfect! That must be where Karrillus and Kaitrinn found those ancient star-maps to Earth that Big Brother was talking about."

"Ice cream! I can't believe it," repeated Mayizim "All this time spent on such a stupid riddle. Humans keep astonishing and disappointing me." The holographic projection of Mayizim hung its head and shook it in disgust.

"Okay, well, thank you," said Molly and began to pull Elliot towards the exit of the Communion Chamber.

"Yes, thank you very much," said Elliot as politely as possibly.

But Mayizim was caught up in a discussion with himself, as if he'd forgotten that he was still communicating with the two human children. "So, what's so special about that riddle, that Karrillus, even when imprisoned and doomed to die, wouldn't reveal it? Plain human stupidity and pride."

"What? Wait!" called Elliot and turned back to the holographic face of Mayizim. "What did you say?"

"I was just pointing out that this riddle was of no special importance at all and will be filed under 'Totally Pointless and Time Wasting Human Word Plays.'"

"No! I mean what you said about Karrillus being imprisoned and doomed to die." A great lump of anxiety was forming in Elliot's chest.

"Oh that. Yes. I've confronted Karrillus every day since his imprisonment to reveal the answer. Every evening I contact him in his dreary cell and ask him to deliver the answer. Every evening he refuses. He's a stubborn and stupid man. It's not like he's got that much time left to live anyway."

"Uncle Karl is alive?" Elliot exclaimed.

"Of course he is. Well, at least for the moment. A month ago he was brought to the dreaded dungeons of the Eternally Sunless Deep."

Elliot's heart fluttered with joy. He'd assumed that Uncle Karl was dead and given up all hope. But he was alive! Uncle Karl was alive! Yes, he might still be in great danger, but at least that was better than being dead.

"Where is this place? How can we find him?" Elliot asked impatiently.

"The Eternally Sunless Deep lies under the old and deserted Great Temple of the Eternal Sun in the Mah'vee Swamplands. It's very hard to reach and very, very large."

"And I guess it's not really deserted?" added Molly.

"No, that's true. It's a secret training facility for the warrior priests who are preparing the coup here on Sku'raan."

"How did you know he was there?" asked Elliot.

"As I mentioned before, since millennia back I've tapped into every communication, surveillance and database network in the Empire."

"Is he alright? I mean is he injured?"

"He's alright and uninjured. Apart from living in a miserable and damp cell, Karrillus is well and as stubborn as always." The face of Mayizim then turned away from them. "Now, you must excuse me, I have other things to attend to. This conversation has really done nothing to enhance my databanks or improve my unimpressive impression of humans. Good day to you all!"

"ZZZZZZZZZZorry! I cannot access the communication network," said Little Brother suddenly. Evidently he had unfrozen from whatever he had tried to say several minutes ago when he tried to access Mayizim.

"Not a problem," thanked Molly. "We've spoken to Mayizim already."

"What? You spoke to Mayizim the Great? I don't believe you! It can't be true! What did it say?" Little Brother sounded hysterical.

Elliot ignored Little Brother and turned to Molly. "We have to find a way to free Uncle Karl. We have to."

"First things first," said Molly. "If we manage to warn the Emperor, he will be able to save your Uncle."

"I guess you're right," agreed Elliot. "But how do we do that? We can't get past those priests."

"You actually *spoke* to Mayizim? I mean, that's not really possible or likely. Mayizim didn't just print out some information for you to transfer to someone else? I mean, did it communicate with you?" Little Brother went on. Elliot and Molly ignored him.

"We have to get into the Imperial Palace," continued Molly as they left the Mayizim Communion Chamber. "That's the only way to reach the Emperor."

"Yes, but how do we do that?" said Elliot. "We've tried already. It seems impossible. He's the most holy and protected man of hundreds and hundreds of worlds."

"I guess we'll have to ask around. Get an invitation to the Imperial Palace or something. I'll start probing around with my PDM and see what I can find."

"What I'm saying is, that *speak* can mean a lot of things," continued Little Brother. "It can be a one-way communication and thus not a real communication, if you understand what I mean. It's unheard of that Mayizim the Great has ever spoken to human children and…"

***

Down in the Plaza of Great Expectations tourists were stopping in the middle of their souvenir shopping to watch the colourful palace guards. More than fifty of the lizard soldiers marched into the centre of the square, led by four red-caped Priests of the Eternal Sun. The lacquered armours and silver weapons of the palace guards gleamed in the brilliant sun. Holy symbols of the Emperor were painted on their crested helmets and on their green and black garments.

"You have your orders," one of the Skar'ley priests said. "Search every street, alley and building for the terrorists." Slowly rotating holographic images of Elliot and Molly were projected from the priest's staff for all the palace guards to see. "Bring them to us – dead or alive."

The hardened palace guards knew well the main purposes of their caste – to obey orders to the letter and servitude until death. As one, they hissed in confirmation and began to spread out over the plaza in four groups.

After the palace guards had left, one of the priests turned to the other three.

"What is happening? Why are we progressing so swiftly with the Grand Plan? Who are these human children?"

"You ask too many questions, young Amha," replied one of the older priests. "You have been initiated and that should be sufficient. Only those who have bathed in the True Light of the Eternal Sun know the full purpose of our plans and our actions here today. Trust in those that lead you."

"I'm sorry. I did not question the wisdom of those that lead us. I simply suspect that something has happened. Something unforeseen. It seems like we are hastening and risking too much. Maybe the Grand Plan is not yet truly ripe for harvesting?"

"Maybe not, maybe not. But despite what we fear, this is the Path that the Eternal Sun has illuminated for us. We are too lowly servants to understand our role here today. Let us continue with the task at hand."

***

In the nothingness of deep space, just outside the star system of Sku'raan – where there are no planets, no light from nearby suns, nothing but stars – a great battle was about to begin. The great asteroid ships tumbled towards their destination. Disguised as a swarm of renegade debris, which often would be attracted to the Oort clouds of star systems, they moved with a hidden purpose. They were but the first of two more swarms of seemingly innocent renegade debris. The asteroid ships had slowed down while bypassing the defence stations on the borders of the Imperial star system in their seemingly innocent course for the Imperial Throne World. As they hurtled along harmless trajectories which would take them out of the star system again, they were largely ignored – until now.

Suddenly space was lit up by fifty small stars, as several Vurite warships emerged from strange wormholes. With engines blazing, they set a course for the asteroid ships. Largely crewless the asteroid ships should be easy pickings for the well-armed Vurite warships. But the number of asteroid ships, the sheer size of them and the fact that most of their hull was protected by super-hardened rock made the battle's outcome uncertain. As every asteroid ship also carried heavy duty meson cannons, they were a considerable threat.

Understanding that the Vurites and Porians meant business, the engines of the asteroid ships blazed into life, revealing what the huge lumps of rocks really were. Torpedoes were fired. Laser shots began to seek out targets and meson cannons fired up. This region of deep space would be empty and silent no more.

***

Elliot and Molly left the Mayizim Halls and returned to the large central stairwell. Three floors below the Mayizim Halls the stairwell was joined by four connecting stairs from different sections of the great Imperial Library. Like the grand stairwell, they were all cut out of glass or clear crystal. Above one of the joining stairs a sign read 'BIOGRAPHIES'.

"Before we leave I want to look for those ancient records," said Elliot and looked up at the stairs leading to the Biography Department. "Even if we can't manage to warn the Emperor, it would be good to have the coordinates for Earth. With them maybe the Hidden Watchers or the King and Queen can help us protect Earth?"

Molly shrugged and followed Elliot up the new flight of stairs.

"What ancient records?" asked Little Brother. "What are we looking for?"

"Mayizim told us about The Testaments of the Lonely in the Biography department, but I can't remember where," replied Elliot.

"He transferred the information to my PDM as we spoke," informed Molly. "It should be under Exploration Era, Section 6F."

"Oh, that's straight ahead and the fourteenth aisle to the left, according to the Wireless Library Map," said Little

Brother. "But… that means that Mayizim actually *did* speak to you. That's amazing! Do you know how fortunate you are? I wish I'd had the chance to speak to Mayizim. What an honour! How did you do it?"

"We gave him the same riddle Uncle Karl and Aunt Kaitrinn gave him," explained Elliot. "He hadn't managed to solve it and was very irritated about it."

"Yeah, and Elliot solved it," said Molly proudly.

"So… what was the answer?"

"Ice cream."

"Ice cream?"

"Yes, ice cream."

"That's odd. Doesn't seem that hard to figure out, once you know the answer," said Little Brother slightly disappointed. "I was expecting something more sophisticated."

"So did Mayizim," said Molly with a snigger.

"Here it is," interrupted Elliot. "Aisle fourteen."

When they turned down the aisle they found a lot more than they expected. Instead of books or crystal data slivers which seemed to be the norm in the Imperial Library, silvery scrolls of a kind of elastic metal lined the shelves. Amongst the sections of shelves, countless ordinary everyday items such as mugs, hats, boots, belts and PDMs were on display under glass casings. Most of them had a kind of personal touch to them in the form of name markings, scribbled texts or colourful decorations. Countless images of the lizard-like Skar'ley men and women were displayed on pillars in the aisle between the shelf sections. Some in the form of simple sketches, others in the form of elaborate paintings, photographs, sculptures or holographic projections. These brave explorers were long dead and the only things they left behind were their anonymous faces and some of their personal belongings. Small texts under the items and faces revealed them to be between eight and six thousand years old. Although Elliot could clearly see that the items were worn from use, they seemed no older than mugs and boots he had seen on Earth. There was nothing antique about them, in the sense that Elliot recognised anyway.

"Wow! This old boot is seven thousand years old," said Elliot admiringly, as he studied a magnetic boot used by ancient mariners to stay on their starship hulls.

"Yeah! Makes you wonder why they keep all this old crap," agreed Molly without much admiration.

"But it's ancient. It used to belong to someone," continued Elliot. "Someone just like you and me… well more like a lizard… but a brave explorer. I wonder what his name was? What he was thinking? What he did in his life?"

"Well, I don't," said Molly flatly. "And these scrolls are really old technology. I've seen people keep plain old books out of sentimental reasons, but not data scrolls such as these."

"I guess what we're looking for should be among these scrolls here." She pointed to Section 6F, which was filled with silvery scrolls. Molly picked one up and unrolled it. Interactive text and image boxes began to fill the scroll as she held it. By touching them with her finger she could jump between sections and pictures or enlarge them to her liking. The unrolled part of the scroll was evidently only displaying a fragment of the scroll's contents.

"They don't look like they do, but these scrolls contain a lot of information," said Molly.

Elliot picked up another scroll and began to eye the contents. Thanks to his Translator Lenses the ancient Skar'ley text reformed into Swedish runes he could read. But because of its age, some words or expressions seemed untranslatable by the Translator Lenses.

"Keep your eyes open for a scroll called The Testaments of the Lonely," said Elliot.

"Eh…. It's actually not one scroll, Master Elliot," explained Little Brother carefully. "It's the whole section. According to the Brief Summary emitted by the shelf transmitters, these twenty-seven scrolls are all referred to as The Testament of the Lonely."

"What? All twenty-seven of them? We'll be here all day and all night if we have to look through them for some kind of information about Earth," moaned Elliot.

"Pass a couple to me," said Molly and sat down on one of the stone benches in the aisle. After having swirled her neck around and cracked her fingers as if warming up, she focused on the scroll. Text and images began to flicker past her eyes at an amazing speed.

"The Speed Lenses allow me to get a grasp of what the scroll is about," she explained. "This way it'll be faster."

"Speed Lenses? I don't have any…" began Elliot.

"Yes, and I can try to search what indexes there are for references to Matalla," said Little Brother helpfully. He extracted his steel tentacles and detached from Elliot. Like a weird briefcase-spider Little Brother began moving between the shelves.

"Okay… then I'll… do something else," said Elliot, without having a clue what he could do to help. He piled some more scrolls on the bench next to Molly and then looked around him. Knowing that standing around impatiently would only make Molly irritated he began studying the many everyday artefacts of the explorers who had written the biographies. The first case was actually empty, having once contained something referred to as the 'SEAL OF THE FIFTH IMPERIAL SCOUT SQUAD'. A small note in the glass case simply stated that the item was on loan to 'LIBRARY CARD HOLDER 167139445-K.U. 451934'. But the other cases were full of both wondrous and sometimes stupidly uncommon things, such as glyphs from extinct civilisations, ancient alien tools, crew workout sweatbands, a worn old glove, a pair of double-toed boots and mysterious ornate nose-hair plyers. In his imagination, he tried to imagine what it must feel like to be the first to explore alien worlds. The excitement, and perhaps even danger, associated with exploration. Then he realised that he was such an explorer. He was the first from modern Earth who had travelled so far out into space. He was an explorer. There certainly had been plenty of excitement and danger in any case.

"I think this is it!" shouted Molly suddenly. She held up a silvery scroll and waved it excitedly. "It was the fifth one I went through. I tried to focus on explorers who lived six and a half thousand years ago. That is the estimate of Earth's discovery."

Molly placed the scroll on a table and all three of them bent over it. Silver text and images began scrolling up and down the scroll as Molly traced her finger over it.

"What does it say?" asked Elliot, barely able to contain his curiosity any further.

"Well, it's written by a Vilia Sama'resh, an engineer aboard the Fifth Imperial Scout Squad exploratory ship *Star Plow*," Molly continued. "Vilia was a veteran from the ongoing Massikita Wars and participated in the expedition which found a place he calls Rum'hamveer – Orb of the Violent Ones. He begins by writing a lot of boring stuff about depression in space, everlasting darkness, sensory deprivation of wind, smells and seasonal cycles, blah, blah, blah. He goes on and on about these things and how they affect the Skar'ley psyche. Evidently he was a bit too soft in the head to go on such a long, long journey in the first case." Molly twirled her finger at her temple to show them the Skar'ley engineer must have been a bit strange.

"Anyway, after two years of travelling they found faint atmospheric traces in a small star system far out in one of the remote spurs of the Sagittarius Arm and tracked it to a small planet dominated by water. He writes:

'*And every continent but one was filled with savages evolved from predators or at least omnivores. They lived in small-to-medium communities and were clearly uncivilised. Despite their closeness to nature and primitive state of existence, these beings would not cooperate amongst communities and would easily turn to violence against members of other communities than their own. We have come to call them the Violent Ones due to their aggressive nature and perfection of physical coordination and effective fighting skills.*'

"These creatures sound nasty," said Elliot. "Does it really describe humans? Does it mention the word 'Matalla'?"

"Well, humans can be quite cruel to each other. But, no, I haven't seen anything about Matalla," said Molly with a disappointed frown. "Actually, the scroll doesn't mention that name at all."

"You must remember, Your Highness, that Matalla was an ancient Atlantean name," explained Little Brother. "It means Land Under Sun and was the name the original Atlantean tribes used for their own world. It is unlikely that the name Matalla would be used by the first explorers."

"Well, does the scroll contain the word 'Atlantis' then?" asked Elliot.

"No. No it doesn't," said Molly after flicking through the texts. "Neither are there any pictures or proper descriptions of humans. Instead, this Vilia keeps going on about his personal feelings towards being on a planet again and feeling the wind brush against his face and his nostrils fill with the putrid, but natural stench of rot and decay. He's a bit sick in the head, I tell you."

"What's that?" said Elliot suddenly and pointed to the symbol of a star. It had seven points interconnected by bold lines.

"That?" Molly read the text again and enlarged the star so it covered the entire scroll. "It says here that it's the symbol of the Fifth Imperial Scout Squad. Underneath it reads '*The Stars Guide Us*.'"

"The Stars Guide Us…" repeated Elliot dreamily. He'd heard this before.

"Ah yes. But the star is also very similar to the seven-pointed star of one of the original Atlantean tribes," explained Little Brother. "It was called the New Star and was a very common depiction among the early Atean nations. I believe it was carried by human warriors for luck during the Massikita Wars."

"That's it! It must be Matalla they found," said Molly optimistically. "It can't just be a coincidence. The Atlanteans probably copied that symbol from those godlike alien explorers. They probably assumed it was magical. It makes sense, doesn't it?"

"But annoyingly enough there seems to be no star map to Matalla. I can't find any linked files in the scroll," said Little Brother. "Isn't that so, Your Highness?"

"Yeah, that's true. There's nothing here." Molly sighed. "I think this scroll is worthless to us. What do you think, Elliot?"

But Elliot wasn't listening. He was deep in thought. As if it was yesterday, he remembered the Nojd's words again.

"… *look to the stars to guide you.*"

The Nojd had been uncertain about the words. He had said that it could even have been '… *look to your star to guide you.*'

As he turned, the Nojd's words over and over in his head, his gaze wandered back to the empty glass case on the shelf.

'Seal of the Fifth Imperial Scout Squad' it read. Inside, the note about it being on loan to someone. 'Library Card Holder 167139445-K.U. 451934.'

Could 'K.U.' be initials? Could it be 'Karillus Ursus'?

Slowly, and as if in trance, Elliot pulled out the star-shaped medallion from under his clothes. Uncle Karl had been here, he was sure. He had borrowed or stolen the medallion from this case. Uncle Karl had sent him the medallion for a purpose. Elliot looked at the star in the scroll again.

It was identical to the star-shaped medallion!

Even the interconnecting lines were visible on the medallion as faintly engraved lines.

Molly didn't say anything. She stared mesmerised at the medallion which dangled from Elliot's hand.

"It's identical!" Elliot stated. "This isn't a medallion made by the original Atlantean tribes, as the Atean engineers on Centus Prime thought. It's a medallion made by those first Skar'ley explorers. See, the lines are placed exactly…"

But as Elliot held the medallion over the enlarged image of the star on the scroll something happened. The star image on the scroll flashed and split into seven parts. These then reformed into countless, lines, numbers and symbols. Behind it all were several clusters of faint stars.

"The map!" gasped Molly. "It's the star map! The medallion activated the map! The medallion itself was a Revealing Key for the scroll."

With her fingers, Molly moved the image around in the scroll, following the lines and numbers. Suddenly stars and planets appeared. Some of them blank orbs, others accompanied with geographical details, numbers and text. Molly then stopped by a planet accompanied by a single moon. Under the planet was the text, 'Rum'hamveer – Orb of the Violent Ones'.

"This is it! It's the star map to Matalla!" whooped Elliot.

"I must agree with Master Elliot," concurred Little Brother. "This is a fully functioning star map, although it's quite old. With some slight alterations due to star drift, this map should be no problem to follow."

"This must be the map Uncle Karl used to find his way to Earth. Can we copy it?" asked Elliot.

"Not right now," explained Little Brother. "The access ports to this scroll are ancient and not compatible with my ports. Maybe the librarians have something we can use to…"

"We don't have time for that," interrupted Molly. "We'll just have to borrow it for a while."

"Borrow it? I don't think something this old can be borrowed. Anyway, we don't have an Imperial Library Card, which is needed in order to…" complained Little Brother.

"Molly's right. We'll have to borrow it and say we're sorry afterwards," agreed Elliot.

"But that's stealing! This is a very valuable and ancient…" proclaimed Little Brother in shock.

But Elliot wasn't listening. Instead he pocketed the scroll and rose from the bench.

"Let's get out of here," said Elliot. "We've spent too much time here. Now we have to figure out a way to warn the Emperor. Maybe we can send him a message or something?"

"I don't think that's possible," said Molly and shook her head. "Any message for the Emperor would be checked for bombs and stuff. He'll have a whole army of people doing just that. That's how it works among royals, trust me I know. The priests are bound to find it. No, we have to find a way to speak to him directly. But, now that we have this map, we could use it as evidence to show him what the priests have been hiding."

With Little Brother hopping after them on his steel tentacles, they left the Exploration part of the Biography Department and made for the grand open stairwell. But as they passed a tall glass window overlooking the stairwell they saw movement. Although the view was slightly distorted through the glass and crystal of the magnificent stairwell, they easily identified several armed palace guards running up the stairs.

"Palace guards!" exclaimed Molly and pointed.

"W-what are they doing here?" asked Elliot, fearing that he knew the answer already.

"They must be looking for us. Look! There's a priest with them as well."

Elliot could see a red-robed priest hurrying behind the armed palace guards. His form distorted like the guards through the glass and crystal.

"Oh no! What are we going to do?"

"I-I don't know," stuttered Molly. "They seem to be searching one floor at a time. They'll be here soon. I guess we could go higher up, but we're already close to the top of the building."

***

In the great stairwell stood the Chief File Backup Manager. Heavily armed palace guards ran past him up the stairs. Their armours and weapons clanked nosily and their gruff voices cut through the tranquillity of the library.

"Tsk, tsk, no running!" the old Skar'ley complained as the palace guards pushed past him.

But the palace guards paid him no heed. They continued up to the next floor and began to spread out and search it. Their grand antique helmets were equipped with modern visors which instantly marked all living organisms with red for easier identification.

"Librarian," hissed a voice behind the old man. The Chief File Backup Manager turned to find a red-robed priest standing directly behind him. The priest was leaning on a staff while trying to catch his breath. Evidently, he wasn't as fit as the much younger palace guards who were running about their duties.

"Librarian!?" replied the Chief File Backup Manager with clear insult in his voice.

But the red-robed priest didn't seem to notice the insult and continued. "Have you seen two small humans here today?" asked the priest sternly.

"Two small humans? Why yes," replied the Backup Manager. "They were here just a couple of minutes ago."

"They were?" replied the priest, hardly able to believe his luck. He pushed a button on his staff and all the palace guards stopped in their tracks and returned to flock around him.

"Where are they now?" asked the priest eagerly.

"Now? I don't know where they went," cackled the Backup Manager. "But I'll tell you one thing, they were running around and shouting – which isn't allowed in the library, you know."

"Yes, yes, but in which direction did they go?" asked the priest impatiently.

"And they were eating ice cream. Ice cream! In a library! Can you believe the youth of today? No… hum… respect and no… hum… personal hygiene."

"Listen here, librarian," interrupted the priest sternly.

"Librarian!? I'm a Chief File Backup Manager you know. Takes more wit and experience to be a Chief File Backup Manager than being a librarian. Most people spend their entire careers without ever…"

"I don't care what you call yourself," interrupted the priest again. This time his voice was cold and hard. "But you'll be calling yourself Chief Stair Cleaner if you don't pull yourself together and tell us where those two humans went." To emphasise his words, the priest cocked his head strangely and made a threatening clicking noise in his throat. His yellow eyes seemed to glow menacingly in the gloomy stairwell.

"Chief Stair Cleaner," whispered the Backup Manager, who now seemed to have acute hearing. "Well… hum… let me see. Yes, yes, they said they were going to see Mayizim. They asked for directions to the Mayizim Halls. Now, I told them that it's a public holiday and I assume they left because…"

The priest wasn't listening to the old man. Instead he looked up the stairwell. Then he saw them. Although there were countless glass and crystal stairs, banisters and walls in the way, the reflections of two human children could still be seen.

"There they are!" he hissed loudly. "Get them! Seize them! In the name of the Emperor, seize those terrorists!"

***

As soon as Elliot and Molly heard the priest and saw him pointing at them, they ran from the tall glass window. Little Brother swiftly jumped back onto Elliot's back.

"Where do we go?" shouted Elliot above the din of the palace guards charging up the stairwell.

"There's nowhere else to go than up," replied Molly, who took Elliot by the hand and pulled him along with her. The two of them dashed to the stairwell and began sprinting up the glass steps. Behind, the palace guards charged after them with raised voices. After having passed the next floor it became evident that the much taller and stronger palace guards were gaining on them. Glancing over the banisters, they could see the grim muscular faces of the palace guards staring up at them as they ran.

Soon they reached the glass dome at the top of the stairwell. Under it were the ornate doors to the Mayizim

Communion Chamber. They knew they would be trapped in the Mayizim Communion Chamber so that wasn't an option. Panting for air, they looked around them frantically. At either side of the ornate doors stood great sculptures depicting wise old Skar'ley of glass holding scrolls in their hands. On either side of the statues were tall glass doors which led out.

"There!" shouted Elliot and ran for the doors. Luckily, the doors weren't locked, and warm, wet air met them as they ran out onto the roof. For a couple of seconds they stopped to scan their surroundings. They were on the roof of the great Imperial Library. The only feature on the walled roof was the great glass dome. Through it they could see the palace guards reaching the landing just below them. All around them were equally impressive and old stone buildings covered in red trees and green hanging vines. But on one side was the broad Plaza of Great Expectations and beyond – the walled Imperial Palace grounds.

Elliot and Molly ran to one of the low walls encircling the roof. Beyond was nothing but thin air. From the wall they could see the distant plaza below. They were really high up, at least on the fifteenth floor. The immense height made Elliot feel nauseous and his legs began to shake. He hated heights!

"There's nowhere to go," stated Elliot, and backed away from the low wall. "We're trapped."

"I don't believe this!" exclaimed Molly. "There are trees and creepers on all those other buildings, but not on this one. We could maybe have climbed down one of them, but no!"

"I saw some trees on a landing below," noted Elliot. "But it must be a jump of six floors or more to get there."

"I'm afraid that wouldn't be so wise, Master Elliot," informed Little Brother. "You see, the human body cannot withstand a fall of that magnitude and would…"

"We get the picture!" snapped Molly. "But we have our shields…"

"I'm afraid your personal shields wouldn't be able to take the strain from such a fall, Your Highness," noted Little Brother. "Also, Elliot's shield was most likely depleted by that laser shot in the Hollow World."

Behind them the glass doors were thrown open. Palace guards rushed out.

"It's over," sighed Elliot and hung his head. "They've got us now."

The palace guards spotted the two children standing by the roof's edge and ran at them. Their weapons were in their hands and grim determination showed in their faces. Far behind them ran the winded priest.

"Seize – *pant* – them! In the – *pant* – name of the Emperor!" the priest wheezed.

Molly suddenly turned to Elliot.

"Do you trust me?" she said gravely.

"What? I… yes I do, Molly."

"Then do as I do," she instructed and climbed onto the wall.

"What are you doing!?" cried Elliot in panic.

The palace guards came closer.

"Just do what I do!" shouted Molly and grabbed Elliot by the neck of his clothes.

Elliot was pulled up on the wall and gasped as he gazed down on the plaza below. The people milling about below looked like tiny ants. Vertigo gripped him and he felt dizzy, cold panic spread through his chest and down his spine. His legs trembled and he couldn't breathe. A breeze he hadn't felt before now threatened to topple him over the edge. It would be a fall to a very messy death.

"No… no!" moaned Elliot in fear and tried to sit down so he wouldn't fall.

"Now Elliot, we jump," said Molly seriously, still holding on to his shirt. She looked pale and in one of her trembling hands she clutched something against her chest.

"What! Jump? Are you crazy?" screamed Elliot, with tears of panic forming in his eyes. He looked down again. Alright, they were cornered, but suicide seemed a little too dramatic, not to say terribly frightening. He would probably die of fright before choosing to jump to his death.

"No! No! Don't do it!" shouted Little Brother from Elliot's back. "I'll die too!"

The palace guards were upon them now. The two fastest lunged for the human children.

"You'll have to trust me!" shouted Molly and grabbed Elliot's hand. Her hand shook, but she held on hard. "Jump!" she whispered and stepped out into the air while tugging Elliot along after her.

"No!" screamed Elliot as Molly pulled him with her. He tried to pull back in panic and for a couple of seconds he struggled to regain his balance. Then gravity got the better of him and pulled him over the edge along with Molly. One of the palace guards made a desperate attempt to grab his shirt as he dove for Elliot.

But the fine fabric passed through the scaly palace guard's hands and was gone.

And Elliot fell.

"Noooooo!" he screamed in terror.

"Noooooo!" Little Brother wailed in horror.

Then his stomach knotted and a thousand needles tingled all over his body. His heart stopped beating and he lost his breath. Without being able to say a word more he plummeted through the air to a nasty death on the hard cobbles below.

Even though his body and his mind were locked in the panic of falling – he knew this was the end.

CHAPTER 8
OLD ACQUAINTANCES AND SMALL FAVOURS

Elliot, Molly and Little Brother fell through the air towards a cold hard death below.

Although the air was warm and damp, it now felt icy cold as it rushed past them. Gravity pulled them mercilessly towards the hard cobbles of the Plaza of Great Expectations. They flailed their arms, legs and tentacles in panic, but nothing stopped their fall.

As the walls of the tall stone building of the Imperial Library shot past them, their lungs once again filled with air so they could scream again.

And they screamed.

They screamed in terror and despair, knowing that in a few seconds they were about to hit the ground. Elliot felt nothing but sheer animal panic. No other thoughts passed through his head. With lightning speed the ground shot up towards them. Suddenly it was just there, everywhere around them.

At the moment of impact a loud buzzing filled their ears and they somehow slowed down. The last fraction of a second left of their lives suddenly became extended to the last two seconds of their lives as a large energy bubble formed around them. Air was pressed out of their lungs and it felt like being squashed under a car or something equally large and heavy. The energy bubble flattened against the ground and then popped with a static crackle. The two children fell, winded but unharmed, the last half metre to the paved plaza.

As Elliot lay there on his back in shock, he heard the energy shield device in his belt sizzle and saw sparks and smoke coming out of it.

"Our… energy…shields," gasped Elliot. "I thought you said they couldn't help us, Little Brother."

"Aga! Aga! Aga!" replied Little Brother tonelessly from his back.

"But they did," said Molly a little shakily, while slowly getting to her feet. "Thank Salank, the good old Squid, for that." Without really thinking, she touched her earlobe, activating her Memo-Hair Gel which immediately re-ordered her braids after the fall.

"How did you know they were strong enough to save us? That was a pretty long fall," asked Elliot as he sat up. He felt sick and his legs still stung from a thousand needles.

"I didn't. Just like Little Brother I thought they couldn't save us. I was counting on my Radorian Saviour Ball instead." She held up the greenish egg in her shaky hand, which obviously hadn't inflated to save them.

"B-but it didn't do anything. It was the shields that…" stammered Elliot.

"Tell me about it! I was really surprised. I thought it would work. It worked when we crashed on that asteroid."

"We could have… we should have…" stuttered Elliot as the horror of their potential mistake sunk in.

"Yes, well," added Little Brother, who now had composed himself from soiling his cache memory. "Your Highness, I think I have read somewhere that the rare Radorian Saviour Balls are constructed for vacuum evacuation, which means they only function in space."

"Now you tell us!" groaned Molly. "It would've been good to know that earlier."

"You didn't ask me. And if you had asked I would have advised surrender and pleading for mercy. It would have been the only sane alternative."

"They wouldn't have spared us!" Molly pointed out. "They want us dead for knowing their secrets."

But Little Brother continued his lecture. "Now standard energy shields can withstand a lot, but not a fall from that height. When you pulled us over the edge, I assumed your shields would be far too weak and tried to calculate my own chances of remaining intact after impact. The odds were very low indeed. You were extremely lucky that Salank altered your energy shields the way he did."

"So, it didn't really go as planned." Elliot's knees felt like jelly as he tried to rise. "Wha-what if the shields hadn't been strong enough?" he said weakly.

"Then we would've died and wouldn't have had to worry about it anymore," replied Molly flatly. Although she tried to sound confident, Elliot could see that she was deathly pale. She had trusted the Radorian Saviour Ball to save them, but it hadn't worked. Instead, they were extremely lucky that the shields had worked.

People stood all around them with mouths open in shock, horror and bafflement. Skar'ley, Idagons, humans and Furanians gawked at the amazing survival of the human children.

Elliot looked down at his still smoking energy shield device.

"Yeah!" agreed Molly. "That one's taken a beating too many. Both the laser shot in that Hollow World and the fall must have been too much. It's burnt out. I'm afraid it won't help you anymore."

"I don't really care," said Elliot. "I survived that." He pointed up at the top of the Imperial Library and shuddered. As he examined the roof, he noticed that none of the palace guards were visible.

"Oh no!" he moaned. "The palace guards are on their way down again!"

"Let's get out of here!" said Molly.

They ran down one of the streets which led away from the Plaza of Great Expectations. The old stone houses around the palace grounds looked like ancient stained and overgrown temples. Between them ran equally magnificent streets decorated with drifting cast-iron lamps, statues which rearranged themselves in different poses, intricate cobble stone patterns and countless flower arrangements. But the two children didn't have much time to take in all the beauty of the city, as they ran for their lives. Somewhere behind them were the palace guards and they had to find somewhere to hide.

The answer came in the form of a canal. Running parallel with the palace wall was a great canal filled with boats, barges, rafts and canoes. It was absolutely packed with

Skar'ley and many of the larger boats, barges and rafts were tied together, forming a floating mat packed with people. Everywhere things were sold or bartered. Fruit, vegetables, spices, clothes, animals and jewellery were but some of the things Elliot could see on the closest boats. They ran along the large stone steps of the canal embankment leading down to the water. It was filled with people plying their goods or on their way to or from the great floating market.

"Here! We can hide here!" said Molly and dove into the crowd of people. Elliot followed her and it was easy to disappear amongst the people who were too busy trading to notice them. They pushed their way along the stone embankment steps, dodging between loud merchants and their stalls.

***

Having stormed out of the Imperial Library and Mayizim Halls, the palace guards now reached the canal. Winded from the run down the library steps and through the streets they stopped to get their breath back. Their yellow Skar'ley eyes took in the great market with despair. Their quarry must be here somewhere, but would they be able to spot them? There were so many people in the market. Although most of them were Skar'ley, there were too many stalls, packed goods, colourful clothing and occasional aliens to be able to spot two small humans.

"Have – *pant* – you – *pant* – found them?" asked the priest, when he eventually caught up with the assembled palace guards. He was exhausted and his legs trembled and ached. His lungs burnt and the long, thin reptilian tongue lolled out.

The nearest palace guard motioned to the floating market instead of answering. The cackle and buzz of the assembled people drowned any other sound. As far as his eyes could see along the canal, there were people everywhere.

"By the Eternal Sun!" he groaned. "We will never find them here."

***

Elliot and Molly crossed the canal by stepping from boat to barge to raft to boat again. In less than a hundred metres the two children had been offered to buy over a dozen varieties of fruit, countless stinking fish, rude rubber toys, something which looked like a sad featherless chicken, a bottle of perfume and an oddly shaped root. The merchants didn't seem to consider the strange fact that two human children were passing through their market, as they only had eyes for potential customers.

When they reached the canal embankment on the other side, Elliot carefully walked up a couple of steps and looked behind them. He could see the palace guards assembled and walking slowly up the other side of the canal, but not really searching the throng of people. After he had seen enough he ducked down again and joined Molly behind a large stall.

"They've lost us – for now," he whispered.

"And we've lost a lot of time," sighed Molly. "It's already noon and we haven't got a clue how to warn the Emperor. We have to find a way to get into the palace."

"A way into the – *chlum* – palace?" repeated a familiar voice behind them.

Elliot and Molly turned to find three S'margs standing behind them. The snake-like aliens with the flat faces peered at them with their sparkling golden eyes. Their multi-tentacled tails held an assortment of items which looked like lucky charms and pieces of paper. The unpleasant odour of the S'margs could be felt despite the many other smells of the floating market.

"Smellies!" said Molly with disgust and held her nose. "Whad do you wand?"

"We overheard your wish to – *chlum* – to enter the Imperial Palace, yes?" said the first S'marg.

"Perhaps to celebrate among the other VIP guests in the Imperial Festival Gardens?" said the second S'marg.

"Maybe we can assist you?" said the third S'marg.

As all S'margs looked identical to Elliot, for all that he knew, the three S'margs could be the same as those he had encountered on The Knot.

"Go away, Smellies!" said Molly brusquely. "We don't need your help."

"No! Wait a minute!" interrupted Elliot. He pulled Molly aside and whispered to her.

"Maybe they *can* help us? Although I didn't think so at first, they actually helped me find the abandoned human habitat at The Knot."

Molly cast a sceptical glance at the three S'margs who stood innocently waiting with their satchels full of presumably illegal goods. "I don't know. I don't trust them," she whispered.

"Neither do I, Master Elliot," whispered Little Brother in agreement from his back. "They are tricksters and liars who will try to steal all our money."

"That's what you said on The Knot as well. But they *did* manage to help us in the end – even if it cost us all the money we had left."

"Hmmm… I bet it was their kind that betrayed us on The Knot," mumbled Little Brother, desperate to have the last word.

But Elliot wasn't listening as he turned to the S'margs who had waited patiently during their hushed discussion.

"Will the Emperor be at the Festival Gardens?" he asked.

"Why, yes of course!" said one of the S'margs.

"He always attends to his invited guests at the – *chlum* – Festival Gardens after he has held his speech to the people at sunset," another S'marg added.

"With our help, you could be one of the lucky few who manage to speak briefly to the Emperor of the Skar'ley," said the third.

"How could you get us into the Festival Gardens?" asked Molly suspiciously. "Isn't it really well guarded?"

"More guarded than – *chlum* – anything else in the Imperial capital," said one of the S'margs. "It has thick walls and surveillance of all known spectrums of visibility as well as light displacement field detection."

"More guarded than – *chlum* – a mother Acid-Wolf's cubs," said another. "It has a lethal firewire perimeter, roving A.I. perimeter mines and thousands of armed guards."

"It is impossible to enter, unless specially invited," added the last. "All guests are DNA verified with their invitation and Truthsayer analysed upon entry."

"Phew! That sounds pretty… well guarded," replied Elliot with a shaky voice. "So, how would you get us in there then?" asked Elliot.

"We might just – *chlum* – know of an alternate way to enter," said a S'marg, winking with one of its big golden eyes.

"Yes, but how?" asked Molly impatiently. "Stop playing silly games, Smellies."

"Well, that information is not for free, young humans," said another S'marg. "We would sadly have to – *chlum* – charge you in order to assist you."

"Alright. How much will it cost us to get into the Festival Gardens tonight?" asked Elliot, knowing that the price he would be given would be exorbitant.

"Two thousand Imperial doubloons," stated one of the S'margs simply.

"Two thousand doubloons!" exclaimed Molly.

"Thieves! Rogues!" wailed Little Brother.

"I-Isn't that a bit much?" asked Elliot quietly.

"We are sorry, but we have our families and our livelihood to think about," explained the S'marg and held up his branched tail-tentacle apologetically.

"There are many people who would sacrifice an arm, leg or – *chlum* – a tentacle for an evening in the Imperial Festival Gardens," explained another S'marg.

"Not forgetting that the penalty for assisting somebody to – *chlum* – unlawfully enter the Imperial Festival Gardens is very stiff indeed," explained the last S'marg. "We have to cover all expenses we might have."

"Yes, yes, alright!" said Elliot angrily. "I understand all that. But we don't have two thousand doubloons."

"Then what do you have? We could settle for, say, one thousand eight hundred."

"Eh… what *do* we have?" Elliot asked Little Brother.

"I was given unlimited funds by the Atean King and Queen, Master Elliot," Little Brother replied. "However, the asteroid crash destroyed much of my decentralised storage nodes and most of the credit records and codes in my databank. All that remains now is small change, taxi money and enough to find you two some cheap take-away meals."

"How much are we talking about in doubloons?"

"Twenty-three doubloons and eighteen talons."

"Well, that doesn't help us much," sighed Elliot.

"Listen Smellie," said Molly angrily. "I won't pay to get into a party like a common street urchin. When father was alive we used to get *invited* to parties like these or even get *paid* to come. This is stupid."

Elliot gently pushed Molly back and smiled. "What she's trying to say is that we don't have any money at all. Even if we, against all logical sense, would consider paying that amount, we can't."

"No money!" exclaimed one of the S'margs in shock.

"A creature without money at the Floating Palace Market is like a boat without a bottom. They sink and are never seen again," explained the second S'marg.

"Well, then we are sorry to have disturbed you," apologised the third S'marg and the three smelly aliens turned to slither away.

"No, wait!" said Elliot. One of the snake-like S'margs stopped in its tracks and turned to face him again. Its long tentacle-tail flexed expectantly.

"Maybe we have something else other than money that would interest you?"

"And what would this be?" said the S'marg hungrily. The other two S'margs also turned to Elliot again.

"Well... I don't know," confessed Elliot and began to rummage through his belongings. Over Molly's shoulders hung the satchel with the serum against the slave genes, but he didn't dare to offer this to the S'margs. Neither could he give them the Orichalcum amulet or the ancient scroll. They were all too important. Apart from that, the only thing of value he had was his wrist communicator, his Mini Earphones and his Translator Lenses. But when he offered these to the S'margs they shook their heads.

"We can get – *chlum* – better equipment than that here at the market for under three hundred doubloons."

Elliot looked at Molly, who sighed angrily. "Alright. You can have my Cyclone XVII Class Orichalcum PDM," she said reluctantly.

"I'm sorry, but these items are of no – *chlum* – interest to us," replied a S'marg.

"Cyclone PDMs are horribly outdated these days," added another. "I'm not sure they would even power a simple timepiece."

"What! This is an excellent PDM and it still kicks ass," argued Molly.

"But what if you get her personal energy shield as well?" said Elliot.

"Energy shields are worth a lot, but still do not amount to the honour of attending – *chlum* – Imperial festivities."

Suddenly Molly lit up. "Alright Smellies! Do you know what a Radorian Saviour Ball is?"

"We do, we do," replied one of the S'margs.

"They are rare and – *chlum* – extremely expensive," added another.

"A marvel of science and a great secret of the Radorians," concluded the last.

"Well, we have one," said Molly and produced the green leathery egg.

The three S'margs gasped in astonishment and drew closer. The foul stink from their bodies made Molly gag and she took a step back, holding her nose.

"You cad have de Savioud Ball if you ged us idto the Festival Gardeds," promised Molly.

"It's a deal!" exclaimed the three S'margs in unison. "Give us the Radorian Saviour Ball and we will – *chlum* – help you."

Molly shook her head and took another step away from the smelly S'margs so that she could talk without holding her nose. "No, no! We won't give you anything until we're inside those palace walls," she said.

The S'margs huddled together and began to whisper. After a few seconds they turned to the children once again.

"We agree! We will see to it that you get inside the Imperial Festival Gardens before dusk today – *chlum*. In return you will give us the Radorian Saviour Ball."

"Then we have a deal," concluded Molly and put away the green leathery egg.

"Good. But then we must also hurry. You must – *chlum* – follow us," said one of the S'margs.

***

Elliot and Molly followed the three S'margs further down the canal and into a small alleyway. From there, the S'margs took a rickety rail bus to a seedier part of the Imperial capital. Although the houses were still of stone, they were narrower and more crooked. Instead of magnificent hanging gardens, they were covered in mould and weed. Their destination was a dodgy bar with a broken neon sign hovering above it. In private booths inside, people sat cast in shadows. Skar'ley barmaids carried trays with food and drink between the smoky booths.

The three S'margs joined a group of creatures assembled around a large table in one of the booths. As Elliot and Molly entered the booth, sounds they hadn't heard before suddenly burst into existence. The loud voices of the assembled and some wailing music filled the booth, but hadn't been heard from the outside.

"Local Sound Wall," explained Molly when she saw Elliot's surprise. "People use them to prevent others from hearing what they're talking about."

Around the table sat two more S'margs, three Idagons and two Skar'ley. All of them eyed Elliot and Molly suspiciously. The foul smell of the S'margs was more intense in this confined space.

"Please gentlemen," said one of the S'margs who had led Elliot and Molly to the bar. "May I present the last two members of your – *chlum* – little expedition to the Imperial festivities."

The six-armed Idagons flailed their arms around. "We paid only for us three," one of them complained gruffly. "We won't pay for them as well." The Idagon pointed a stubby finger at Elliot and Molly.

"We agree!" said one of the Skar'ley, which Elliot realised was female. Her clothes were jewelled as well as her metal head crest. "It is bad enough to travel with foul Idagons, but to be accompanied by noisy humans is intolerable! Really!"

"I agree, of course," said the other male Skar'ley with a tired and bored voice.

"There is no need to worry. These – *chlum* – clients will pay for themselves," replied another S'marg.

"They also wish to participate in the festivities," said a third S'marg, "but for entirely different reasons we guess."

"As long as they don't get us caught, I don't care what they'll be doing," said the gruff Idagon.

"As long as they have the taste not to disrupt this finest of moments of our distinguished culture with shrewd drinking, shouting and fighting, isn't that so my dear?" added the snobbish female Skar'ley.

"Of course, my dear," replied the tired looking Skar'ley.

Elliot and Molly didn't understand a thing. The Skar'ley evidently wanted to attend the party as they seemed to be snobs or nobles. But what were the Idagons doing here?

"What are the Idagons doing here?" whispered Elliot.

"Probably up to some of their usual tricks," answered Molly. "You know how they are. Remember the Galactic Olympic Games and the fake asteroid field in the Ash Plains?"

"You have seen the legendary Snabvarru Spunge Asteroid Field?" exclaimed one of the older looking Idagons, whom evidently had overheard them. He smiled and rubbed his six hands happily.

"You are lucky indeed. It was a marvel of creation and the dedication of a lifetime of Snabvarru the Ever-Sneezing. It was thought long lost. Oh joy that it still exists to trouble the space lanes."

"Do you always play tricks on people? Is that all you do?" Molly asked the Idagon with an irritated tone.

The Idagon looked shocked and drew back, all six eyes blinking rapidly.

"All we do? Of course not! We also sing, drink, play sociable games of chance and offer our services in the entertainment and transportation business."

"So what are you doing here?" asked Elliot suspiciously. "Are you going to play any tricks on the Emperor?"

The two Skar'ley turned to stare aghast at the Idagons.

"I'm afraid that our – *chlum* – clients enjoy the full discretion of our services," a S'marg quickly interrupted.

"This means that they are not obliged to reveal what their business is," another S'marg explained.

Elliot concluded that the greedy S'margs intended to get all five of them into the Festival Gardens somehow. Obviously the Idagons were up to something dodgy, but hopefully harmless.

"May we remind you once again to use the same – *chlum* – discretion once inside the Festival Gardens," said a S'marg. "We wish to remain anonymous suppliers of guests to the palace and would ask you to please refrain from mentioning how you got in."

"So, how *do* we get in?" asked Elliot again.

"We take you, of course!" said the inconspicuous salt shaker on the table.

"What? Who?" said the two Skar'ley and looked around for the source of the voice. The three Idagons however turned their eighteen eyes to the salt shaker in disbelief.

"Ah, yes!" exclaimed one of the S'margs nervously. "Our transport agency is… in contact with us through this… device."

"Transport agency?" exclaimed the snobbish female Skar'ley. "We've paid an exorbitant amount of money for the privilege of attending the festivities our kind Emperor in his grace forgot to invite us to. We do not expect to travel in second or third class!"

"Certainly – *chlum* – not!" assured one of the S'marg with his large golden eyes doing their best to look sincere. "The trip must however be done discretely and therefore our agent will – *chlum* – shield you from unkind eyes until you are in the palace. It is a simple procedure."

"Procedure!?" noted the other Skar'ley with a tired and gloomy look. "That sounds more like a kind of operation, dear."

"Indeed! We have not paid to undergo unwanted surgery, cosmetic or otherwise."

"We assure you it is nothing of the kind," a S'marg said with emphasis and waved with his branched tail-tentacle. "Our agent will render you unseen to the palace guards and their equipment and then reinstate you upon arrival. It is totally painless and reasonably safe. Let me show you!"

As the S'marg pulled the talking salt shaker towards him, another S'marg touched a small wall panel, which immediately rendered the Local Sound Wall opaque. The dark wall now prevented anybody from seeing what was happening in their private booth.

The first S'marg directed a small opening on one side of the salt shaker towards the Skar'ley and pressed a hidden button on its side.

"Oh, it's an old-fashioned cam…" began the snobbish Skar'ley – and then vanished.

"What?!" exclaimed the Idagons in unison and jumped back. "Did you disintegrate them? Were they teleported into the palace somehow? Were they made optically invisible or physically insubstantial?"

"I'm afraid it's a more complicated procedure than so," said another S'marg.

"And a more secret procedure," added the last S'marg.

"Alright! Let's get on with it!" said Molly suddenly, surprising everybody. "We don't have all day! Just get us into the palace and you can keep your secrets." She handed over the Radiorian Saviour Ball as payment to one of the S'margs.

The S'margs nodded their flat faces in approval and re-arranged the salt shaker's opening towards Elliot and Molly.

"I hope you know what we're doing," whispered Elliot. "Because I…"

Then there was nothing.

***

The next thing Elliot experienced was pain. Something stung his arm and he jolted upright.

"Ouch!" he exclaimed, but immediately got a hand clamped down over his face.

"Good! You're finally awake! Now don't make any more noises!" whispered Molly next to him. Elliot could see that they were in a small and dirty room with discoloured metal walls. Molly sat next to him, looking very alarmed and glancing around to see if anybody had heard Elliot's shout. A long sliver of light pierced the cold room's gloom. It came from a bulky metal door which stood ajar. As Elliot collected his legs under him he saw the long and thin metal needle jutting out of his arm. It was this needle that had awakened him. To his horror, he also saw another ten needles jutting out of his other arm and his legs. He even had one at the top of his head.

"You were quite hard to awaken," said Molly apologetically, as if sticking her friend with a dozen needles was nothing out of the ordinary.

"Ouch!" whispered Elliot as he began to remove the needles. While Elliot was doing this, Molly leaned close again.

"I think we have been pressganged!"

"Pressganged?"

"You know, drugged and thrown on board a ship heading for the farthest reaches of the Spiral Arm. When we wake up it will be too late to return and we'll be forced to work as slave labour until the end of our days or until the foreman whips us to death."

"What!?"

Oblivious to her horrendous and surreal statement, Molly continued explaining. "It was my adaptive antidote nano hives which saved us!"

"Oh, them!" replied Elliot meekly and remembered she had spoken about these on The Knot.

"Yes, the antidote nanites revived me and I managed to hack the door system."

A bunch of wires were hanging out of a wall panel next to the door and smoke curled up from them.

"You're sure you hacked the system?" asked Elliot. "It looks like you…"

"Yes, yes, so I smashed it okay. These systems are really alien. Like nothing I've ever seen before. And also, the PDM seems shut down. Must've been something the S'margs did."

"Where did you find these needles?" asked Elliot bewildered as he removed the last one from his leg.

"Oh, there were heaps of them in that box over there," Molly answered and waved absently towards a dirty bench with all kinds of tools.

"Where's Little Brother?" Elliot asked suddenly. He looked around frantically.

"He's here!" answered Molly and patted the black case which now had retracted its tentacle straps. "It seems he's also been shut down somehow when the S'marg's drugged us. I can't activate him."

"I hope he's okay," muttered Elliot, feeling sorry for his synthetic friend. "What's… what's out there?" he continued and pointed towards the heavy steel door.

"Take a look for yourself," Molly answered and rose to stand by the door with Little Brother in her arms.

Elliot rose unsteadily. His legs felt heavy and his body slightly numb, as if just roused from sleep. When he peaked out of the thin opening of the door he saw a railing and confusing, blurry landscape beyond. It was full of colourful clouds, mounds or mountains which passed by. It was clear they were on a moving craft of some sort, the humming of the engines also confirmed this. But parts of the blurry landscape outside somehow also seemed to move on its own accord, as if he was looking at blurry clouds moving at different speeds.

"What is that?" he whispered.

"I think it could be some kind of gas giant atmosphere," replied Molly. "It could be the composition of the atmosphere that causes the blur to our eyes."

"It's nothing of the kind!" replied a loud and proud voice just outside the door.

The door suddenly swung open letting in more light. Elliot and Molly jumped back, Molly somehow producing a cruel-looking cutting tool she must have found on the tool bench. Just outside the bulkhead door stood a stick-insect-thin creature with a colourful red and black uniform filled with countless medals, golden cuffs and brass buttons. Its head resembled that of a hammerhead shark with two bulging black eyes and mouth ringed by a neatly trimmed silver beard. Its hands were humanoid but had a dizzying amount of thin fingers or tendrils which held something which clearly must be a rifle.

"Who are you, what do you want ,why have you pressganged us, how dare you!" shouted Molly and waved her makeshift weapon menacingly.

"I am Manivar do Shala kep tam Uwari," answered the figure proudly and bowed all the way down to the floor with his strange head.

"I dare to say I am the captain of the *Pudding Maker* and your humble servant on this journey. You have not been pressganged or kidnapped in any way against your will. Instead you are safely on your way to your destination."

"Then why did you drug us?" demanded Molly and pointed the cutting tool at his face.

As if daring Molly, the creature took a step closer to her weapon until its face was inches away from it. It held its back straight as it boldly answered. "We did not drug you. We simply persuaded some of the nerve cells in your brains to cease communicating and increased the production of your hormones which entice you to sleep."

"That's the same thing!" hissed Molly and stepped even closer to the alien. Her nose nearly touching his... facial protrusion.

"I would argue differently. But nonetheless, it was paramount that you were rendered unconscious and unaware of this voyage."

Molly was about to say something again when Elliot stepped up and forced himself between them.

"Why should we remain unaware? Where are we going and why aren't we going directly to the Festival Gardens in the palace?"

"But you *are* going there. Straight there, as fast as the engines of the *Pudding Maker* can deliver you." The captain gestured out towards the blurred, colourful clouds. "See?"

Elliot and Molly gazed out at the dizzying landscape not understanding anything.

"What was your name again?" Molly asked menacingly.

Not understanding her tone, the creature once again bowed proudly. "I am Manivar do Shala kep tam Uwari, Captain of the…"

"Well… Manny…. you'd better explain fast what's going on or I'll turn your innards to outards!" roared Molly and punched a hole in the air with her makeshift weapon.

Blinking in shock, more at his new nickname than Molly's display of violence, Captain Manny took a step backwards.

"I… I've never…" He then composed himself with a snort and glared at Molly while beginning to explain.

"We had to render you unconscious so that you wouldn't experience nor understand the re-sizing effect. Very few are aware of this technology and we – as well as our business partners – would like to keep it that way."

"What do you mean re-sizing?" asked Molly suspiciously. She turned and whispered conspiratorially to Elliot. "Uncle Frej had some kind of re-sizing power, but I was told it was naughty and unhygienic. I'm not sure I approve."

But Elliot wasn't really listening. Instead he took in the strangely moving unfocused clouds around them and realisation struck him.

"You've shrunk us! Somehow you've shrunk us!"

"That's correct," Captain Manny replied beaming with pride. "The effect won't last forever though, as the relative distances between your molecules will force themselves back to their natural equilibrium, but it should be long enough for this journey."

Elliot now understood that the objects around them was actually the normal… sized… world. The colourful things were somehow too big to be focused on and for some reason moved in slow motion. But if he squinted he thought he could make out the towering upper body and face of a humanoid creature far away in the distance. Other towering and blurry objects moving slowly in different directions must be other people or even buildings. They had been reduced to dust mote size!

"You're Zip Zaps!" Molly exclaimed.

"Hrmph! That's a much-abbreviated name for a race which has conquered the known galaxy."

"Well, nobody really noticed you conquered it…" Molly pointed out.

"Well, one day they'll be sorry for ignoring us."

Ignorant of the conversation, Elliot turned back to Captain Manny.

"Why is everything moving so slowly?"

"It isn't! We are moving faster!" Captain Manny explained. As it was clear that the human children didn't understand, he explained further.

"We're moving faster than the objects around us, relatively speaking, so at our reduced size we experience this as everything moving slower. It's a bit hard to explain but has a lot to do with relative inertia in relation to speed and size, topped with a complicated relation to molecular composure."

Elliot shook his head, trying to ignore the dizzying and incomprehensive facts. "But what does all this mean? How long will this journey take?"

"Oh, no more than two days!" replied Captain Manny.

"Two days! But we need to be at the Festival Gardens tonight!"

"And you will be. When I say a two-day trip I mean this relative to your current size. It will seem like two days to you here aboard my fine ship, but we'll arrive in your grossly slow and… larger… time only twelve hours after we departed."

"But I thought time went faster when we're smaller…" Elliot began.

"It is all very, very hard to explain," Captain Manny said dismissively. "But I assure you that you will arrive at the time and the place agreed with our business partners."

"Your business partners!" Molly cut in, while putting away the cruel-looking cutting tool. "You mean the S'margs? They've known all along about your ability to shrink things?"

"Yes of course!" beamed Captain Manny with pride. "This has enabled us to pursue a lucrative partnership for more than six hundred years… that's ten years to you."

"I understand," said Elliot. With your small non-detectable size you and the S'margs can smuggle people and goods in and out of nearly any place in the Spiral Arm. That's why you normally keep your passengers unconscious, so your smuggling won't be known."

"Smuggling, makes it sound so illegal. We have conquered the galaxy after all and everything we survey is at our disposal."

"As long as nobody notices…" Molly mumbled.

"What is it that you're intending to do inside the Imperial Palace… apart from smu… transporting us there?" Elliot asked.

"We do not call it the Imperial Palace. We have so far found no palace there and don't understand what all the fuss is about. For us it is known as the Fabulous Mines of Varania. Precious metals, food chemicals and raw ores of nearly every sort can be found there. Tens of thousands of our people gloriously work in the mines there… more or less voluntarily. The *Pudding Maker* plies this route regularly and transporting you is good cash on the side for us."

"The *Pudding Maker*?" asked Elliot, while Molly moved to the railing to watch the view.

"It's as good a name as any!" stated Captain Manny with challenge in his eyes.

Elliot didn't pursue the subject any further. He'd understood from the haughty comments at the secret meeting of the Hidden Watchers that the Zip Zaps might well be hot-heads and didn't want a conflict over the peculiar and sensitive name.

Instead he joined Molly at the railing and tried to focus on the blurred objects all around them.

"This is amazing, isn't it!" he exclaimed. "When you thought the universe couldn't get any bigger, we became smaller."

"Well, I guess it's amazing," agreed Molly reluctantly. "I'm however more concerned where these Zip Zaps have been and what they've seen." She nodded towards Elliot's pants and he suddenly blushed.

"I… I don't think they really want to… I mean… I don't think they would actually see any details… of things…"

"They'd better not!" said Molly menacingly, in a way only she could when threatening an entire alien species.

***

True to his word, the trip to the Fabulous Imperial Palace Mines of Varania took two days. During this time, Elliot and Molly were shown around the transport ship known as the *Pudding Maker*. Captain Manny began by showing them all the amazing weaponry to protect them against pirates and ensure their dominion of the known universe. It was admittedly quite an impressive arsenal of cannons and torpedoes, but Molly quietly suspected they would hardly make a dog itch if given a full barrage. They then toured the engineering bay, the storerooms (containing the sleeping Idagons and Skar'ley, amongst other things) as well as the shining bridge. Everywhere they went, uniformed Zip Zaps snapped to attention when Captain Manny approached.

The Zip Zaps had the means to communicate with and view the larger world, but it made little sense to them. So after spending an hour of explaining the various charted obstacles on the way (read: people), Captain Manny invited them to dinner in the Captain's mess. The Zip Zaps ate large fluffy balls of different colours, but with very little taste. But somehow they delighted in the taste and were visibly invigorated to the degree of involuntarily sending off sparks and excusing themselves as if burping.

When enquiring about Little Brother, Captain Manny became very serious. Communication with his superiors had cleared the newly awakened human children, but he wasn't allowed to re-activate the molecular activity of the A.I. until they had arrived and been re-sized. As long as they weren't in any danger, Elliot and Molly agreed to keep the secret of the S'marg and Zip Zap inconspicuous transport network.

The next two days and nights they wandered the deck looking out at the strange landscape or stayed in the luxurious cabin Captain Manny arranged for them. Elliot became more fidgety with nervousness with every day that passed. It was hard to convince his mind that the few hours they had left to warn the Emperor had been drawn out to two days. Both he and Molly grew more and more impatient and often found themselves pacing back and forth on deck. Uncle Karl was still alive – for now. This brought great comfort to Elliot, but he knew that this wouldn't last. The bloodthirsty priests could kill him any moment. They desperately needed to warn the Emperor and save… everyone. The weight of this responsibility was crushing.

***

During the last day, the blurry landscape had changed to more green and brown, which Elliot and Molly assumed and hoped were the Imperial Festival Gardens. When darkness finally descended, they understood that the evening in the real slow-time world had arrived. It was finally time to depart and Captain Manny brought Molly and Elliot to one of the larger cargo storerooms. A huge and strange machine covered one side of the room and was pointed menacingly at them.

"It is time for us to part ways," Captain Manny began ceremoniously. "You have arrived at your destination, but we must continue onward to ours – the Fabulous Mines of Varania. But rest assured that you have both made a lasting impression upon us all. We will always remember you as… people we met."

With those words he stepped carefully aside and signalled his technicians who began adjusting levers and pressing buttons on the menacing machine pointed at them.

"What will that do to us?" Elliot asked nervously.

"It's a smaller version of the Transmatter Tower in the Stinking Plains which re-sized you. It will return you to your original size with minimal discomfort."

"The Transmatter Tower? You mean the salt shaker on that table? Isn't that for eating?" asked Elliot.

"Salt shaker? I don't know what you're talking about? We have seeded Transmatter Towers everywhere throughout the conquered galaxy for the purpose of transmuting material and energy. I have admittedly heard reports of grossly oversized aliens robbing them of their power crystals for food, but I'm sure that's all exaggerated. Now, please remain still while we home in on your molecular activity."

"I hope this won't hurt," said Molly with a finger of warning raised. "Because if it does I'll…"

Then there was nothing.

CHAPTER 9
HIDDEN TRAITORS AND DEADLY ASSASSINS

A large purple shrubbery with white flowers rested silently in the warm and humid night. Shrubberies are normally always silent, but this particular shrubbery kept extra still and silent so as not to disturb the slender, singing trees surrounding it.

Suddenly the air distorted with a loud pop and two human children seemed to materialise out of thin air.

The two children landed hard on soft grass with an "Ouch!" Their bodies itched and they drew themselves up while rubbing their arms and legs. They felt sore from a stinging pain, a bit like intense sunburn on the inside of the skin and skull.

"That really hurt," whispered Elliot with a gasp.

"They'll pay…" whispered Molly.

But then the real-size world returned to them in full. The smells came first. All around them were new and exotic smells of vegetation, which hadn't been available to them in the Zip Zap's miniature world. As a matter of fact, smells hadn't really been strong at all and now they raced back with a vengeance. It was dark, except for faint lights that shone through the high vegetation that surrounded them. When they looked up they could see the dark brown night sky, polluted by the myriad of lights from the great city below it. The looming dark shape of a great hovering building could be seen to their left. Myriads of dimmed lights shone along its sides. Two glistening beautiful moons dominated the rest of the night sky. One amber and one light purple. Somewhere close they heard music and laughter.

The Idagons and Skar'ley which had also been smuggled into the palace by the Zip Zaps were nowhere to be seen. Doubtlessly, they had been deposited somewhere else in the Festival Gardens.

"That was… strange," Elliot pointed out. "A bit like a dream."

"A long dream," added Molly.

"I don't remember anything," informed Little Brother cheerfully. "There was a power surge and now we're here. I seem to have suffered a temporary shutdown. What happened?"

"That's a bit hard to explain," said Molly, remembering her and Eliot's promise not to reveal the S'marg and Zip Zap secret of smuggling re-sized people and goods. "Let's say the S'margs are very good at smuggling things into the palace without the Skar'ley noticing."

"How do we know this is the Festival Gardens?" Elliot wondered.

"Listen to Singing Trees, Master Elliot," replied Little Brother. "These rare plants are only found in the Festival Gardens."

When they stopped talking and listened they could hear a faint, high-pitched singing noise and realised it came from the tall slender trees with cauliflower tops which stood all around them. They were also surrounded by high purple bushes and when they squinted out through the branches they could see lights and people.

They were in a vast garden or park surrounded by high fortified walls. Towering over the gardens to one side were the pyramid-shaped palace buildings with their many forested walkways, terraces, spires and balconies. The large spherical main building hovered impossibly in the air, its countless windows spreading light in all directions. The bottom of the floating palace sphere nearly touched the tip of the large pyramid. It was an amazing and impossible sight.

The garden itself was filled with peacefully floating lights in paper-like lanterns. They cast a smooth and soothing glow over the countless people that passed between amazing alien flower arrangements and beautiful trees and bushes. Fountains and statues dotted the gardens and small houses could be seen as silhouettes in the gloom. The people moving through the garden seemed to be mainly Skar'ley with elaborately crested headpieces and richly adorned clothes. But there were also several elderly humans, hard-drinking Idagons, fair Vurites, babbling Furanians and silent Grunans. Here and there Elliot could see containment boxes of Radorians.

"This has to be the Festival Gardens," Molly whispered next to him. "Look, there are priests and royals everywhere."

"Yeah, and palace guards," added Elliot.

They could see the armoured palace guards along paths and on the walls and walkways of the palace. They were everywhere.

"What time is it?" Elliot said suddenly.

"It's forty minutes to midnight!" Little Brother confirmed cheerily. "We haven't missed the magnificent fireworks."

"That means we still should have some time to find the Emperor," Molly said.

"Yes, we're here *and* still in time," Elliot said with a relieved sigh. "Everything still seems to be as normal. The Emperor must still be alive and well."

"All we have to do now is find him," said Molly. "As its close to midnight, he's already held his speech. He must be here somewhere among his guests. Let's go and see if we can find him."

"How do we recognise him?" wondered Elliot.

"I don't think it will be that hard," said Molly. "We find the most well-guarded, most beautiful, most waited upon person here in the gardens, and that should be him."

***

Elsewhere in the palace, a Skar'ley servant looked again at the beautiful and enormous golden mirror of the Setting Sun reception hall. The gold along the frame seemed stained. He rubbed at it with his cloth. But nothing happened. Upon close inspection he saw that it was actually pockmarked and worn, as if something was eating the gold out of the frame, one tiny, microscopic bite at a time.

"Strange," the servant mumbled to himself. This was just like the silver spoons in the Cupboard of Splendid Preservation. What could it be?

With a shrug, he then decided that this must be some kind of aggressive pollution and made a mental note to notify the East Wing Manager about this. He continued his round of dusting without being able to zoom in on the huge gold mine fields of the Zip Zap workers on the golden frame.

***

The two children exited the shrubbery from which they had overlooked the gardens and set off down one of the paths. Under two gently drifting lanterns stood a group of Skar'ley who spoke gently to each other. In their hands were elaborate glasses with colourful drinks and small paper umbrellas – which proved that some things were truly universal. As Elliot and Molly passed the Skar'ley, they stopped talking and stared at the two children. But they didn't stop them or even talk to them.

Further ahead a couple of priests stood huddled under a gaunt tree with leaves that sparkled in the gloom.

"Priests up ahead!" hissed Elliot and pulled Molly away from the path. "We better avoid them."

"Yeah," agreed Molly. "Them and everybody else we might know."

As carefully as possible they continued their exploration of the Festival Gardens. Sometimes they used the paths and sometimes they cut across lawns. All around them the tall slender trees sang beautifully and luminescent insects buzzed gently through the night gloom. It was a warm and pleasant night, with wonderful scents from unseen flowers drifting across the many paths. The Festival Gardens were huge and slightly disorienting in the gloom. Adding to the confusion were the floating tubes of water, like hovering streams, which criss-crossed the Festival Gardens and drifted gently in the breeze. Elliot and Molly had to dodge or crawl under them to get past them. Fish could be seen swimming in them and water plants bobbed on the tubular surfaces. When putting their hands into the water they became wet, but no water spilled down on them.

"Weird!" was all Elliot could say.

Here and there they would meet occasional strollers or small groups of people who were roaming the gardens, but none of them seemed important enough to be an emperor. They tried to look inconspicuous when passing people, but always took shortcuts to other paths over the grass or through shrubbery, whenever they saw a priest. As they reached the more central parts of the Festival Gardens, they could see that there were a lot more people milling under a couple of pavilions with warm yellow lights. That was where the music originated from as well.

"I bet that's where we have to go," said Elliot and pointed.

"We won't be able to move around there without the priests seeing us," informed Molly.

"I guess so. But we have to speak to the Emperor. If we can only get to him, it won't matter if the priests spot us."

"Priests!" hissed Molly suddenly and pulled Elliot aside. They ducked behind one of the slender singing trees as a party of priests came up the path towards them. Two floating lanterns followed the priests and their revealing lights came steadily closer.

"They're coming our way," moaned Elliot as he glanced around the tree.

"Let's go through here," said Molly and led the way through a large bamboo-like arrangement. They half ran through the tall but dense fronds, eager to get away from the priest. Not seeing where the concealing shrubbery ended in the gloom, they suddenly burst out onto another path and ran into a group of people. Elliot accidentally brought one of the bamboo-like branches out with him and let it snap back across the arms of a Skar'ley, whose drink was knocked out of his hand. Molly bumped into an elderly moustached Atean who stumbled backwards.

"What in the name of…?" shouted the Atean with mounting anger.

"I'm sorry, I'm sorry, I'm sorry!" repeated Elliot and picked up the glass he'd knocked out of the Skar'ley's hand.

"Yeah, we're sorry," said Molly while trying to slip away.

"What in the blazes? They're children!" said another elderly Atean with a long white beard. His elderly wife grabbed the glasses hanging around her neck and put them on to peer at them. In doing so, she leaned close enough to Elliot so as to kiss him if she'd wanted to. Her enlarged blue eyes fixed on Elliot as he tried to back away.

"Oh, it's those two children the King and Queen had as guests. My word, I thought they were dead!"

"What? The Atean children?" said one of the Skar'ley with a raspy voice.

Molly grabbed Elliot's hand and pulled him away from the people. The loud excited voices would surely attract more attention.

"Elliot? Elliot Stormsson?" said a familiar voice suddenly.

Elliot turned around and saw a figure emerge from the group. He was shorter than the others, as if he was half sitting. The reason for this was the strange multi-legged chair which bore him.

"Ambassador Horus?" said Elliot carefully.

"Elliot! It *is* you. You're alive!"

Ambassador Horus came into the light of one of the drifting lamps. As his legs were of no use to him, he was seated in his slightly spider-like chair. A long, silver robe adorned with red flowers and patterns covered most of his body and his mechanical chair. His still-brown hair was tied into a complicated knot at the back of his head and in his hand he held a drink.

"This is amazing!" Ambassador Horus exclaimed. "It's a miracle! You're both alive!"

Elliot flinched every time Ambassador Hours raised his voice, afraid that priests would notice them.

"What are you doing here? How did you survive the Cruelie attack?" Ambassador Horus went on.

"Well we…" said Elliot hesitantly.

"Elliot!" hissed Molly and pointed towards the group of priests that came up the path. Two lamps drifted over them, so it was probably the same party of priests they had avoided before. Their path probably encircled the shrubbery they had darted through.

Ambassador Horus saw Molly's nervousness and stopped talking. He followed her gaze and noticed the priests.

"The children!" continued the Ateans happily. "They're alive and healthy!"

"Just wait till I tell my wife about this!"

"I bet they're up to some mischief, children always are, the lucky little devils."

"Can I have a picture taken with you together with the Ambassador?"

But Ambassador Horus saw that Elliot and Molly were desperately trying to get away from the party of important Skar'ley and Atean nobles.

"Please, ladies and gentlemen," said Ambassador Horus, raising his arms. "The children have a very hectic schedule tonight, being the most distinguished guests of the Emperor. You will see more of them later. I guarantee that you'll have a chance to speak to them then."

He then led Elliot and Molly away from the path. As soon as they stepped in behind two large bottle-shaped trees, Horus' face became concerned.

"What's going on? Why are you sneaking around the Festival Gardens? I didn't even know you were here, let alone that you survived the attack."

"Well, we managed to get out of the ship and were saved…" Elliot began again, but broke off as he felt Molly stepping on his foot. She was right. They weren't sure Ambassador Horus could be trusted.

"That was lucky. Well we also managed to get out of the ship. Actually, all of the crew managed to get into the lifeboats," Ambassador Horus explained. "We were then rounded up by the Cruelies who shipped us off to be sold as slaves. Luckily a Vurite ship intercepted the slave ship."

"Yeah we heard…" said Elliot. He really wanted to trust Ambassador Horus. He seemed to be a genuinely nice man. But they couldn't afford to risk anything when they had worked so hard to come this far.

"I was devastated, and so was Captain Asetos, when we learnt that the two of you weren't among the survivors," continued Ambassador Horus. "We thought you were dead. Everyone did."

"We need to speak to the Emperor," Elliot said suddenly.

"Speak to the Emperor?" Ambassador Horus was surprised by the sudden demand, but nodded thoughtfully.

"Well, of course you should. After all, you were invited here as distinguished guests."

"Can you take us to him?" Molly asked.

"That shouldn't be a problem. He should be in the Floating Flower Pavilion right now."

"Then can we go now, please? We have to see him at once," pleaded Elliot.

"I don't understand…" began Ambassador Horus and then trailed off. He saw how frightened and concerned the two children seemed.

"Alright, we'll go to see the Emperor at once. Then maybe you can explain what all this is about and how you escaped the attack without the Cruelies capturing you."

"I promise we will. We'll explain everything," Elliot said solemnly. "Just take us to the Emperor."

Ambassador Horus nodded and gestured for them to follow him.

Despite being confined to his mechanical chair, Ambassador Horus could move swiftly. The thin metal legs clinked as they moved across the gravel of the path. None of them said anything as they walked towards the ten or so lit pavilions. As they drew closer, Elliot and Molly could see musicians atop tall pillars and people dancing strange Skar'ley dances below. Long, multi-layered tables were laden with food and drinks of all sorts and large rose-like flowers drifted around the pavilion area in the light breeze.

Regal Skar'ley with adorned and crested headpieces and shiny clothes dominated the scene. But several Atean nobles could be seen here and there with impossibly large hats and colourful clothes. Giggling and intoxicated Idagons which looked like dressed up six-armed monkeys were among the guests, as well as Furanians, who instead of wearing clothes had knotted their furs in complicated patterns. Three containment boxes holding Radorians were placed close to the dance floor and countless Grunans with red, thrashing hair braids moved around serving them. Groups of slender and fair Vurites could be seen here and there, standing relaxed with dumb but bright smiles. Their leader however, had a Porian attached to his head and seemed to study the party carefully with unseen eyes. Even some yellow Sarapids moved among the important guests on their many tentacles. Under a lamp, Elliot caught a glance of two almond-eyed Snakirra talking to some Skar'ley priests. But even stranger creatures walked among the guests. They were all a chaotic mix of animal parts and carried musical instruments. Elliot guessed they were Sha Kiff entertainers.

As they moved into the light, people stopped talking and stared at them. The Ateans knew immediately who they were, while the Skar'ley understood they were unusual. A murmur spread among the guests and people parted in front of them as Ambassador Horus led them forward. Soon they saw a large party of palace guards stationed in a circle around the central pavilion. A handful of Skar'ley and a couple of Ateans were sitting and talking with drinks in their hands. The centrally placed figure drew all the attention however. He was dressed totally in gold and carried a large gold and blue headpiece with three crests that met at the forehead. Above his head hovered three small metal spheres, covered by a dozen small lenses. The spheres slowly circled the gold-clad man's immediate surroundings, like three small moons orbiting a planet.

That had to be the Emperor. He had to be the reason for all the palace guards.

Elliot suddenly felt very nervous. He didn't know what words to use or how he was going to explain to this all-mighty Emperor about the conspiracy of the Priesthood, the secret asteroid fleet and the humans of Earth who were going to be enslaved.

The Emperor looked up from his conversation when he saw people parting for Ambassador Horus and the children. His reptilian eyes widened and he couldn't believe what he saw.

But the Priests of the Eternal Sun had also seen Elliot and Molly. Among those high-ranking priests that stood assembled close to the Imperial person himself, was the High Priest Skauda'tesh. He noticed the two children at the same moment as a flustered priest ran to his side to report the children he had seen. Reacting as swift as a viper, he stood up and raised his voice.

"Assassins! Guards, guards! Seize the Atean Children!"

At the mention of the word 'assassin' chaos erupted. People let out shrieks of surprise or fear. Guests stopped dancing or shuffled to their feet if they had been sitting. Waiters stopped and dropped their trays. Meanwhile, the palace guards jumped to attention. They drew long, crystal swords and laser gun barrels extracted from their forearm armour plates. They stepped together, shoulder to shoulder, facing outward, creating a living wall around the Emperor. Energy shields crackled into existence, originating from the small hovering orbs, forming a dome over the Emperor and his guards.

"The children are carrying bombs! Seize them! Protect the Emperor!" Skauda'tesh continued. His hoarse voice somehow cut across the chaos and frightened voices of the guests and he pointed accusingly at Elliot and Molly.

"What?" said Ambassador Horus and stared in surprise at the children.

"It's not true!" shouted Molly. "We don't have any bombs. We don't have any weapons at all."

"It's the priests who are trying to kill the Emperor," shouted Elliot and backed away. "It was *they* who tried to kill us in the Dead Worlds Cluster."

"But, but, it was Cruelies that attacked us. I don't understand. Why...?" said Ambassador Horus in a confused voice. Ambassador Horus looked both scared and disappointed, but didn't have time to say anything else before angry palace guards pushed him aside as they ran up to seize Elliot and Molly.

"Assassins! Murderers!" Skauda'tesh continued to bellow.

"No! It's not true!" shouted Elliot. He tried to meet the Emperor's eyes, but the palace guards were already escorting him away from the potential danger.

"Please, Mr Emperor, you have to listen to us. You're in danger!" shouted Elliot.

But even if the Emperor had heard him, he didn't turn or even look at them. Instead he followed his guards to safety.

The palace guards seized Elliot and began to pull him away from the Emperor. Even Molly was caught by the guards, but put up a vicious verbal fight.

"Get your filthy Scalie hands off me, your flea-ridden sons of..."

But the grips of the palace guards were hard as iron and their bulky armour slammed into their faces. They saw nothing else now, but the angry palace guards. A transparent crystal sword came up to Elliot's throat. It looked very, very sharp and he could see his own scared reflection in its glossy surface.

The Emperor was leaving. Soon, they would be alone with the priests. Elliot knew this was their only chance. But what could he say to get the Emperor's attention? Suddenly he had an idea.

"Emperor! Emperor, listen to me! Karrillus Ursus is still alive. I know where he is. He found Matalla. It still exists."

"Silence dog, or we'll cut your tongue out!" said one of the palace guards.

Skauda'tesh pushed through the throng of priests standing around Elliot and Molly.

"What do we have here?" he said menacingly with his cruel and harsh voice. His yellow reptilian eyes were narrow and his two nose slits wide open, as if sniffing for something. Elliot knew that Skauda'tesh's harsh voice and the dark, stained scales surrounding his eyes were the only evidence left of his Has'pleen body which had been altered by the Flesh Smith to look like an ordinary Skar'ley.

"So, the two troublemakers come to the cake, like wasps to sugar. Is that not how you would express it humans, hmmm? What is it that you do to wasps when they irritate you, hmmm? Yes, you swat them, don't you?"

Elliot said nothing. He just glared as hatefully as he could at the evil priest.

Molly on the other hand had plenty to say.

"Go and eat yourself, you stinking piece of shredded skin." She spat at Skauda'tesh, who seemed perplexed at Molly's extremely aggressive behaviour.

"Enough of this! These assassins are a threat to the Emperor, take them away!" Skauda'tesh hissed.

"Wait just one moment!" a stern Skar'ley voice said. The palace guards immediately moved aside to give room for the Emperor himself.

"My Emperor," gasped Skauda'tesh who seemed genuinely surprised at the Emperor's sudden appearance. "Light Manifest of the Eternal Sun, what are you still doing here? You must be taken to safety. You must stay away from these assassins."

"Emperor, don't listen to him!" said Elliot. "He's lying, he's…" but Elliot's words were cut off as the crystal sword was pressed harder against his throat. It felt like the edge would cut clean into his flesh at any time.

"Isn't this the two human children I invited to these festivities?" the Emperor asked Skauda'tesh sternly.

"These? I think not, O Father of Society," replied Skauda'tesh quickly. "Those children were killed by the Cro'lichks in the Dead Worlds Cluster. These must be impostors, organic constructs, robots or Sha Kiff impersonators. They are deadly assassins, although they do not look it."

"I think I have sufficient guards to protect me from these… deadly assassins," interrupted the Emperor and stepped up to Elliot. "My Beholders detect no Sha Kiff or robots, nor any hidden weapons on them."

For a couple of seconds the great Emperor of the Skar'ley looked Elliot and Molly up and down, while his

Beholder orbs circled over them. His yellow reptilian eyes were cold and scary. His green scaly face totally inhuman, and somehow even more lizard-like than the other Skar'ley. As if he somehow was closer to nature and held a rawer, more primitive life force within him. The larger scales around his nose slits, his eyes and his lipless mouth gave him a wrinkled and elderly appearance. Like a wise old man.

"I am glad, young humans, that you are still alive," said the Emperor finally. "Any loss of life, especially that of younglings, is a terrible tragedy. My heart broke at the thought of my invitation having led to your deaths. But you mentioned my old friend Karrillus. Rumours say he found Matalla. Rumours also say he's dead. You now claim to know where he is?"

The palace guards holding Elliot moved the sword away from his throat to allow him to answer. Elliot looked into the large yellow eyes of the Emperor and shivered.

"I… I thought he was dead," stuttered Elliot. "I thought the Hunter robots had killed him. But now I heard he's alive, but a prisoner…"

"Protector of Our People, be wary of these humans. They pose a danger to you," interrupted Skauda'tesh in a whisper. He had sidled up to the Emperor like a snake. The High Priest was obviously bothered by the Emperor speaking to the human children.

"He's the real danger, Emperor," said Molly and pointed at Skauda'tesh. "Him and all the priests."

The Emperor turned to Skauda'tesh who shrugged, as if he didn't know why the human children acted so strangely.

"They lie. They are confused. They are assassins' weapons…" whispered Skauda'tesh.

"We're not! *You* tried to kill us," said Elliot and pointed his finger accusingly at the High Priest. "*You* told the Cruelies where to find us in the Dead Worlds Cluster. But we survived and we've come here to warn the Emperor about your plans."

This time it was the Emperor who interrupted them. Most of the guests were returning now, curious to see what was going on and he was clearly disturbed by all the prying eyes. He held up his hand to silence Elliot.

"We will withdraw to the palace to discuss these matters further," the Emperor ordered. "The Festival Gardens is not the place to discuss accusations such as these."

The Emperor turned and headed for the entrance to one of the palace buildings. His palace guards trooped after him, acting as a living shield and moving the curious noble onlookers aside. The big palace guards that held Elliot and Molly lifted them off the ground and carried them head over heel after the Emperor.

"Ambassador Horus!" the Emperor said as he passed the shocked human. "You reported these human children dead, didn't you? Please come with me."

Ambassador Horus jumped when hearing his name. As quickly as the mechanical legs of his chair could carry him he followed the Emperor.

"You too Skauda'tesh, old friend," the Emperor said. "It's only right that the High Priest of the Eternal Sun is allowed to defend his honour when it's at stake."

Skauda'tesh and his retinue of priests bowed in obedience and followed the Emperor.

The gold-clad Emperor led all of them through the Festival Gardens and into one of the immense and ancient palace buildings. Guests of all species stood gawking at the spectacle as the troop passed them. Just inside the palace was a large room, adorned with gold, red and blue. The Emperor stopped there and turned once again to his retinue.

"Leave your priests outside!" the Emperor ordered Skauda'tesh.

Skauda'tesh bowed and waved his priests off with a gesture of his hand. However, Elliot also noticed other kinds of hidden hand signals between the High Priest and his servant that the Emperor didn't see.

The palace guards then began to search Elliot and Molly. They took Molly's PDM and Little Brother from Elliot's back. Also the satchel with the anti-slave-gene serum was taken from them. Even Ambassador Horus was checked and his walking chair powered down with a sigh. The High Priest of the Eternal Sun was, however, not searched and stood silently to one side while the guards worked. Clearly, the palace guards had no trust in the humans, while trusting their own priests fully. This was a mistake, thought Elliot and it made him feel uneasy. After they were done searching the humans, the countless palace guards then positioned themselves either outside or inside the doors of the room, ready to defend their Emperor.

The two great doors closed behind them and the Emperor finally had the privacy he demanded. Everyone in the room, except the Emperor himself, seemed uneasy and nervous. Elliot fiddled with the hem of his clothes and Molly pressed her earlobe, so that the Memo Hair-Gel in her hair began fixing her braids, which had been ruffled by the palace guards.

"So," the Emperor began, breaking the nervous silence. "Let us sort this mess out and prevent any more shouting to upset this most glorious of days. Could someone please explain to me what these human children are doing here? I was told they were dead. Ambassador Horus, what do you have to say?" the Emperor stepped up to Ambassador Horus who sat slumped in his powered-down chair.

"My lord, I don't know," Ambassador Horus replied. "We fled in the escape pods when the Cro'lichks attacked the *Warhammer* in the Dead Worlds Cluster. All escape pods except one were accounted for. That last one never jettisoned and crashed with the ship. It was assumed that the children had been on board either this escape pod or on the ship itself. We were shocked when we found out. We presumed them dead."

"But they evidently aren't dead, as my Beholders can confirm. According to their readings, these human children are identical in appearance, body mass, voice, retinal patterns, smell and colour to the two children that departed from Centus Prime as invited guests of the Skar'ley Empire."

The Emperor then turned to Elliot and Molly. "So how *did* you survive that attack?"

Elliot and Molly looked at each other. Molly nodded to Elliot to explain.

"Well, you see Mr Emperor, we *did* crash. The escape pod didn't work. I believe it had been sabotaged and wouldn't release. The ship hit that asteroid and was as good as pulverised. We only survived thanks to our Radorian Saviour Ball."

"I have heard of these items. They are very rare. It was fortunate indeed that you had one," said the Emperor admiringly. "So you survived the crash of the *Warhammer*. But I was told there were no signs of survivors among the debris."

"Surely somebody must have seen our footprints around the place?" protested Molly. She then remembered how the Furanians had said that nobody knew they were alive when they had revived them. Maybe they had somehow covered their tracks?

"But we did survive… kind of," explained Elliot. "I guess we actually did die, but that was after the crash. We ran out of air on that asteroid and suffocated. We were then found and revived by Furanians who had something called an Organic Jumpstarter."

Elliot didn't know what to tell the Emperor after that. He had promised not to tell anybody about the Hidden Watchers, but he didn't know how to continue if he didn't.

"The Furries then helped us look for a place called the Ash Plains," Molly quickly continued. "We had intercepted a secret and coded message for the traitor on board the *Warhammer*. No doubt it was this traitor who somehow messed up our coordinates from Otherspace, so we exited far away from our escort. The coded message said something about an ancient plan and a Flesh Smith living in the Ash Plains."

"A Flesh Smith!" gasped the Emperor in shock. "But that's impossible. The Flesh Smiths are long dead. Merely legends by now. You cannot possibly…"

"With all respect, Emperor, not all of them are dead," replied Elliot quickly. "One is still held prisoner in a secret Hollow World in the Ash Plains. That Flesh Smith told us how he had helped previous Emperors heal the Skar'ley during the Curse of Decay. The existence of the captured Flesh Smiths has since that time been erased from your records.

"So, you… spoke to a Flesh Smith?" the Emperor said doubtfully.

"Yes, and it was he who revealed the priesthood's old conspiracy to kill you and take over the Empire. In order to do this they plan to enslave humans of Earth and use them as soldiers."

"Flesh Smiths? Secret conspiracies? Human slaves from Matalla?" murmured the Emperor with disbelief.

Skauda'tesh chuckled. "There are no Flesh Smiths anymore. These… humans… are lying. They are evidently hiding something. Maybe they have been somehow altered or brainwashed? They could be dangerous."

The Emperor shook his head, clearly feeling that the truth was too amazing to be believed. Instead he focused on something else.

"So, what does your fantastic escape have to do with Karrillus Ursus? Karrillus was a very good friend of mine. For a human, he was very calm and good natured."

"Your priests hold him prisoner here on Sku'raan," answered Elliot. "He's held in a dungeon under an old swamp temple. Mayizim told us."

"Mayizim told you?" the Emperor once again looked shocked. "Mayizim *spoke* to you?"

Once again Skauda'tesh chuckled aloud.

"Yes, he did," replied Elliot, trying to ignore Skauda'tesh's annoying chuckling.

"Yes, they actually did speak to Mayizim," sighed Little Brother.

The Emperor looked over in surprise to the sulking black briefcase held in one of the palace guard's hands.

"He's a Stage Ten Artificial Intelligence," apologised Elliot.

"O Great Spokesman of the Eternal Sun," Skauda'tesh interrupted. "These children evidently don't know when to stop lying. Their minds are feeble and no doubt dangerously disturbed. They miraculously survived a crash in an asteroid field? They secretly met with a long dead Flesh Smith? They have spoken to Mayizim the Great and they claim I'm heading a secret conspiracy that wishes to enslave old humans? Please let your security officers interrogate them before they do something dangerous. Keeping you safe is the only concern we have at the moment…"

Elliot started to get angry. "No, no, no. Don't listen to him! Listen to me. We *did* survive that crash. The Furanians *did* revive us. We *did* find a Flesh Smith in the Ash Plains. That Flesh Smith told us everything about the conspiracy that threatened the Empire and the Spiral Arm."

"Lies and fantasy," Skauda'tesh sighed and sat down calmly.

"No, it's not lies," said Elliot. "Give me time and I'll tell you everything. I'll even tell you how they plan to kill you."

"Please, O Father of Our Race. Don't waste your time with these creatures," sneered Skauda'tesh where he sat in his chair. "Your guests are waiting and the festivities are drawing towards their end."

But the Emperor didn't reply. He looked from Skauda'tesh to the children.

"We have some more time before midnight," the Emperor finally said calmly. "Until then you have to tell me everything, young human, starting with your life on Matalla."

And so Elliot did. He told the Emperor how he'd been brought up in an orphanage on Earth. He told him briefly about Sweden and how Uncle Karl had visited him at school for the first time. He then continued with his journey to

Kiruna and his flight from the Hunter robot. When he retold the story, it felt like it was a hundred years ago. So much had happened since then. After having told the Emperor about the destruction of the *Ursa Major* and Big Brother he continued with his adventures on The Knot and his meeting with Molly.

The Emperor listened intently and didn't interrupt. Skauda'tesh, on the other hand, sighed on several occasions and shook his head.

When Elliot began to tell the Emperor about his invitation and the attack on the *Warhammer*, Ambassador Horus nodded in agreement. "That's what happened, my lord. Just as I told you."

"I do not doubt the words from your mouth, Ambassador Horus," said the Emperor and put an arm on his shoulder. "What I do doubt is this whole tale."

But Elliot continued. He told the Emperor how they had been found by Furanians but skipped the whole part with the secret assembly of the Hidden Watchers. He then retold their search for the Flesh Smith in the Ash Plains and their dangerous exploration of the Hollow World. When he described the asteroid ships being built and the ancient plan to enslave the humans of Matalla with the slave genes being spread in secret, the Emperor's eyes opened wide with amazement.

"We have proof of this," insisted Elliot. "We have the anti-slave-gene serum the Flesh Smith gave us in the satchel your guards took. In the Has'pleen ship we stole, we have two Has'pleen prisoners and a Furanian that was altered by the Flesh Smith to help us escape." Elliot then produced the scroll 'Testaments of the Lonely'.

"This old scroll contains the coordinates for Matalla. It wasn't destroyed or deleted by the priests and Mayizim, as the other sources were. This once survived, thanks to the fact that nobody suspected there would be a map hidden inside it. This is what Uncle Karl and Aunt Kaitrinn found. This is how they found Matalla – Earth as it's now called."

The Emperor looked at the scroll and was about to say something when the captain of his palace guards suddenly held up his hand for attention and approached the Emperor.

"Sire, we are receiving emergency reports of a battle on the rim of the Sku'raan system." The captain listened intently to his helmet microphone while he reported the details haltingly.

"Show me," the Emperor ordered.

Immediately the air in front of them began to flicker. Between the three hovering Beholder orbs a large triangular holo-screen formed. The screen was black with countless small white dots.

"Stars!" Elliot realised. It was as if a window into deep space had been opened. They must be looking at the transmission from a ship or guard station at the rim of the Sku'raan star system.

"There appear to be several thousand large ships headed for Sku'raan," the captain of the guard explained. As he pointed, the large image zoomed in on some of the dots and revealed them to be a great swarm of asteroids. Like dark ominous carpets, the three flattened swarms of asteroids tumbled towards a small and distant sun which Elliot understood was the sun of the Sku'raan system. But these were no normal asteroids. Here and there he could see manoeuvring jets firing as the disguised ships corrected their courses to avoid tumbling into each other. The reason for their manoeuvring could soon be seen. Twenty or so sleek, snaking ships darted between the asteroid ships on the outskirts of the first swarm. Like a pack of wolves, they were upsetting the herd of asteroids.

"The ships seemed to be engaged in battle," the captain of the guard said. Along the fringes of the great swarm, Elliot could see flashes from laser fire and explosions from pummelled asteroid ships that lit up the darkness of space. The sleeker ships were much faster and seemed to be crafted from some wet-looking metal or porcelain. The blasts from the asteroid ships reflected harmlessly off their blue, glowing energy shields. The asteroid ships, however, were being destroyed one by one.

"Asteroid ships!" the Emperor confirmed grimly.

"I think those other ships are of Vurite manufacture, but our sensors can't get any detailed readings."

"Vurite warships," said the Emperor silently. "Legend says that they are summoned from distant and forgotten parts of the galaxy when the Spiral Arm is in danger."

"Should I order the Heart Fleet of the Imperial Navy to intercept?" asked the captain of the guard nervously.

"Do it!" the Emperor ordered. The captain of the guard nodded and began speaking into his helmet communicator. Elliot could see that the Emperor now looked heart broken. Something told Elliot that the Heart Fleet wouldn't be able to stop the Priesthood's immense fleet of asteroid ships.

"On the rim of the Sku'raan system," mumbled the Emperor in disbelief. "That's the very heart of the Empire. How could so many ships…?"

"We told you," said Molly. "The priests built them to look like asteroids. They've probably drifted past the other

Imperial systems unnoticed. You have to destroy them now, before they are manned by human slaves."

The Emperor turned his back on the large holo-screen where the distant battle continued. Instead he faced Skauda'tesh with a sad expression.

"What is going on? What have you got to say to all of this, Skauda'tesh old friend?" The Emperor now seemed tired, as if everything he'd heard somehow had broken him or confirmed his suspicions. He drew himself up regally and fixed his yellow eyes on the High Priest. "I'm sure there is a perfectly sane explanation for all this madness, isn't there Skauda'tesh?" he added tiredly.

Skauda'tesh rose from his chair and cleared his throat. "My reply is simple," he began in his harsher and deeper voice. Then, with a blur of motion, he suddenly drew something from his red cloak. It was a gun of some sort, with a wide and flat barrel. Skauda'tesh flung his arm out and across the perimeter of the room in a wide arch. The gun gave off a high-pitched sound and the very room seemed to distort, as if the air froze and cracked like ice. When viewing the room through the strangely distorted air, the walls seemed to splinter for a brief second and then quickly rearrange themselves back to normal again.

"Look out!" shouted Elliot and ran for cover. But there wasn't really anywhere to go except behind Ambassador Horus' powered-down chair. Elliot threw himself behind it. The Emperor ducked while the captain of the palace guards ran towards Skauda'tesh. Molly turned the other way and ran towards one of the high pillars of the room. She dove in behind the pillar just in time as Skauda'tesh drew his gun across that part of the room.

Skauda'tesh continued his sweep across the room. The air crackled and distorted in the wake of the gun's nozzle. All the palace guards that were caught in front of the strange gun seemed to freeze with their weapons half raised. Even the captain of the guard seemed stunned and perplexed. He stepped uncertainly back to the Emperor.

When Skauda'tesh had completed a full circle he turned his attention back to the centre of the room again and smiled.

The Emperor stood crouched by Ambassador Horus and watched in shock as his palace guards looked around themselves in disbelief, as if they couldn't recognise where or who they were. His own captain sat down heavily at his feet.

"Guards! Seize the High Priest!" the Emperor ordered and straightened.

But the guards didn't reply. Instead, one of them fell giggling to the floor while two others only said "duhhhh!" The three palace guards by the door began to fight over the nice and shiny helmet of a fourth, while the captain of the guards stared in fascination down the barrel of his gun.

"I said seize him!" the Emperor repeated. "Seize the High Priest! What's the matter with you?"

None of the palace guards did what the Emperor told them. They were busy investigating their immediate surroundings, which suddenly had become perplexing and extremely interesting to them. One guard however met the Emperor's eyes and grunted eagerly in understanding.

With a blood-curdling war cry he then flung himself hard against one of the pillars and began to wrestle it.

"What...?" exclaimed the Emperor in shock.

Ambassador Horus also looked around in disbelief. "There's something wrong with them," Ambassador Horus said, pointing out the obvious.

"It's the Synaptic Erosion Gun!" cried Elliot from where he stood behind Ambassador Horus. "He's destroyed the minds of the palace guards."

"How very observant of you, young human," Skauda'tesh said with a cruel smile. "You are correct. Most of the synaptic connections of their minds have been overloaded and severed, leaving them confused and as intelligent as carrots."

"You did that to poor Aunt Kaitrinn as well, you monster," spat Elliot.

"Yes, I believe that was her name. A pity she has problems remembering it herself. She was a most meddlesome human. At least she retained some basic functions though. The Synaptic Erosion Gun isn't as effective on humans as on Skar'ley."

"By the Eternal Sun! That's what happened to my Gatekeeper Visa'taum," the Emperor gasped. "We found him sitting babbling to himself in his quarter this afternoon."

"Yes. Old Visa'taum proved to be quite a nuisance. I find the worst type of servants to be those that think too much."

"Guards! Security! Beholders!" shouted the Emperor to the closed doors.

"I'm afraid it won't help calling for your guards outside either," mused Skauda'tesh. "My priests have activated a Virus Door Lock which has sealed off this room. Neither can the concealed weapons of your Beholders be directed against priests. We have seen to that a long time ago."

From outside the room they could hear shouts of anger and someone began to bang on the reinforced doors.

But they didn't open.

One of the palace guards suddenly ran up to the Emperor with a stupid smile and tried to grab his enchanting and oh-so-beautiful golden headpiece. But before he reached his target the palace guard bounced back and fell over. He had hit a large energy field which grew out around the Emperor and now encompassed Elliot and Ambassador Horus, who was sitting helplessly in his powered-down chair.

"What have you done? How long will they... stay like this?" the Emperor asked Skauda'tesh in disgust, while looking at the palace guard crawling at his feet.

"I'm afraid the effects of the Synaptic Erosion Gun are permanent, unless reversed by me," replied Skauda'tesh while positioning himself right in front of the Emperor, Elliot and Ambassador Horus. "However, copies of the victims' functioning synaptic connections are scanned and stored in the gun before it fires. The right equipment could possibly restore their minds with the help of this mapping. But your palace guards will remain lolling idiots until I find a reason to restore them."

✳✳✳

From the corner of his eye, Elliot could see movement. It was Molly. Skauda'tesh had forgotten about her or missed entirely that she had hid behind one of the pillars. Now she was creeping from one pillar to the next. Without trying to look directly at her, Elliot tried to figure out what she was doing. She wasn't going to try to grab the Synaptic Erosion Gun was she? That would be too dangerous. Skauda'tesh stood in the middle of the room, right in front of the energy field dome that held the Emperor, Elliot and Ambassador Horus. She couldn't possibly approach Skauda'tesh without being seen.

***

"But why? Why are you doing this, Skauda'tesh?" asked the Emperor sadly. "Those ships really *are* yours, aren't they?"

"They are the fleet of the Vengeful Sun. They will erase all sin and decadence from the Empire."

But you are the High Priest. You should be protecting the Empire, not trying to destroy it."

"Protect the Empire? But that's just what I'm doing. That's why you are at my mercy," snarled Skauda'tesh. He flung an arm out theatrically and looked for a moment like a giant red crow with his headpiece bent low. "For more than a millennium the Skar'ley Empire has degenerated and diminished. As a race we have fallen. Our ethics and our morals are flawed. We are no longer a vibrant and expansive people. We are no longer the same glorious race that our forefathers released unto the stars. Our culture has grown stagnant and foul."

Skauda'tesh then pointed at the Emperor. "Why has this happened? We priests know the answer, even if you and your fat nobles are too weak and blind to notice it. It is because of a failing bloodline of weak Emperors. It is because of weaknesses of the flesh that were never removed after the Curse of Decay. It is because of age-old meddling by foreign races and conspirators who want only our docility or our destruction."

"We, the true and ever loyal servants of the Eternal Sun, will restore our people, our culture and our Empire. But without the flawed line of Emperors. Without the bonds put upon us by other species. Only those who can truly see and understand the will of the Sun that Lives Forever can rule the mighty Skar'ley."

"You're mad," the Emperor said flatly. "To do this you would have to kill me and all of my kin."

"That will be no problem. Your deaths will be the dawn of a new era. An era free from your feeble kin who have proven themselves unable to lead and protect the Skar'ley."

"How dare you!" roared the elderly Emperor with a loud and commanding voice that surprised Elliot. "I am the Emperor of the Skar'ley. You cannot lift a hand against me. It would mean the end of your soul and eternal damnation into the Darkness." The Emperor then took a step towards Skauda'tesh to intimidate him.

But Elliot grabbed the Emperor's arm and whispered, "No. He's a Has'pleen. He wouldn't hesitate to kill you."

"What? A Has'pleen?" said the Emperor loudly and once again in shock.

"The Flesh Smith has altered him to look just like a normal Skar'ley. But if you look closely you can see his darker eyes and hear his hoarser voice."

"Once again you are correct, human whelp. I'm Has'pleen and proud of it. Only a Has'pleen can distance himself from the people and do what must be done for the good of the Empire."

***

Molly had silently managed to reach two palace guards who were wrestling each other at the doors to the room. It seemed they were trying to steal each other's boots. Lying discarded to one side of them was the black briefcase of Little Brother and Molly's PDM. Ever so carefully she tried to reach for her PDM without Skauda'tesh noticing. Carefully she groped for the PDM, but it was too far away. She glanced carefully around the pillar and could see Skauda'tesh with the dreaded gun. To reach the PDM she would have to leave the protection of her pillar. Skauda'tesh would undoubtedly spot her doing it. One sweep with that gun was enough to turn her brain into jelly, and she didn't want that. She tried again with her foot, to see if she could reach further. But it was no use. The PDM was too far away. It was either dart out and get it, or give up trying.

Suddenly a steel tentacle snaked around the PDM. It belonged to Little Brother. Then, ever so slowly, he pushed the PDM towards Molly.

"Thank you, Little Brother!" whispered Molly when it was close enough to grab.

"No problem, Your Highness," whispered Little Brother in reply. "What are you trying to do?"

"If he can hack the door system and plant a virus, so can I. I'll try to open the doors."

"Good idea, Your Highness," whispered Little Brother.

Sitting behind the pillar, Molly conjured up the holo-screen and her fingers began to run across the holographic keyboard.

***

On the large holo-screen the battle on the outskirts of the Sku'raan system continued. Although the Vurite warships were faster and better protected, they were now encountering problems with the innumerable asteroid ships. A hundred or more ships synchronised their fire and directed it at one Vurite ship at a time. In a blinding volley of laser lights, one Vurite warship at a time tumbled away with overloaded shields and hull sections peeling off like petals of a flower in the wind.

The Priesthood's fleet had been surprised and initially suffered heavy losses. Now the battle was turning.

"So, you plan to murder me with your own hands and take my place," the Emperor said loudly. "The people won't follow a murderer, you know. They will fear and loathe you. You will have broken everything that is holy and sacred to a Skar'ley, in deed and in mind."

"You are right of course, my dear ex-Emperor. Killing you myself wouldn't make sense. No, instead I will let somebody else do this for me. Someone the people can hate. Someone I in turn can exact the people's vengeance upon."

Skauda'tesh raised the hand not holding the Synaptic Erosion Gun and pointed a long, thin finger at them.

"Ambassador Horus," Skauda'tesh said with his voice unusually low and hoarse. "Rise!"

Elliot and the Emperor turned to the Atean ambassador. Instead of looking scared and bewildered, Ambassador Horus' eyes were now glazed, as if staring at something in the distance.

"Yes, Master," Ambassador Horus replied with grim determination and rose from his chair. His legs were thin from little use, but held him nevertheless.

The Emperor gasped again. "Horus, you can walk!"

Skauda'tesh laughed. "He's always been able to walk. Nobody has ever known however, himself included."

'*Toothless will be fanged when the moment is right*' Elliot remembered the words of the Has'pleen priests they had captured on board the scout ship. Ambassador Horus was the assassin.

"Ambassador Horus – hold the Emperor, if you please!" Skauda'tesh ordered.

With a swift movement, Ambassador Horus grabbed the sword out of the scabbard of the captain of the guards, who was sitting at their feet examining his gun. It was a long sword made out of clear crystal. Ambassador Horus' grimly determined face could be seen through it.

Elliot jumped up and tried to stop him. But Ambassador Horus was surprisingly strong and easily knocked Elliot aside. Understanding that Ambassador Horus was dangerous, the Emperor turned to run. But with another swift movement Ambassador Horus caught the hem of the Emperor's cloak and pulled him back. Like a well-trained dancer he swirled the Emperor around and laid one of his arms across his throat. Caught in a vice, the Emperor found himself pinned with the long and sharp crystal sword to his throat.

"Bravo! Well done!" congratulated Skauda'tesh and applauded. The sound of his hands clapping was like dry sticks being knocked together. "That went better than expected."

"Let me go!" rasped the Emperor hoarsely. Ambassador Horus' grip was so hard he could hardly speak.

"As you can see, Ambassador Horus obeys only me now. Such is the power I have over him, and over all Matalla humans."

"The slave genes," said Elliot darkly.

"But – *gasp* – Ambassador Horus is not from Matalla," protested the Emperor.

"There you are wrong," replied Skauda'tesh. "We have known about Matalla's location for quite some time. During the centuries when our people suffered the Curse of Decay, many historical records were lost. The Emperor, and even the High Priests of that time, forgot many of their ancient secrets. Archives were accidentally destroyed or neglected. Among those secrets was the location of Matalla, and the fact that the Cro'lichks never destroyed it. My predecessor found the long lost and forgotten coordinates to Matalla over six hundred years ago."

"You hid the information and cleansed the databanks together with Mayizim," Elliot accusingly pointed out.

"Not to begin with. The Emperors began our work. When the humans became too dangerous and were spreading without control after the Massikita Wars, they hoarded the Cro'lichks into this part of the Spiral Arm. Deep space explorers had encountered the Cro'lichks and knew how dangerous they could be. By luring them closer and closer with the promise of fresh worlds to conquer, the former Emperors managed to guide them straight into the cannons of the Ateans. It was hate at first sight and a war was inevitable. During the following Annihilation Wars it was easy for the Emperors to use clever manipulation of facts and records along with a tight Skar'ley defence in the Matalla system to fool everybody, including the Cro'lichks, that Matalla had been destroyed."

"But why?" Elliot asked.

"Who knows what the Emperors of that time thought? They were already getting weak and decadent. Maybe they hoped to eradicate the human gene pool? Maybe they believed humans were so poorly adapted to their new colonies that they would dwindle without their homeworld?"

"So you – *gasp* – enslaved the humans you – *gasp* – found on Matalla?" the Emperor said.

"In a way, yes. Although they're not aware of it, most of them carry the slave genes that allow us Has'pleen to control them. Those few that seem immune to the slave genes are being eradicated by Hunter robots as we speak. Just like Elliot's parents and he himself would have been if he had had the wits to surrender to the inevitable."

"You… killed my parents," said Elliot in shock and in anger. He already knew this, but hearing it directly from Skauda'tesh made tears of sorrow and anger well up in his eyes. All the misery of his life, his upbringing at the terrible Höder orphanage, was Skauda'tesh's fault. At that moment, Elliot hated the lizard-like alien more than anything he had ever hated in his life.

"Yes, I did. I killed them," hissed Skauda'tesh. "Although I didn't do it personally of course, I simply ordered the Immunity Strain to be eradicated." Skauda'tesh seemed to enjoy the moment and continued his gloating. "Yes, I sent those Hunter robots after you. My spies and Hunter robots then found you on The Knot and followed you to Centus Prime. I prepared the trap for you and I altered the Otherspace exit coordinates so you would be separated from the escort ships in the Dead Worlds Cluster. I informed the Cro'lichks of your coming there. I sabotaged your escape pod. But you were tenacious and stubbornly evaded the inevitable. You should both have died many times over! If only you'd had the courtesy to die quietly, it wouldn't have to end in this very, very messy way."

The evil High Priest then raised a scaly fist to the air and said aloud, "Once again humans will serve the Skar'ley as soldiers – but this time we will control them. With the humans, we will restore the Empire and bring order to the Spiral Arm by spreading the light of the Eternal Sun to all species and worlds."

"You – *gasp* – are truly mad," the Emperor said. "Your Has'pleen blood has maddened you."

***

"Damn!" Molly whispered. "I can't get wireless access to the doors. I need a direct connection through the port by the doors."

"Maybe I can help you," whispered Little Brother and began snaking one of his steel tentacles towards the doors. With a faint click, he connected to the small port beside the door. Another tentacle connected to Molly's PDM. Immediately Molly gained access to the doors, but found a strange and complicated code barring her way.

"So, you're the big scary Virus Door Lock. Let's see how tough you really are," she whispered defiantly.

***

The banging on the doors to the room intensified. The Emperor looked hopefully at them, but they didn't open.

"The doors are made of reinforced Turanium and the Virus Door Lock is very advanced," Skauda'tesh said with a pleased smile. "It will take them quite some time to break through. Before that, all will be over."

"This – *gasp* – Empire is not yours. It does not belong to priests and – *gasp* – it never will," the Emperor wheezed in

Ambassador Horus' hard grip. "The Heart Fleet will destroy those ships of yours."

"Have you not been paying attention?" Skauda'tesh said with a pitiful sigh. He pointed to the great holo-screen where the Vurite warships clearly could be seen scattering to get away from the combined onslaught of the asteroid ships.

"They… they're fleeing," Elliot said and felt his heart sink.

"Yes. They might individually be far superior, but they are vastly outnumbered. Also, your pitiful Heart Fleet is outnumbered and will be destroyed – unless I order them to stand down and succumb to the new reason and order of the Empire."

"But how have you manned them?" asked Elliot. "I thought you hadn't enslaved the humans of Earth yet."

"Not all of them. Not all of them. But over the last six hundred years many humans have disappeared from your precious little world. Most were unwanted and will never be missed. Others stumbled upon our activities and were abducted. All of them share the fate of dear Ambassador Horus. Some serve us now as spies among the Ateans, while others have been waiting in hibernation for this moment. These humans are loyal and have been trained to fly our ships with their excellent reaction speeds and multi-tasking skills. The rest of humanity on Earth will, however, serve us as soldiers in the coming cleansing of the Spiral Arm."

"You will never succeed," said the Emperor. "The Vurites, the Vo'Orrns and…"

"What about them? They are weak and will never be able to stand against the might of the Imperial Navy and our new fleet. Do you think we have not calculated the strength of our adversaries?"

"You – *gasp* – underestimate the power of freedom."

"Enough of this!" snarled Skauda'tesh. "It is time to put an end to this pointless debate. Ambassador Horus – kill the Emperor."

Time seemed to freeze. Elliot saw Ambassador Horus grip the sword handle tighter, clenching his jaw tight, preparing to cut the Emperor's throat. The crystal sword gleamed fatefully against the green Skar'ley throat.

There was nothing anybody could do.

"No!" shouted Elliot in desperation. But he knew nothing would stop the blade of the enslaved Ambassador Horus. The Emperor was as good as dead.

But nothing happened.

Ambassador Horus still held the sword, but blinked uncertainly and looked at Elliot.

"I said, kill the Emperor!" Skauda'tesh repeated angrily.

"Don't do it, Ambassador," said Elliot carefully. Ambassador Horus once again hesitated. The Flesh Smith's words suddenly came back to him.

'*…she had the power to break the hold upon her kinsmen with the Words of Reason.*'

The Flesh Smith had been talking about his secret alteration of one of the human captives six hundred years ago. His clever deception of the Skar'ley Priesthood. Genes that could liberate the enslaved humans. Elliot carried these genes. He had these Words of Reason. His words and his voice somehow broke Skauda'tesh's hold over Ambassador Horus.

'*…your words can break their bond.*'

"Kill the Emperor! Do it now! Strike!" howled Skauda'tesh in rage.

"Don't do it!" said Elliot again calmly. "Put down the sword!"

Incredibly enough, Ambassador Horus did what Elliot said. The crystal sword was slowly and hesitantly lowered. The ageing ambassador looked confused and scared.

"Ambassador Horus! I gave you a direct order. Obey me or be punished," roared Skauda'tesh.

Ambassador Horus flinched at every venomous word Skauda'tesh spat, but he didn't raise his sword again.

"Don't listen to him," said Elliot and put his hand on Ambassador Horus' arm. The old man was trembling. "You don't have to do what he says. You never have to obey him again."

With a groan of disgust, Ambassador Horus let go of the crystal sword. It fell with a clatter to the floor. As if suddenly remembering that he couldn't walk, the old man fell to the floor. The sudden strength and determination was now gone.

"What is the meaning of this?" growled Skauda'tesh.

"This is the secret weapon of the Flesh Smiths," said Elliot defiantly. "Their surprise gift to you. I carry the genes that allow me to break the control you have over your human slaves. I can speak the Words of Reason. And I will do it over and over and over. Until the crew of those asteroid ships are free. Until all humans you have enslaved have rebelled against you."

"The immunity strain!" said Skauda'tesh with sudden realisation. "That treasonous animal! We thought it was only a stubborn combination of genes that made some humans immune to control. We should have eradicated it as soon as we discovered it."

"Eradicate it? You mean kill the humans that carried it? Like you killed my mother and father?" Elliot could feel his blood run cold at the notion. They had been killed and he had become an orphan just because of their genes.

"You, like your parents, do not fit into the Luminous Plan. If it hadn't been for the meddlesome Ursus family you wouldn't even stand here today."

"But *I am* standing here," Elliot said with anger building inside him. "Uncle Karl made this happen. Thanks to him I escaped the Hunter robots. Thanks to him all this has finally been uncovered. You can no longer kill the Emperor and I will free all humans you ever enslave."

Skauda'tesh growled angrily. "Curse you! But the game is not over yet. If I cannot have the Emperor's life, I will have his mind."

Skauda'tesh raised the Synaptic Erosion Gun and pointed it at the Emperor. But just as he was about to fire the dread weapon, a steel tentacle rose up from underneath and grabbed it out of his hand. Another four steel tentacles wrapped around Skauda'tesh from behind.

"What?" the High Priest exclaimed.

It was Little Brother who desperately tried to help Elliot, Molly and the Emperor.

"Quickly! Run for it! I'll hold him," cried Little Brother.

But Skauda'tesh had no intention of giving up so easily.

"No! I will have no more of this," Skauda'tesh bellowed. With those words he pressed a button on his staff and struck the floor hard. A bright flash dazzled them all and was followed by a loud thunderclap. A charge danced over Little Brother's tentacles and the black briefcase that was his body. The steel tentacles writhed and flailed uncontrollably and let go of Skauda'tesh. All around the Emperor, similar electric discharges could be seen as his energy shield seemed to be eaten away by something. The large holo-screen showing the victorious asteroid ships moving relentlessly towards Sku'raan flickered and disappeared, Then, with a sad whirr and some blue electric discharges, the three hovering Beholder spheres fell to the floor with loud clangs.

"You think you can resist me with your simple tricks, but you're just postponing the inevitable," rasped Skauda'tesh. He stood triumphantly before them, holding his staff high. Behind him, the noise at the door seemed to intensify, but without any indication of anybody breaking through.

"Your shields and weapons will not work now, dear Emperor," Skauda'tesh snarled. "Your Beholders are dead and your guards reduced to lolling idiots. Do not think that the child and the cripple can save you."

Skauda'tesh then twisted off the tip of his staff and poured out something which looked like black sand onto the floor. As it fell it twitched and lumped together in the air. The air in the room began to stir and Elliot could feel a faint wind rushing inward towards the pile of black sand at Skauda'tesh's feet. With faint sparks deep within the pile, it began to writhe and coalesce into something. Ever so slowly the pile of black sand rose from the floor and began to form a bulky pillar.

"You monster!" shouted the Emperor. "Technoid nano-bots! You break the holiest and most fundamental principles of life by carrying them. Unleashing them here could mean disaster for all of Sku'raan. You're insane!"

Elliot shuddered as he remembered the microscopic spider-like creatures with glistening metal skin and wriggling antennae which he'd seen when investigating the *Ursa Major* with the Nav-Globe. They had been used for repairs and fault finding and could combine into larger, more complex machines. The thing that was forming in front of them must be comprised of millions upon millions of the tiny robots. He also remembered Big Brother saying that nano-bots were banned on most worlds, especially the Empire.

The black pillar quickly grew larger than Skauda'tesh himself and loomed over him. A great bulky head, four arms and three massive legs could now be discerned in the chaotic whirling mass.

"I'm *not* insane," Skauda'tesh snapped while he approached them menacingly. "I have means of controlling the countless microscopic nano-bots. As you can see, they are self-replicating, growing and copying themselves with whatever matter they can find." Skauda'tesh pointed to the creature and Elliot could see that the once polished floor was now rough and pockmarked, as if the creature was grinding away pieces of it.

"They grow and are forming into the perfect killer. Together they have the power of a raging Bulgran Lion. Even alone, one of them can tear and rend your tissue until, inevitably, you are pulp. Resistance is useless. Trust me when I say that there will be absolutely nothing left when they are finished with you."

Like a stumbling or flowing creature of darkness, the figure began to lumber after them. Black dust trailed down its flanks to the floor, but somehow clung to its main frame, like slimy black tendrils which refused to let go. It raised its huge arms to strike at them while Skauda'tesh's evil laughter echoed through the room.

Behind the pillar, Molly heard the evil laughter and risked a quick glance. She saw the huge black figure lumber after Elliot and the Emperor who fled to the other side of the room. Lying in a lifeless bundle of steel tentacles on the floor was Little Brother. Molly suspected that the poor A.I. had taken quite some damage from the energy surge. But sitting behind the pillar had saved her and her PDM from the effects of the energy surge. Her PDM had only flickered and frozen for a heartbeat and then continued. Trustworthy old Atean craftsmanship she thought. But without Little Brother's connection to the door, she could do nothing else. On her holo-screen in front of her, she could see that her program had decoded and eaten away at most of the Virus Door Lock program. The modifications of Salank the Sarapid had been very helpful. Her PDM was now more powerful than ever. It had nearly dissected the Virus Door Lock enough to get around it. But now she had to connect with the door again before the Virus Program reconfigured to protect itself.

A loud crash made her jump. Parts of a pillar came tumbling across the polished floor.

"Just a few moments more," she whispered to herself and began to crawl towards the door.

The black construct was surprisingly fast and had shattered a pillar with a mighty blow from one of its thick arms. It moved in a calculating way and tried to corner Elliot and the Emperor. So far they were still faster than the nano-bot construct, but Elliot noticed that it got faster for every second it pursued them. The surface of every piece of finely decorated wall, floor or pillar that the thing passed, was blasted and ground into their fundamental particles in order to increase its mass and microscopic numbers.

Running and ducking blows, Elliot and the Emperor darted back and forth across the room. Having gained much speed, the black nano-bot construct rapidly came closer, like an ominous demon cloud. It lunged at them and they quickly dove for cover behind a pillar, as alabaster and tiles from the wall where they had stood rained down over the floor. Unfortunately, the pillar they had dived behind was already occupied.

"Ouch! Watch where you're going," complained Molly, as they tripped over her crawling form. With a thud, both of them landed on top of Molly.

None of them had time to say anything else before the nano-bot construct was over them again. Two powerful arms reached behind the pillar to grab them. Elliot and the Emperor rolled away. But Molly still lay flat on her back after Elliot and the Emperor had tripped over her.

Like a bird of prey, the nano-bot construct hovered over Molly for a moment, then engulfed her. She screamed loudly as the inky blackness transformed into a black cloud that covered her.

But her energy shield flickered to life. Thousands upon thousands of microscopic robots tore at her shield, trying to get at her, but couldn't get through. If she hadn't had the shield, her flesh would have been peeled away like sand in a strong wind.

"Molly!" shouted Elliot in panic, as he saw her writhing in the black inky cloud. He stood up and began to run towards her.

"No!" she shouted and held up a hand towards him. Through the raging black particle storm he could see her gesturing to him. "Take my PDM to the door!" she screamed, her voice hardly distinguishable in the buzzing of the energy shield. With great effort, as if a strong wind or force held her in place, Molly then threw her PDM out of the nano-bot cloud which was eating away at her shield. It slid to Elliot's feet and stopped.

"Take it… to the door! Open… it!" Molly shouted. Elliot could see that she was frightened and her shield was weakening for every second that the nano-bot monster tore at it. Through the dark swirling haze her large blue eyes met his for a moment. Fear, but also hope and trust in him were in her eyes. Elliot didn't know what to do. Molly would die if he didn't try to help her. He didn't care about a stupid door. But what could he do? It was easy to see that it wouldn't help to hit or kick the nano-bot cloud.

"Open it… Earth Boy!" Molly commanded and pointed to the door.

Elliot swallowed hard and turned to the door. But as he swirled around he came face to face with Skauda'tesh. A strong and scaly hand grabbed his wrist and began to wrest the PDM from his grasp.

"I'll take that!" Skauda'tesh growled. With a hard yank he pulled the PDM out of Elliot's hand.

"No you won't!" a voice said suddenly.

Standing to one side of the High Priest, was Ambassador Horus. He pulled back his fist and then struck Skauda'tesh squarely on the jaw. The yellow reptilian eyes of the High Priest opened wide in surprise and then rolled upwards.

The PDM and his staff dropped out of his hands as he tumbled lifelessly to the floor. His staff landed with a clatter on the stone floor, but jumping forward, Elliot caught the PDM with a yelp, just before it landed.

Ambassador Horus stood over the bundle of red cloaks which covered the unconscious High Priest. He looked at first with surprise at his fist and then grinned triumphantly.

Behind them Molly suddenly began to scream in pain. Her shield was flickering on and off, close to overloading completely from the strain of the nano-bots. Here and there her clothes were being rapidly eaten away as the shield failed.

Elliot turned to the door and frantically examined it. He soon saw the lifeless steel tentacle lying right under a small port next to the door. Without thinking more about it, he pressed the PDM against the port.

Nothing happened.

"Elliot! Help me!" Molly screamed in real terror now.

Tears ran down his cheeks as he saw Molly writhing in pain within the dark cloud. He felt so helpless, but he had to do something to help her. She was his friend and it didn't matter if he sacrificed his own life to help her. He couldn't stand by doing nothing, so he prepared to dive into that black cloud and fight with his hands and feet. It would be pointless he knew, but better than standing there staring at Molly being eaten alive.

Just as he was about to let go of the PDM the door shuddered. At last the PDM overcame the Virus Door Lock. With a hiss it opened.

Grim-faced palace guards rushed in, some with gleaming crystal swords, others with short laser rifles. They quickly identified the Emperor and rushed to his side, pushing Elliot violently out of their way. One of them even levelled his rifle at Elliot, preparing to remove what he considered a threat to the holiest of holy people in the Skar'ley Empire.

"No!" called the Emperor. "The children are my saviours. Destroy the nano-creature before it consumes us all."

Not really knowing what to do, the palace guards charged the whirling black cloud that surrounded Molly. As soon as they reached the black mass, it engulfed them. Their energy shields flicked and buzzed violently in the maelstrom.

But the palace guards could do nothing to harm the nano-bot construct. Instead it pummelled their shields and overloaded them one by one. As it began to convert the metal of their armour into more copies of the microscopic robots, it grew in size. Although the palace guards could do no real harm to the nano-bot construct, they made it move away from Molly who lay lifeless in its wake. Her clothes were tattered and her skin red and sore. She lay on her stomach with her hands covering her face. Her energy shield flickered weakly and then died.

Elliot ran to her side and rolled her over. Ambassador Horus also came to Molly's side. His face twisted in concern for the young girl. Even Molly's face was red and sore, as if she had burnt it. Her hair was ruffled and looked slightly shorter.

"Molly! Molly!" Elliot called and took her limp body in his arms. "Wake up! Please wake up!"

Behind him the palace guards were screaming in agony now. But instead of fleeing they continued their pointless battle with the invulnerable nano-bot construct. They were loyal until death and had trained their entire lives to protect their beloved Emperor. The Emperor himself was being ushered out of the room by other palace guards not engaging the creature, but he stared in horror at the thing that had been unleashed in his palace. The creature had begun to give off a strange and scary buzzing sound that changed in frequency and tone, as if a million tiny voices were slowly growing in strength.

Molly's eyes slowly opened and she looked tiredly at Elliot who held her. In a routine gesture one of her hands rose up to her earlobe and activated her Memo-Hair Gel.

"You're alive!" Elliot exclaimed. "I knew it! You're alive." He was beside himself with relief and joy. He thought Molly had died. Ambassador Horus also smiled with relief and patted her on her hand.

But Molly didn't say anything. She simply turned her tired eyes towards the buzzing black thing that loomed from the ceiling of the room. It seemed to have more physical mass now, denser somehow. As the palace guards fell unconscious from their injuries one by one, it began to move towards the open door – towards freedom and more open space to expand into.

Molly lifted a tattered arm and pointed at the floor. She still didn't say anything.

"What…? I don't understand what you…" stammered Elliot. But then he saw what Molly was pointing at – Skauda'tesh's staff. The long metal staff lay on the floor where Skauda-tesh had dropped it. Although the staff seemed untouched, there was no sign of the High Priest. He was simply gone. Where Skauda'tesh had fallen, there was only a large pockmarked hole.

The nano-bot monster had devoured him!

Understanding what Molly meant, Elliot leapt to his feet and ran over to the staff. The black cloud hesitated and then loomed over him.

"I hope I remember what he did," gasped Elliot as he pressed a button on the staff and slammed it into the floor.

Another blinding flash temporarily blotted out everything in the room. A deafening thunderclap echoed throughout the palace.

The black whirling nano-bot construct in front of Elliot was pierced by the light and countless tiny sparks seemed to ignite its denser inner core as the microscopic robots short circuited. The buzzing reached a high-pitched crescendo that sounded eerily like a living thing. Then it exploded, like a big sack of black flour, engulfing the room and billowing harmlessly to the floor.

The nano-bot monster had been destroyed.

A fine black dust billowed out of the room. It fell heavily on the polished floor outside. Nervous and wounded palace guards stood staring into the mist with their crystal swords drawn. Their once shiny and polished armours were half eaten away.

Suddenly three figures staggered out of the black cloud, coughing and wheezing.

It was Ambassador Horus and the two children.

As if celebrating their survival, thousands of bells and chimes began to ring out the midnight hour and the Massikita Victory Memorial festivities reached their crescendo.

***

Oblivious to what had happened in the palace, the fireworks teams let off their rockets at midnight. This was a time of joy and happiness. The legendary defeat of a terrible enemy and the union of two great species. A great hiss of rockets deafened all other sounds of the great bustling Imperial capital as the fireworks climbed towards the gleaming stars and shining moons. Then, one single rocket exploded in a bright red plume and ignited a shockwave of rockets in all directions. In a crackling instant, the entire night sky of Sku'raan became covered in beautiful flowers of all colours. After unfolding to their full extent, they slowly faded and began to rain down on the city as glistening silver droplets, multiplying the stars in the night sky a thousand-fold. Wave after wave of fireworks blossomed over the happy and celebrating citizens of the Imperial capital, who sang to the heavens in joy.

***

In the Imperial Palace, two children jumped happily up and down, holding each other's arms. Black soot puffed from their clothes every time they landed, but their grimy faces were split in pearly white smiles as they laughed and whooped at the magnificent fireworks above them.

Palace guards stood all around them, injured, tired or wary of an unseen enemy. But the joy of the two children was infectious and smiles began to show in the corners of their flat reptilian mouths.

Even the great gold-clad Skar'ley Emperor smiled. He knew there was still much to do, but for now they were safe. Thanks to the two human children who danced and skipped happily in front of him.

ENDINGS

The dreaded dungeons of the Eternally Sunless Deep
The ancient and half-sunken temple deep in the Mah'vee swamplands was crumbling and nearly completely covered in moss and orange weeds. Green swamp water reached far up its sides and only a few hovering lights at the dark entrance gave any clue to the old ruin still being used.

A flock of bat-like birds with long snaking necks scattered from their perches as ten figures suddenly emerged from the dark entrance. Nine Skar'ley palace guards escorted a tired white-haired man with a big beard and belly.

"Uncle Karl!" Elliot exclaimed and ran from the shuttle which had barely landed on the small stone causeway leading to the dark temple entrance. His heart raced with anticipation and he could feel tears of joy welling up in his eyes. The flight to the temple had built up a big nervous lump in his chest. During the entire flight he had thought of nothing else other than getting to the dread prison temple of the Has'pleen before it was too late.

"Elliot? Is that you?" Uncle Karl croaked unbelievingly. He blinked and held his hand up to shade him from the bright light of Sku'raan's sun. His long blanched mane of hair and his big white beard were a wild tangle, but his eyes still crinkled with life and joy.

Elliot ran along the crumbling old causeway and threw himself into the burly man's arms. Not until he hugged the bulky explorer did the lump in his chest finally loosen.

"Uncle Karl! I'm so glad you're still alive. I'm sorry I didn't find you sooner!"

Uncle Karl held Elliot tightly and gazed with wonder at the other people emerging from the still whining Imperial shuttle. There were more palace guards, but also someone he recognised – his friend Ambassador Horus. But Horus was without his walking chair and standing on his own two legs, presenting a broad smile. He also saw a young human girl with blonde braids, and a black suitcase with metal legs.

"I… what… how… where?" began Uncle Karl.

"We saved you! We stopped them! The Emperor is safe! Earth is safe!" Elliot exclaimed while continuing to hold Uncle Karl tightly. The old man smelled of mouldy old dungeons, but still felt warm and comforting like he remembered him from his visits to the school and orphanage.

Uncle Karl stopped trying to understand and instead began to laugh. It started as a quiet chuckle and then grew to a loud and booming laughter. He laughed and laughed and at the same time raised Elliot to the sky and whirled him around.

"Elliot Stormsson! I don't know what you've done, but I know I was right about you. You're a very exceptional boy."

When the others drew close, Uncle Karl also embraced Ambassador Horus. He laughed and shouted with joy, but never let go of Elliot.

Molly stopped two steps away from the laughing and hugging people. Her heart raced with joy, but she felt awkward and a bit of an outsider. She had never met Elliot's fabled Uncle Karl, but could feel the contagious joy of the old man spreading through everyone. Even the Skar'ley palace guards surrounding the growing group hug began their hissing laughs.

Suddenly Uncle Karl stopped laughing and nodded at Molly.

"And who's this, young Master Elliot?" he said with a warm smile.

"This is Molly, my best friend," answered Elliot proudly from deep within Uncle Karl's embrace. "She's a real princess and she helped me with everything. Without her we wouldn't have managed to save you." His eyes rested warmly on Molly who suddenly felt embarrassed.

"Well," said Uncle Karl dragging all his hugged friends towards Molly. "If she's a friend of yours, she's a friend of mine as well." Uncle Karl then pulled Molly into the great group hug before she could escape and began laughing again.

Little Brother also joined the group hug with his steel tentacles and Uncle Karl whooped as he recognised him.

For a long time, they just laughed and laughed…

The Imperial Palace
The sun was setting over the Imperial Palace on Sku'raan. Its last golden rays bathed the terraced pyramids of the palace in golden light and reflected off the crystal windows and orichalcum rooftops.

The countless flying vehicles flittering between the massive, plant-covered stone buildings of the city glinted in the orange sunset light. To the citizens of the Empire, it was business as usual.

The Skar'ley Emperor looked out over his great city and sighed. It had been a long day – a long week, as a matter of fact. With his arms behind his back he drew in a fresh breath of air and contemplated the week which had passed. It had started with the annual celebrations of his forefathers. Proper ceremony had been followed and the Empire had prepared for a weekend of celebrations. But instead of the usual festivities the Emperor had barely escaped an assassination and the glorious Empire of his ancestors had nearly been usurped by power-crazed priests.

It had taken him more than a week to round up all the conspirators, which meant most of the higher caste of the Priesthood of the Eternal Sun. Although the Has'pleen were scorned by all and could easily be banished, the remaining priests who had been fed Skauda'tesh's and his predecessor's lies would be harder to bring back to the fold. But with the Has'pleen gone, there was at least no risk of violence, as a Skar'ley could not and would not harm a member of their own species.

The dangerous ideals and demands of the Priesthood to reinstate the Imperial glory would have to be battled with debate and, maybe in some cases, met. Many priests were remorseful and more than willing to help reinstate proper moral values again through their love of the Eternal Sun. Others still harboured the feeling that the Empire no longer was true to the ideals of the Eternal Sun and Lifegiver. His people would feel the repercussions of this near rebellion for quite some time. It would inevitably lead to a change in their attitude towards religion and their place in the Spiral Arm. All Skar'ley feared change and so did the Emperor. But he hoped it would be a change for the better.

Thanks to the selfless acts of the two human children, the Emperor still lived and peace endured. They had risked their lives many times to save the Emperor, as well as their own people and the Spiral Arm, from death and chaos. Also, Tavvin the Furanian and Captain Destroyer the Cro'lichks had Elliot and Molly to thank for their lives. The thawing had been painful for them, but they had been grateful that the human children had saved them from the cruel clutches of Has'pleen priests. Even though they didn't yet understand it, the human slaves of the Has'pleen ships had also been saved by the brave children. With his Voice of Reason Elliot had broadcast his message of freedom to the enslaved crews of the asteroid ships who had immediately rebelled against their masters. The great armada of the Priesthood had ground to a halt and been peacefully incorporated into the Imperial Navy.

But what about Skauda'tesh? Had he truly been devoured by the nano-bots? There was certainly no trace of him anywhere. Even if he was dead, had the treacherous High Priest planted any more surprises for the Empire before his death? But despite the fear of future dark surprises, there was hope that Skauda'tesh's ill deeds could be reversed. Already the synaptic mapping locked inside the Synaptic Erosion Gun had after a week of therapy restored the minds of the palace guards and poor Visa'taum.

And what would be the fate of the hapless human abductees that had manned the asteroid ships? Many of them had been abducted when very young and hardly remembered where they came from. Others had, through cryosleep, been separated for so long from Earth that they would not recognise it or its people. Some, however, wanted to go home. The Emperor hoped that he had done the right thing by sending them to the Atean Star-Kingdom. The humans would now have to decide what to do with them. Hopefully, the thousands of young people would rejuvenate the Star-Kingdom and bring much joy and happiness – maybe in the form of new children? King Lukas IV and Queen Sibylla II would certainly have plenty to do in the next couple of years.

And what should be done about Earth itself? The King and Queen were already on their way to Sku'raan to discuss their options. Should they contact the people there? Should they and could they let them continue their lives uninterrupted, in ignorance of their neighbours in the Spiral Arm? Earth was truly a great responsibility. Whatever option they chose, the anti-slave-gene serum had to be released to the populace of Earth. In secret, if that was necessary. Now he began to know what his ancestors must have felt like when they had decided Earth's fate so long ago. This time he wanted to do things right, though. He hoped the retired Ateans would prove wiser in this matter, compared to their younger and more restless ancestors.

The Emperor had much to thank the two children for and knew that he had not rewarded them enough.

He then smiled, realising that his extravagant worldly rewards meant little to the two children. Being reunited with his Uncle Karl had meant more to Elliot than anything the Emperor could ever give him. Even Molly could no longer be tempted with worldly treasures. All her life she had been pampered with gifts and lived in extreme luxury, but slowly she had come to understand that wealth and power are not everything. The Emperor believed that Molly had never been more happy in her life than when Uncle Karl and Elliot had pulled her into their embrace – and into their family – on the crumbling footsteps of that old swamp temple.

With another sigh, the Emperor looked up at the darkening sky. Already the first stars were visible and the luminous amber and purple moons of Sku'raan were making their dramatic entrance on the night sky. Somewhere among those stars was Earth's sun – Sol. It held so much promise and so much uncertainty. His gaze then settled on another star – twin stars actually – although their individual lights couldn't be discerned from this distance. It was Canosis, the twin suns around which Centus Prime orbited. At least in that system he was sure there were six people that most certainly would be celebrating and laughing together.

Centus Prime

The flying car settled down on the pearly white sand dunes of Lanmaar, just as Centus Prime's first sun began to climb over the blue horizon. Waves broke gently upon the sandy beach and the yellow crab-like creatures were already skimming the surface of the water, snapping at small fish. Summer was here and the place was tranquil as usual.

Even before the small landing steps had unfolded, Elliot jumped off impatiently and landed in the soft sand. He'd been awake long before dawn, restlessly waiting for the car to take them from the Three Moon Palace. Yesterday, when they arrived from Sku'raan in a grand Imperial warship, they had been received as heroes. That evening had been full of ceremony and celebration, but Elliot hadn't had time to think about anything else other than getting to Lanmaar. Uncle Karl, on the other hand, had nicely dodged the King and Queen as well as Quetzalcoatl, the royal advisor, and departed to see his sister in Lanmaar. Elliot and Molly had, however, been forced to spend a restless evening at the palace first.

Behind him, Molly and Little Brother got off the flying car. Molly had new Atean clothes and Little Brother walked proudly on his steel tentacles. The white-moustached driver and the two elderly servants who were supposed to carry their luggage blinked in the bright morning sun and fought the urge to retreat back into the gloom of the car.

Beyond the sand dunes stood Aunt Kaitrinn's white house. Pink flamingo-like birds waded in the small private lagoon and countless flowers nodded in the gentle sea breeze. The house seemed peaceful and serene, as if no time at all had passed since Elliot was here last.

"It's… beautiful," said Molly coming up alongside Elliot. "Just like you said it would be."

"Yes," agreed Little Brother. "The angles of the roof are true monuments to mathematical balance and serenity."

Elliot didn't reply. Instead he looked intently at the house. There was somebody sitting on the porch.

Treading through the white sand he made his way to the house. Silently, Molly and Little Brother followed him. As they drew closer they could see that the figure was draped in a blanket to keep the morning chill away. When the second sun rose over the horizon, the warm and golden morning sunlight reached the porch and reflected off the frosty white hair of the person sitting there. As Elliot set his foot upon the porch the figure looked up.

It was Aunt Kaitrinn.

The face of the old woman seemed tired and worn, yet her eyes were full of energy.

"Elliot Stormsson, I presume?" said Aunt Kaitrinn as Elliot walked up the porch steps.

Elliot stopped in his tracks. "You remember me?" he said.

"Of course I do. How could I ever forget our conversations here on the porch… and all those wild pranks you told me about."

"They did it! They restored your memory!" Elliot exclaimed and ran forward.

Aunt Kaitrinn laughed and stood up with her arms open. Without hesitation, Elliot ran into them and hugged the old lady. Uncle Karl and Johanna stepped out on the porch when they heard all the commotion. The big man let go a rumbling laugh and Johanna smiled warmly.

"You did it, Uncle Karl! You restored her memory," said Elliot happily and smiled at Uncle Karl.

"Yes. As that vile serpent Skauda'tesh said, the Synaptic Erosion Gun wasn't as effective on humans as on Skar'ley. With the synaptic mapping it was fairly easy for the doctors to restore Kaitrinn's broken mind last night."

"All thanks to you," said Kaitrinn joyfully and rustled Elliot's hair. "You're our little hero you know." She hugged Elliot once again.

Molly stood on the porch feeling awkward. Her heart leapt in joy at seeing Elliot reunited with Uncle Karl and Aunt Kaitrinn. His joy and the warmth of their bond were easily felt. But Molly also felt lonely. Although she, Elliot and Little Brother hadn't known each other for very long, they seemed strongly bonded. She had never really had a family like this. Yes, her royal family had been huge, but always cold and formal. She sighed and fiddled with her braids absentmindedly.

Suddenly Elliot turned to Molly and gestured for her to come closer.

"I'm not a hero," he said. "It's Molly who's the hero actually. She decrypted that message that unveiled the conspiracy. She got us out of all kinds of sticky situations at The Knot and on Sku'raan. She even flew that Has'pleen ship and opened the door to let in the palace guards."

Molly could feel her cheeks redden. "No… I didn't…"

"Elliot's right. You're a true hero," said Uncle Karl and stepped over to Molly. "Actually, you are all heroes. All three of you. Molly Asir, Little Brother and Elliot Stormsson."

Uncle Karl then gave Molly and Little Brother a great bear hug and dragged them to the others. Laughing, Uncle Karl and Aunt Kaitrinn hugged Molly, Elliot and Little Brother as hard as they could. Aunt Johanna also joined in.

When finally Uncle Karl let them all go, he wiped his tears of laughter and straightened up.

"Now I know there's a lot of crab fishing, swimming and sand running to be done, but first we have to say this." Aunt Kaitrinn stepped up to his side and put her arm around his waist.

"All three of you must know that you are welcome to stay here as long as you want. Forever, if you wish. Our home is your home."

"Thank you!" said Elliot, Molly and Little Brother in unison.

"But by 'forever', we mean 'forever'," added Aunt Kaitrinn. "This could be your home, if you want to." From her pocket she produced a sheet of interactive paper with moving text, instructions and pictures on and held it out for the children to see.

'Adoption Form' the headline blinked on the paper.

"You… you… want to adopt us?" said Elliot, hardly believing what he'd seen.

"Well… yes," said Uncle Karl and scratched his big white beard. "All three of you! If you'd like us as parents… or grandparents, that is. I promise we won't nag you and tell you to clean your rooms and hard discs all the time."

"There's plenty of room in this family," explained Aunt Kaitrinn. "We would be very glad indeed to have you in it. Besides, I think we would make quite a good team. Karrillus and I need extra crewmen on our next expedition to the Vanishing Nebula."

"What do you say?" bellowed Uncle Karl expectantly. "Do you want to be part of the Ursus family?"

"Yes, I do!" exclaimed Elliot. He couldn't believe it. He was finally getting adopted. This was something he had wished for all his life.

"I… guess…" began Molly uncertainly. She then lit up with a warm smile and hugged Aunt Kaitrinn. "Yes! Yes, I would very much like to have a family."

"I am overwhelmed by the warmth and welcome I have felt. Despite our difference in molecular structure…" began Little Brother. But before he had time to continue his speech, Uncle Karl laughed loudly and gathered everybody in another bear hug.

Elliot and Molly laughed and hugged each other. There was still an ongoing investigation conducted by the King and

Queen and Earth was about to be rediscovered. But all that had to wait. Elliot, Molly and Little Brother had new families now. The same family! They were safe and tomorrow just had to wait.

As the twin suns rose and spread their warmth over the blue sea and pearly white sand dunes, the party at the Ursus beach house was just about to begin.

The Höder Orphanage

Gottfrid had awakened in a foul mood and someone would pay. Hugin and Munin had been barking all night and he'd hardly slept at all. Also, in the middle of the night the headlights from a passing car had filled his room with blinding light and awakened him. On top of this, the infernal winter wind had howled and rattled the windows of the old orphanage all night.

As he stepped out into the cold corridor he growled to himself while pulling on his mittens. This would be a dreadful morning. He could feel it in his old bones and through the cold slippers on his feet. Gottfrid hated having to leave his warm and comfortable sanctuary in the morning just to teach these worthless and unwanted children some manners and some healthy respect for their elders. But maybe his bad sleep could be remedied with some good and healthy belting of a mischievous child. He polished his small round glasses and put them back on his long and crooked nose.

"Mr Samuelsson! Mr Samuelsson!" cried the two nurses, Mrs Eskilsson and Mrs Jansson, in unison as they came running down the corridor. They were in a fit as usual. There was always something wrong with the plumbing, with the heating or some child that had misbehaved.

Mr Samuelsson!" the two nurses cried as they ran up to him. "The children! The children!"

"What about them!" snarled Gottfrid. "What have they done now?"

"They're… they're…"

"They're what?"

"They're gone, Mr Samuelsson," the two nurses said sheepishly.

"What do you mean, gone?" Gottfrid replied angrily. The two nurses didn't reply, just pointed shakily at the dormitories. Gottfrid could sense a cold feeling of dread growing within him as he ran with creaking knees to the dormitories. When he rushed into the girls' dormitory he found it empty. Not a single child could be seen amongst the unkempt beds. The boys' dormitory was also empty of children, but now he noticed something else. All the toys and clothes of the children were gone as well.

His eyes were suddenly drawn to the bedside table of one of the beds, the bed which had belonged to that bothersome rascal Elliot Stormsson. That troublesome boy, who had run off in the middle of the night and embarrassed him in front of the Factory Director. On the bedside table lay a small glass marble. It gleamed in the morning light. Gottfrid picked it up and looked at it closely. He was astonished to see a miniature version of Elliot jumping around on a sunlit white beach in shorts. The boy then suddenly pulled down his shorts and showed Gottfrid his bottom. Then, with a pop and a hiss, the marble disintegrated and blasted Gottfrid's face and spectacles with red dust. The two nurses yelped in surprise and fright while Gottfrid staggered back and fell onto a bed. The red dust made his throat and nostrils itch terribly and he began coughing and sneezing violently.

Before Gottfrid had time to compose himself he heard Jonas the Janitor calling from below.

"Mr Samuelsson! Mr Samuelsson!" Gottfrid could hear that Jonas was concerned, as his tone bore a hint of panic.

"What now!?" he howled in rage and sneezed one more time.

"It's the police, Mr Samuelsson. They're here to talk to you about mistreatments and such. Mrs Fagerlund is with them. She says she has a letter from the mayor declaring that she is the new manager of the orphanage."

In truth, it *was* the most dreadful morning in Gottfrid's life…

The Hidden Watchers

Sishra the Snakirra stood gazing out at the sunless void. The pinpoint stars reflected in his large and black almond-shaped eyes. In reality, the void wasn't really sunless. It was full of stars. All of them suns and potential centres of life. The round observation window was huge and his thin frame could hardly be discerned against the backdrop of space. Despite its size, the observation window was just a tiny speck in the gargantuan and chaotic sprawl which was The Knot.

Sishra's long spider-like fingers played over a carefully sealed small metal box. Thoughtfully he placed it in an ejection tube and closed the small hatch with a hiss.

"It has to be done," boomed an artificial voice from behind him. Sishra turned to the Vo'Orrn tank behind him. The large glass wall separated him from the huge worm-like creature that swam in the dark, cold, pressurised water. Having evolved deep under the ice crusts of a distant planet, the Vo'Orrns couldn't endure light. Not even the faint light of the stars.

"I agree," Sishra said. "It would be too dangerous to let them live and thrive."

"Their doom was sealed a long time ago. It would be too dangerous to change this now," the Vo'Orrn's voice boomed from the speaker in the glass wall.

Sishra nodded and lifted his hand to the button.

"I was just thinking how clever they were. They nearly fooled us," Sishra mused.

"The cunning of the Flesh Smiths is well documented," agreed the Vo'Orrn. "I doubt this will be the last we see of them, even though we destroyed the hollow moon."

"We were lucky to get our hands on these seeds before anybody else did," said Sishra.

"Even luckier still that the children didn't spread these microscopic spider seeds they were unknowingly carrying on themselves to other worlds than Sku'raan. Those infectious microscopic, multi-legged spiders were the true seeds of the Flesh Smiths and would have remained unnoticed if it wasn't for your foresight, Sishra. We were lucky that you survived the battle of the Ash Plains. We were equally lucky that we discreetly managed to contain the infection in time without anybody noticing. No Flesh Smiths will be born out of people infected by their seeds."

Sishra nodded. "At least not today," he added and pressed the button. The metal box was jettisoned out into space and the small charges inside it exploded. There was a brief flash and then the box was gone.

"I assume the altered Furanian has been taken care of?" the Vo'Orrn asked.

"Yes," replied Sishra. "The genome reconstruction serum actually seems to be working. We can detect no tricks of the Flesh Smith. I assume the Furanian will return to his former self within another two weeks. Luckily the memory of his meeting with the Flesh Smith is very vague – perhaps due to the trauma of his death, rebirth and cellular reconstruction. He will be a more-than-usually-confused Furanian for the next couple of months."

"At least he still has life. That is more than could be expected from such turmoil," said the Vo'Orrn solemnly. "If this serum is so successful in reconstructing an old race such as a Furanian, it should have no problems removing the slave genes from the younger humans of rediscovered Matalla."

Sishra nodded and looked dreamily into the murky waters of the large Vo'Orrn tank for a moment before he spoke again.

"What about the human children and those explorers – the Ursus? They know too much about us."

"We will watch them," replied the Vo'Orrn. "But most probably they will fit into our plans anyway. Their inquisitiveness will serve us well, as they are resourceful and have a sense of adventure, which is unlike any of their race. Most likely they will continue to make amazing discoveries or uncover more long-forgotten secrets. What they learn will be beneficial to us all. And when they get into trouble, we will try to be there to help them."

Sishra nodded and turned to the stars again. Those small pinpoints of light held so much promise and so many mysteries. Who were the Founders and why were many of their ancient artefacts and ruins re-activating after such a long time? Where did the Cro'lichks come from and what were they fleeing? Why were some of the distant stars in the Perseus Arm of the galaxy clustering together at speeds faster than light? What would happen in the far future when the Massikita returned to this part of the galaxy?

It was a pity that he would never solve these mysteries in his lifetime. After all, he and even the gigantic construct of The Knot, were mere short-lived specks of dust in the vastness of the galaxy. The Snakirra let his gaze wander out among the countless stars and his mind was soon lost in the enormity of it all.

———

And so the great adventure ended. It had started with a sad exceptional, yet ordinary star princess who had been sent to bed for being naughty; and an ordinary, yet exceptional orphan boy from Sweden who received a mysterious parcel. It ended on exotic Centus Prime, throne world of the old Atean Star-Kingdom, with two children and an A.I. finding friendship and a new family far, far out in the vast but amazing depths of space.

When contemplating all the extraordinary things these children experienced, it would be very wrong indeed to say that adventures never happened to ordinary people.

So, what could be a better ending than for them all to live happily ever after?

Nothing you say?

Well… what about the promise of daring explorations, exciting new adventures and dark mysteries among the myriad of stars of the Spiral Arm?

For once an adventure gets hold of you, other adventures are drawn to you like moths to a flame.

THE END

*Do you want to stay updated about
upcoming books in the Atean Chronicles?
Are you interested in more personal details
about Elliot, Molly and Little Brother?
Would you want to know more about the
alien worlds and their inhabitants?*

*Visit
www.jcmansell.com*

James Mansell was born in northern England, but has lived in Sweden most of his life.

His passions in life are is his family, exploring the world and sharing his rampaging fantasy with others, through writing and roleplaying games. Storytelling, either verbally, through games or in written form has always been a big part of his life.

Fantasy and science-fiction have been his steadfast companions and mental escape throughout his life. Works of scientific and historical facts as well as works of fiction are consumed eagerly to feed more ideas and stories. Unfortunately, there just doesn't seem to be enough time to pen all crazy stories down.